The Prince of Lies called into the dark and silent prison: "I am Cyric, Lord of the Dead and God of Strife. I am here to bind you to my service, Kezef."

A rumbling growl rolled out of the shadows.

"No god of Faerun would loose the Chaos Hound of his own free will." The inhuman voice was low and full of malevolence. "So you must be no god."

"If you lavish godhood on the pretenders who chained you here, then you're right. I am no god," Cyric countered snidely. "I'm very much more than that."

The Chaos Hound moved into the light. The beast resembled a huge mastiff, as large as any draft horse Cyric had seen in the streets of Zhentil Keep. Teeming maggots were his fur, the coat shifting incessantly over barely covered sinews and bones. His pointed teeth glittered like daggers of jet. A tongue oozing tatters of corruption lolled to the Hound's chin, poisonous spittle dripping in sizzling drops to the ground.

A short length of chain, forged by the God of Craft himself, held the beast in place. The links clattered sullenly as Kezef settled onto his haunches and looked the Prince of Lies in the face. "What dark task would you have me complete?"

A wicked smile creased Cyric's lips. "I want you to find the soul of Kelemvor Lyonsbane."

FORGOTTEN REALMS
FANTASY ADVENTURE

FORGOTTEN REALMS

FANTASY ADVENTURE

PRINCE of LIES

James Lowder

TSR Inc.

PRINCE OF LIES

Copyright ©1993 TSR, Inc.
All Rights Reserved.

First Printing: August 1993
Printed in the United States of America.
Library of Congress Catalog Card Number: 92-61091

9 8 7 6 5 4 3 2

ISBN: 1-56076-626-3

TSR, Inc.
P.O. Box 756
Lake Geneva, WI 53147
United States of America

TSR Ltd.
120 Church End, Cherry Hinton
Cambridge CB1 3LB
United Kingdom

Author's Note

Five years ago, I was handed my first big assignment as an editor for TSR's book department: the Avatar Trilogy. Little did I suspect at the time that my office would soon become home to something game designer Jeff Grubb liked to call the Avatar Vortex. Anyone who crossed my threshold from July 1988 to October 1989 ran the risk of spiraling down into that maelstrom of Avatar products: novels, game modules, and comic books. Some folks made the descent willingly, others shouted a bit as they went under, but from its inception the Avatar Project owed its vitality to a large team of creative people.

With all that history in mind, it shouldn't be surprising that this Avatar-related novel owes much to the work of others:

To Scott Ciencin and Troy Denning, the better parts of Richard Awlinson, who penned the original trilogy and broke me in as an editor.

To Jeff Grubb, Karen Boomgarden, Ed Greenwood, and all the creatives who worked on the game department side of Avatar. The vortex would have been pretty lonely without your cheerful company.

To Mary Kirchoff, who assigned the Avatar Trilogy to a green editor, then taught him enough as a writer that he could add a chapter or two (or twenty) of his own.

To J. Robert King, who showed astounding grace under fire in the editing of this manuscript.

And most especially to my wife, Debbie, who has weathered the five-year-long Avatar maelstrom with good cheer. I doubt this is the last we'll see of Cyric, but it's nice to know you'll be around to keep him quiet during *Jonny Quest* the next time he drops by for a lengthy stay.

PROLOGUE

Gwydion was doomed, but he kept running anyway.

Dubbed "the Quick" by the sergeant of his company in Cormyr's vaunted Purple Dragons, Gwydion had bested everyone who'd ever challenged him in a footrace. He could dash from one end of Suzail's expansive Promenade to the other without breathing hard, while the pretenders to his title fell to panting long before they'd reached Vangerdahast's Tower, less than halfway along the course. As a scout during the crusade, he outran three Tuigan cavalrymen to deliver a report to King Azoun. So unassailable was his reputation that none of Gwydion's otherwise skeptical fellows had thought to question him, even though no one else had witnessed the amazing feat.

Yet, even Gwydion doubted his fleetness of foot could save him now—no more than Lady Cardea's priceless elf-crafted bow had kept her alive; no more than the myriad enchantments of Aram Scragglebeard had whisked him out of harm's way. No, the carrion crows filling the iron-

1

gray sky were there as much for him as for his fallen companions.

As he scrambled to the foot of the cliff, Gwydion looked back up to the plateau. Twilight shadows draped the rocky face, the cloak of darkness broken now and then by long, glinting icicles or patches of snow. And at the trail's start, haloed by the sun setting at his back, stood the giant. He resembled nothing so much as a tower perched on the high ledge—his boots small gatehouses, his hands thick balconies, his horned helmet the peaked and merloned roof. He stood unmoving, staring at Gwydion with frost-blue eyes. Then the giant leaped forward.

"Torm's heart!" Gwydion gasped, sprinting away at top speed.

The falling goliath seemed to fill the sky, and his shadow engulfed the fleeing man. With surprising agility, the giant bounded once, twice, and finally a third time as he ran down the steep rock face. His iron-shod boots sent boulders cascading around the petrified sell-sword. Billows of powdery snow swirled into the air as the rocks hit the clearing. The carrion crows flapped to a safer vantage, black spots moving in the glittering mist of snow.

As the giant landed, the ground trembled for miles around, and many darksome creatures in the Great Gray Lands of Thar were shaken from their unquiet slumbers. "You cannot run from Thrym!" the titan bellowed, brandishing a battle-axe adorned with the feathers of griffons and giant eagles.

Gwydion charged across the open ground, heading for the fast-flowing river a few hundred yards away. If he could make the boat they'd secreted there, he might be able to lose Thrym. If not . . .

Gwydion gritted his teeth and ran.

The clearing sloped away from the cliff, its blanket of new-fallen snow broken only by scattered boulders, clusters of gnarled yew shrubs, and the churned tracks left hours ago by Gwydion and his two fellow treasure-hunters. He stayed in those tracks as much as possible, hoping to avoid the deep drifts and sinkholes hidden beneath the snow. On her way to the giant's lair, Cardea had stumbled into one such hole—a particularly deep fissure. She'd have blamed the sprained ankle for her poor showing against Thrym, Gwydion thought grimly, if she weren't lying in two halves up on the plateau.

He risked a glance over his shoulder. Thrym lumbered after him, surrounded by a haze of snow. For every five of Gwydion's steps, the giant took only one. And he was still gaining ground.

By the time Gwydion spotted the fissure that had done Cardea so much harm, he could smell the stench of the uncured hides Thrym wore beneath his breastplate. The sell-sword let his knees buckle beneath him, and he tumbled painfully into the fissure. Then, clutching his bruised ribs, he tried his best to shrink into the hole.

Running too fast to stop quickly, Thrym leaped over the scar. He swung his axe as he passed, but the awkward slash did little more than fan another thin cloud of snow into the air—that and frighten all thoughts of the river and the boat from Gwydion's mind.

As the blade hissed close to the mercenary's face, he saw only the blood coloring the chipped head. The gore's from Cardea and probably Aram, too, Gwydion thought, though he hadn't stayed long enough to witness the old mage's grisly end. The next blow will probably end this sorry adventure and my career as a sword-for-hire.

"Anything, Torm," Gwydion shrieked. "I'll do anything if you let me live to see Cormyr again." The sell-sword's plea to the God of Duty was utterly insincere, as were all the oaths he'd sworn in times of desperation, but it did not go unheard.

3

Come to me, Gwydion.

No more than a whisper, the words echoed insistently inside his head. Then a warm, flickering light appeared before the man's tearing eyes. It beckoned the sell-sword, wordlessly ordering him to tunnel into the snow that filled the fissure. Gwydion did so without hesitation, without doubting for an instant that some greater power had taken pity on him. Such things weren't uncommon in Faerun, a land where the gods took on mortal avatars from time to time, and miracles were limited only by faith and imagination.

After scraping forward a dwarf's height, Gwydion felt the packed snow beneath him shift.

Go deeper, the voice instructed. The words banished the chill from his trembling limbs and masked the pain in his raw and bleeding hands.

Through the cold blanket overhead came Thrym's bellowed curses. The footsteps were getting close again, the ground trembling beneath the giant's iron-booted gait. Gulping a breath, Gwydion tore into the packed snow beneath him like a vole burrowing away from a ravenous fox. Then, quite suddenly, the shroud of snow covering him was gone, brushed away with one swipe of Thrym's callused hand.

"Ha! You think you can fool me with an old trick like this?" Thrym mocked. His voice was as cold as the icicles hanging from his dirty blond beard.

Gwydion looked up at the giant. Thrym's iron boots stood like prison walls to either side of the fissure. Legs clad in motley furs led up to a battered breastplate that had once been the front door of a Vaasan palace. The giant's face, three stories above Gwydion, was mostly hidden by his unkempt beard and huge helmet, but his blue eyes glittered through the tangle. Those eyes narrowed as Thrym lifted the axe high above his head.

Have no fear, the voice purred in Gwydion's mind. *I have heard your plea.*

The snow beneath the sell-sword fell away. With a shout of surprise, Gwydion slipped into the hole and careened down a worn chute of marble. Above him, the giant's axe struck the ground, sending a shower of snow and dirt clattering down the chute after him.

Gwydion tumbled and slid just long enough to right himself. No sooner had he done that than the chute deposited him into a small, man-made chamber. He sat there for a time, stunned, bloodied, covered with dirt and dripping wet from the snow. He noticed none of those discomforts. Neither did he hear Thrym's shouted promises of horrible tortures, dire rites of pain, and suffering perfected by frost giant shamans over the centuries.

"It is your duty to bow before your god."

It took a moment for the command to seep through the mist of fear and awe floating over Gwydion's thoughts. Then he blinked, mouthed a wordless prayer, and dropped his forehead to the smooth marble floor. The god let Gwydion stay in that uncomfortable position for quite a long time.

"You may look upon me, Gwydion," the god said at last, and the sell-sword meekly raised his head.

It took some time for Gwydion's eyes to adjust to the wonder-bright radiance filling the chamber, but when they did, he saw that the stranger was tall, at least twice the height of a man. Waves of power, of steel-fisted authority, radiated from the armored figure like heat from a raging fire. He held up a gauntleted hand, and Gwydion's wounds were healed. Fear and confusion fled the sell-sword's mind as divine knowledge engulfed him. A cool clarity of thought settled over Gwydion, and this new understanding trumpeted one seemingly undeniable fact until it shook the core of his being: He was in the presence of

Torm the True, God of Duty, Patron of Loyalty. Of that Gwydion had no doubt.

Torm's ornate armor, more ancient than any preserved in Faerun, was hued dusky purple, mirroring the customs of the greatest warriors dedicated to his cause. Spikes carved from the bones of the first evil dragon slain in his name jutted from the cops at his elbows and knees. Points of light scintillated like a thousand tiny stars on the twilight canvas of his breastplate. Eyes like twin suns shone from Torm's helmet as he held a rose-red short sword toward Gwydion, point leveled at his chest. The blade pulsed with the rhythm of a beating heart.

"Men call me Torm the True because I value loyalty above all else. They call me Torm the Brave because I will face any danger to prove my respect of duty." The god touched the sell-sword's shoulder with the rosy blade. "Any who would call himself my follower must do the same."

"Of c-course, Your H-H-Holiness," Gwydion stammered. A frisson of fear tingled down his spine. "I understand."

"Once you understood," Torm said flatly. "But you have strayed far from the path of obedience and duty."

The words echoed from the god's helmet like a ghastly warning sent from inside a coffin.

"When you fought under King Azoun's banner, you knew honor. You did me great glory in your battles against the Tuigan barbarians and shone as a true knight of my church. But then you left the Purple Dragons, refused your duty to strive for law and justice. And for what—to become a mercenary, an adventurer hunting the land for profit."

When Gwydion merely bowed his head in shame, Torm continued. "You came to Thar seeking the treasure of the frost giants, but you have discovered the only reward they offer to greedy fools is a quick death. For your allies it is

6

too late. For you, there is still a chance, still a way for you to regain your honor."

"Anything, Your Holiness," Gwydion said. Tears of contrition streamed down his cheeks as he struggled to his feet.

"Then behold the final resting place of Alban Onire, Holy Knight of Duty, known in his day as a foe of all evil giants."

Torm floated to one side, revealing a handsome young man lying in state upon a stone bier. He was clad in armor much like the god's. The plate mail looked newly polished. The smell of fresh oil came from the armor's straps and the leather belt holding the gem-encrusted scabbard.

Gwydion licked his lips nervously. "I've heard stories of Alban Onire, but—" He glanced at the sparkling armor, the peaceful expression on the corpse's features. "But he died centuries ago."

"This place has been made holy in honor of Alban's great deeds," Torm said. He, too, turned to gaze on the fallen knight. "His soul is at rest, but his body will not return to dust until someone worthy comes forward to take his place as bane to giants and dragons." Slowly he held a hand out to Gwydion. "Once you were blessed in my sight. You can be again, but only if you shake off your cowardice and take up the burden of Alban's legacy."

The sell-sword tried futilely to keep his surprise from his face. At first he couldn't imagine why Torm would choose him. His mind raced, searching for some reason for this great honor. He'd fought bravely as a Purple Dragon, facing death a dozen times on the crusade alone. Perhaps that was enough. Stories of other blessed warriors flooded his mind, tales of men and women empowered by the gods to be their agents in Faerun. It didn't take long for those visions of glory to overwhelm his doubts.

"Lord, I am not worthy," Gwydion said, though he was

now certain he deserved whatever honors Torm might heap upon him. He solemnly fell to one knee in a show of humility.

Torm gestured with his own rose-hued short sword. "Rise, heir to Alban's greatness, and claim your blade. Some bards call it Titanslayer, and with good reason. No giant may harm you so long as you wield this sword. One touch of its enchanted steel will topple the mightiest titan. Use it well."

Gwydion moved to the edge of the bier, lifted the scabbard, and drew the sword. The weapon was weighted perfectly, its grip solid and reassuring in his hand. He slashed the air. The blade moved like an extension of his arm or even his very soul. He smiled and held Titanslayer up so he could watch the light dance up and down the keen edges of the silver-white blade. With this sword, he could carve a wide place for himself—for Torm, he corrected hastily—in the history of Faerun.

"Thank you, O holiest—" He swallowed the remaining words and looked around in shock.

Torm was gone. So was the body of Alban Onire. Gwydion stood alone in a small dark cavern, the only light in the place coming from the chute to the surface. He reached out with chill fingers for the bier, finding a rough outcropping of stone that held a few ancient bones and some rusted pieces of armor. I've allowed Alban to go to his rest at last, the mercenary thought proudly.

He gripped the sword and, feeling reassured by its weight, strode to the chute. A circle of dim light marked the top—sunlight, the sell-sword realized with a start. The God of Duty and the sharp blade of Titanslayer had captivated him far longer than he'd imagined.

Bracing his legs against one wall, his back against the other, Gwydion struggled up the incline. Trickles of water slicked the stone, making the climb perilous. He slipped twice. Both times the accident sent him back a few feet before he managed to stop his descent. Once, Titanslayer slid from its scabbard, but he caught the hilt before the weapon tumbled back into the darkness. As he gently replaced Titanslayer in the scabbard, the sell-sword had a fleeting vision of Torm's wrath. It took him a long time before he could still his trembling enough to continue.

Finally he scrambled out of the chute, into the fissure that had first sheltered him from Thrym. Gwydion felt fatigued from the long climb, but anticipation of the fight to come gave him renewed strength. He peered out of the rocky scar and spotted his foe.

Thrym lazed against the cliff, dozing in the early morning sunshine. The few crows left in the clearing hopped along his arms and legs, feeding on the insects in his filthy clothing. A mouse peeked out from under the giant's breastplate, causing a flurry of activity. The crows darted after the rodent, but Thrym started awake at the hungry cawing. He swatted at the birds, and they scattered into the sky. Only when Thrym's rumbling snores once again shook the yew shrubs and drowned out the murmuring river did the crows land and renew their feast.

"In the name of Torm, stand and face me!"

Slowly the giant opened his ice-blue eyes and stared down at the little man standing before him. After a moment, he rubbed his entire face with one beefy hand. When Thrym looked again, much to his surprise, the thief was still there.

"It is my duty as a knight of Torm to allow you the chance to surrender," Gwydion said.

The giant lurched to his feet, and the sell-sword had to fight the urge to flee back to the hole in the ground. Instead, Gwydion tapped the long-unused well of his courage. He felt the cold waters of resolve still his trembling soul, douse the ember of panic burning in his breast.

"I should warn you," Gwydion announced grandly, "I wield Titanslayer, bane of all evil giants. You cannot harm me while I have this sword." He held the weapon high, marveling at how the sunlight played off the blade.

Thrym narrowed his eyes in confusion. He reached for his axe, which lay against the cliff like a toppled tree, and hefted it to strike. "Mad as a tarrasque," he muttered and brought the axe down.

Gwydion saw his sword arm hit the ground an instant before he felt the giant's axe cleave his shoulder. The limb convulsed, and the fingers released the long, blackened bone they held so desperately. There was no Titanslayer, no gift from the gods. Then the pain shrieked through the sell-sword's chest, along with the dim realization that he was lying in the snow, covered in his own blood.

"Torm," Gwydion whispered as the giant brought his axe down for the killing blow.

I

LIFE UNDERGROUND

*Wherein an unexpected journey leads Gwydion
the Quick to the maker of his doom, and the
mighty Torm dutifully attempts a defense
of the dead man's honor.*

Fervent voices filled the air. Cries of joy, hopeful whispers, and murmurs thick with a desperate longing for salvation merged to become a blanket of sound over the Fugue Plain. The tangled weave of voices held a certain weird power, soothing in its constancy, exciting in its boundless optimism. Such were the prayers of the recently dead.

"Silvanus, mighty Oak Father! Gather me into the great circle of trees that is the heart of your home in Concordant!"

"We are the Morninglord's children, born again into his eternal care. Let us rise, Lathander, like the sun in spring dawning, to renew our spirits at your side!"

"O Mystra, divine Lady of Mysteries, this servant of your great church asks humbly to be shown the secrets of magic, to be taken into the weave of sorcerous power that enfolds the world!"

In the clear sky over the endless, chalk-white plain, a burst of light announced the arrival of a god's herald. The hulking, golemlike creature was a marut, carved from a block of onyx as large as any castle in Cormyr, ensorceled to do the bidding of its divine creator. It hovered above the throng and studied the assembled souls with a pair of eyes that burned like sapphires in its round, stony face. Wide plates of armor and intricately carved bands of hammered gold could not hide the marut's broad shoulders or thick-muscled arms. Its aura of resolute power, of unyielding strength, likewise could not mask the glint of wisdom in its steady gaze.

The souls crowding the endless plain looked expectantly up at the marut. The herald presented one massive hand in a sign of benediction. As it spread its blunt fingers wide, a blue-white nimbus appeared against the marut's dark palm. The soft glow grew, forming a circle of stars. Red mist flowed in a thin stream from the circle's center.

The shades recognized the holy symbol. From all parts of the Fugue Plain, a cry went up: "Mystra!"

Jagged shafts of light erupted from each of the thousand stars and seared the plain in a sudden hail of lightning. The bolts struck the worshipers of the Goddess of Magic, blasting away the cares and concerns that had hardened like shells around their souls in their years of mortal life. The servants of Mystra cried out joyously. Bathed in the power and love of the Lady of Mysteries, they stretched their arms wide and floated up toward the circle of light. One by one, Mystra's faithful became like glittering stars. When all had been lifted from the crowd, the herald closed its hand and disappeared.

As one voice, the souls on the Fugue Plain resumed their chants: "Hear my sword upon my shield! I summon you, O Lord of Battles, and demand my commission into your great army in Limbo. My victories in your name are legend, the host sent to this field of the dead before me without number. Astolpho of Highpeak fell to my ever-sharp blade, and Frode Silverbeard. Magnes, son of Edryn, and Hemah, foul knight of Talos. . . ."

Gwydion the Quick stared at the armor-clad man as he hammered his sword against his riven shield. The warrior bellowed a seemingly endless list of names, pausing only to shout for Tempus to rescue him from this dull place. Gwydion had stumbled across other worshipers of the war god on the Fugue Plain. They were all the same—boastful of their victories and anxious to join the god's army, where they could spend the rest of eternity in glorious, unending combat.

The sell-sword mournfully shook his head and shuffled away. On every side, men and women sent up prayers to their patron gods. Bards and rangers dedicated to Milil formed huge choruses, chanting their praise of the Lord of All Songs. A solitary devotee of Loviatar moved through the throng, scourging himself with a barbed whip, oblivious to all around him. The bards momentarily parted for this frenzied shade, discord overwhelming their song. The interruption soon passed, however, and the praise of Milil floated once more into the air, born aloft on harmonies so perfect they soothed even the savage minions of Malar the Beastlord.

And in the midst of this tapestry of sound, Gwydion the Quick found himself mute.

He'd appeared on the Fugue Plain some time ago, though he found it hard now to tell how long. At first the sell-sword dared to hope he'd dreamed his death. After all, his body seemed solid enough. His sword arm was attached to his shoulder again, the other fatal wounds miraculously healed. The fur-lined cloak he'd bought for the trip to frigid Thar was free of bloodstains. Tunic and breeches and high leather boots all seemed perfectly new.

But images of his severed arm lying on the frozen ground and Thrym's bloody axe descending for another blow still dominated his memory. Gwydion need only call these vivid scenes to mind to know his fate had been sealed. He had passed beyond the realms of the living, into the lands of the dead.

The notion neither frightened the sell-sword nor awed him. From the instant he'd found himself standing in the midst of the teeming throng, a thick shroud of indifference had clouded his thoughts. He moved in a fog, taking in the strange sights and sounds as if they were no more unusual than those to be found in any marketplace in Suzail.

Gwydion understood just enough theology to identify the crowded expanse around him as the Fugue Plain. Long ago, in his days as a Purple Dragon, he'd guarded a diplomatic caravan to Bruenor Battlehammer, dwarven lord of Mithril Hall. A traveling priest of Oghma had bored him witless during the trek north with complicated explanations of the route a soul took on the way to eternal peace. Now, Gwydion would have given almost anything for a lecture on what lay in store for him beyond the Fugue Plain.

Turning his back on the worshipers of Milil, the shade tried once more to call on Torm. The words came out as a horrible croak, just as they had each time he'd attempted to pray—to Torm the True or any other god. He couldn't even form the litany in his mind. In vain he fought to remember the prayers, but the words simply vanished from his thoughts before he could focus on them.

One of Milil's bards paused in her song to stare at Gwydion. When the sell-sword met her gaze, she looked away, but not before he noted the terror clouding her eyes.

That fear proved contagious. A softly glowing ember, it flared in Gwydion's mind and burned away the shroud of uncaring still fogging his senses. What if Torm has taken my voice as the price of failure? A chill ran down Gwydion's spine. No, he reminded himself. I was tricked. Some mage —some very powerful illusionist—led me to my doom.

He shrieked and whimpered, but not a single word escaped his lips. The ember of fear burst, showering fragments of panic across his thoughts. He was cursed. Whoever had cast the illusion had stolen part of his soul. . . .

Gwydion felt burning tears well up in his eyes, but when he tried to blink them away, he found he couldn't close his eyelids.

The shades of the Faithful jostled Gwydion as he broke into an aimless run, their souls as tangible as his own strangely physical form. Some prayed more fervently as the gibbering sell-sword shambled by. Others turned their unblinking eyes on the lost soul. They were struck by the sorrow etched on Gwydion's face, but fearful to cease their own murmured prayers to comfort him, lest they, too, be cut off from their gods.

Gwydion stumbled through the milling crowd. The faces blurred before his eyes, and the prayers became a meaningless cacophony. He grabbed a young woman wearing a silver disk of Tymora and shook her roughly. Someone had to lift the curse! In reply to his gurgled plea, the woman knocked Gwydion's legs out from beneath him with a sweep-kick, then backed away.

"He looks like one of ours," came an inhuman voice.

"Nah. Just another of them cracked doommasters. Beshaba attracts that sort of trash."

The coarse, profane voices jarred against the sacred prayers, startling Gwydion out of his frenzy. He leaped to his feet and spun around, only to come nose to stomach with the most horrifying creature he'd ever seen. Its head had belonged to a huge wolf at one time, but the rest of its grotesque form had been patched together from a dozen other animals. Striped fur bristled in a mane that ran from between its pointed ears down its hunched ogre's back. Bright red scales plated the rest of the thing's body. It had a pair of human arms ending in hands that were little more than claws. These the creature rubbed together nervously. Four enormous spider legs waved and clutched the air beneath the other arms. Serpentine coils supported the monstrous torso, writhing and twisting beneath its bulk.

"You're cracked, Perdix," the beast said, saliva drooling from his wolfish jaws. "This one's for the city. It's obvious! Look at his face. He's been crying."

Perdix folded his leathery wings and hopped closer to Gwydion on a pair of skinny legs that bent backward at the knees. Rubbery yellow skin covered his body, which was as thin and wasted as that of a drought-starved child. With the single blue eye in the center of his wide face, Perdix looked up at Gwydion. "Well?" he asked impatiently, thin tongue flickering over gleaming white teeth. "Get praying, slug."

Frantically Gwydion tried to shove the little creature out of the way, but two sets of spider legs closed around his chest and pulled him backward. The wolf-headed thing glowered down at the sell-sword and placed clawed hands to either side of his head. "You heard Perdix," he hissed. "Let's hear your best holy day shout."

As before, a pitiful croak escaped Gwydion's lips when he tried to call on Torm.

Perdix shook his head. "For once you're right, Af. I was certain he was a doommaster. They're always getting into rows with Tymora's lot." He held out a set of night-black manacles. The iron rings clicked open, revealing sharp spikes pointed inward. "Now let's not have any trouble from you, slug."

16

One glance at the shades nearby told Gwydion he was alone in this. The others had turned their backs on him, leaving him to his two hideous captors. The Faithful close by formed a wide circle. They had their faces turned to the sky, their hands clenched together in white-knuckled devotion or crossed devoutly over their unbeating hearts.

Gwydion cursed them wordlessly and struggled against Af's implacable grip. His panic had subsided to a slow-burning dread, allowing him to think a bit more clearly. The endless hours of drill on Suzail's parade grounds came back to him then, his training in hand-to-hand combat. He laced his fingers together and pounded Af in the jaw. At the same time, he drove both heels down on the creature's snaking coils.

Af growled in annoyance at the blows, but silently reminded himself there would be trouble if he twisted the prisoner's head off. Instead, the denizen bit down on Gwydion's hands as he raised them to strike again, clamping his jaws just hard enough to pierce the flesh.

In that instant, Gwydion realized the giant's axe hadn't liberated him from pain.

"Tsk. Isn't that always the way?" Perdix sighed. "No matter what I say, you slugs try to fight anyway." He hopped high off the ground and clamped the manacles onto Gwydion's wrists.

As the iron rings clanked shut, their spiked interiors bit into flesh. Then, as if the taste of the shade's essence had suddenly woken them from rusting slumber, the spikes twitched to life and burrowed deeper still. They dug into bones, twisted sharply, and shot straight up Gwydion's arms. Blinded by the pain, the shade screamed a long, yowling wail of agony.

For the first time since Gwydion's arrival on the Fugue Plain, the sounds from his throat rang clear and true.

* * * * *

When the haze of pain cleared from his eyes, Gwydion found himself in a noisy crowd gathered outside a great walled necropolis. His whole body ached terribly, but the manacle spikes seemed to have stopped driving into his arms. Af had a clawed hand clamped on one of Gwydion's elbows. Perdix held the other in cool, webbed fingers. A charnel house stench hung over everything. Gwydion found tears streaking down his cheeks, not from the pain in his wrists, but from the choking smell of death and decay seeping into his nose and mouth.

The gates towering before him would have dwarfed Thrym or any other giant in Faerun. Dark and foreboding, they reached up into a sky swirling with red mist. To either side, past the hulking gatehouses, high, pale walls stretched to the horizon. He was too far away to be certain, but Gwydion thought the walls were moving. It was almost as if each brick were shifting constantly, writhing as though it were alive.

All around the sell-sword, the crowd of whimpering, bawling shades pushed closer to him. Each had been bound at the wrists by manacles, and, like a reluctant steer before a slaughterhouse, every damned soul was herded along by a pair of monstrous denizens. The creatures were kin to Perdix and Af, but only in their sheer grotesqueness. They'd been formed by insane mixings of animals and men, plants, or even gems and metals. They flew, slithered, and crawled along, prodding their prisoners with suckered fingers or jabbing them with sharp spines.

The crowd surged forward, pressing Gwydion up against the closest of the twin gatehouses. The tower's surface was hard and dark, and it felt oddly warm against the sell-sword's face. He pushed away to get a better look at the small, roundish blocks. They weren't stones, he decided, but fist-sized lumps of . . . *something*. He peered closer, then recoiled in horror.

"Hearts!" he shrieked. "The tower's made of human hearts!"

Af snorted. "Bright boy. The gates are, too." He lowered his snout and stared into Gwydion's terror-filled eyes. "Bet you can't tell me what kind."

"Oh, leave him be," Perdix said. "He doesn't look like a priest to me. They're the only ones who care about such trivia."

"Cowards' hearts," Af gloated, ignoring Perdix completely. "They don't make as good a wall as heroes' hearts, but then, we don't get many heroes here."

Perdix shook his head in disgust. "Tsk. You're so proud of the blasted things, you'd think you built them yourself."

"I did!" Af bellowed. "At least, I was around here when they was first put up!"

Gwydion finally found his voice. "Torm, save me!" he shrieked.

Every denizen in earshot turned to Gwydion, and a webbed hand clamped over his mouth. "None of that, slug," Perdix hissed. "There's one god in the City of Strife, and he don't like his subjects calling out to any of the others. We don't care if you get in deep with him the first day you're on your own, but right now you're our charge. This reflects bad on Af and me."

"And we certainly don't need the grief," the wolf-headed denizen grumbled. He balled one taloned hand into a fist and brought it hard against Gwydion's jaw. Bones shattered. Teeth spilled from the shade's mouth like marbles from a torn bag.

Perdix frowned. "You're our own worst enemy, Af," he sighed, wrapping one leathery wing around Gwydion to shield him from further blows. "If he can't speak, they'll be really miffed at the castle. Remember what happened

19

last time, when you twisted that shade's head off?"

Af slithered sideways on his coils. "Aw, this'll heal before he gets in to see him. 'Sides, he was calling on another power. You know the rules about that."

Reluctantly Perdix agreed but was careful to impose himself between Gwydion and Af until the gates opened.

Horns sounded from high in the gatehouses, and the dark doors creaked apart just wide enough for three men to pass through, shoulder to shoulder. Denizens shoved their wards through the gap, then followed close behind. The shades tried their futile best to resist these last few steps into the City of Strife. The matter was always decided by the steady push from the thousands of damned souls milling behind the reluctant prisoners.

A straight boulevard led away from the gates, lined on both sides by hundreds of skeletal guardians wielding pikes and spears. The undead soldiers existed solely to abuse the newly damned and their captors. With their razor-sharp weapons, they sliced off chunks of flesh that were quickly ground into paste beneath the mob's feet. Along the boulevard, hungry things with haunted eyes waited impatiently in the shadows, hoping to recover some morsel.

Had anyone passing through the gates needed to breathe, the press would have suffocated him before he'd gone a dozen steps. A constant drone filled the air. This wasn't a tapestry of prayers, as on the Fugue Plain, but a shrill curtain of vile curses and anguished cries. Near the gates, the noise was so great no one bothered to speak below a shout. Thankfully, the twisted, scarred, ten-story brownstones that made up the skyline muted the sound as the mob approached the city's center.

Time blurred for Gwydion as he made his way with countless others to the heart of the City of Strife. Only the steady healing of his jaw marked the passing of the hours.

He could feel the bones knit, the new teeth pushing through the raw gums. The pain still plagued him, blurring his vision and scattering his thoughts, but it had lessened to a continuous, throbbing ache. Gwydion wondered dully if his capacity to feel such mundane agony had been stunted. After all, the pain from the spikes buried in his wrists had diminished, too. In his heart, though, the sellsword knew better than to hope he'd be immune to torture after this. The denizens would invent new kinds of pain for him if the old ones wore thin.

Finally the mob crossed the living bridge that spanned the gurgling black ooze of the River Slith, then dashed through the open gates of the great palace at the center of the necropolis. Hemmed in by defensive walls newly built of the purest diamonds, the shades were allowed to rest. Most of the damned collapsed, exhausted by the run. Not Gwydion the Quick. He stood, unfazed by the marathon, staring up at the shadowy heights of Bone Castle.

The keep reached high into the red sky. Its lowest floors were wrought of skulls that looked out sightlessly on the courtyard. Higher up, other bones found their way into the architecture, forming fantastically spiraling frames around windows, sturdy braces for balconies. Winged denizens used these balconies to enter the palace or launch themselves into the mist swirling around the upper stories. Higher still, the tower's jagged peak disappeared into a thick miasma of smoke and fog.

"Awright," Af barked. "Time to go."

The keep's front door had opened, and the denizens were scrambling around the bailey, roughly rousing the shades. Gwydion was still on his feet, so he was the first to be ushered forward.

"Please," the sell-sword said miserably. "I think there's been a mistake." His jaw clicked painfully with each syllable, and his teeth felt loose, but at least he could talk again.

"See," Af chimed. "I told you his jaw would heal before we got in to see the prince."

Scowling, Perdix grabbed the chain between Gwydion's manacles and yanked him toward the keep. "What kind of mistake? You think you don't belong here, slug?"

"I don't even know where here is!" Gwydion shouted.

"Ho ho! One of the Faithless, eh?" Af rubbed his spider legs together gleefully as he slithered alongside Gwydion. "Then it's into the wall for you."

"He isn't one of the Faithless," Perdix scoffed. "He cried out for the Fool outside the gates. That's why you busted him in the jaw, remember?" The denizen turned his lone blue eye on Gwydion. "You believe in the gods?"

"Of—of course," he stammered. "Someone cast an illusion that caused my death. I was a warrior of—"

"Don't you learn?" Perdix snapped. "Isn't one crack in the jaw enough? You can't say any of the gods' names down here—excepting Lord Cyric's, of course." He pulled Gwydion to the threshold of Bone Castle. "You're in Hades, in the City of Strife. Since you couldn't pray to any of the other powers out on the Fugue Plain, you get sent here, to be judged by the Lord of the Dead himself. If you're smart, you'll keep quiet. Sometimes Cyric goes easy on the first soul of a new lot, but only if he isn't a whiner."

"You're getting soft," Af snorted. "I say we crack his spine so he ain't got no choice but to whine at the prince."

Perdix shrugged. "Be my guest, but don't forget who has to see the slug's punishment is carried out. If he gets off easy, we dump him in the boroughs and be done with him."

Gwydion opened his mouth to speak, but Af silenced him with a vicious snarl. "I guess you're right," the denizen grumbled through wolfish teeth. "But it sure woulda been nice to see this slug take a bit of the old man's wrath."

Af and Perdix hustled their charge past the massive slab

of carved onyx serving as the main door, into an entry hall built upon a floor of seamless crystal. Colored glass fibers spun by the drow of Menzoberranzan had been woven into beautiful tapestries that covered the bone walls. The hangings depicted the atrocities the dark elves regularly visited on the peace-loving people of the North. Yet those scenes were but a child's dark fancy compared to the things Gwydion glimpsed through the floor.

"In here, slug," Perdix said, his rasping voice lowered to a respectful whisper.

The room beyond the ghastly entry hall was large, but sparsely furnished. A podium stood in the center, a wide ribbon of parchment hanging from its top and curling down its single leg. To its right sat a bulky chair. The ancient throne had been weirdly beautiful long ago, with scrollwork carved in hypnotic patterns over much of the night-black wood. In recent years, some vandal had chipped away at the arms and legs with a blade. Rubies had once formed a circle on the back that would appear as a crystalline halo to anyone looking at the man seated there. Half the gems were missing now, the crimson circle broken and ragged.

Light bleeding in through the room's stained glass windows painted everything the brown of dried blood. Thousands of skulls lined the walls, their mouths open in perpetual, silent screams. Thick rolls of parchment had been stuffed into each maw. Spider webs hung from the skulls like banners in a dining hall, and tiny white eyes peered out from between the decaying skulls in every part of the room. Somehow Gwydion knew these weren't rats, but something far more malevolent.

The denizens brought their captive to the podium and forced him to his knees. Af and Perdix followed suit, prostrating themselves as much as their twisted forms would allow.

No sooner had the creatures touched their foreheads to the floor than the seneschal of Bone Castle appeared at the podium. The monstrous scribe's smooth, gray face held no features other than a pair of bulging yellow eyes. His body was nothing more than a shadow-filled cloak, which rose and fell upon a wind Gwydion could not feel. With white gloves supported by unseen arms and hands, the creature produced a quill pen and positioned it steadily over the scrolled parchment.

From every corner of the library, every skull and roll of parchment, cockroaches skittered into the light. The insects dropped to the floor with a patter like a hard autumn rain. Large and small, black and brown and white as bone they scrambled toward the empty chair. Gwydion felt the roaches racing over his legs, across his back, but the denizens grabbed his hands when he tried to swat them away.

The insects scaled the chair's battered legs, heaped themselves into a hissing pile upon the seat. And then the cockroaches were gone, melted together into the form of a rather mundane-seeming man, lean and hawk-nosed and apparently quite bored. He slouched low in his seat, his legs crossed at the ankles, his arms draped loosely at his sides. His clothes were hardly regal—high boots, drab black trousers, leather scabbard, and a shapeless crimson tunic bearing the emblem of a black sunburst and skull. Only his short sword and his circlet of white gold marked him as someone important in Bone Castle, though the crown seemed to be intended less as a show of power than as a device to hold the man's long brown hair back from his eyes. Yet for all this apparent ennui, an air of tension hung around him like a pestilent cloud. No matter how far he slouched in the chair, he was still a coiled serpent, ready to strike at the slightest provocation.

"Hail, Cyric, Lord of the Dead, greatest of all the powers

of Faerun," Perdix said, kowtowing.

Af repeated the gesture. "Hail, Cyric, Prince of Lies, slayer of three gods."

The Lord of the Dead fidgeted, as if he were anxious to be elsewhere. Whether the impatience was purely for show or merely the echo of some habit of Cyric's from his mortal life was unclear, but like all the greater powers, the Prince of Lies wasn't limited to a single physical incarnation. Even as he held court in Bone Castle, his divine consciousness manifested in dozens of avatars across the universe, answering the prayers of his faithful, sowing strife and discord wherever it would take root.

"Let's get this over with, Jergal," the Lord of the Dead murmured.

The seneschal leveled his gaze at Gwydion, and the shade felt something cold and inhuman slither across his mind. It burrowed into his memories, rooting through his life like a rat in so much refuse. Gwydion tried to look away from Jergal's lifeless eyes, but he found himself paralyzed. Then, as quickly as it had begun, the interrogation was over.

You are Gwydion, son of Gareth the blacksmith. The disembodied voice was as chilling as Jergal's mental probe. *Born in Suzail thirty winters ago, as time is reckoned there. In your life you have been a soldier and a sell-sword, though your only true gift was your fleetness of foot. This you used mostly to win petty wagers. No great happiness touched your life, nor any great pain.*

"Wait a minute," Gwydion sputtered. "What about Cardea or Eri? I loved—"

You believed in the gods of Faerun, but worshiped them only in times of danger. You named the Fool your patron, but displayed neither great courage nor any loyalty to his causes throughout the last years of your lifetime.

Cyric yawned. "Your deeds have branded you one of the

False," the Lord of the Dead said without thought. "No god will accept you into his paradise, so you are my ward. As such—"

Gwydion leaped to his feet. "I died fighting for Torm! He must—"

The name of the God of Duty had barely left the shade's lips when a short sword pierced his throat. Gwydion hung, impaled on Cyric's blade, twitching and coughing. A chill unlike any the shade had felt in life or death spread from the wound, leaching his very essence. The short sword pulsed, and its blade darkened slowly from pale red to deep crimson.

The Lord of the Dead turned cold eyes on Af and Perdix. "Someone should have informed him I alone may repeat the name of another god in the City of Strife."

"We—we did, Your Magnificence," Perdix said. "But he thinks there's been some sort of mistake. He claims someone tricked him and—"

"Everyone thinks there's been a mistake when they end up here," Cyric noted. "You two will share this one's punishment for a time, just so you'll be more diligent in preparing the shades to meet me in the future." He slipped his sword from Gwydion's throat and let the shade drop to the floor.

"Thank you, Your Magnificence," Af said. Both the denizens prostrated themselves before their master.

"As for a fate . . . We haven't sent Dendar any souls recently, right, Jergal?"

The Night Serpent would be glad for your generosity, the seneschal agreed. *She has not tasted the marrow of a fresh soul in quite a long time.*

Cyric slouched back into his chair. "Then it's decided. Take the shade to Dendar."

As Jergal scratched notes with careful, precise strokes of the pen, the denizens grabbed Gwydion. The shade,

27

though weakened by the abuse, fought them. He gasped something at Cyric, but the words wheezed from his punctured throat like steam from a hot kettle.

The untempered astonishment in Gwydion's eyes caught Cyric's attention. The Lord of the Dead gestured, and the shade's wounds healed instantly. "You recognize me?" he asked, idly striking the chair's leg with his sword.

Gwydion pointed to the blood-red blade. "It was you," he gasped. "You came to me in Thar. You pretended to be—"

The Fool, Jergal prompted. *Each god has a name more appropriate to his or her stature in our realm. The God of Duty is known here as the Fool.*

"You pretended to be . . . the Fool," Gwydion said. Speaking the blasphemous name made him wince. "Why? Just to trick me into throwing myself at the giant like a lunatic?"

"Exactly so," came a deep, booming voice from the doorway to the library. "That is just the sort of petty amusement Cyric makes for himself."

Jergal, Gwydion, and the denizens spun around to find a massive figure standing before them. His ancient armor was stained dusky purple, with elbow and knee cops wrought of dragon bones. Light glinted like stars on his breastplate, even in the badly lit library. He radiated power, stern and unforgiving.

"Oh no," Perdix whispered. "Not *him*. Not *now*."

Torm the True strode toward Cyric. His armor clanked as he walked, the sharp sounds echoing off the walls like distant cannonades. At Gwydion's side Torm stopped and removed his helmet. The shade had never seen such a perfectly handsome young warrior. The light of righteousness flashed in his blue eyes. Unwavering courage set his square jaw.

"Release this soul," Torm ordered. "You drew him into

your realm through illusions and perfidy. You cut short his life through deception."

The Lord of the Dead sat back in his chair and scowled. "Oh, come now, Torm. You didn't journey all the way to Hades for this worm. You have bigger giants to slay—isn't that how the expression goes amongst your Tormites?"

"*Tormish*," the God of Duty corrected stiffly. "And Gwydion's fate alone is enough to bring me to your loathsome court. He called upon me. I am answering his prayer."

A cry of relief escaped Gwydion's lips. "Thank you, Your Holiness. I knew you wouldn't let a faithful—"

"Don't shower him with praise just yet," Cyric interrupted slyly. "Torm cares nothing for your soul. He has enough power to enter my city uninvited only because you spoke his name aloud. You've provided a convenient way for him to make himself unwelcome in my home."

The anger Torm had been fighting to suppress boiled over. He raised a mailed fist and shook it at the Prince of Lies. "I have a duty to my worshipers. Men call me Torm the True because I value loyalty above all else. They call me—"

"They call you Torm the Brave because you are too stupid to cut your losses and abandon a failed fight," Cyric hissed. "I know the litany quite well. I repeated it rather dramatically to Gwydion in Thar not too long ago."

Torm took a menacing step toward Cyric, who still had not risen from his chair. "We get to the meat of the matter quickly. That's unlike you."

"Ah, you came here to inform me you are unflattered by my impersonation." The Prince of Lies laughed. "It was quite good, I assure you. Apart from the sword, I had you to a T." He stood and stretched. "Still, I'll give you a chance to save this poor, abused soul."

"You admit your sins?" Torm asked, narrowing his eyes suspiciously. "Gwydion is free to leave?"

"I admit nothing," Cyric said, "but I'll give you the chance to rescue this would-be Tormite." He kicked Af out of the way and raised Gwydion by the shackles. "Before you take him under your armored wing, though, you must convince me he will have a home with your faithful. I cannot release a soul from my realm without such a guarantee."

"If not with me," Torm began, "then with—"

"You cannot speak for the other gods, Torm. I'm surprised you would be bold enough to try."

The God of Duty flushed. He turned his steady gaze on Gwydion and said, "I can offer you sanctuary, but only if you are truly one of my faithful. Will you prove your devotion to me?"

The shade stepped forward, away from the cringing denizens and the weird, silent seneschal. "Of course," he said.

Torm straightened his fingers and held his hands out, palms to the floor. The sickly glow from the windows revealed myriad tiny runes carved into his gauntlets: on the right hand, the word for duty in every language ever known; on the left, the same for loyalty.

It was whispered that Torm could be destroyed if all those words were lost. To prevent this disaster, some Tormish novices spent their first year of servitude sequestered in tiny cells, where they repeated one of the words for duty or loyalty, mantralike, throughout their waking hours. The most devoted of them even kept up their assigned chant in their sleep.

"Read any word from either gauntlet," Torm said solemnly.

Gwydion squinted at the armor, then looked up at the God of Duty. "I . . . I see no writing, Your Holiness."

A genuine sadness filled Torm's eyes. "The pact I have with my church is clear, Gwydion the Quick. I cannot accept your soul if you cannot pass this simple test." The anger returned then, flaring hotly. He faced Cyric. "You will pay for this. I'll make certain of that."

The Prince of Lies turned his back on the armored god and walked slowly to his chair. "Af, Perdix, take Gwydion and stick him in the wall. Watch over him until I summon you again."

Silently Gwydion looked to Torm for aid, but the God of Duty shook his head. All the shade's hopes died. Head down, he let the denizens lead him away without a struggle.

As soon as the prisoner had left the room, Cyric waved a hand, idly dismissing Torm. "Go on, report his punishment to the Circle. I know perfectly well the wall is reserved for the Faithless. I put the worm there for one reason: I want you to know for the rest of eternity you made things worse for him by sticking your square jaw where it didn't belong."

"The law that governs—"

"My whim is law in the City of Strife," Cyric snapped. "You'd be well-served to remember that, especially since you are trespassing. If I happen to summon a few hundred pit fiends to escort you out . . ."

"You threaten me!" The God of Duty transformed, his handsome features becoming leonine. "I could slay every pit fiend in your hellish home," he roared.

"But they would keep you occupied for quite some time," Cyric cooed. "Long enough for me to visit your churches in your guise and start a holy war. You wouldn't have the might to stop me, either. After all, Torm, you are only a demipower."

Torm stalked to the edge of the library. His lion's face was locked in an angry snarl. His golden mane bristled around his head like a halo. "You are unfit to be called a greater power." With a flash of blue light, he was gone.

The Fool is lucky he cannot know how dangerous you truly are, Your Magnificence, Jergal noted.

Cyric drew his short sword again and stared intently at the crimson blade. "If he did, I would simply deal with him as I did Bhaal and Myrkul and Leira. In fact, I might kill him anyway. My sword has gained a taste for the blood of gods." He ran his hand gently along the blade. "Haven't you, my love?"

Only if it is blood spilled for you, a seductive, feminine voice purred. The spirit of the sword curled contentedly in the mire of Cyric's consciousness, as dark and vicious as any of the corrupt thoughts lurking in the death god's mind.

II

BOOK OF LIES

*Wherein the three hundred ninety-seventh
version of a book detailing Cyric's life receives a
very harsh review indeed, much to the dismay
of the scribes and illuminators
in Zhentil Keep.*

Bevis had been an illuminator for fifteen years, and he
couldn't think of an instant when he'd enjoyed his job. He
hated the perpetual ink stains blotting his fingers. The
sour-smelling paints made his eyes run, and he never finished a day's work when his hand wasn't cramped to the
wrist. The problem was, Bevis had no other skills he
might put to legal use and even less bravado with which to
cut himself a niche in Zhentil Keep's sizable and thriving
underworld.

And so he plodded through the days, providing artistic
embellishments for dull collections of sermons, tedious

accounts of local battles, and pompous autobiographies by guildmasters hoping to buy a place in Zhentish history. Bevis found the work he did on penitentials a bit less tiresome. Such books detailed the penance demanded for various sins and usually contained vivid scenes of denizens torturing souls in the City of Strife—just in case the faithful needed to be reminded of the penalties for shirking. Like all the other miniatures Bevis drew, the horrific images originated in a pattern book. Still, copying denizens was more interesting than repeatedly scribbling the holy symbol of Mask on cheap paper intended for thieves' guild ransom notes.

The volume in Bevis's uninspired care at the moment had snared his attention more completely than even the most gruesome penitential. He'd been hired by the Church of Cyric to clean up the gatherings of finished pages before they went to the stationer for binding; even with the mysterious shortage of scribes and illuminators in Zhentil Keep, the clerics had rudely informed Bevis that his skill wasn't up to standards to provide any borders or miniatures for this important work. After scanning the first few pages, he was inclined to agree.

The parchment was the finest he'd ever seen, thin and flexible and textured perfectly to hold ink and paint. Ornate display scripts written in bold red ink called out the intention of each new section. Weird borders of bestial denizens lurked around the text, apparently warning the squeamish reader away from the knowledge they guarded. Large squares of rubbed gold foil served as backdrop for the miniatures. The most elaborate of these depicted cities under siege by unnatural monsters and the gods themselves being cast from the heavens.

"Ah, the Time of Troubles," the illuminator whispered, then nervously scanned the cavernous room surrounding him.

The priests had gone back to the warmth of the temple long ago, leaving Bevis alone in the crypts. A ring of braziers drew a wide circle of light around him, but he still had the uneasy feeling someone hovered just out of sight. After a staring into the darkness for a time, though, the illuminator decided he was being foolish. He was alone. The priests would never know he'd disobeyed their strict orders and read just a small part of the book.

The Wrath of Ao, the page before him declared in grand, noble letters. The section described how the overlord of the gods, angry at the theft of the Tablets of Fate, had banished the deities of Faerun from their eternal palaces in the heavens. The gods-made-mortal were forced to walk the world in mortal avatars until the tablets were returned. In their wakes, chaos and strife erupted. Magic became unstable, clerics could no longer call on their heavenly patrons to heal the sick, murder and violence seized even the West's most civilized nations and city-states.

This was all the stuff of history, and in the decade since the Time of Troubles, dozens of treatises had been written to explain the calamitous events. Bevis had even illuminated one, five years back. Yet something about this telling drew his interest. He felt strangely compelled to read on. Collecting the gatherings before him, Bevis sorted them into a ragged-edged pile.

The Theft of the Tablets—well, that goes before the section I just read, he thought. *The Betrayal of the Guild*— this history isn't limited to the Time of Troubles. It's about Cyric before he became a god! *A Childhood in the Shadows. Kelemvor and the Ring of Winter. The Knightsbridge Affair. . . .*

Breathless, Bevis scanned the first page of each gathering. An illumination showed Cyric in his days as a young thief, sneaking up on an unsuspecting guard atop the black walls of Zhentil Keep. The next entry told of his first meeting with Midnight, the sorceress who would quest for the Tablets of Fate alongside Cyric, the cursed warrior Kelemvor Lyonsbane, and a vain priest named Adon. Little did Cyric or Midnight suspect that first night in Arabel they would recover the tablets and be rewarded by Lord Ao with a place among the gods.

A violent miniature bright with the sheen of gold caught Bevis's eye as he turned to the next gathering. The artist had created a ghastly scene of slaughter in a halfling village. Zhentish soldiers spitted small women and children on pikes. The houses and barns burned in gold foil while severed heads with ink-black eyes looked on. And in the center of the carnage stood Cyric, a rose-red short sword clutched in his bloody hands. A halo of darkness foretold his future divinity.

The display script next to the gory scene proclaimed its topic simply: *Black Oaks and Godsbane*.

So it came to pass that Cyric freed himself from the company of the whore Midnight, the preening Adon of Sune, and the cursed swordsman Kelemvor Lyonsbane. He gathered around him, in the days that followed, a small force of Zhentilar and made them prophets of his ascension. He crossed the Heartlands with these soldiers, striking down any who challenged his vision of a world free from the hypocrisy of Law and Honor.

The blood of doubting kings stained their blades, the brains of foolish sages spattered their armor. Yet each shattered skull or riven heart recruited twin heralds to Cyric's cause. In the mortal realms, the corrupting corpses reneged their challenges to his greatness with silent screams and faces frozen with terror. In Hades and the other heavenly realms, the newly liberated souls arrived with a proclamation: Make ready, for a god comes who will take all the vast universe for his domain.

Once his message had spread and the people realized that freedom could only be earned through Might, Cyric found himself welcomed as a conquering hero by many cities and towns. They hung garlands around the necks of his men and presented lavish feasts in his honor.

Yet some isolated hamlets—like the halfling village of Black Oaks—remained blind to Cyric's glory. The stunted creatures that dwelled in Black Oaks shunned him and threatened to call down the wrath of the feeble icons they worshiped. Even then, a month before his ascension from the top of Mount Waterdeep, Cyric knew someone of his stature could not tolerate such insults.

With fire and steel, he scourged Black Oaks from the map of Faerun. As his Zhentilar burned the squalid houses, Cyric herded the halflings together and beheaded them one by one. The heads were set in neat rows, like gawking, bloody cabbages awaiting harvest; Cyric then cursed the bloated lumps of bone and flesh to an unending living death. To this day, the ravaged skulls speak to all who look upon them, decrying their foolishness.

Because his blade had been so dulled by his tiresome work upon the halflings, Cyric sought another to replace it. He liberated a powerful enchanted sword from the hands of Sneakabout, the greatest warrior in Black Oaks and the only one to escape the village that day. The spirit of the blade had broken the halfling's will, making him an unquestioning slave. There was no shame in this, for until Cyric held her, the rose-hued sword had been unconquered. Great was the line of soldiers and kings destroyed trying to bend the blade to their purposes, but only Cyric had sufficient will to triumph over her.

The enchanted, rose-hued sword served Cyric well, shielding him against the chill winds of Marpenoth, healing the wounds he received in the fierce battles for the Tablets of Fate. In return, Cyric rewarded her with blood. Like all who serve him selflessly, the sword received that which she desired most.

Fane, a Zhentilar officer, was the first to give his life to the blade. The halfling Sneakabout was next. Yet the essence of these men would prove to be mere scraps before the banquets on which the blade soon feasted.

At Boareskyr Bridge, Cyric slew Bhaal, Patron of Assassins, Lord of Murder. So great was the chaos unleashed at Bhaal's death that the Winding Water still runs black and poisonous from Boareskyr Bridge to Trollclaw Ford. Every creature that drinks of the river dies cursing those who stand against Cyric, for such resistance is futile, as the poisoned water surely proves.

Bhaal was not the last god unmade by Cyric's hand. Atop the tower of Khelben "Blackstaff" Arunson, a mage known as a foe of both Zhentil Keep and her agents, Cyric faced his united enemies, for Midnight had allied with Myrkul, the fallen God of Death. Together they had hatched a cowardly plan to place the Tablets of Fate—and thus all the lands of Faerun—into the hands of those gods who worshiped Law and Good above all sense. Cyric slew Myrkul for turning against his worshipers. With a single stroke of his enchanted blade, he sliced the god's avatar in two. The corpse dissolved into ashes, which rained down upon Waterdeep, melting away buildings and roads.

Kelemvor Lyonsbane died that glorious day atop Blackstaff Tower, too. And the traitorous Midnight would have followed her lover to destruction had she not called upon her magic to flee from Cyric's wrath. It is because of this cowardice that Lord Ao commanded Midnight to abandon her name when he raised her up to take the place of the destroyed Goddess of Magic. And so it was that Midnight became Mystra.

Thus has the enchanted, rose-hued short sword come to be known as Godsbane, for no other weapon in the history of Faerun has been used to strike down the powers that rule over the mortal realms.

Bevis closed the gathering. Reading in the braziers' flickering light had given him a throbbing headache, and his mouth was strangely dry. He rubbed his temples and squeezed his eyes shut for a moment, hoping to banish the ache, but the grisly illuminations flashed in his mind. The words of the history echoed in his thoughts like a siren song, calling him to read on. Perhaps it was a spell-book of some sort, disguised to appear as a life of Cyric. Or perhaps the clerics had placed a curse on the pages to punish anyone who might read it uninvited.

His heart pounding, Bevis overturned the stack of pages in search of a clue. The scribes' guild in Zhentil Keep required its members to place a colophon on a manuscript's final page. Usually these personal notes—written in the guild's esoteric code—expressed the scribe's relief at having completed the book, along with a prayer that he be paid well for his efforts. For dangerous tomes, the colophon warned other guild members to browse the text only at their own risk.

The colophon for this volume was longer than most. It started with the common exclamations of relief and complaints of cramped hands, then moved on to hopes for a pretty wench and a pint of fine ale. The final section of the colophon had been obscured by hasty crosshatching, which indicated the lines should be scraped from the parchment before binding. The marks made the text difficult to read, but Bevis was not unpracticed in deciphering such puzzles.

From the god's mouth to my pen, in this, the tenth year of Cyric's reign as Lord of the Dead. Three hundred ninety and seven versions of this tome have come before. May it please my immortal master not to use my skin for the pages of the three hundred ninety-eighth.

With a cry of horror, Bevis pushed the gatherings away. They fluttered from the table and settled to the floor like vultures dropping around a corpse.

"That's hardly the way an artist should treat the work of his fellows," said a voice from the shadows.

Bevis spun around. Someone was there, in the darkest part of the crypt. "P-Patriarch Mirrormane?" the illuminator stammered, cautiously reaching for his penknife.

"Hardly." The man lurking in the darkness stepped forward. He was young and lean, with a catlike grace that betrayed his training as a thief. Brushing aside his black cloak, he planted a hand dramatically on the hilt of his short sword. The weapon hung from a loop on the man's belt, its rose-hued blade unmasked by a scabbard. "Did you enjoy my book?"

The illuminator mouthed a reply, but the words wouldn't leave his throat. The hawk-nosed man stalked closer, his footfalls utterly silent on the crypt's cold stone floor. He bent down and retrieved a gathering, one that depicted the Lord of the Dead, then held the page up next to his face for Bevis to compare. The miniature was a remarkable likeness, right down to the halo of darkness.

"Oh gods," Bevis managed to gasp as he crumpled to the floor.

Cyric's cruel smile widened. "No, the only one that matters."

* * * * *

Bevis hung limp against the stone pillar, blissfully unaware of the three figures gathered around him. The ring of braziers still burned brightly, but they were no longer needed. With only a thought from Cyric, light had filled the catacombs, revealing every inch of the uneven stone floors and low vaulted ceilings.

"I wish Fzoul would hurry up!" Xeno Mirrormane shrieked. The high priest's silver-white hair curled wildly around his head as he stalked forward, waving the steaming iron rod at Bevis. The priest's thin frame was hidden by the bulk of his dark purple robes. "I want to get started on this spy before dinner."

The fat nobleman lounging nearby yawned and held a scented handkerchief to his bulbous nose. "Your departed brother would have been proud of the way you wield that thing, Xeno," he drawled through his square of patterned Shou silk. "You have taken to your newfound role as patriarch admirably. We are all grateful you could replace Maskul after he passed away so, er, mysteriously."

"Spare us your innuendos, Lord Chess," Cyric said. "You know Xeno murdered Maskul. Your spies informed you of the deed even before the dagger found his heart. It shouldn't have surprised you, though. After all, Xeno serves me, and I am the Lord of Murder, am I not?"

The facade of foppishness slipped, and the ruler of Zhentil Keep withdrew the handkerchief from his face. "Of course, Your Magnificence," he murmured.

"Tell me, Chess," Cyric demanded sharply, "do you still pray to Leira for a way to hide your disgusting gut from your courtesans? Illusions only conceal so much, you know."

Flushing in embarrassment, Chess straightened his bulk against the crypt's stone wall. When he looked to Cyric for some sign of approval, he found the god's avatar had wandered away into the cavernous catacombs, leaving him to wonder just how the Lord of the Dead had intercepted prayers sent to another in the heavens.

The crypts had once held the honored dead of Bane—priests and warriors and accomplished statesmen who had dedicated their lives to the former God of Strife. After the Time of Troubles, when Cyric had taken Bane's mantle, he directed his minions to plunder the places sacred to the Black Lord. They defaced the beautiful marble statues and tombs before they smashed them to rubble. The remains of Bane's faithful they dumped unceremoniously into the River Tesh.

The Church of Cyric had yet to create enough of their own martyrs to fill the now-desolate crypts, so the space was used for other purposes. A group of church assassins had taken to meditating amidst the rats and spiders and more chilling creatures that stalked the dark catacombs. Apart from them, and the few church wizards who conducted secret experiments in the crypts, the expanse of vaults and chambers remained empty. They wound unused beneath the vast complex of temples and monasteries dedicated to the Prince of Lies.

Cyric paced uneasily across the ragged indentation where a marker had once graced the floor. *Perhaps I should let Xeno enshrine the scribes who labored on the early versions of the* Cyrinishad, *he mused. That would fill this place up soon enough. I might even give the scribes' bodies back, if the clerics wish to bury what's left of them.*

The Prince of Lies closed his eyes and listened. The unending shrieks of the men and women who had penned the failed tomes filled his ears, even from their place of fiery imprisonment in the throne room of Bone Castle. . . .

A jarring clatter chased the wails of the damned from Cyric's consciousness. He glanced back at the others; Xeno had dropped the iron into a brazier for reheating. The thought of entombing the patriarch with his murdered brother flashed through the death god's mind—pleasant repayment for this incessant shrieking and fidgeting—but amusement quickly drowned Cyric's annoyance.

Cyric had taken on a physical avatar for this visit to Zhentil Keep, something he'd seldom done since becoming a god. He preferred instead to haunt the dreams of his worshipers as a bloody wraith or manifest as a cloud of poisonous smoke before his enemies. He'd forgotten what it was like to perceive the world through senses easily plagued by distractions. The strange feeling was pleasant, in a nostalgic way, and it softened his dark mood just a little.

The echoes of Fzoul's footfalls preceded him into the crypts. When he appeared at the base of the stairs, he showed no signs of having hurried to answer Cyric's call. In fact, from the ceremonial dress he wore, it seemed as if the priest had taken the time to array himself for the meeting. The weird radiance lighting the catacombs made Fzoul's black armor appear slick, like a snake's scales just after it molts. Once the holy symbol of Bane had graced the breastplate. Now it was blank, a midnight sky devoid of stars. Bands of silver plundered from the centaurs of Lethyr Forest bound his long red hair in a braid and ringed his drooping mustaches.

Fzoul slid the gloves from his hands one long finger at a time, then folded the dragon-leather gauntlets and slipped them into his belt. "Your Magnificence," he said without reverence or enthusiasm. The priest dropped to one knee and bowed his head, more to hide the look of disdain on his harsh features than to show his submission.

Cyric's cruel laughter filled the crypts. "Your reluctance only makes your worship that much sweeter to savor, Fzoul. I know you hate me. You've hated me ever since I put that arrow in you at the Battle of Shadowdale." He smirked. "Tell me, do the war wounds hurt on Bane's old high holy days?"

Fury flashed like lightning in the priest's eyes. He gritted his teeth to hold back a bitter reply.

"That's right, Fzoul. Send silent prayers to every dark power in the universe," Cyric said. "The other gods can't bring Bane back, and they'll do nothing against me." The mirth had fled his voice now, and his gaze pierced the priest's soul.

Slowly Fzoul stood. A pall of fear had damped the jagged streaks of anger. "So you have proved, again and again over the last ten winters, Your Magnificence."

To break the tension that had settled over the group, Lord Chess smiled broadly and clapped a hand on Fzoul's shoulder. "Tell me, how go things with the Zhentarim? Have your mages found any trace of Kelemvor Lyonsbane? Damned strange, his soul missing for all these years." He beamed foolishly at Cyric. "Your Magnificence killed him too well, I fear."

Godsbane stirred uneasily against Cyric's thigh. *I long to drink the blood of all these prattling apes,* the rose-hued sword purred in the god's mind.

The dark smile returned to Cyric's face as the sword shared visions of carnage with him. The Prince of Lies dwelled upon those; Fzoul's precise uninteresting explanation for the Zhentarim's inability to find Kelemvor's soul lodged itself in another part of Cyric's immense consciousness.

The Lord of the Dead didn't particularly trust the Zhentarim. Since the destruction of their immortal patron, Bane, the Black Network had continued to subtly undermine the lawful kingdoms of Faerun by means of spies and assassins. The mages who controlled the group had proved annoyingly loyal to the memory of Bane or, even more infuriating, to the Goddess of Magic. Still, Cyric recognized their usefulness, especially for matters that required the services of talented sorcerers.

"And the oracles can find no trace of Lyonsbane," Fzoul concluded flatly. "If his soul fled your wrath and hides in the realms of the living, some great power is shielding him from our magic."

Cyric frowned. "The same as every report for the past

ten years," he rumbled. "Mystra is behind this, or one of her allies. But they won't keep Kelemvor hidden from me forever, not after the *Cyrinishad* steals their worshipers away, eh Xeno?"

The patriarch cackled madly and lifted the stack of parchment from the table. "You're fortunate, Fzoul. Someone else has given the book its first review—part of it, anyway." He gestured to Bevis with his chin. "We'll put the brand to him and see if he believes it."

"Don't worry, Fzoul," Cyric murmured as he passed close to the priest. "You'll get to read the book next if this little experiment proves successful. That's why I called you here. I want you to be the first to see the error of your ways."

After shaking Bevis awake, Xeno held the hot iron rod against the man's bare feet. The pain sent the illuminator into an agonized swoon. As soon as his mind cleared, the smell of his own charred flesh made the gorge rise in his throat.

"I'm sorry," Bevis choked. "I know I wasn't supposed to read it. B-But once I started, I couldn't stop."

Xeno howled triumphantly. "Couldn't help yourself, you say?" He waved the smoldering iron in front of Bevis's face. "You wouldn't lie about that, would you?"

"No!" the prisoner shrieked. "P-Please. I won't tell anyone what I read. I won't tell them what the book says!"

Rubbing his double chin, Lord Chess scowled and shook his head. "That's not the point at all. We'd really rather you tell everyone."

Bevis looked hopefully into the foppish nobleman's eyes. "Then I will. I'll stand in the streets and shout the story over and over. Look, my daughter used to be a scribe, an excellent one, too. She quit the guild, but I'll get her to help copy the text if you want. . . ."

"This is getting us nowhere," Fzoul snapped. He grabbed

the red-hot iron from the patriarch. "We want to find out if he believed the book, not if he can be bullied into becoming a town crier for the church."

At a nod from Cyric, Fzoul Chembryl started a long, systematic torture of Bevis. For more than an hour the illuminator endured the pain. He repeated much of what he'd read from the *Cyrinishad,* word for word. The passages were set into his memory with a brilliance undimmed by the priest's most ingenious use of his dagger or the hot iron—until they came to the death of Myrkul and the battle atop Blackstaff Tower.

"I can't remember that part of the story," Bevis shouted through scorched and bleeding lips.

Xeno frowned. "Don't believe him."

"Of course not," Fzoul snapped. He wiped his sweaty brow with the back of one hand, then flicked the salty liquid onto Bevis's flayed cheeks. When the illuminator stopped howling, the priest asked quietly, "Who destroyed Myrkul?"

"It—it was in the other book," Bevis said. "The one about the Time of Troubles I worked on years ago." He began to laugh uncontrollably. "The only book I read from cover to cover, that history was. I thought—"

"The destruction of Myrkul," Cyric prompted impatiently. He unsheathed Godsbane, for some part of him knew the answer before Bevis gave it.

"Midnight killed Myrkul," the illuminator whispered, rolling his eyes back until the whites showed. "But it hurts to think that now, even though the other book said it was true. And Cyric waited in the tower and ambushed Midnight and Kelemvor and the other one, the scarred priest. And he stabbed Kelemvor in the back and stole the Tablets of Fate. He ran away because Midnight would have—"

The crimson blade pierced the man's side, cutting off

his rambling reply. Bevis had time to gasp once as Godsbane drained every drop of blood from him. Then Cyric reached into the corpse and yanked the soul free. Phantasmal and shimmering, the soul seemed to be formed of light, but once he was in the City of Strife, Bevis would be as corporeal as all the other shades—and as vulnerable to eternal torture.

One hand tight around the soul, the Lord of the Dead turned eyes brimming with hellfire on the three mortals in the crypts. "We will start again three days from now, at sunset," he shouted. "Have a scribe ready in the usual place. Find the one who penned this piece of rubbish—" he pointed Godsbane at the gatherings, and the ink disappeared from the pages "—and add his skin to the parchment for the next volume. I'll send a denizen to collect his body when you're done flaying him."

Xeno dropped to his knees. "But we've no more scribes in the temple," he said, his voice quavering. "We've even used up all the guild members we arrested."

The soul in Cyric's grasp burst into flame. "This one said he had a daughter who could write," the god shouted over Bevis's cries for mercy. "If you have no one left, find her. I'll decide if she's worthy of serving me when I meet her." And with that, the Lord of the Dead vanished.

Lord Chess waved his scented handkerchief before him, trying vainly to drive away the stench of charred flesh. "This book will be the ruin of Zhentil Keep yet," he mused, though his voice betrayed little concern.

One silvery eyebrow raised in suspicion, Xeno Mirrormane said, "Sounds to me like you're doubting the god's powers, Chess. I could have you killed for that."

"Don't be melodramatic," Fzoul snapped. "He's only stating the facts of it. If Cyric can find the right scribe and the right wording for his book, he'll have the perfect weapon to convert everyone in Faerun—in the world, even." He thumbed through the blank parchment gatherings. "He was close this time. The artist nearly believed the whole thing, even though he'd read the truth before." Fzoul shook his head. "Read the *Cyrinishad* and believe in it, no matter what it says. Why do you think Mystra denied Cyric the magic to create the book himself? Or why Oghma denied him the services of his eternal scribes? Without worshipers, the rest of the pantheon will disappear, just as if they never existed."

Xeno pulled the pages from Fzoul's hands. "Mystra and Oghma cannot stop Cyric's faithful from creating this tome. And there are many who believe everything His Magnificence tells us even without the *Cyrinishad*. To us, there are no other gods."

"That's the most frightening thing of all," Fzoul said and turned to leave the crypts.

III

POINT OF VIEW

*Wherein Mystra meets with the Circle of Greater
Powers to censure Cyric and discovers that, even
in the heavens, guilt and innocence
are a matter of perspective.*

To each of the gods, the Pavilion of Cynosure appeared
as something different. Sune Firehair saw a vast hall filled
with mirrors to reflect her perfect beauty. Tempus envisioned a planning room deep within a fortified redoubt.
Maps and charts of legendary wars fought by the Lord of
Battles covered every wall, every table. The Great Mother,
Chauntea, perceived the place as an endless field fertile
with wheat. The crops waved slowly in the autumn wind,
eternally ready for harvest.

The gods in the pavilion saw each other with disparate
faces as well. Lathander Morninglord viewed the powers
gathered there as either shafts of light or dark clouds,

forces that augmented or obscured the glorious sunrise of renewal he fostered in the world. For Talos the Destroyer, bellicose Master of Storms, the gods devoted to good or law were islands of annoying calm in the roiling thunderheads before him.

As one facet of her consciousness manifested in the pavilion, Mystra noted with a mixture of amusement and bewilderment that, as always, Lathander and Talos had positioned themselves as far apart as possible. To the Goddess of Magic, the other gods appeared as human mages. Their gorgeous robes were drawn from the magic weave that surrounded Faerun, the web of enchantment from which all sorceries originated. The pavilion itself was a wizard's workshop, filled with bubbling beakers and jars of every arcane substance known to man or god.

"Tell me, O Lady of Mysteries," asked a melodious voice, "have you ever considered why the Morninglord and the Destroyer can't seem to put their differences aside, even for an instant?"

Mystra turned to find Oghma at her side. The God of Knowledge and Patron of Bards bowed and took the goddess's hand. Her dainty alabaster fingers glowed like streaks of moonlight against his dark skin as he raised them to his lips.

The Goddess of Magic smiled at Oghma's gallantry. "Their feud is no mystery," she replied. "It's simply a function of their offices. Renewal and destruction are not particularly complementary pursuits. It's nothing more than that."

"Really?" Oghma said. "When you look around you now, what do you see?"

"A workshop for training mages," she replied.

"And what do the others see—Talos and Lathander and the rest?"

The goddess balked at the insistent tone in Oghma's

voice. "Why do you ask?"

"I'm the God of Knowledge," Oghma said dismissively. "Just exercising my divine curiosity."

From the slight smile on the god's lips, Mystra could tell the reply was hardly the whole truth. Still, there was little to be lost in answering him. If nothing else, it might lead her closer to discovering the real purpose for his prying.

The Goddess of Magic took Oghma's arm in hers and moved gracefully to one of the circular tables scattered about the workshop. The train of her blue-white dress floated behind her like gossamer wings. "Since I see a mage's laboratory, the other gods probably see the pavilion as something familiar to them. Their minds put a facade over the bland reality of the place, making it into something that reflects their office in the pantheon. I suppose you see a library of some sort."

Oghma nodded. "But if I wanted to see the pavilion as something else, or see the reality that underlies the facade my mind has created—what then?"

"You could will your consciousness to do so," Mystra said.

"You're certain it's that simple, are you?" A flicker of disappointment crossed Oghma's expressive features. He fell silent for a moment, then noted abruptly, "Not to change the subject, but I have considered your proposition concerning the Prince of Lies. I don't think it would be wise of me to take a more active stand against him at this time."

"But the *Cyrinishad,* and Leira's disappearance—"

The God of Knowledge held up a restraining hand. "I won't go back on my word to you. The scribes in my domain, and any who worship me in the mortal realms will not aid Cyric in completing the book."

Oghma frowned severely, and his voice took on a decidedly pedantic tone. "But beyond that, I think any open

51

challenge to Cyric—about Leira's disappearance or anything else—would be ill-advised for both of us. You don't understand the way the rest of the Circle thinks, and until you do, any direct confrontation might very well strengthen his position."

"So that's what your little interrogation was about," Mystra said coldly. "You presume a great deal, milord. Don't think the fact that I was once mortal prevents me from understanding the politics of the pantheon."

"I would never slight your humble origin," the Patron of Bards replied. "In fact, I believe the mortality you once faced grants you a rare and wonderful trait for a goddess: humility. Since you aren't so foolishly certain of your own perspective, you might be able to understand how the gods limit one another, how their nature binds them."

"Ever the accomplished bard," Mystra scoffed. "If you offend someone, immediately dole out a compliment to assuage any hurt feelings."

"I count many painfully honest scholars amongst my faithful, and not all the bards who do me worship are flatterers," Oghma replied. His voice was both musical and precise, a chorus of master storytellers speaking in harmony. "Some of the greatest harpers in my kingdom lost their lives because they couldn't tell a king he was handsome or wise or generous when it was not so."

Oghma clasped Mystra's hands in his. "Your name alone shows the truth of your mortal humility," he said. "When Ao raised you up from the mortals, you could have remained Midnight. But you chose instead to adopt the name of the goddess who preceded you."

"It was a political move," she replied ingenuously. "It insured the church's stability. As I said, I'm not as naive as you think."

Oghma ignored her blunt claim. "Because you call yourself Mystra, there are some in the world who say Midnight of Deepingdale never existed, that she is a myth."

The Goddess of Magic shrugged. "There are also some who say Cyric is a myth, though he's spent the last ten years forcing his name upon the worshipers of Bane, Bhaal, and Myrkul. At this moment there are forty-eight bloody battles being fought in the Heartlands because of his pride, his vanity, worshipers killing worshipers over the true name of their god. That's simply foolishness."

"Perhaps. But his name will figure prominently in the tomes that tell the history of Faerun, whereas your mortal name will one day fade away." Oghma smiled. "I see by your face you're not concerned with history, though you should be. After all, control of history is at the heart of Cyric's mad plans. It's the reason he strives to create his much-feared book."

"Pardon me," a deep voice interrupted, "but Cyric is concerned merely with power. The *Cyrinishad* is a means to that end." Torm the True bowed formally to Mystra, then Oghma. "I do not mean to challenge your conclusions, Binder of All Knowledge, but I've had much traffic with the Prince of Lies of late, and I believe—"

"We are not here to discuss what you *believe,* Torm," said the blind man who had suddenly appeared in the pavilion's center. His features were square and unforgiving, like the cut of the magical robes Mystra perceived as his raiments. In his left hand he held a silver balance. His right hand had been chopped off at the wrist. "We are here to discuss the *facts* of Cyric's transgressions, the things you say you witnessed in his realm. When that's done, we shall bring the full weight of the law against him."

Talos paused in carving his name into the tabletop before him. "I say we just waylay him and spread his remains across the planes," he joked, twirling his silver dagger menacingly.

Tyr, the blind God of Justice, prodded his long white beard with his stump and turned sightless eyes on the Destroyer. "You will be given your turn to speak. Hold your peace until then." For a reply, Talos snorted and sliced a long sliver of wood from the tabletop.

"And so begins another conference of the Circle of Greater Powers," Oghma whispered to the Goddess of Magic. "Rather similar to every other meeting, don't you think?"

Mystra had to admit that Oghma was right. The greater powers met infrequently, since problems rarely arose that concerned all of them. Yet, in each of the few meetings Mystra had attended, Tyr had presumed to take control of the Circle, and Talos had disrupted it. Then, as now, Oghma had placidly noted every word and every action of his fellow immortals, while Tempus impatiently suggested his divine army be mustered to solve even the most delicate dilemma with sword and shield.

Mystra realized then that this was the very conclusion Oghma had been laboring to get across: after centuries of interaction, the gods had become predictable. Tyr could be counted on to promote all causes furthering law and good in Faerun. Talos would just as surely oppose such measures, striving to create chaos and, at least as Tyr defined it, evil. In the same way, the viewpoints of Talos and Lathander made it difficult for them to find any common ground.

Difficult, she decided, but not impossible. Surely the gods could break these patterns, could realize that theirs was not the only perspective in the universe.

Slowly Mystra scanned the Pavilion of Cynosure. Ten of the eleven greater powers were in attendance—all save Cyric. Most of the gods had gathered around tables crammed with flasks and beakers and spell components. The trio of deities devoted to chaotic pursuits—Tempus,

Talos, and Sune, the Goddess of Love—fidgeted in their seats or roamed around the perimeter. In the center of the room, Tyr held court from a podium, methodically listing the rules by which the gods would proceed with the hearing. To his right stood Torm. The God of Duty was only a demipower, but Tyr had sponsored him to speak to the Circle because of his recent conflicts with Cyric.

"And I think it best for us to begin with the testimony of Torm the True," Tyr droned, "for his charges against the self-styled Prince of Lies bring us together now."

As Torm took the podium, Mystra paused to consider her own position in the room. The pavilion resembled laboratories common in Halruaa and Cormyr and Waterdeep, places civilized enough to support schools where mages could be taught the rudiments of the Art. Tyr, and now Torm, had taken the place reserved for the instructor. The other gods were students. As in any school, some paid careful attention to the lecturer—like Oghma—while others waited for the time to pass so they could escape.

In her version of the pavilion, Mystra had not cast herself in the role of either teacher or student, but as an impartial monitor. In the mage schools she'd seen in her youth, the most powerful sorcerer never taught. He or she sat quietly in the back of the room, watching the class, ready in case someone should cast an enchantment that misfired or grew dangerous.

"Cyric is a threat to all of Faerun," Torm began, gesturing broadly. The robes of magic Mystra perceived hanging from his square shoulders were dimmer than those of the greater gods, signifying his lesser status. "As all of you know—"

"If we already know, why tell us again?" Talos shouted impatiently.

Tempus stopped poring over his maps long enough to snort his agreement, and the Goddess of Love giggled into her dainty hands. Of the remaining gods, only Tyr really seemed offended by the outburst. The God of Justice sneered in the direction of the Destroyer's voice, then motioned for the God of Duty to continue.

"What you *don't* know," Torm said sharply, glaring at Talos, "is that Cyric has been impersonating other gods, causing mortals weak in spirit to kill themselves with reckless acts. He chooses only those men and women who have yet to earn a god's favor through devoted worship. They die before their time and become prisoners in the City of Strife."

Torm went on to describe how Cyric had fooled one particular sell-sword, a Cormyrian named Gwydion the Quick. He dealt with the heart of the incident briefly, but his speech didn't end there. In detail, he described how Cyric's offenses assailed the honor of each and every god. Torm followed this diatribe with his expected tirade on duty, calling the Circle of Greater Powers to stand against the blackguard Lord of the Dead.

As Torm spoke, Mystra found herself wondering exactly how the God of Duty saw the pavilion. Breaking into the demipower's thoughts proved much easier than the Goddess of Magic expected. His mind was a simple and orderly fortress of purest white stone, built around a vast temple to duty and honor. Armored knights stood silent vigil upon the walls. Whether they didn't sense Mystra's presence or dismissed her as an ally was unclear, but they let her pass through the gates unchallenged. Once inside, she could look out through Torm's eyes.

To the God of Duty, the Pavilion of Cynosure appeared as a pillared extension of his own castle. Marble columns lined the hall, with thrones at the foot of each. In these rested the gods, huge armored warriors with shields bearing their holy symbols. Some, like Tyr, wore bright plate mail, magnificent and glittering. The less the god supported law, the dimmer the gloss on his armor, the shabbier his cloak and boots and gloves.

Torm kneeled in the center of this impressive gathering. His plate mail shone less brightly than Tyr's, but it was much more ornate and weighted with badges of honor. Mystra was awed by the overwhelming sense of duty that pressed down on the demipower. And as the goddess looked closer, she saw thin chains of shimmering gold linking the God of Duty to each of his fellow deities. Some chains were thicker than others, but these links of obligation extended from Torm's hands to every other god in the pavilion.

"What says the Goddess of Magic to Torm's proposal?"

The words registered in another part of Mystra's mind, a section she had left focused on the demipower's speech. Like all the other deities, Mystra possessed an intellect capable of performing a hundred different tasks simultaneously. While a small part of her mind had explored Torm's perspective, another facet listened intently for the prayers of her faithful. Others kept vigil over the magical weave surrounding Faerun, or monitored the progress of Cyric's book, or catalogued each new spell and enchantment created in the world. The most important of these facets, the nexus of her being, controlled the various lesser incarnations, creating or destroying them as necessary.

Now the Goddess of Magic abandoned Torm's perspective and focused more fully on the Circle. Tyr had once again taken the podium. His blind eyes were directed at her. "Do you think we can force Cyric to free this Gwydion fellow and the other souls wrongly imprisoned in the Wall of the Faithless?"

"Possibly," Mystra said.

Torm stepped forward again, blustering happily, "Of course, this great wrong can be righted! The laws established in the Realm of the Dead for the treatment of the Faithless—"

"Were ratified by the Circle of Greater Powers when Myrkul reigned in the City of Strife," Oghma noted coldly. "Cyric has always claimed himself free of laws established by the trio of powers he replaced."

"Besides, the whole point of *forcing* Cyric to do anything in his realm is moot," Lathander added glumly. He stood and straightened his robes. "We have no power in the City of Strife. We can't even enter it unless we're invited. And the Wall of the Faithless is clearly within the boundaries of Cyric's kingdom." He sighed. "Do you think logic or reason will persuade him to free those souls, with no threat of force behind it? I'm not one to abandon hope, but even I see this as futile."

Mystra shook her head in disbelief. "If we band together, we can show Cyric our displeasure. If we're silent, we're tacitly consenting."

She stalked toward the podium. Both Torm and Tyr gave her a wide berth. "When Cyric started work on his infernal book," Mystra began, "I denied him the use of magic to create it on his own. Oghma denied him the services of the eternal scribes to complete it in the heavens. This left him to call upon his worshipers to create the *Cyrinishad*. These sanctions worked, did they not? The book remains but a dark grail for him."

"I would not discount the possibility of one of his mundane servants writing the tome he desires," Oghma warned. "As you should well know, Mystra, mortals can accomplish a great deal given the right motivation."

The Goddess of Magic nodded, but the resolve in her glowing blue-white eyes never faded. "Nevertheless, we have forced him to work within the code the rest of us follow. We can do so again with the imprisoned souls—" she paused and scanned the faces of the assembled powers

"—and we can do so with the disappearance of Leira."

The gods shifted nervously at the mention of the missing goddess. "Let's get back to the matter at hand," Oghma suggested. "The mistreatment of the shade Torm saw—"

"Cyric's crimes against the Balance are the true matter at hand," Mystra hissed. When no one disagreed, she pressed on. "Leira hasn't shown herself since the Time of Troubles. It's obvious to me that she's gone. Someone destroyed her."

"Leira is the Goddess of Deception," Oghma noted. "This wouldn't be the first time she obscured her whereabouts from us, simply to prove her power to hide outstrips our ability and patience to seek."

After yawning loudly, Talos dismissed the topic with a wave of his hand. "Someone's answering the prayers of her faithful. That's all that matters."

"And if that someone is Cyric?" Mystra asked. "He already has the power of three gods. Do any of you wish to see him take the power of a fourth?"

A subtle shift in Talos's expression told Mystra that even the Destroyer trembled at the prospect of confronting Cyric about Leira's disappearance.

"Someone must be aiding him if he's kept the crime hidden this long," Torm offered boldly. "Mask, perhaps?"

Tyr nodded sagely and ran gnarled fingers through his long white beard. "The Lord of Shadows would have much to gain from an alliance with Cyric. As God of Intrigue, Mask could bury all clues of Leira's murder so deep even a god's eyes might miss them."

"Perhaps," Mystra said. "But if Cyric destroyed Leira and took on her worshipers, he's added God of Deception to the rest of his titles. He might not need Mask's help to hide his crimes."

An uncomfortable murmur broke out in the pavilion,

and Oghma turned pleading eyes on the Goddess of Magic. Mystra ignored him, though, and said, "I call upon my right as a member of the Circle. I demand Cyric and Mask be brought before Lord Ao for judgment."

The response to this proclamation was instantaneous; the gods sent countless incarnations winging across the planes to summon the two errant deities. A burst of darkness and a sickening stench of brimstone heralded Cyric's arrival in the Pavilion of Cynosure. His robes glowed almost as brightly as Mystra's, crackling around his thin frame like a cloak of fire. But brightest of all was the enchanted sword at his side. The rose-hued blade burned with such magical radiance Mystra found it difficult to look at it for long.

Cyric sneered at the other gods, his face twisted with hatred. His dark eyes glittered malevolently as he turned to Torm. "You've whined loudly enough to get an audience, I see. That's not so surprising, I suppose—though I can't imagine why the rest of you have bothered to call me here."

"To answer certain charges," Tyr said stiffly.

"Charges!" Cyric scoffed. "If Torm the True told you I'm guilty of breaking some cosmic law, you'd be fools not to believe him. He can't lie, the dolt, and I'm not going to waste my time trying to get you to believe otherwise."

"Then you admit to impersonating other deities," Torm said. He leveled an accusing finger at the Lord of the Dead.

"Of course."

"And of unfairly sentencing souls to the Wall of the Faithless?"

Cyric snorted. "You were there, Torm."

"And of continuing work on your infernal book, intending to use it to undermine all other faiths in Faerun?"

"Didn't I just tell you I admit to everything you can

charge me with, you dimwitted tin warrior? The real question is, what can any of you do about it?" Cyric rolled his eyes in disgust and faced Mystra. "He's almost as dull as Kelemvor, eh Midnight?"

The goddess returned Cyric's cold gaze evenly. "What about the death of Leira?" she asked tonelessly. "Do you admit to that?"

One eyebrow arched, the Lord of the Dead leaned back against a table. "Upon whose testimony are you accusing me of harming the elusive Lady of the Mists? As I remember, the Circle of Greater Powers cannot try me for a crime without testimony or evidence."

"We have only our suspicions," Mystra said calmly, "but I've demanded the Circle call upon Lord Ao and ask him where Leira is. Do you have any objections? Actually, they don't matter, so don't bother voicing them."

The Lord of the Dead and the Goddess of Magic stared at one another. The twitch in Cyric's left eye told of barely subdued rage, while the hard line of Mystra's mouth, the tension in her limbs, revealed an overwhelming revulsion for the creature of darkness she had once called friend.

Cyric closed his hand tightly around the hilt of his sword. The gesture's meaning was not lost on Mystra; that blade had nearly drained her life atop Blackstaff Tower, after Cyric had used it to kill Kelemvor Lyonsbane. He would repay her for humiliating him before the Circle. Godsbane would taste her blood again.

"We yet await Mask's arrival," Tyr announced. "Only then may we summon Ao."

"Don't delay on my account," said a smooth whisper. The words hissed like a black silk cloth polishing a sharp blade. "I've been here for quite some time."

As one, the gods turned to find Mask standing at the very edge of the pavilion. Darkness clung to him in thin wisps, passing over his bright robe of magic like clouds over a full moon. Black gloves covered his hands, and a loose-fitting mask concealed his features. Only his eyes were visible, twin pools of red flashing and ebbing as he spoke.

"Should I join my fellow conspirator?" he asked glibly. Without waiting for a reply, the Lord of Shadows slid with feline grace past Mystra to stand beside Cyric.

"Hear our plea, great and wise overlord," Tyr began without prelude. "We seek your wisdom."

The other gods picked up the evocation, repeating it over and over. Their voices grew louder, the words more strident. They called until they howled like mad things—all save Cyric, who stood mute and sullen in the midst of the riot.

Mystra winced at the discord, yet some part of her reveled in the painful cacophony and drew strength from it. She screamed along with the others until she saw that the Pavilion of Cynosure was trembling. The laboratory her mind had cast as a facade over the place warped, then unraveled like a worn tapestry. The tables melted, then the ceiling and walls. The floor went last, wafting away in a haze of unreality.

The gods found themselves surrounded by a vast sea of emptiness. The prayers of Mystra's worshipers faded in her mind to distant, feeble cries as more and more of her consciousness was drawn into the void. The mortal world became a desert oasis seen through a heat haze, faint and shifting, more ghostly than real. Then, suddenly, the sea of emptiness transformed into a night sky filled with a million stars. And from each pinpoint of light radiated a spectrum of subtle, unearthly hues and a chorus of terrifying heavenly voices.

Keepers of the Balance, you have summoned me needlessly.

The words insinuated themselves into Mystra's mind, demanding the attention of every facet of her divine intellect. She reeled at the force of the million stern voices rebuking her, the myriad angry flashes filling the darkness around her.

Know you now that Cyric and Mask did murder Leira, Ao boomed. *Yet they have done nothing that is outside their natures. Cyric is Lord of Murder, so he should strive to blot out even the lives of gods. Mask is Lord of Intrigue, so he should strive to conceal such deeds.*

The facade of a wizard's laboratory began to reappear before Mystra's eyes, and the voices of her faithful grew stronger. The stars faded, leaving phantom afterimages burned into her mind. Ao offered a final warning, full of dark portents: *It is your responsibility to stand against Cyric—just as it is his to destroy you if you fail. Such is the way of the Balance.* Mystra knew the words were meant for her more than any of the others in the pantheon.

In the center of the pavilion, Cyric crossed his arms over his chest. "Is there anything else?" he asked smugly.

Tyr took a step toward the Lord of the Dead, his fist raised before him. "There will be justice done for this crime."

"Didn't you hear Ao?" Cyric scoffed. "There was no crime. Leira died because I willed it." He drew Godsbane and leveled the blade at the God of Justice. "Any of you could be next. That's my place in the Balance: To weed out the weak from this pathetic pantheon."

Dutifully Torm stepped between Godsbane and his patron. A sword appeared in his hand, gleaming silver and edged sharply enough to slice a rainbow into separate bands of color. He tapped the blade in warning against Godsbane, then planted his feet in a practiced fighting stance. "We will not fall as easily as Leira."

Mask flinched as the gods flicked the tips of their swords together. "This isn't the time, Cyric," he counseled, "not in the open, not when there are so many against you."

"Spoken like a true coward," Torm snarled. "You might as well try your luck now, Mask. From this day forward we'll remain vigilant against your treachery."

Lowering his pen and parchment to the table before him, Oghma raised empty hands to both Cyric and Torm. "We cannot bring Leira back, but perhaps we can reach some agreement. Release the souls unfairly imprisoned, and we—"

Cyric laughed bitterly. "I will do with Gwydion the Quick as I wish. I may release him; I may torture him forever." He slowly lowered Godsbane and sheathed her. "But none of you will influence his fate. Until now, I have occasionally welcomed you or your envoys into my domain. No longer. As of this moment, the City of Strife is completely closed to the pantheon."

"You asked before what we could do against you because of your crimes," Mystra said. Her words were edged sharper than Torm's sword. "I have your answer—and yours as well, Mask. As Goddess of Magic, I forbid you both from drawing on the magical weave."

"What!" Cyric shrieked. "You can't deny me magic. I must answer the prayers of my faithful. And the City of Strife—"

"Is not my concern," Mystra interrupted. "Your minions may still use magic, and your worshipers will be granted spells, but you, Cyric cannot draw the magic for a single cantrip."

Mask bowed his head, hiding his glowing red eyes from Mystra. "I acted only by my cursed nature, Lady. I can do little but plot intrigues and further the place of thieves in the world. Is there no way I can escape this punishment?"

"Forswear any alliances with Cyric," Mystra said without pause. "Swear that you will not aid him again."

The Lord of Shadows replied just as quickly. "Of course, Lady."

"You cowardly bastard," Cyric shouted.

He started toward Mask, but Mystra gestured grandly. A shimmering wall of force blocked his path. The Lord of the Dead struck the wall, and the robe of magic he wore began to fade. The brilliance drained from the raiments like water. The cast-off magic pooled on the pavilion's floor before vanishing, evaporating into the air like summer rain.

Cyric clutched his head and screamed in impotent rage. His features blurred, and three dozen faces appeared on his head—shouting vile curses, answering his minions' questions, stalking the nightmares of men and women across Faerun. Stunned in his sudden loss of power, the Lord of the Dead had lost all control of his myriad selves. They sprouted from his body like cancerous growths, swearing dark oaths, shrieking their displeasure.

For a time the rest of the pantheon watched in fascinated horror as Cyric fought to regain control. When finally he managed to subdue the warring facets of his mind, he no longer appeared as the lean, hawk-nosed mortal Mystra had known during their quest for the Tablets of Fate. His skin had blistered and hardened into a smooth red hide. His muscles rippled on his thin frame, bands of steel corded beneath his flesh. From his gaunt, almost skeletal face, eyes like dark suns burned with unending malice.

"Without magic, all your incarnations will share this hideous face," Mystra said. "Submit to the Circle's will, and you will be allowed to heal yourself."

"Submit to the Circle?" Cyric repeated, his voice sepulchral. "The *Cyrinishad* will bring this entire pantheon to its knees." He smiled viciously and leveled a gnarled finger at Mystra. "But while I wait for my mortal minions to complete my book, I'll search for the soul of Kelemvor Lyonsbane. His suffering will be your particular reward, Midnight."

The Lord of the Dead patted the rose-hued sword at his side and chuckled. "You're leaving me Godsbane? That's surprisingly kind of you."

"I won't destroy something wrought from the weave simply because you own it. Besides, you'd be hard-pressed to stand against a seasoned mortal soldier without something to protect you." She returned his cruel smile. "Now, if you ask nicely enough, I'm certain one of the other powers would be kind enough to transport you back to the Realm of the Dead—unless you plan to walk."

Talos took a tentative step forward, looking to Mystra for some sign of approval. The Goddess of Magic nodded, and the Destroyer took Cyric's arm and disappeared.

"You cannot maintain this ban for long, Lady," Oghma whispered as soon as Cyric had departed. "If he should lose control of the Realm of the Dead . . ."

Mystra turned to the God of Knowledge. "That's why I left him the sword," she said distractedly. "He can maintain his power with that, but he shouldn't be able to harm any of us. That should give us time to shore up our houses against his next onslaught." The Goddess of Magic bowed hurriedly and excused herself, vanishing from the Pavilion of Cynosure in a burst of blue-white light.

She returned to her throne room, at the heart of her magnificent palace. There Mystra buried her face in her hands, trying to banish a chilling image from her memory. She knew it was futile. For the rest of time, the horrid sight would haunt her.

In the instant before Cyric disappeared from the pavilion, Mystra had slipped into his mind, hoping to catch some glimpse of his twisted perspective. The contact was brief. The ever-vigilant spirit of Godsbane had sensed an intruder and pulsed forward, an amorphous red-hued mass of evil. But before the Goddess of Magic fled, she

66

saw for a moment the world from the eyes of the Lord of the Dead.

A red haze of pain mingled with black clouds of strife and despair. At the center of this roiling chaos stood the Prince of Lies. The Pavilion of Cynosure had no other features, the gods and goddesses no faces or forms. They spoke with Cyric's own voice, and their words came to him as unruly comments from his own mind. He was utterly alone.

IV

SOUL SEARCHING

*Wherein the Prince of Lies uncovers clues of
many sorts, and Gwydion the Quick learns
that there are things to fear in the
City of Strife, even for a dead man.*

Cyric sat brooding in Bone Castle's immense throne
room, continually replaying in his mind his humiliation at
Mystra's hand. Each time he reached the moment when
the goddess denied him contact with the weave, Cyric
imagined some wildly twisted version of the actual event.
In one he shattered Mystra's arcane shield and struck her
down with Godsbane, thus adding God of Magic to his
growing list of titles. In another the weave itself revolted
against Mystra. Or the gods of chaos rallied and descended on her like a pack of winter-starved wolves. Or
Ao himself manifested to prevent her from abusing her
power so flagrantly. . . .

The variations were endless, and in certain dark corners of Cyric's mind, some of them dropped like seeds into the mire of delusion and fantasy. In days or months or years, as time was measured in the mortal realms, these notions would blossom into false memories. The noisome thoughts would vie with the truth, creeping around it with leafy tendrils, draining it of vitality. Then these lies would become Cyric's only memories of the meeting, transforming it into a triumph.

"Glorious," Cyric muttered as he envisioned himself dripping to the elbows in Mystra's blood. He could almost taste the crimson liquid on his lips

Revenge will be yours, my love, Godsbane purred. The spirit of the sword pulsed inside the swirling chaos of Cyric's thoughts. *Just as soon as you put your plans into motion.*

"Eh?" Cyric grunted. "My plans?"

To find Kelemvor. To finish your tome.

The Prince of Lies rubbed the sword's pommel. "Right now a hundred plots are coming to fruition, a thousand agents are on the move. . . ."

His mind raced as he considered the monstrous assassins he'd sent to stalk Mystra's clerics in Sembia. They trailed the goddess's minions from beneath the ground, in the guise of mutated moles, and from the skies as human vultures. Press gangs on the Fugue Plain were also just now grabbing Mystra's faithful. They would be rushed into the City of Strife before the maruts could escort them to paradise. In Zhentil Keep, the search for his new scribe was almost over. The soldiers had learned the whereabouts of Bevis's daughter from a parchmenter. In hours, she would be ready to begin the new *Cyrinishad*. There were other schemes, too—the desecration of Torm's shrine in Tantras, the disruption of the holy rites of Tyr in Suzail, the betrayal of Mask's agents in the city watch of Waterdeep. . . .

And in every temple dedicated to Cyric, every coven of worshipers, circles of clerics and powerful mages sought the soul of Kelemvor Lyonsbane.

For a decade, Cyric had turned his worshipers' magic to the task. He little believed the mortals would find the errant soul, since only a deity had the might to shield Kelemvor for so long. But each oracle and priest scrying for the hidden shade put the deceitful god's power to the test. Now the number of seekers had been swelled by the faithful of Leira.

It hadn't been difficult to win the cooperation of the church hierarchy—a finely polished tale of their goddess's murder at the hands of Kelemvor had been enough. The truly fervent had been the easiest to convince, the quickest to join the hunt for the renegade soul. The fear of offending the new God of Deception swayed other important clerics, especially the men and women who had dedicated their lives to the art of illusion. Assassins had dealt with those too vocal in their opposition. And once the high priests were brought in line, Cyric could count on the rest of the church to follow them like mindless sheep.

Your Magnificence?

The words echoed inside Cyric's thoughts. It wasn't the cool, feminine purr of Godsbane, but a chilling, inhuman voice. Cyric looked out on the long, narrow throne room and found Jergal before him. The seneschal cast his gaze down to the floor. White-gloved hands floated up and folded palms together in a show of submission. *I am sorry to disturb your reverie, but emissaries of the Shadowlord are at the gate again. They beg to deliver a gift from their master.*

"Kill them all," Cyric said coldly. "Then send their heads back to Mask, along with their gifts. Sooner or later he'll give up—or run out of emissaries."

Godsbane stirred uneasily. *You might be able to use his aid, my love,* she said.

"He wants to apologize for his cowardice, not buy back an alliance with me. He fears Mystra too much to break his promise to her—not this soon anyway."

Cyric leaped suddenly to his feet, sending Jergal floating backward to avoid being trampled. The seneschal's empty black cloak fluttered and danced. "There's something odd about this," the Lord of the Dead hissed. "Mask is risking Mystra's ire just sending messengers to me."

Perhaps the gifts hold the key, Godsbane suggested.

"Hmmm. Have you examined the gifts, Jergal?" Cyric asked.

The seneschal nodded. *Arquebuses, Your Magnificence. All the emissaries have carried arquebuses. No written message, though all the rifles bear the symbols of both the Shadowlord and the Gearsmith.*

"Why would Mask offer me Gondish rifles? Gond himself has sent me a dozen such contraptions in the past. He thinks they'll make any army invincible, the dolt." Cyric snorted. "How can they be any threat at all when they blow up in soldiers' faces as often as they fire correctly?" The Prince of Lies rubbed his pointed chin. "Anything else special about them? Are they enchanted somehow?"

Jergal shook his head. *No, Your Magnificence. I examined them myself. They are simple contraptions of metal and wood, like everything else the Gearsmith builds. The only thing unusual about the gifts is that the bearers had strict orders from the Shadowlord himself to present them to you in this room.*

Face rigid with concentration, Cyric paced away from his throne and down the length of the long audience hall. Chained to the pillars along either wall were three hundred and ninety-seven souls that burned without diminishing—the scribes who had failed in creating the *Cyrinishad*. One other shade writhed in fiery torment: Bevis the Illuminator. He hung from the ceiling halfway between the throne and the doors, suspended spread-eagle by chains of red-hot iron. As they entered the hall, supplicants would hear Bevis's whimpers. The other Burning Men had long since screamed themselves mute.

Muttering incoherently, the Lord of the Dead stalked through the long shadows warping across the hall. He glanced up at some of the other trophies as he passed them, his mind veering wildly from his consideration of Mask's strange gifts. Here was a ghastly canvas painted by a worshiper of Deneir, the red and brown pigments nothing less than the blood of her children. Next to it hung an axe used to enforce the judgments of a mad king who ruled in the name of Tyr. A glass case at the base of one pillar held a single silver nail with which a man devoted to Sune had blinded himself after receiving a vision of the goddess, convinced he would never see anything so beautiful again.

In fact, much of the hall had been dedicated to displaying badges of other gods' shame. Cyric had meant these trophies to unnerve the deities when they visited, but in his isolation, they served only to remind the Lord of the Dead how easily worship could be twisted.

The greatest symbol of that truth was Cyric's throne itself. The Prince of Lies had built the hulking, grotesque chair from the bones of men and women who died mistakenly believing themselves saints—a worshiper of Chauntea who slit his wrists thinking his blood would make the crops grow faster; a druid devoted to Eldath who drowned everyone who wandered near a certain secluded pool because they upset the peace of the place; a knight of Torm who tortured anyone he caught in even the most insignificant lie. . . .

As he approached his throne once more, Cyric stopped and stood absolutely still. Amongst the other relics was the hand of a Gondish ironsmith. The man had bled to death after lopping off his left arm in hopes of replacing it with a mechanical limb built from blueprints he'd dreamed the night before. As his lifeblood drained away, the smith raved about an army of unstoppable mechanical warriors, men in living Gondish armor greater than any artifact wrought by magic. The idea of Gond's machines making Mystra's weave superfluous was near to Cyric's black heart, and one he had discussed many times with Mask.

"Greater than magic," Cyric whispered. "Of course."

The Prince of Lies smiled and gestured to Jergal. "Pen and parchment," he said impatiently. He took the items that appeared in the seneschal's gloved hands and scribbled a lengthy note. "Take this to Gond," he told the phantasmal creature when he'd finished. "No one else is to know of this message. Make it clear to the Gearsmith this is so. Tell him I'll pay whatever price he asks, but the consignment is to be kept secret. See that the emissaries are killed before you go, but keep one of the arquebuses. That will be answer enough for the Shadowlord."

Bowing deeply, Jergal took the parchment and backed away, keeping his bulging yellow eyes fixed on the floor until he reached the doors.

The Shadowlord is a worthy Lord of Intrigue, Godsbane said once the seneschal had gone. *A novice could learn much from him.*

Cyric settled back in his grisly throne. "Actually, I was just thinking how much he's learned from me. . . ."

A flutter of light appeared somewhere in a remote part of Cyric's consciousness, causing his mind to race and seek it out. The Prince of Lies found his thoughts drawn to the small section of his mind devoted to hearing the prayers of his faithful. A braying voice called to the Lord of the Dead with a fervor even he found hard to ignore.

"O mighty Cyric, judge of the dead, master of the damned, hear me! I have glorious news from your most holy of churches in Zhentil Keep."

When Cyric focused on the prayer, the visage of Xeno Mirrormane appeared before his mind's eye. The high priest's silver hair was wild around his glowing face. His eyes shone with a mad happiness. "Yes, Mirrormane," Cyric replied flatly.

"O great Prince of Lies, the priests of Leira have news," Xeno burbled. He smiled like a drunkard happily lost in his bottle. "Lord Chess himself led their vigil—under my supervision, of course—and they had a most magnificent vision, a most—"

"Get on with it," Cyric snapped.

"Kelemvor Lyonsbane," Xeno said. "The priests have divined that his soul is in the City of Strife somewhere."

"Where in the city?"

"They cannot tell exactly. Some power still tries to block their magic."

Cyric withdrew his consciousness from his faithful priest and focused once again on his throne room in Hades. His voice tight with excitement, he shouted for his denizens. They would scour every inch of the city, burn down every structure if need be. Kelemvor could not escape; no one left the Realm of the Dead without Cyric's permission. If he was trapped there somehow, all that remained was to flush him out of hiding.

As he formulated his plans for the search, the Lord of the Dead cursed Mystra again for robbing him of magic. But then another thought presented itself fleetingly. Mystra was the one who'd been hiding Kelemvor all along, masking his presence within Cyric's own realm since she had no way to rescue him. The death god had no doubt of that. But now that she was expending so much power to guard the weave, she'd missed the prying magic of Cyric's new followers. The Prince of Lies smiled. That had the ring of truth to it. . . .

Cyric's mind spun away, embellishing the plot he'd just created. He was soon certain there could be no other explanation for Kelemvor's elusiveness. But now Mystra had let her guard slip, and Cyric would have his revenge. He imagined a thousand new tortures to be played out on Kelemvor's soul. The fantasies stretched across his mind like a web shimmering silver in the swirling darkness.

* * * * *

"Stop your whining, Perdix," Af grumbled. "I'm climbing as fast as I can."

The wolf-headed denizen pushed himself past another level in the Wall of the Faithless. He climbed slowly, planting spider legs between the rows of writhing souls that made up the wall, then pulling his long, serpentine coils up the steep face. "I don't see why you needed my help, anyway," Af grunted.

Perdix hovered just out of striking range, wings beating furiously against the fetid air. "You've never had to get someone out of the wall before, have you?" he puffed. "Tsk. You should know it'll take at least the two of us. After all, you built the thing single-handed didn't you?"

"I never said that!" Af shouted over the agonized moan emanating from the wall. "Don't be so facetious, or I'll club you one. You need—" With his human hand, Af clamped the mouth of the nearest shade closed. The souls of the Faithless cried out continually; that's why the wall had been built with the souls facing into the City of Strife, so that, in their torment, the unquiet spirits could serenade the Lord of the Dead. "Damn whiners," Af said bitterly. "Worse than living downstairs from a banshee."

"I knew a banshee once," Perdix said wistfully. "Lovely lass, but you're right, they are a bit hard on the ears." He scanned the wall with his single blue eye. "Almost there,

Af. Just two or three more levels—well, possibly ten, but that would be the most."

After passing thirty rows of souls, Af reached the spot where they had left Gwydion the Quick. Like the Faithless stacked around him, the sell-sword twisted and cried out. Some of his agony was caused by the greenish mold that held the souls in place. The living mortar grew between the shades, sending painful rhizoids into any of the unfortunates that stopped moving.

"What do you know," Perdix exclaimed as he looked at Gwydion's pale face, "he's still got a tongue. He learned something after all. I thought for sure he'd try calling out to another god again." He wrinkled his face in distaste. "Those beetles they use to eat the tongues out of troublemakers . . . brrr."

"Yeah, yeah. Let's just get this over with."

Af placed his human hands to either side of Gwydion's head and leaned back. Slowly the denizen worked the soul out of the wall, though the Faithless to either side tried their best to hold the sell-sword back. It was Perdix's task to deal with these jealous shades. The little denizen tore at their arms and hands with gleaming white teeth.

When Gwydion was free of the other souls and the green mold, Af hefted him over one hunched shoulder and started back down the wall. "You're a lucky boy," the denizen grunted. "I woulda bet anything Cyric was going to leave you in there forever."

"W-Why free me?" Gwydion gasped.

Perdix hovered close to the soul's ear. "Cyric wants all the denizens—that's us—and the False who aren't being tortured for something specific—that's you—to search the city," he said. "You're going to help us look for a fellow named Kelemvor Lyonsbane, some old enemy of Cyric's who's hiding out here."

Numbly Gwydion turned his head to look out over the

City of Strife. The wall of writhing bodies encircled the hellish place, reaching high into the air. Denizens crawled or flew to the high ramparts. The bestial creatures carried screaming souls to be stacked atop the wall like so much cordwood. As far as Gwydion could see, he was the only one being taken down.

Inside the Wall of the Faithless, ramshackle buildings clustered in decaying boroughs. All these structures had been built on the same pattern: ten stories with square windows and a flat red roof. They only differed now in how ruined they were. In some places, huge fires engulfed whole blocks. In others, denizens tore the buildings down brick by brick, creating huge piles of rubble. Other denizens bombarded the boroughs from the air with javelins of lightning; these darksome beasts soared over the necropolis on massive wings of flame that cut through the choking shroud of fog like shooting stars.

And in the center of this destruction stood Bone Castle. From this distance, the pointed white tower seemed to be nothing more than a distant church spire, a haven of law and peace that might be found in any city in the Heartlands. Yet Gwydion knew that, within its protective curtain of diamond and moat of black ooze, Bone Castle harbored the most dangerous agent of chaos. Thoughts of Cyric and the madness he'd glimpsed in the god's eyes haunted Gwydion the rest of the uncomfortable way down the wall.

"Awright," Af said. "End of the line." The denizen shrugged and unceremoniously dumped the shade onto his face.

Gwydion pushed himself up from the base of the wall, spitting a mouthful of dust. Here, the Faithless were quiet, having long since been crushed into immobility by the thousands of others atop them—and thereby conquered by the mold holding them in place. The sell-sword shuddered as he found himself leaning against the fungus-eaten features of a shade. Only the man's staring eyes remained free from the green mold covering him.

"Well," Perdix asked lightly, "now that we've got our ward, where do you want to start? The marshes on the far side of the castle?"

Af wrinkled his wolfish snout. "Nah. How about the Night Serpent's lair? She gets fed about now, and it'll be easier if we try to talk to her *after* she's eaten."

"She frightens me," Perdix said bluntly.

"But we have to see her sooner or later, right?"

"I suppose," Perdix sighed. "We'll do the marshes after that."

The two started away from the wall, Af slithering, Perdix hopping on thin legs. After a few steps, both denizens turned around. "Well?" Perdix asked. "You don't have any choice in this, slug. Come on." The denizen's tongue darted out between each word, punctuating the command.

Gwydion shuffled forward. There was no point in resisting; the denizens were Cyric's agents, and the Lord of the Dead had already proved to the sell-sword how completely he owned the souls in his domain. As he fell into step with Af and Perdix, Gwydion picked away at the mold that had worked its way into his matted blond hair and the rags that had once been warm winter clothes. The shackles had been removed from his wrists when they put him in the wall, yet Gwydion still found his hands incredibly clumsy. His fingers felt no more agile than stumps of wood.

The trio passed through dark alleys, where souls with indistinct yellow-gray faces and expressionless gray eyes huddled in doorways. Sputtering lamps set on windowsills cast sickly yellow light into the gloom, along with fetid black smoke that made Gwydion's eyes sting and his skin burn. Denizens passed in pairs, rousting the faceless shades or moving into the buildings themselves. These other denizens always gave Af a wide berth. Surprisingly, most of them nodded respectfully to Perdix, as well, offering solemn greetings to the diminutive creature.

"These shades all look alike," Gwydion observed dully after a time. His voice was a rasping whisper from screaming for release from the wall.

Deftly Af slithered to the top of a pile of broken stone that blocked the alley. "Yeah. So?"

"So how do we recognize Kelemvor when we find him?"

With two leaps, Perdix hopped over the mound. "Oh, we'll know him all right. There are only three sorts of beings in the City of Strife: denizens, the False, and the Faithless. All the denizens—souls like me and Af here, who used to worship Cyric—are transformed when we arrive here into forms that'll be more useful in our new line of work." The yellow-skinned denizen flapped his wings proudly. "Makes it easy to tell the jailers from the inmates, too.

"Anyone stupid enough not to believe in the gods is stuffed into the Wall of the Faithless," he continued, "so we know where that lot can be found." Perdix folded his wings again and sighed. "That just leave slugs like you— the False, the people who didn't make the list for any god's eternal reward."

The alley emptied into a small plaza surrounded by more buildings. A shade wearing drab gray rags moved away from the denizens as they approached, neither hurrying nor tarrying. Perdix gestured at the faceless soul. "The False who came here before Cyric took over are easy to spot—they're the ones that look like this sorry slug. The old Lord of the Dead used to think it was the worst thing possible to forget your life and your identity once you came here." The denizen laughed. "The new lord of the dead is a lot more creative than that. Anyone who arrived after Cyric claimed the throne retained his own appearance and has marks on his wrists from the shackles."

Gwydion nodded. "So Kelemvor will look like a shade,

but he won't have any scars on his wrist."

"And he'll be roaming about, which is getting more and more rare," Perdix added. "Cyric's started locking the False into unique tortures created to punish whatever bad things they did in their life—like that slug there."

Gwydion followed Perdix's gaze to a spot in the center of the plaza. There, a soul stood chained to a statue of a river spirit. The scantily clad stone nymph held a jug from which poured a steady stream of water. Iron bands kept the soul's head and legs rigid against the stone, and his arms ended in blackened, scarred stumps too short to reach the sparkling liquid. The water rained down before the red-haired shade, fell to the parched ground, and evaporated.

"Torture helps you slugs remember why you're here. The pain reminds you of every misstep you took that led you away from the truth of the world," Perdix noted as he hopped up to the shade bound to the fountain. "Like old Kaverin here. He thought he could outlive Cyric and out-smart him, too."

The red-haired shade opened his mouth to speak, but all that came out were wisps of blue flame. Kaverin's lifeless eyes grew wide as Perdix hopped beneath the water. The little denizen threw back his head and gulped mouthful after mouthful of the cool, clear liquid. Af soon joined his partner, and the two tormented the prisoner by soaking themselves.

"No drinks for you today," Perdix taunted.

Kaverin thrashed against his bonds frantically. His screams were gouts of fire.

"Yeah. None for you today," Af repeated, then gestured to Gwydion. "But you can take a drink if you want."

When the denizens stepped aside, Gwydion walked slowly toward fountain. A small silver cup lay at the statue's base, well out of Kaverin's reach. The sell-sword glanced at the denizens, but they merely watched without comment as he took the cup and filled it. He hesitated for a moment, then brought the water to Kaverin's parched lips.

The red-haired shade flailed madly, knocking Gwydion onto his back. Over the laughter of the denizens, the sell-sword heard Kaverin curse vilely. "You bastard," he hissed, thin rivulets running down his chin. He spit the rest of the water at Gwydion. "They start all over again now—five years wasted! I didn't want the water. I didn't want your help. You'll pay—"

The flames rekindled in Kaverin's mouth, burning away the rest of his threat. Perdix lifted the cup and battered the imprisoned shade with it, then tossed it down and hopped to Gwydion's side. "He'll never forget that you made his torture worse," the denizen said flatly. "Of course, you won't forget it either."

Impatiently Af gestured for Perdix to follow. "Enough of the civics lesson," he grumbled. "We've got to get to the Night Serpent, remember?" Shaking his lupine head, Af slithered across the plaza, into another alley.

At Perdix's prompting, Gwydion struggled to his feet, then set off at a jog after the brutish denizens. He soon found himself padding through grim streets crowded with the faceless, emotionless shades of the elder False. The sight of so many damned to an eternity without hope or love or fear sickened Gwydion, but there was something about his surroundings that preyed in more subtle ways on the sell-sword's mind. The buildings, the streets, even the humid, stinking air seemed just as cold and hopeless as the souls of the damned. Something inside Gwydion warned him the city itself would try to leach away any true emotions he would feel if he shook off the shroud of despair that had settled over him.

At last the boroughs gave way to an uneven field of rubble, beyond which lay the city's heart—Bone Castle itself.

Gwydion and the denizens struggled through the shattered stone and twisted metal to the mouth of a vast cave, near the oozing river that served as the castle's moat. Stalactites and stalagmites lined the gaping hole like stone teeth. Orange steam hissed between the jagged points in a steady, sibilant flow, and dark water from the River Slith pooled around the entrance. The ground underfoot was marshy and foul.

Af clamped a hand on Gwydion's shoulder. "Stay behind me and keep your mouth shut," the denizen ordered gruffly.

Gwydion watched as Perdix flew to the cavern's mouth and called out. "Envoys from Lord Cyric," the little denizen announced, his voice quavering noticeably. "Mistress Dendar?"

A grating sound echoed from the cave as something enormous shifted position. Two eyes appeared in the darkness. They were the sickly yellow-black of rotten eggs, with slitlike pupils. "What do you want with the Night Serpent?" she hissed.

"Lord Cyric wishes us to search your cave," Perdix explained meekly, crouching behind a stalagmite. "There is a shade hiding—"

"Ah. He is hunting Kelemvor again, is he?" the thing sighed.

Gwydion thought he saw a flash of blood-drenched fangs in the cave's murk. The sight stirred some vague horror in him, resurrected some long-forgotten terror.

"Your master fears his old friend—or was he a foe?" The Night Serpent chuckled. "I don't think Cyric himself remembers."

"Lord Cyric fears nothing," Af growled.

"I have reason to know otherwise." A square snout edged closer to the mouth of the cave. The Serpent's scales glowed with a thousand hypnotic hues of darkness. "The unremembered nightmares of gods belong to me as much as those of mortals . . . and Kelemvor Lyonsbane haunts Cyric's nightmares. He frequently leads a revolt in the City of Strife, a revolt that brings your prince low."

The Night Serpent tilted her head slightly. "But, come, you may search my cave. I have nothing to hide from Cyric, least of all his nightmares."

Perdix started forward tentatively while Af grabbed Gwydion with one hand and climbed boldly into the cave. Light from the swirling crimson sky reached shallowly into the murk, revealing a wide stone floor littered with bones. Only the tip of the Night Serpent's snout was visible, but it was as large as a noble's town house in the richest part of Suzail. The yellow eyes seemed to hover in the darkness, twin pools of cunning and malice.

Those eyes focused on Gwydion as he entered the cave. The slitted pupils dwarfed the trembling soul. "I was sorry to see you die, Gwydion," the Night Serpent hissed. "Your nightmares were delicious."

"B-But I never had nightmares," the sell-sword replied meekly.

The bloody fangs flashed again—a smile, perhaps? "If you'd remembered them, dear Gwydion, I couldn't have made them mine." The Night Serpent tilted her head slightly. "Come, now. Has the world grown so smug that you know nothing of Dendar the Night Serpent? Don't the elders teach the poem any longer?"

Gwydion's memory stirred, and he heard his grandfather's voice repeating a childish rhyme:

> *"In Shar's domain of night I rest,*
> *So dreams may show me how I'm bless'd.*
> *If screams of terror break my sleep,*
> *Then Dendar's sunk her fangs too deep."*

A shudder wracked the sell-sword. Dendar was a myth meant to frighten children into going to bed when their parents wanted—or so he'd always believed. His grandfather had told him that the Night Serpent ate the horrible dreams of disobedient boys and girls, growing fat so she could rise from Hades at the end of the world and swallow the sun. Each nightmare you couldn't remember was another pound of flesh on Dendar's bones.

The Night Serpent nodded her black snout, recognizing the fright in Gwydion's eyes. "Ah, I see you *do* know me. I'm relieved."

"Er, excuse me, Dendar," said Perdix, "But you're blocking the way. We can't go any farther into the cave unless you give way."

"My body has grown so large only my head has room to move," the Night Serpent said. "So the mouth of the cave is the only place big enough for anything to hide—and, as you can see, there is nothing here." Dendar swept her snout slowly back and forth over the pile of bones. "I like to think my predicament means the world will end soon."

Perdix nodded with all the enthusiasm he could muster. "We can only hope. Well, we'll be going. Let Cyric know if you see anyone suspicious lurking around your cave."

"Certainly," the Night Serpent purred.

"Come on, Af," the little denizen said. He turned to his brutish fellow, but found the wolf-headed creature frozen in place. "What is it?"

Af lifted a misshapen skull from the scattering of bones beneath his coils. "These are from denizens," he murmured.

"Of course," Dendar said nonchalantly. "They don't taste very good—not as good as a fresh soul, anyway—but Cyric throws in a few denizens along with the shades for variety. The whole idea of a levy is for show. The forgotten nightmares are food enough for me, as you might guess from my bulk."

"But we're his *servants*," Af said to no one in particular. He shook the denizen's skull until it broke. "Cyric can punish us or torture us, but we're not supposed to be destroyed. The levy should be drawn from the False!"

"How can you destroy a soul?" Gwydion asked. "I mean we're already dead."

"There are ways to pass beyond death," Dendar hissed with smug self-satisfaction. "But your denizen friends would have no reason to seek out oblivion. They're happy with their lot in death. As for the False or the Faithless—well, Cyric has absolute command over their fates. They can't die unless he wills it, and he only sends shades to oblivion after he tires of torturing them."

"Let's talk about this on the way to the marsh, all right? We don't need to bother Dendar with it." Tugging on one of Af's spider legs, Perdix hopped toward the cave mouth.

"No!" Af barked. "There's a pact. I was there when it was signed. Cyric himself told us—"

Sudden, bitter laughter filled the cavern. "And you believed him?" Gwydion scoffed.

Perdix and Af glared at the shade with hate-filled eyes. When he didn't stop laughing, they beat him viciously, but even their blows and threats couldn't stop him.

The look of helplessness on Af's lupine features had shown Gwydion that the denizens had no more power than he, that they, too, were victims of Cyric's madness. With that realization, the shroud of despair slipped from his soul and a giddy dream took root in his thoughts: the False and the denizens were brothers in damnation. Why couldn't they rise up and free themselves from suffering?

It was the Night Serpent who finally silenced Gwydion's mad laughter. She turned one yellow eye on the shade and said, "Oh yes, dear Gwydion, dream of freedom. But remember, where there are dreams, there are always nightmares."

V

AGENT OF HOPE

*Wherein the daughter of Bevis the Illuminator
begins a new, and likely short-lived, career
as a scribe for the Church of Cyric.*

Rinda owned the entire building, but that really wasn't saying much. The sad, one-story hovel squatted in the poorest part of Zhentil Keep, among the unlicensed brothels, the gin mills, and the broken-down homes of escaped slaves and men too besotted by drink to be of use to anyone. In another quarter, the place would have been condemned. Rats maintained a thriving colony in the rafters. Dry rot had claimed large sections of the floor where the boards had not already collapsed into the foul mud below. On cold Marpenoth days like this, the wind whistled through chinks in the walls, promising four more months of relentless cold.

Rinda barely noticed these blights. She spent as little

time as possible in the hovel, using it only for sleeping and eating and sometimes scribing false traveling papers for runaway slaves or assassin-plagued merchants. It made Rinda uncomfortable to do the work there, but with most of the men and women who came to her for help, she had no other choice. Her clients often called darkened doorways home; to keep a steady hand in those dank places was close to impossible.

She'd refused a position in the scribes' guild to help these people, something her father had argued against right up until the instant she walked out of his house, two years past. Rinda didn't miss him. He was a bitter man who hated his lot in life. He could never understand her need to help others, the drive that made life worth living in a bleak place like Zhentil Keep.

Whenever she tried to rest, Rinda found herself troubled by thoughts of those more unfortunate than she. And so she spent most of her waking hours on the streets, helping the Keep's downtrodden as best she could. Some days, this meant arranging temporary shelter for a destitute family or forging letters of passage for a soldier deserting the Zhentilar. On other days, she roamed the inns and taverns, teaching the prostitutes and petty thieves how to read and write.

This particular day had been spent in the marketplace, begging money for bribes. The Zhentarim mages who watched over the slums cared little if Rinda helped a few escaped prisoners slip away down the Tesh. They demanded a price for their silence, though. Now, as she huddled against the cold in her hovel, Rinda tallied up the few coins she'd scrounged.

"I don't have nearly enough." She sighed raggedly, then counted the coppers again. "Not even close. This will mean trouble for the girls hoping to run away from Madame Februa."

Rinda turned thrillingly green eyes on the dwarf lounging by the door. He tilted precariously in a rickety chair, his heavy boots up on a table. His clothes were unkempt leathers, his beard and hair a tangled mop of black and silver. One gray eye peeked out from under a bushy brow. A brown eye patch circled with silver studs hid the other. "I hear Lord Chess cried himself to sleep when he learned Leira was gone," the dwarf noted. He blew his drooping mustaches away from his mouth and added venomously, "That bloated sack of orc dung."

"Hodur, you know I hate it when you ignore me like that," Rinda said angrily. "If you want to talk about something else, just say so."

The dwarf smirked. "All right, then. I want to talk about something else. Anything's fair game, just so long as it ain't how little food there'll be this winter or how the Zhentilar beat up on prisoners or anything else about the riffraff around here." He paused to scratch furiously under his beard. "You're the most depressing person I've ever met, you know that?"

The young woman dropped the copper coins into a chipped teacup. "So why are you always here?"

"Maybe I like to be depressed," Hodur replied. "I've always heard we dwarves are supposed to be melan—uh, meloch—er, unhappy. A street preacher in the Serpent's Eye talked about it once. He said it's because we're a doomed race. Not enough little dwarves to carry on our crafts and our wars, so we've got no future." His voice painted the words with emotions he'd meant to hide. "Or maybe I ain't got nothing else to do. No work for a stone-cutter with mitts like these," he said, holding up palsied hands. They trembled in fits and starts.

Tactfully, Rinda let the subject drop. She pried up one of the few sound floorboards and secreted the cup in the mud beneath. The ground squelched nastily as she set the treasure in place. "So what's this about Lord Chess?"

"Oh, nothing important," the dwarf conceded. "I just heard he was all tore up when Cyric announced to Leira's priests that the goddess was gone."

Rinda smiled knowingly. "He hasn't been a practicing cleric in years. All he'll miss are the banquets the Leirans threw—masks required, no debauchery too unusual, and no questions asked."

"How would you know?"

With mock sweetness, Rinda held her hands to her cheeks. "Why a dwarf told me," she said. "How else?"

Hodur laughed, his mustaches flapping in front of his mouth with each loud bark. "You know, it must be pretty rotten to be a Leiran right about now. I mean, rumor is Cyric's the one that done her in, right? But if you kill yourself in despair over it, you just end up in the dark-hearted bastard's domain anyway!"

"Careful," Rinda warned. "You don't know who's listening."

"Why is it human gods have nothing to do but plague their worshipers with quests or eavesdrop from the heavens so they can squash anyone who says something bad about them?" The dwarf dropped his feet to the floor. The chair creaked dangerously as he shifted his weight. "You don't find dwarven gods wasting time like that. Moradin and Clanggedin and their lot have better things to do with their time—you know, crushing the orc gods' armies or insulting Corellon Larethian and the other immortal elvish sots."

"It's not the gods I'm worried about," Rinda said. "It's the clerics—and the Zhentilar. Patriarch Mirrormane has asked Lord Chess to make speaking out against Cyric or the church equal to treason. And Chess is coward enough to make the army support Mirrormane's wishes."

"The Zhentarim won't stand for that," the dwarf said, dismissing the notion with one trembling hand. "And they're the ones who really run this place."

Rinda's green eyes grew thoughtful. "We can only hope that's still true," she murmured. "They're a lot less dangerous than Cyric's men. . . ."

"I never thought I'd hear you say a good word about the Black Network," Hodur exclaimed. He clapped his hands together. "Could it be the truth of the world has penetrated that ridiculous armor of good intentions you've hammered out for yourself?"

"I see the world a lot more clearly than you think," she said. "But there's nothing wrong with hoping things might be better than they seem. The—"

A pounding on the door cut Rinda short and startled Hodur to his feet. "Open up in the name of Cyric," a deep voice boomed.

Cursing into his beard, the dwarf rushed to the other side of the room, where a lantern sat upon a long bench. He grabbed it roughly. "Get a flint," he hissed as he dumped oil on a nearby pile of parchment.

Rinda scowled and gestured for him to stop. "If this were a raid," she whispered, "they wouldn't have knocked."

Despite her own reassurances, Rinda overturned a mug of water onto a forged set of identity papers as she moved to the door. No sense taking too many chances.

The two men standing on the threshold were typical of the thugs the Church of Cyric employed. They leaned against the jamb, idly picking splinters from the rotting wood with shivs. One was fat, with a bristling beard and heavy-lidded eyes. The other was small and lithe. His round-shouldered stoop and the dark rings circling his eyes made Rinda think of the weasels that lived in the river outside the city. Both men wore fur-trimmed cloaks over their shabby clothes. Only their red armbands identified them as churchmen, emblazoned as they were with Cyric's holy symbol—a leering white skull surrounded by a black sun.

"Let's see," the small one said. He unfolded a ragged scrap of paper. "Brown hair. Medium height. Slender build." Wrinkling his face, he squinted up at Rinda in the failing afternoon light. "Yeah, green eyes, too. This is her, Worvo."

"You Rinda, daughter of Bevis the Illuminator?" the fat one asked. Even his words were bloated, full of round vowels and slurred consonants.

Rinda crossed her arms over her chest. "And if I am?"

"Just answer the question, awright?" The weasely thug spit onto the street and looked around. "We ain't got all day on this."

Like a barricade being rolled into place, Hodur swaggered between Rinda and the thugs. "You got the wrong place. There ain't no Rinda here."

Worvo blinked a few times, then let his mouth hang open in an idiot's gape. "We do? There ain't? Hey, Var, if this ain't—"

"Of course it's her," Var snapped. "She's supposed to be smart, right? A scribe." He gestured to Hodur's eye patch with his dagger. "Even a blind old gin-head like this could see she ain't like anyone else around. Her clothes are clean. She's even bathed this month, from the looks of her." He licked his thin lips. "And she's even awake during the daytime. Probably the only woman within a mile of here who don't wake up at sundown—unless her little one-eyed friend here just got her out of bed."

Hodur balled one trembling hand into a fist and grabbed the front of Var's tunic with the other. Both thugs leveled their knives at the dwarf, but Rinda pulled him back from the door before trouble could start. She'd seen Hodur fight. Despite his infirmities, he was more than a match for the two scruffy churchmen—and five more like them. But if a scuffle broke out, the watch might show up, and that meant trained killers. Probably mages, too.

"It's all right, Hodur," she said calmly. The hard look in her eyes cowed the dwarf, and he stepped back into the room.

"So are you Rinda or not?" Worvo asked.

"Yes. What business does the church have with me?"

"Like I said before, you're a scribe, right?" Var nodded for her. "The church needs your services. That's all you need to know."

Rinda frowned. "But I'm not a member of the guild. They can't hire me if I'm not—"

"I didn't say you was going to get paid for this," Var said. He turned to his fat companion. "Did I say this was a paying job?"

"Uh, no, Var."

"See, I thought I was being perfectly clear." He reached out and took Rinda by the arm. "The church wants a scribe with some smarts, and you fit the bill. So, let's get going, awright?"

Rinda reached around the doorjamb and grabbed the thin cloak that hung by the door. "Stay here until I come back, Hodur. Don't worry. I'll be all right."

Flanked by the churchmen, she hurried away from her home, through alleys shrouded with the lengthening shadows of twilight. "Where are you taking me?" she asked.

"Not far," Var replied. His beady eyes darted back and forth, taking stock of every figure huddled in a darkened doorway, every drunkard weaving in his path.

He's no fool, Rinda noted. This part of the Keep often proved a deathtrap for those unfamiliar with the things that stalked its night—the press gangs and assassins and lurking creatures hungry for human flesh. Worst of all, though, were the *naug-adar*, the Zhentarim wizards who roamed the alleys in search of subjects for their sadistic experiments. No one was safe from these "devil dogs," not even men wearing Cyric's holy symbol.

"Er, we was supposed to tell you he's dead," Worvo blurted. "Your father, I mean. Three nights ago."

"Yeah," Var added. "Right after he recommended you, he had a accident in the crypts below the temple. The church buried him there as a martyr."

"How nice," Rinda said flatly. She swallowed hard to drive down the lump in her throat—not of sadness, but of rage. Betrayal was nothing new to her, especially from her father. What infuriated her now was the thought that Bevis had given over his only child to the Church of Cyric, and he hadn't even saved himself by doing it.

* * * * *

Rinda smelled the parchment-maker's shop long before she saw it. The stench of animal skins and fetid barrels of standing water wafted from the place, making the whole alley stink like an abattoir. From the amount of activity on the street, though, it was obvious the neighbors had gotten used to the unpleasant odor long ago.

In darkened doorways, scantily clad girls called out to anyone sober enough to walk on his own. And if a passerby happened to stumble, they descended on him like crows on a battlefield, taking everything of the slightest value. The body picked clean, the women hurried back to their cold, lightless perches, hacking and coughing from long-untreated maladies.

A pack of grubby children poured out of a rookery at one end of the street. They howled like wolves and overturned everything in their path not nailed down. Before that horde of flying feet and unwashed faces, men and women scattered. The prostitutes slammed their doors closed, waiting for the mob to pass, and Rinda and her escort pressed themselves against a wall. The churchmen drew their daggers to warn away the urchins. Fortunately, the pack seemed more interested in making noise than preying on anyone in particular.

As the children passed and the howling died down, a drunken chorus of bawds took command of the night air. At a tavern down the way, they belted out a paean to Loviatar, punctuating the end of each verse with a loud clattering of mugs on tabletops. Rinda thought she heard the sharp crack of a whip, too—a common enough sound at dusk in Zhentil Keep.

"This way," Var murmured through the handkerchief braced against his mouth and nose. He tugged her toward a small shop crushed between two higher buildings.

Light bled out through thick, latticed windows on the lower floor, pooling in the street. That revealed enough of the place for Rinda to see it was a one-story workshop, with two floors of living quarters over it. The upper windows were either boarded up or dark. As she had suspected from the smell, the sign above the door proclaimed it the abode of a parchmenter.

Six Zhentilar stood before the shop, a wall of chain mail and bared swords. These were elite soldiers, Rinda guessed, maybe even part of Lord Chess's personal body-guard. They stood at attention, watching the passing prostitutes and drunkards and feral children.

Var lowered his handkerchief as he approached the Zhentilar, then batted Worvo's down as well. The soldiers greeted him in return with a picket of raised blades. "Scribe for Patriarch Mirrormane," Var said to the nearest soldier.

After a moment, the man nodded his square chin and let them pass. Rinda shuddered as the light played off the soldier's face. The long scars marring his cheeks announced to the world that his tongue had been removed.

The shop door creaked open. Patriarch Mirrormane appeared on the stoop, wreathed by light and rubbing his hands together nervously. "Ah, at last," he said, then fished two silver coins from the pocket of his long purple clerical robe. "Well done."

Var and Worvo took the coins eagerly, their disgust at the alley's smell driven away by greed. "Our thanks, Patriarch," Var offered. He bowed grandly and kissed the death's-head ring the high priest wore. When Worvo lumbered forward to do the same, Mirrormane waved him away.

"One of the Zhentilar will escort you out of here," the patriarch said as he pulled Rinda into the shop. The door slammed closed on the thugs' further exclamations of gratitude.

From the steel in Mirrormane's eyes, Rinda knew that Var and Worvo would be dead before they made three blocks. It was a common practice for Cyric's church: hire a messenger, then kill him once he'd completed his task.

The patriarch's face was a mask of wrinkles, his silver-white hair a nest of snakes. He smiled in a poor imitation of warmth and gestured for the scribe to move into the room. They were alone amongst the tilting shelves and rolls of finished parchment.

"You are to be blessed with a rare opportunity to serve the church," the patriarch began. "Lord Cyric has need of your skills as a scribe."

Rinda slipped the cloak from her shoulders and shook her dark curls into place. "Begging Your Holiness's pardon," she said, "but I'm not very religious and, I'm sorry to say, a rather poor scribe. If I had any skill at all, I'd be part of the guild."

"We've been checking up on you, Rinda," Xeno returned sharply. "You turned down a spot in the guild, not the other way around. And for what—to go off and do good deeds for thieves and drunkards."

The thin facade of pleasantness shattered. With every word, every gesture that followed, the patriarch teetered on the brink of mad rage. "We know everything about you. Don't think for an instant your actions go unnoticed, that you do anything in this city we do not condone." He chuckled. "The hope you foster, the dreams you nurture —they help our causes in ways you can never understand."

"This is hardly the way to win her cooperation," a voice said coolly from the back of the room.

The patriarch dropped to his knees and pressed his palms together in fervent prayer. "Forgive me, Your Magnificence, forgive me. But she is an unbeliever. She profanes your—"

"Enough," the man said. He stepped into the room with casual grace, eyeing Rinda openly. His gaze made her skin crawl. "Perhaps an unbeliever is just what we need to win over the other fools who cannot see the light."

For a moment the scribe wondered who this lean, hawk-nosed man could be to make Patriarch Mirrormane kowtow. He appeared to be no less than half the priest's sixty years, and his clothes marked him as nothing more influential than an underling in the city's thieves' guild. His leather boots were worn at the heels. His cloak was clean, but a little threadbare. Only the ancient rose-hued short sword on his belt told of wealth or power.

"I am Lord Cyric," he announced, then paused for a reply, for Rinda to bow or avert her gaze. When she merely stood and stared, a smile crept to his lips and crinkled the crow's feet surrounding his dark eyes. "You're a skeptic. That's good."

Patriarch Mirrormane slipped a dirk from the sleeve of his robe. "Kneel," he hissed.

"Oh, let her alone," Cyric said. He studied the scribe a

moment longer, then added, "Get out, Xeno. I think we'll get started now." The patriarch scurried backward to the door and disappeared into the night.

The realization that this was indeed the Prince of Lies crashed in on Rinda, and she began to tremble uncontrollably. Like rainwater, her cloak slipped through numb fingers to pool on the dirty floor.

Cyric ran a slender finger across her lips. "A skeptic, but wise enough to fear me, too. Better and better."

"I—I don't—"

Cyric silenced her with a gesture. "You're here to listen, not talk. Come."

He took her hand and led her to the part of the shop where the parchment was prepared. Vats of water and lime stood along one wall, filled with soaking animal skins. Circular wooden frames held skins already softened in the tubs. Beneath each one, wet piles of fur mounded where the parchmenter had begun scraping the skin to the necessary thinness. Rinda had seen such workshops before, and she could tell at a glance this one produced parchment of especially low quality. The water in the tubs was dirty, the curved scraping knives dull and rusted. The skins held in the frames were riddled with holes from careless handling and blotched from the filthy surroundings.

"I would never ask you to waste your time writing on parchment like this," Cyric said, watching the scribe as she took in her surroundings. "For notes it's fine, but never for a finished book." He patted her hand. "The parchment I use is made much more carefully, from much rarer stock."

"I don't understand," Rinda managed at last.

"Don't worry. You will."

Cyric paced around the huge room, taking in the drying racks crammed with badly cut sheets and tables piled high with account books. "I always begin the story in this place because I was born here." He stopped and rested his hands on his hips with theatrical flair. "Hard to believe, but this is the birthplace of a god—well, the house that used to stand here was, at any rate."

Slowly Cyric turned and stared into Rinda's green eyes. A jagged lance of fear bit into her heart. "I am going to tell you a story," the Prince of Lies said. "And from it you will write a book, one that will inspire men to worship me. The mages in my church have created special inks and parchment. They wrote special prayers that must be incorporated into the text exactly where they dictate, in the precise form they dictate. There will be illuminations and special bindings . . . but your work is the most important."

He crossed to Rinda's side once more and laid a gentle hand on her shoulder. "If you succeed, you'll be worshiped, praised in the annals of my world as a herald of the new order, an angel of knowledge to rival Oghma himself."

An unvoiced question hung in the air. Cyric paused only an instant before he answered it. "If you fail—" a shadow passed over his face, and he dug his fingers into her shoulder until the nails drew blood "—I'll drag your screaming soul down to Hades and hang you in my throne room next to your father."

* * * * *

From the *Cyrinishad*

It is said that Tymora and Beshaba wager for dominion over each and every soul born into the world. Lady Luck flips her silver coin, and the Maid of Misfortune calls heads or tails. If Beshaba guesses wrong, then Tymora showers the happy soul with good luck for the rest of his life. It is also said that the Maid of Misfortune rarely loses such contests.

Only one man in all of history escaped their cruel game—Cyric of Zhentil Keep. Even before he first walked the world as a mortal, Cyric had the will to resist the random call of Fate and make his own fortune. As his newborn soul stood before the goddesses, he cast a light upon Tymora's silver coin, blinding them to his presence. The deities never saw the coin fall, never settled their wager for Cyric's destiny. Thus was he born into the world without any fate save the one he himself could forge.

In the squalor of Zhentil Keep's slums, the man-who-would-be-a-god took on the shell of mortality for the first time. His mother, a beautiful bard with a mind as quick as Oghma's, had foreseen her child's greatness in a dream. She hid the infant Cyric from his father in the back alleys of that grim city, for the man was a leader of the Zhentilar and an agent of the Black Network, faithful to the god Bane. The God of Strife, too, had foreseen Cyric's potential mightiness. Fearing the only mortal unbound by Fate, he sent his agents throughout the city to slay the child.

On the hottest night in Flamerule, in the grips of the most brutal summer ever visited on Zhentil Keep, the assassins caught Cyric's mother and murdered her. Among the first to drive a blade into the woman's heart was her lover, the father of her son. Yet Cyric himself escaped their daggers by crawling away into the sewers. Gore-smeared and alone, he fought for life when any other human child would have withered and died. The blood of rats became his milk, and the motley skin he tore from the vermin became his blankets.

At dawn the next day, Cyric struggled back into the light, hardened like a thrice-tempered sword by the murder and his hunger and the Flamerule heat.

A Sembian vintner named Astolpho, traveling in the poorer sections of the city to sell his wares, discovered the infant Cyric and secreted him away. He had little idea that he'd become the means of the child's escape from a bloodthirsty pack of soldiers and Zhentarim mages. All he saw was a baby, dirty and abandoned. Like many, he could not gaze past the mortal facade hiding Cyric's greatness from the world.

For a dozen years Astolpho the vintner and his wife raised the boy amongst the trappings of wealth so common in the merchant-kingdom of Sembia. Cyric, ever disdainful of luxury, used their money and power to educate himself, to gather all the knowledge he could about Faerun and the lands he would one day rule as Lord of the Dead. The ever-jealous gods watched the child grow, frightened by his power, yet unable to drive him toward any destiny but the one he had chosen for himself.

Still, the gods Cyric would one day destroy—Bane and Bhaal and Myrkul—attempted to fight his growing strength and wisdom in any way they could. Bane created dark rumors about the boy, isolating him from the wealthy circle in which his parents traveled. Myrkul struck a deal with Talona, Lady of Poison, to plague him with diseases. And Bhaal sent his most subtle assassins to hunt the boy. But Cyric had turned his early suffering into a shield no god could shatter. He destroyed their minions wherever he found them and conquered hardships cast before him as if they were nothing but blunted caltrops strewn before a juggernaut.

The last of Bane's minions that Cyric faced in Sembia were Astolpho and his wife. The God of Strife had purchased their loyalty, promising to end the ill-fortune that had brought the man's business near to ruin. In return for this empty dream of renewed prosperity, they tried to prevent the young boy from leaving Sembia to seek his fortune. Yet the bonds of familial duty and feigned love they wielded were no match for Cyric's razor-sharp mind. He rejected their wealth and comfort, striking out to see the world he had only viewed through the eyes of bards and historians.

Astolpho's corpse was found spiked to the town gates,

flayed like the rats that had sustained Cyric in the Keep's sewers so many years before. No one ever found the remains of the vintner's wife, so expertly had the boy hid them throughout the town. To this day, nothing can lessen the smell of death hovering over the place, or silence the ghostly, tortured cries that nightly fill the air.

And so Cyric came to travel the Heartlands, amassing his own hoard of knowledge from the coins of experience he gathered along the way. The fearful gods, certain of their impending doom, tried their best to hold him back, but he was beyond their feeble grasp. He learned to fight as well as any soldier in Faerun and to live off the land in even the most inhospitable climes.

At last he returned to the city of his birth, for no other place in the world could match the cruelty and everyday horrors of Zhentil Keep. In short, it is a city where the cowardly veil of Civilization is thinnest, where men and women pass each day with the realization that Existence is Pain, and Death is the only water to ease suffering in the wasteland. That knowledge was Cyric's birthright, and the time had come for him to claim it. . . .

VI

SECRET PASSAGES

*Wherein the Prince of Lies expounds upon the
motivational uses for fear, and Rinda gains a
very powerful patron who has another version of
Cyric's life to set down on parchment.*

As Cyric stepped through the portal, the illusion masking his hideousness melted away. Gone were the humble clothes and roguish good looks. His face hardened into a rigored mask, blood red and gaunt. The flesh vanished from his fingers, leaving them little more than daggers of bone. A robe of darkness cloaked his lithe frame. The shadowy vestment was patterned only with a gleaming white skull that seemed to float over the god's heart.

On the other side of the enchanted gateway lay the parchmenter's shop. Mirrormane and his tongueless Zhentilar escort prostrated themselves in the center of the room, bowing toward the portal. Behind them, Rinda kneeled in shocked silence. None of them could see Cyric as he stood in Bone Castle's huge throne room. Yet as the Prince of Lies glanced back at the scribe, he wondered how she would react to his inhuman face. Perhaps, he mused, *I will honor her with it once she's completed the book.*

Was the illusion satisfactory, Your Magnificence? Jergal asked. He floated at Cyric's side, ever ready to do his unholy master's bidding.

The Lord of the Dead grunted noncommittally and stalked toward his throne. It wouldn't do to admit a lackey had proved useful in masking his lack of magic. "What news of the search for Kelemvor?"

The denizens have completed their sweep of the city, the seneschal began. He paused just long enough to dispel the portal he'd created, then hurried after the god. *The news is not as good as I had hoped it might be.*

"Don't be coy," Cyric snapped. "Did they find him or not?"

No, Your Magnificence.

"Then they obviously aren't looking hard enough!" Cyric shouted. He drew Godsbane and turned on the seneschal. "You promised to see to this matter, Jergal. I didn't leave a facet of my mind focused here because I trusted your word. Am I to take this failure as a sign you've come to the end of your usefulness?"

Jergal bowed, turning his bulging yellow eyes to the carpet. *I can only hope not,* he said fearfully.

The Prince of Lies ran the flat of his blade over Jergal's skull. Godsbane pulsed a deeper red, humming like a galleon's rigging in a gale wind. "Kelemvor is near," Cyric murmured. "I can almost smell the unwashed lout."

He turned the blade so it nicked the seneschal. An unearthly howl of pleasure went up from Godsbane as she gulped Jergal's yellow, poisonous blood, draining his life-force away. The stoic Jergal flinched, then trembled in agony, but he never cried out, never raised a hand to defend himself.

After what seemed like an eternity, Cyric took the blade away. *Please, my love,* Godsbane purred. *He has betrayed your trust. He does not deserve to live.*

"Enough," Cyric said. He sheathed the sword and raised Jergal to face him. The seneschal's yellow eyes were dim, the gray skin on his skull mottled with festering blotches of purple. "Remember this pain. If you fail me again, I will make it last forever."

The phantasmal creature nodded weakly. *I exist only to serve you, Your Magnificence.*

Rubbing bony hands together, Cyric paced to his throne. He shifted his robe and settled into the ghastly chair. "They need to fear me. That's the heart of this problem, I think."

All living creatures fear you, Jergal said from the foot of the throne. He gestured to the trophies of pain and suffering displayed about the room. *You dwell in the darkness of men's souls.*

"Not mortals," Cyric corrected. "The denizens." Impatience flashed across his blasted, hellish features. "They've lived too long in this city believing themselves safe from my wrath."

They fear your tortures, Jergal offered.

"But torture is finite. Utter destruction is a different matter entirely. The False and the Faithless may welcome oblivion, but not the denizens. This is their heaven, after all. Why leave it?" Cyric ran one finger along Godsbane's red blade. "For a moment, when the sword had her fangs in you, you thought yourself doomed."

Jergal shuddered. *Yes.*

"I think it made you see the error of your ways, did it not?"

Of course, Your Magnificence. I'll not fail you again.

"And neither will the denizens, if we give them a glimpse of oblivion." Cyric steepled his fingers before his mouth and tapped his thumbnails on his chipped teeth. "They cannot truly fear me unless they know the price of failure is destruction. And if they do not fear me, they are useless as servants."

There is the matter of the pact, Jergal said quietly. *Your faithful are supposed to be safe from destruction, so long as they continue to worship you.*

Cyric looked up at Jergal, surprise in his red-rimmed eyes. "Are you suggesting I cannot do with the citizens of my city as I please?"

No, the seneschal replied. *Merely reminding you that the laws of the realm—*

"I've sent denizens to their doom from the first day of my reign," Cyric drawled. "The hour in which I ratified that foolish pact I also condemned a dozen to become part of the Night Serpent's levy."

They had broken from worshiping you, Jergal offered.

"Ah, but who is to say what I consider true worship?" Cyric asked. "Today I've decided that the hunt for Kelemvor is a holy quest, so from this moment on, all who fail in that quest are traitors." He studied his seneschal for a moment. "Perhaps this devotion you have to law is blinding you to your duties."

Jergal looked into his master's eyes. *It is part of my nature, Your Magnificence. When I was created to oversee the castle, I was given that trait so I could be trusted to uphold my obligation. I am faithful to the Lord of the Dead even before myself.*

"Once you were loyal to Myrkul," Cyric noted.

Yes.

"And now you're loyal to me?"

You are the rightful lord of Bone Castle, Jergal replied evenly. *And as long as you are, I will do anything you ask—*

except betray you.

"Then I wish you to break the pact with the denizens," Cyric said, searching for some sign of displeasure in Jergal's dull yellow eyes. "Have one thousand of them publicly tortured, then give them to the Night Serpent or bathe them in water from the River Slith. Either way, they'll be destroyed." He drummed his fingers anxiously on the arms of the throne, then murmured, "That isn't enough."

Destroy one for each hour that passes without Kelemvor being found, Godsbane suggested darkly.

Cyric giggled like a madman. "Better still, destroy one of the spineless curs for each *minute* that goes by without the holy quest being fulfilled." He curled his bony fingers around the sword's pommel. "That will set them on his trail like hounds, eh?"

Like Kezef himself, Jergal offered.

Cyric paused, then a sick smile crept across his lips. "Kezef," he murmured. "Of course."

The Circle of Greater Powers has forbidden traffic with Kezef, Godsbane warned, trepidation in her voice.

"Since when have you cared what the Circle proclaims?" Cyric snapped. "Have they not broken their own laws by denying me magic?"

Godsbane did not reply, but Jergal said, *Of course, my lord. You are above their laws. You have every right to unleash the Chaos Hound.*

"My cup," said Cyric, the smile still creasing his seared lips. "Then arrange for my passage to Pandemonium."

The seneschal held out his hands, and an ornate silver chalice appeared, encrusted with hundreds of tiny rubies, each in the shape of a sundered heart. The ever-full cup contained the tears of disillusioned dreamers and broken-hearted lovers. The drink was bitter, but to Cyric it tasted like a priceless wine, aged to perfection.

"To oblivion," the Prince of Lies offered solemnly, "and to Kezef." He lifted the cup to his lips and drank deeply.

* * * * *

Dawn in Zhentil Keep. Rinda made her way through squalid alleys, her hands cramped from taking notes for hours on end, her vision blurred from lack of sleep. She welcomed the chill morning with its bite of sleet in the air. It kept her from completely losing track of her surroundings.

This street was wider than most, which meant a clear path through the offal and garbage dumped from the buildings' upper floors. Ragged refugees slept in every open doorway, the detritus of Zhentish society. Most of them came here to die, in places the dawn never seemed to touch with its healing light and soothing warmth.

Rinda glanced up only to find the rising sun hidden behind the huge spires of Cyric's temple. They loomed, black and twisted, like blind giants standing watch over the city. No, the scribe reminded herself, not blind. The Church of Cyric has a thousand ways of seeing into the hearts and minds of the Zhentish.

"Help me, missy. In the name of Ilmater."

The man sprawled against the Serpent's Eye. His haggard face and scraggly beard were limned with frost. His nose was blue from cold. Holding shaky hands out to Rinda, he pleaded, "A copper, missy. Anything."

The scribe stopped and crouched before him. "I've got no money, but I can bring some clothes here for you." She glanced up through the tavern's windows. Dark. "Will you stay here for a while? The Serpent's closed, so they won't chase you away."

Slowly the man nodded. "You have anything for me to drink till you get back, missy?" He reached under his tattered tunic and pulled out an empty bottle. "That'll keep me warm as any rags. . . ."

"No," she said firmly. Rinda stood and turned away. "I'll send someone with the clothes as soon as I can."

It never helped to get angry with the poor wretches—not when gin was cheaper than food and more plentiful than clean water—but Rinda always found herself railing inwardly whenever she came across someone crippled by drink. Without hope, they drowned the sting of each passing day with a ten-copper bottle. Hodur had been like that when Rinda first found him, but the dwarf had managed to pull himself out of the gutter. Maybe this old man could, too.

The swell of hope washed against the events of the night before and dissipated. Rinda closed her eyes for an instant, willing the dark monolith of despair to crumble. It wouldn't. As large and as immovable as the black spires of Cyric's temple, the tower of hopelessness dominated her thoughts; the Prince of Lies had taken control of her life, at least until this damned book of his was done.

No, she chided herself sharply. He'll take control of my life only if I let him.

After all, she wasn't being held prisoner—despite what Patriarch Mirrormane had suggested. If she arranged her time carefully enough, there might still be a few hours a day to devote to the unfortunates. And there were always men and women who needed her help. . . .

When she finally arrived home, Rinda found the door hanging open slightly. More from habit than concern, she scanned the alley, looking in the doorways and windows of the surrounding buildings for signs of trouble. If robbers or ruffians were waiting in the house, there'd be a lookout posted—someone like the unshaven man watching her from the second-story window across the street. Scowling, Rinda moved away from the door. No sense in walking into a trap alone when she could muster a few friends to help out.

"Hey, Rin! Where you going?"

Hodur's gruff voice stopped the scribe short. She turned to find the dwarf standing in the doorway, his beefy hands planted on his hips. "I was getting worried. It ain't like you to stay out all night."

Rinda sighed in relief. "You shouldn't leave the door open like that," she said. "Not even when you're around. You never know who might wander in."

Just before she followed her friend inside, Rinda looked up at the window across the way. The unshaven man was still there. One elbow planted on the sill, he cupped his chin in his hand. Brazenly he returned the scribe's gaze, with eyes that betrayed more intelligence than his demeanor suggested. He lowered his arm, revealing the grinning white holy symbol of Cyric on his purple clerical robes.

"So you're not a prisoner, hmmm?" Rinda muttered to herself and slammed the door closed behind her.

Hodur had already dropped into his chair by the door, though he didn't plant his feet on the table as he usually did. The stained and scarred tabletop was crammed with bowls and mugs. He'd only cleared one small circle, at the center of which squatted a leather cup full of dice.

Another man—or, more precisely, an elf—sat across from Hodur. He watched Rinda enter, his back painfully straight, his shoulders set squarely, in military fashion. A neat gray tunic draped his thin frame. The material was clean, though a few stubborn bloodstains marred the sleeves. In one hand he held a deep-sided bowl. Carefully, with long, thin fingers, he drew a wriggling beetle from the dish and popped it into his mouth.

"Ivlisar," Rinda greeted stiffly.

The elf nodded, crunching the beetle. A smile stretched across his narrow face as he held the bowl out to the scribe. "I only take 'em from the graves of the bright blokes I dig up. The way I figure it, if they eat the brains of the stiffs, and then I eat 'em—"

"No," Rinda snapped, holding a hand out to ward off the bowlful of beetles. She moved to a neat pile of clothes on the floor and grabbed two tunics she'd taken from the rubbish heap outside a Zhentilar garrison. "Hodur, I need you to take these over to an old man outside the Serpent's Eye. He'll freeze to death if he doesn't put something between him and the wind."

"Later," the dwarf replied. "We need to talk."

"Talk," she scoffed. "You have dicing to do, you mean. Look, it won't take very long. And I'm sure Ivlisar would be happy to go for a walk with you." She gave the elf a stern look. "Don't give the old man anything to drink. If I find out you did, you're not welcome here again."

"A bit of the blue ruin never hurt nobody," Ivlisar said defensively. "'Sides, Hodur isn't pulling your leg. We're set to have a bit of a parley, dear lady."

"Ilmater give me strength," Rinda hissed. She tucked the clothes under her arm and headed for the door to the back room. "Fine, then. I'll go myself. Did you put those spare gloves back here?"

Panicked, Hodur leaped to his feet. "Rin, wait! There's—"

Rinda couldn't hold back her gasp of surprise when she saw what lay beyond the door.

An orc in leather Zhentilar armor lounged on her bed, his muddy feet propped on her pillow. He turned his gray-green face to the scribe and wrinkled his piggish snout disdainfully. Another man, clad in stylish clothes and a rich, double-lined cloak stood before the chest where Rinda kept her few belongings. In his hands was her most treasured possession—a globe of enchanted glass. Locked within the glass was a panoramic view of a lovely, verdant hillside in the Moonshaes.

"Get out!" she roared. "Now!"

The shouted command startled the orc enough for him to roll to his feet. The other man turned slowly to Rinda, then held out the glass globe to her. "These are quite rare," he said. "And quite beautiful. Your taste is to be applauded."

"Quite a compliment coming from you, Lord Fzoul," Rinda said coldly, recognizing the man at last.

When Rinda didn't take the globe, the red-haired man gently replaced it in the chest, then bowed formally. "My reputation precedes me," he said archly, "and from the tone of your voice, it has not presented my best face."

"You got more'n one?" the orc grunted. He shrugged and turned to Rinda. "This her? She don't look like much."

Fzoul rolled his eyes. "As you will find, Rinda, General Vrakk prides himself on being blunt. It might appear that he is quite stupid, but don't let him fool you."

"Me get commendation from King Ak-soon himself for fighting Horde," Vrakk crowed. He slapped his broad chest and grinned, an act that made the sizable incisors jutting from his lower lip almost touch his snout. "Big hero in crusade."

"If you two are here to arrest me," Rinda said, "get it over with. If not, get out. I won't have soldiers or Zhentarim scum—no matter how well-mannered—in my home."

A large hand pressed against Rinda's back. "They're here to help, Rin," Hodur murmured solemnly. "We all are."

"Help what?" the scribe said. "Ruin my reputation with the neighbors? Their kind isn't well liked around here, you know." She crumpled the tunics into a tight ball.

Fzoul stepped gracefully around Vrakk. "I assure you, Rinda. No one saw us enter. No one will see us leave."

She took a step back from Fzoul, bulling Hodur out of the way. "What about the church watchdog across the street—or did you miss him? Or maybe he's one of your lackeys. . . ."

"Hardly," Fzoul said. He paced Rinda carefully, keeping

close to her as she backed across the room. He took his eyes off the scribe once, and then only to nod to Ivlisar. "I'm afraid we can't let you leave just yet," the Zhentarim agent noted as she got close to the door.

Glancing over her shoulder, Rinda found the elf blocking her way. He leaned against the door, munching on beetles and smiling fatuously. "No walking until you hear what we have to parley about," Ivlisar said, then used a long finger-nail to dislodge a stray leg from between his teeth.

"Yeah, just sit," the orc rumbled. "We tell you what to do."

The pig-snouted soldier locked a hand onto Rinda's shoulder, intent on pushing her down into a chair. At first she seemed to comply, to bend with the pressure from his grip. Then, suddenly, she twisted and flung the tunics at Vrakk. The orc swatted them away from his face, but as he did, Rinda planted a kick in his stomach. With a porcine grunt, Vrakk buckled over.

Rinda turned to give the same to Ivlisar. The elf dropped his bowl, allowing the beetles to scuttle away. "Please, dear lady," he said. "This is a terrible mistake."

Fortunately for him, the scribe only managed one step toward him before she was tackled from behind. As she rolled onto her side, kicking furiously to free her legs, Rinda looked down at her attacker. She expected to see Fzoul or even Vrakk holding her down. But it was neither of them.

Hodur clamped her ankles tight within the circle of his brawny arms. Rinda could feel the dwarf's drink-palsied muscles trembling, even through her boots. "Please, Rin," Hodur said. "We don't want Cyric to do to you what he done to all them others."

"Like your father," Fzoul added coolly. "I saw him die, you know. It was quite unpleasant." He knit his gloved fingers together. "And Cyric will kill you, too, if you fail."

Rinda stopped struggling. "Maybe I won't fail."

"Then you have much more to fear than death," Fzoul said. Even through his veneer of civility, Rinda could hear the unaccustomed ring of truth in his voice. From the look of distaste on Fzoul's face, he found being honest unpleasant.

Hodur looked up at her, his dark eyes full of watery sincerity, like a wounded hound's. "Listen to him, Rin."

"Seems I don't have much choice," she said. When Hodur loosened his grip, she pulled her legs free and pushed the dwarf away.

"He lucky," Vrakk wheezed, gesturing with his snout to Hodur. "That why he capture she-cat like you." Bracing his stomach he tottered to a chair. As he slumped into it, the orc added, "Stupid *dglinkarz* like him not good in fighting."

"Orcish is a right charming language for curses," Ivlisar noted cheerily. He gave up scanning the room for his scattered breakfast and turned the bowl upside-down on the crowded table. "All right, Lord Fzoul," he drawled, settling onto the floor in front of the door. "Let's get this over with. Like dear Rinda, I've been up all night, and I need my sleep. Bodies don't dig 'emselves up, you know."

Fzoul offered Rinda a hand up, but she ignored it. Instead, she sat cross-legged in the center of the room. "He's right," she said. "Let's get this over with."

"We know Cyric wants you to create a book of his life," Fzoul began without preamble. "What you cannot realize, and what the Prince of Lies will not tell you, is the purpose of that book." He paused dramatically. "If written correctly and imbued with the right prayers, the right hymns, and the right illuminations, it could coerce anyone who reads it into worshiping Cyric."

"So?" Rinda asked, stifling a yawn. "What makes that different from any church's holy text? The priests want you to believe what it says is true, otherwise, it's a waste of parchment."

"But with this book, you'll have no choice but to believe it," Hodur said. At Rinda's disbelieving look, he nodded solemnly. "Anyone who reads it or has it read to them will believe Cyric is the only god worth worshiping."

"Then the other gods. . . ."

"Will fade away," Fzoul said. He dusted his palms together, as if dismissing the rest of the heavenly pantheon. "Giving Cyric complete control of Faerun and every soul in it, living or dead."

"And I'm supposed to stop him?" Rinda asked. "He's a god—a *god!*"

Ivlisar enthusiastically applauded her observation. "It's nice to chat with someone else who sees backstabbing a deity as just a bit ludicrous."

"You're all lunatics," Rinda said, then shut her eyes tight. "Or I'm dreaming."

"More like a nightmare," Hodur offered. "But this is all as real as the rats in this place and deadly serious to boot. We need your help, Rin. There's a lot of us in the Keep's underground what hate Cyric more than anything, but we need you to help us discredit the book."

Fzoul stepped forward. "Indeed. We have many allies: priests of Bane and Myrkul and Leira, who all want Cyric overthrown; mages and illuminators and men with enough common sense to see the Prince of Lies will be unhappy until the world is a smoking ruin—you'll have the skills of all these people at your disposal."

"No forget my warriors," Vrakk grunted.

"The orcs in the Zhentilar are none too pleased with the army's new restrictions on their kind," Fzoul clarified. "It seems Cyric questions their loyalty. Only humans go to his realm when they die, so he feels orcs like Vrakk here have no reason to fight for him. The priesthood pressured the Zhentilar into limiting the orcs' promotions and assigning them tasks of only minor importance."

Vrakk ground a beetle beneath his heel, then scraped the remains onto the edge of a chair. "We make them priests sorry they no like us."

"Some of the merchants will fight, too," Ivlisar chimed in. "We have a great deal to lose. We in the medical arts—"

"Body snatchers, you mean," Hodur scoffed.

The elf stuck his chin out haughtily. "I prefer resurrection men, actually." Turning back to Rinda, he continued. "We in the medical arts got lots of contacts, what with knowing the mages and herbalists and gravediggers and all. No one but the priests are getting rich off Cyric ruling the Keep like it was his manor house. Just imagine how much worse it'll be when he's got no competition at all!"

"And what about you?" Rinda asked, eyeing Hodur suspiciously. "Who do you represent?"

"N-No one," the dwarf stammered. "I just promised to smooth over an introduction for them all, after they heard the church picked you as the next holy scribe."

"Of course Hodur had to report your predicament to me anyway," Fzoul noted. "As a member of the Zhentarim, it was his obligation. . . ."

Rinda stared in disbelief. "You traitor," she hissed. "How long have you been a spy? How long?"

"For years before he met you," Fzoul said. "We sent him here to pose as a drunkard, to get inside your operation. You were getting so good at smuggling people out of the city, we were worried someone really important might slip by unnoticed. Of course, I tell you this only because I want us all to be honest, now that we're fighting a common foe."

"Rin, I never—"

"Don't pretend to be sorry," the scribe snapped. "Even if you meant it, Hodur, I wouldn't believe you. Gods, I always told you to be careful what you said around here, but I never thought you were the one spying for the Zhentarim."

"Be a realist about this," Fzoul said. "We are offering

you a way to prevent an apocalypse." He smiled knowingly. "You could kill yourself, of course, but since you've never been particularly faithful to any of the gods, you'll just end up in Cyric's realm. There's no other way out, I'm afraid. It's us or him."

Rinda stood and walked to the closed front door. "This is all moot anyway," she said bitterly, pointing in the general direction of the lookout across the street. "The watchdogs Mirrormane set outside here will have heard the fight and our argument. This will all go right back to the patriarch, and that means the end of this conspiracy."

"Hardly," Fzoul said with unbearable smugness. "The spy in the building across the way, the one on the roof, and the others planted around the neighborhood will only see and hear and smell what we want them to. The same with Cyric. Oh, don't look so surprised. Do you really think he'd let such an important person wander around in the slums without watching over you himself? We had to take care of that prying eye before we spoke to you."

"But you can't blind a god. That would take—" She swallowed and glanced nervously around the room.

Yes, Rinda, a soothing voice said from everywhere and nowhere, from within the piles of parchment and the shabby walls, from within Rinda herself. *It would take another god to hide your actions from the Prince of Lies. Cyric's dark deeds worry many in the heavens, and the time has come to act against him and his book of falsehoods.*

"Why me?" Rinda asked, her mind struggling to stay above the swells of confusion. "What do you want from me?"

The same thing Cyric wants from you—your skill as a scribe, as a writer of tales, the voice explained calmly. *I, too, wish you to set down the story of Cyric's life, but I will tell you the truth. And with this true life of the Prince of Lies, we will show those who worship him just how deluded and dangerous he can be.*

The room warped before Rinda's sleepy eyes. The piles of rags, the rickety chairs and tables, the gathered conspirators—all these twisted and flowed like images in an imperfect mirror. When at last they stopped, the people and objects disappeared in a flash of unreality. Behind this crumbled facade lay the dark tower of hopelessness built of Cyric's plans for her. Now, however, it was no longer a lone spire in an open sea of possibilities. A thousand other spires, just as black, just as foreboding, jutted up around it. They filled the world from horizon to horizon.

"When do we begin?" Rinda heard herself say. It was what she was supposed to ask, she knew, just what the mysterious god had expected.

The reply, too, was eerily familiar. *Right now,* the god said, the voice filling her mind with long-hidden truths about the Lord of the Dead. *Of course, we shall begin at the beginning. . . .*

* * * * *

From *The True Life of Cyric*

Though men may try to wrest the reins of their destiny from the gods, they are all born at the mercy of Nature, bound in a hundred ways to those around them. This is how the gods insure mortals are tied to their world of toil and sorrow. Cyric of Zhentil Keep was no exception.

In the hottest Flamerule to ever grip the Keep, Cyric was born to a destitute bard, so lacking in skill she could not earn a copper singing on street corners. Like many desperate women in the slums, she got what little money she could selling her body to the officers in the Zhentilar barracks. Thus was Cyric's paternity sealed in shame, and his fate set for the next decade.

Hoping to gain pity from the Zhentilar who fathered her child, Cyric's mother went to him and pleaded for a few silvers to feed his son. The man, a low-ranking lout of little substance and less ambition, denied ever having bedded the wench. When she persisted in her claims, he threatened to kill her and sell the child into slavery.

In the days that followed, the mother and child lived off the kindness of others—tavern keepers and scullery maids, street singers and pickpockets, who all gave what they could to keep the two alive. Yet the gods had not finished casting lots for Cyric's future, or the story may have ended there. Driven by greed and hatred, Cyric's father returned to the slums. He killed Cyric's mother, taking the screaming, mewling child as payment for his inconvenience.

Sold into slavery before his first step, before his first word, Cyric was transferred like so much veal to the merchant-kingdom of Sembia. There, childless families often purchased babies, since fortunes went to state coffers if not passed from father to child. Astolpho the vintner bought Cyric for a middling sum. In the years to come he would curse the purchase as the worst investment he ever made.

Cyric grew up in the lap of luxury, wanting for nothing. For a time, he seemed content and even happy. As the years went on, though, he became aware of the subtle scorn of his fellows and their parents. It wasn't until he was ten winters old that he learned the reason—his birthright was not the cultured palaces of Sembia, but the back alleys of Zhentil Keep, feared throughout Faerun as a city of great evil and corruption.

Torn by shame and desperate for his parents to prove their love for him, Cyric made a show of running away. Before his parents could mount a search, though, he was captured by the local watch and returned home. News of the incident spread throughout the merchant palaces, adding to the mistrust centered on the boy.

Cyric remained in Sembia for two more years. Astolpho's

business faltered, his social connections withered. Subtle shows of disdain became open displays of scorn. When Cyric, now at an age when he should have been learning his father's trade, confronted his parents about his origins, they offered no excuses for their actions—though they noted more than a little regret at having taken a Zhentish child into a civilized home. When Cyric threatened to leave, Astolpho and his wife didn't raise a hand to stop him.

Servants from Astolpho's house found the bodies of the vintner and his wife the next morning. From the small, muddy footprints around their beds, it appeared that someone had crept into the room and murdered them in their sleep. Such was Cyric's blooding, a cowardly strike against an elderly rich man and his overfed wife.

In the days that followed, Cyric made his way north, through Sembia, toward the black walls of Zhentil Keep. There, he thought, the murder of his parents might buy him acceptance. Yet the young man had little experience in surviving outside the tapestried walls of a merchant's home; within a tenday, he was at the edge of the Dales, close to starvation and delirious from fever.

What happened next may have been Tymora smiling on the unfortunate boy, or Beshaba raining more hard luck on him. Whether good fortune or ill, the Zhentarim agents that happened on Cyric in the wilderness saved his life. They also put him in chains in preparation for the slave markets at their final destination—Zhentil Keep.

So it was that Cyric returned to the place of his birth, once more bound in chains, once more at the mercy of slavers and merchants. . . .

VII

PANDEMONIUM

*Wherein Mystra and her patriarch debate the
limitations of godhood, and the Prince of Lies
demonstrates the true power of chaos.*

With her grip of ice, Auril the Frostmaiden had plunged
Cormyr into the coldest days of a long and bitter winter.
Snow lay thick over the entire kingdom of Azoun IV.
There would be no sight of green for months to come. The
country, like much of Faerun, slept under death-white
cerements—except for the gutted shell of Castle Kilgrave
and the lands that surrounded those stony ruins.

The snow and ice had vanished from those hills,
replaced by a green and lush carpet of life. Jungle foliage
spread in riotous tangles around tranquil fields of gorgeously hued spring flowers. Birds too hearty or sickly to
fly south for the winter frolicked amidst suddenly ripe
fruits and abundant seeds. Confused badgers and rabbits

nosed cautiously from their burrows to wander across the verdant hills, their winter coats stifling in the springtime warmth.

Then, without warning, the mock spring fell away, and the Frostmaiden's cruel fingers spread winter across the land once more. Birds plummeted from the sky, killed by the slash of icy winds sweeping across the fields. Flowers bowed beneath ever-deepening snowdrifts. Vines and trees and hedges withered under a cloud-filled iron-gray sky. Animals cowered against the gale, their homes hidden from them by a thick carpet of sleet.

The cold wind intensified, even beyond Auril's wont, and shrieked across the hills like a grief-maddened banshee. In an instant, the trees and shrubs and every other hint of spring were swept from the land. The stiff corpses of birds were blown up into the sky. The blast stripped the fur and flesh from the rabbits, leaving tiny ice-limned skeletons huddled in the shadows of snow mounds.

Such was the way of wild magic.

"I can't believe it has been ten years," Adon said sadly. "We watched the Goddess of Magic *die* here a decade ago. Who'd have thought it would cause all this?"

The cleric pulled his cloak tighter around his shoulders, though there was little need. The globe of magical energy surrounding him and his companion kept out the cold and shielded them from the wind. "It really seems like yesterday," Adon murmured. "Though I suppose you don't notice the passing of time the same as you used to. . . ."

Mystra neither turned nor spoke, and the comment fell away unanswered. The current Goddess of Magic stared out at the blizzard and watched the plants and animals die. She gritted her teeth as the magical chaos threatened to warp even her sorcery, but the wave passed, leaving her shield intact.

Suddenly uncomfortable, Adon chattered on to fill the

silence. "Still, the land has healed quite a bit since then. Used to be bubbling tar pits as far as the eye could see—well, mortal eyes anyway." He laughed boldly. "Does Helm realize how much spite went into naming this place the Helmlands? I suppose he only thought he was doing his job, killing Mystra and all."

"Helm sees the world as nothing but some vague prize to be protected from an even more vague adversary," Mystra said.

"That would have to be Mask, I suppose. Who would the God of Guardians hate more than the Patron of Thieves?"

Slowly Mystra turned blue-white glowing eyes on her patriarch. A decade ago, when he first met the mortal mage named Midnight, Adon had been a dashing young priest of Sune Firehair. Barely twenty and untutored in the harsher lessons of life, he joined Midnight, Cyric, and Kelemvor Lyonsbane on an adventure that quickly became a quest to find the gods-wrought Tablets of Fate. His faith in himself and the unpredictable Goddess of Beauty shattered when he was scarred by a lunatic. The man who became the high priest of the new Goddess of Magic was much more worldly, much more wise than the vain young dandy who first left Arabel scant months before.

The Lady of Mysteries could see that worldliness in everything about her old friend. His brown hair was shot with harsh streaks of silver. Tiny wrinkles surrounded his green eyes. His cleft chin had kept its strength, his features their sharpness. Only Adon's scar had faded. Once an angry red streak running from eye to jaw, the trail of the old wound was now a puckered line, pale against his tanned face. It was as if the priest's acceptance of the wound had healed it just a little.

"Cyric will be sending more assassins," Mystra noted. "You must take care."

Adon nodded, his hand straying to the mace that hung from his belt. The worn patch on his leggings told any observant man the priest rarely traveled without the weapon. "They've tried before, Lady. Besides, the ring you crafted has done an admirable job in warning me of their presence."

"Cyric's planning to strike against the church," Mystra said darkly. "Your death would be a prize to him second only to finding . . ." The words trailed into silence.

"He'll be sorry if he ever finds Kel," the priest said. Brushing a lock of raven-black hair from Mystra's brow, he looked into her inhuman eyes. "Somehow Kel has kept himself hidden all these years. For all we know, he's safe somewhere, plotting revenge against Cyric."

"The sentiment's appreciated, Adon, but I'm no love-struck child to be consoled by such hopeful fancies," Mystra chided, though she smiled just the same. "I can only hope one of the other gods is hiding Kel's soul, waiting to barter with me for some favor."

Adon shrugged. "Kel tricked Bane into removing the Lyonsbane curse from him when he was alive. If he's clever enough for that, he may have his revenge yet." He caught the sadness crossing Mystra's delicate features, like storm clouds over a sun-bathed rose garden, and unsubtly changed the subject. "The church in Tegea is doing fine," Adon offered. "The village is thriving, and we've gone a long way in reversing the duke's curse. Corene—"

"I know how my church fares, Adon. You are doing an admirable job, and your protege has become an outstanding cleric in her own right." Mystra paused and looked out at the blizzard. "She's quite beautiful, and she cares a great deal for you."

"*Midnight,*" Adon said, the name full of his devotion and respect. "You didn't bring me all the way out here just to

125

talk about Corene."

The goddess smiled sadly. "No. I brought you here for a more important reason. I thought seeing this place would help you to understand what I want to tell you."

Her gossamer robes flowing around her like moted sunlight, Mystra began to pace up the hill. The protective globe moved with her, and Adon fell into step at her side. "I need someone to talk to," she began.

"I'll try to help," Adon said softly. "But another god might see—"

"That's the very heart of the problem, Adon. The other gods can't see anything but their own narrow visions of the world."

The Lady of Mysteries gestured idly to the hillside, buried now beneath a mountain of snow. Even as she pointed, the ice and snow melted away, revealing a plain of black rock. The icy skeletons of rabbits and foxes shuddered to life. Howling in agony, they began to battle like crazed knights at tournament.

"I've never told you why the Helmlands are like this, why wild magic acts the way it does, have I?" The goddess continued without awaiting an answer. "In some places, where the avatars did the greatest destruction in the Time of Troubles, the very cloth of reality was worn thin. And here, where Mystra's dying energy blasted the land like a million Shou cannons, that fabric is the thinnest of all."

"What does this have to do with how the other gods see the world?" Adon asked.

"Where the fabric is so thin, the Balance is unstable," Mystra explained. "The land swings back and forth between the powers, letting each have dominance over the area for a brief while. The verdant spring we saw was the work of Lathander. Then Auril took the land back. Now—" she looked out over the battling skeletons on the featureless field of rock "—this could be the work of Cyric. Or

126

Talos." Sighing raggedly, the goddess closed her glowing eyes. "And the gods never know that they're doing harm. They can't see how plunging the world from winter to summer might destroy everything."

"Can't you show them? If you can see the danger—"

"That's just it," Mystra said, anger making her eyes flash. "The gods see the world as if it were merely a field to be won or lost. But each is playing a different game. Talos seeks to destroy everything, while Lathander plots and schemes to bring about rebirth. They only notice the others in the pantheon when they get in the way."

Adon shook his head. "I'm sorry, Lady, but I just don't understand. I mean, they're gods, aren't they?"

"Yes," Mystra said ominously. "They're gods. But that doesn't mean all that you believe, all that the priests propose in their sermons and tracts. I've been inside their minds. I've—" She paused, studying the mad battle taking place on the stone field. "Perhaps there's another way to show you. . . ."

Mystra gestured subtly, and they vanished from the Helmlands. But when the goddess and her patriarch appeared an instant later at their destination, the scene around them was no less chaotic.

"Where's the light, Gareth? Don't leave me in the dark with them. They're crawling over everything. . . . Ai, get them away from my eyes!"

"The angels have fangs. The angel have fangs!"

"The Serpent took them all! She swallowed all my dreams. . . ."

Adon cupped his hand over his mouth and pinched his nostrils shut. The stench of the place was horrible. He glanced around frantically. Piles of damp, dirty straw lay everywhere. Some of these makeshift beds were occupied by dozing lunatics, others by rats or roaches or worse. In the shadowed corners of the large, dim room, vaguely human figures squatted or brawled or howled. Many inmates had huge cages strapped to their heads or thick wads of cloth wrapped firmly around their hands. The rest were clad in rags, though the place was cold enough for breath to turn to steam.

But what Adon would remember most from that hellish place was the high-pitched, terrified screeching of the madmen.

"The angels have fangs!" A thin half-elf with long brown hair and a pale beard reached out for Adon with trembling hands. "You must warn everyone. The angels have fangs."

Mystra turned the half-elf toward her. "Sleep, King Trebor," the goddess soothed, passing her thumbs lightly across his eyes. He slumped to the ground, though the shudders that wracked his frame showed that slumber provided no escape from his troubled thoughts.

"You know him?" Adon gasped. "Where are we?"

"I know all these unfortunates," Mystra said. "They are as much my children as the mages and scholars who flock to the temple in Tegea. Magic brought them all here." The goddess turned to her patriarch. "This is an asylum, Adon. It's run by the Golden Quill Society in Waterdeep. The bards have taken pity on these men and women, sorcerers warped irrevocably by magic gone awry. They put them here and care for them as best they can."

"Gods, better to kill them than this," Adon said. He had to shout to be heard over the keening.

Mystra shook her head. "Cyric's realm awaits most of them, those who hadn't devoted themselves to a god before magic warped their minds." To the unasked question in Adon's eyes, the goddess added, "I take all those I can, but Ao proclaimed at the beginning of time the gods may reward only their faithful with paradise."

"Magic did this?" the patriarch mumbled, staring at a poor, cowering wretch with neither mouth nor eyes.

"Necromancies and thaumaturgies should never be cast lightly," Mystra replied, "for the power of the weave can destroy as well as create. And even my hands cannot heal their minds, though I have spent hours upon hours here trying to comfort them."

Anger began to show in Adon's eyes. "If you wish to prove the gods can be heartless, you've wasted the lesson," he shouted. "Sune abandoned me when I was scarred, remember? I have no illusions about the world, Midnight. Either tell me how to help these men or take me away from here."

The Lady of Mysteries turned away and walked toward a grizzled old man hunched beneath a thickly barred window. A few of the lunatics quieted as she passed, as if her presence offered them a glimpse of sanity. As soon as the goddess moved away, though, they resumed their howling.

"Come here, Adon. I want you to meet Talos," Mystra called.

Still tense with anger, the patriarch stalked to Mystra's side. "Have you lost enough of your humanity to make light of these wretches?"

"Hardly," Mystra said, her blue-white eyes snapping fire. "Look again, Adon. I know you're bright enough to understand this."

The madman was naked, his hair long and unkempt. With blue eyes narrowed in suspicion, he watched the patriarch closely. All the while, he plucked the beard from his chin one whisker at time. He dropped the hair onto the floor around him, which was already crowded with the unraveled threads of his blanket and the cloth shreds that had once been his clothes.

"Go ahead, Adon," Mystra said softly. "Try to stop him."

The patriarch reached out and stilled the man's hands. The lunatic trembled, watching Adon with watery eyes.

After a moment, when he thought the inmate had calmed, Adon released him. The bony fingers flew to the offending beard and tore at it again, neither faster nor slower than before.

Mystra laid a gentle hand on Adon's shoulder. "What does he see when he looks at you?"

"Someone stopping him from plucking his beard out. Maybe not even a person. Maybe I'm just some huge paralyzing shadow or a set of chains. . . ."

"So now you've met Talos," Mystra said flatly. "Or one very much like him. This poor man destroys whatever clothes or bedding they give him. No one can figure out why. His mind is set on it, and if they keep him chained too long, he stops eating, stops sleeping. They let him out like this now and then to tear something up. And like the gods, he's only aware of anyone around him insomuch as they help or hinder his mad view of the world."

"But surely the gods—"

Mystra shook her head. "Their minds are more expansive, but just as limited in perception."

"Then how can they communicate?" Adon asked. "If they're madmen, they shouldn't be able to agree on anything."

"Something in their consciousness must translate what the other gods say," Mystra replied. "They're all looking at the same reality, but seeing it in myriad ways. Talos can see nothing but a world that must be destroyed." She swept manically across the chamber to a man with his knees pulled up tight to his chest. Bloody tears streamed down his sunken cheeks. "And this is Ilmater, who sees only the suffering of Faerun. His cell mate is Gond, the Wonderbringer, whose mechanical marvels will spread across the world like a clockwork army." Mystra gestured to a bald dwarf busily constructing a tower from shattered chains and fractured servings bowls.

Finally, the Goddess of Magic came to a young boy, his face twisted into a hideous mask by some misfired enchantment. He primped and fussed over the tufts of hair sprouting from his blackened scalp. "You already know Sune Firehair," Mystra said. "It doesn't matter that he's a man, of course. We gods can be whichever sex we choose. . . ."

"And you?" Adon asked bluntly. "What is the face of your madness?"

"Ao allowed me to keep something of my humanity, but that means I can see all the others are mad," Mystra said. "Talos has no idea how the others perceive the world. I, on the other hand, can share in his and every other god's twisted visions. In the end, that could make me the maddest—"

Mystra stiffened in pain and clutched her side. Cyric had wounded her there a decade ago, during the battle atop Blackstaff Tower. "It was only a matter of time," she hissed.

His hands held out to the goddess, Adon rushed forward. "What is it?"

"Cyric," the Lady of Mysteries said through clenched teeth, though now her face was contorted with anger, not pain. "He's striking against the weave. I've got to stop him."

The inmates howled at the sudden burst of blue-white radiance as Mystra disappeared. Even through their madness-fogged brains, they felt some unknowable pain at the use of sorcery in their midst, the damnable Art that had done them all so much harm. And in the center of all the shrieking and screaming, Adon of Mystra stood in silence, with tearing eyes.

He made his way to the door and pounded on the thick metal with his mace. The guards hadn't noticed the presence of a goddess. He hoped they would hear his calls now and take them as something more than the unusually lucid cries of one of the inmates.

"Warders!" he shouted. "I am here from the Church of Mysteries. Open this door, for Mystra's sake, and bring some water."

The priest turned back to the dim room. He laid his fine cloak over a shivering, rag-clad man chained to the wall. Then, choking back his gorge at the stench of offal and disease, he kneeled next to the scarred boy who Mystra had called Sune.

"You look quite handsome today," he said soothingly as he wiped grime from the boy's arms with his handkerchief. Something like a smile crossed the lunatic's lips.

Adon shuddered despite himself. "Maybe the scholars were right in this much," he murmured. "Perhaps the gods can't live without their worshipers after all."

* * * * *

Deep within the maze of lightless, hope-forsaken tunnels known as Pandemonium, Cyric raised Godsbane and slashed again at a glowing curtain of magical energy. The short sword bit into the seemingly insubstantial wall with a screech that sounded like an axe sliding on slate. A thin gash opened for an instant, then sealed itself, just like every other hole the Lord of the Dead had cut in the curtain.

The magic wounds me, Godsbane whispered in Cyric's mind. *Is there no other way?*

Bemused, the Prince of Lies stepped back from the enchanted barrier and looked up. The glittering wall stretched for miles, sealing off the circular tunnel completely.

Cyric drew his mouth into a grim line and rubbed his chin with gnarled fingers. "The gods must have drawn the wall directly from the weave when they imprisoned Kezef," he mused. "This will prove more difficult than I thought. . . ."

The words, though whispered, echoed down the huge

tunnel. Sound built upon sound until the utterance was a howling chorus of nonsense. The winds of chaos that perpetually tore through the slick-walled black caves carried the noise away, then returned it an instant later accompanied by a thousand agonized screams. The cacophony would have deafened any mortal ears, but to Cyric the sounds of Pandemonium were soothing, the swirling miasma of darkness and choking fog a comforting cloak.

"There's no way around it," the death god muttered into the maelstrom and lifted Godsbane once more.

My love, beware! Mystra—

A bolt of sorcerous might struck Cyric in the back. The blow spun the Lord of the Dead around. Eyes wide with shock, he faced his attacker, then glanced down at the smoking hole in his chest. Godsbane slipped from his numb fingers and clattered to the ground. Cyric slumped forward into a lifeless heap.

Mystra took a step toward the Prince of Lies, then stopped, startled motionless by the body before her. Had she so overestimated his power? He had no magical defense, but all the gods had innate powers granted them by their very godhood, not drawn from the weave of magic. The blow shouldn't have—no, *couldn't have* harmed him so mortally—

The Lady of Mysteries cursed and lunged forward, but she moved too late. A blade cut a trail down her back, from her shoulder to her waist. Pain blossomed at the core of her being as the sword tried to drag her lifeforce from her. Yet the wound was too shallow, the contact to brief for any real harm to be done.

"I'm amazed you attacked me here, Midnight," Cyric said. The Prince of Lies smirked at his lifeless twin, then stalked toward the goddess. The light from the magical wall made his features look all the more demonic. "Pandemonium is a place of chaos, after all, and you should know I'm quite at home in chaos. . . ."

Mystra backed to the glowing wall and created a magical buckler. "The Circle decreed this barrier should never be crossed by god or man," she shouted. "And without magic, you are no match for me, Cyric. Give this up before I'm forced to destroy you."

The mock corpse dissolved into a pile of ashes and was borne away on the cyclonic winds in the tunnel. The true Prince of Lies paused to take in his adversary's threatening stance, then laughed. "You wouldn't kill me even if you could," he scoffed. "That would upset the Balance."

Cyric allowed the winds of chaos to flow over him, through him. He channeled their might like sorcerous energy and dissolved into a swarm of flies, which split into two smaller clouds. The winds tossed the buzzing insects to either side of Mystra. There, they reformed into twin images of the Lord of the Dead. Two identical rose-hued short swords bit into the goddess's arms, knocking the arcane shield from her grasp.

"But I care nothing for the Balance," the death god hissed.

Time-dusted memories of mortal pain and a sick sensation of fear crept into Mystra's mind. She felt the awful tug of Godsbane on her spirit, the leaching of her power and the tingling of energy as it dripped like blood from her wounds. Mustering the strength to fight back, she let her hands fall against the glowing prison wall. The raw magical essence pulsed against her fingers.

With a defiant shout, she tore two handfuls of energy from the curtain. The globs of power, drawn from the heart of the weave, flared in her grasp. Lithely they slithered up her arms, pushing the blades away and forming armor more adamantine than any forged by the dwarven gods or their minions. Mystra vanished, only to reappear a dozen yards away. Now she, too, held a weapon—a staff of light that burned like the sun itself.

Yet before she could lift the staff against Cyric it transformed into the dripping, razor-edged blade of Godsbane. Then the Prince of Lies was kneeling next to Mystra, gripping the sword by the hilt. Savagely he drew the blade through her hands as if her fingers were a living sheath. Godsbane dug deeply into the goddess's palms, nearly severing all the fingers of her left hand.

"I lured Leira to Pandemonium," the Prince of Lies cackled. "If there was anything left of her avatar it'd still be blowing around in here."

Cyric vanished as Mystra launched a glittering swarm of meteorites toward him. He rode on a swell in the winds until it left him standing high on the wall. "Killing her was even easier than killing you will be," he crowed. "I must be almost as powerful here as in Hades. Must be the natural chaos of the place. Or perhaps I'm just very good at being the Lord of Murder. What do you think?"

Mystra called forth a sphere of prismatic energy to shield her from the next attack. No sooner had the globe formed than Godsbane slammed against it. The force of the blow alone sent cracks snaking along the twinkling, spinning globe.

Cyric kicked the shield. "One for you," Mystra heard him mutter just before he disappeared again.

The Goddess of Magic took quick stock of her wounds. They were serious, but she could heal them given a moment to concentrate. And then she would—

Cyric loomed over the sphere, gigantic and menacing. He lifted the magical globe in one hand and brought it up to his red-rimmed eyes. "What will happen if I eat this, I wonder?"

Glittering energy leaking from a half-dozen wounds, Mystra looked up at the Prince of Lies. He was right: in Pandemonium, he had the advantage. The chaos made him strong, but Cyric's real weapon was his unpredictability. "The other gods will stand with me," Mystra said bitterly, then disappeared, fleeing to her palace in Nirvana.

"So what?" Cyric said. He watched the prismatic sphere drip through his fingers like water, then let the chaos winds wear away his gigantic facade until he stood no taller than he had when but a mortal.

The Circle fears the Chaos Hound almost as much as it fears you, my love, Godsbane offered. Her purring voice was thick, drunk on the goddess's lifeforce. *We must be cautious.*

"Caution is for those who cannot see the future," Cyric noted as he walked casually to the curtain. "And my future contains only what I will it to hold."

Two fist-sized gaps marred the glowing prison wall where Mystra had torn away the mystic energy. They were small wounds, but large enough for Cyric to exploit. "You see," the Lord of the Dead said mockingly. "Just as I had planned. The Whore opened wide the gates for me."

He lashed out with Godsbane, tearing the rents wider. The shriek of the blade as it split the damaged curtain filled the tunnel and echoed throughout the dark realm of Pandemonium. The babel made its way through the endless, windswept tunnels, and creatures more malefic than any in the nightmares of men or elves or dwarves cowered in terror. They knew that, after millenia untold, a madman had come to free the Chaos Hound.

VIII

HOUNDS AND HARES

*Wherein Cyric makes a perilous bargain with
the Chaos Hound, Mystra discovers a strange
visitor in the House of Knowledge, and a
long-dead, but much-discussed hero
finally makes his entrance.*

As he stepped through the ragged hole in the wall,
Cyric entered a place both silent and dark. The howling
winds and the baleful moaning, so deafening in the caverns beyond, did not reach into the dank chamber. The
sorcerous curtain cast no radiance here. Even the light
that should have crept in through the hole was damped
somehow.

There is still time to reconsider this, Godsbane hissed in
Cyric's mind. The blade now shone dim and sickly in the
darkness, though Mystra's lifeforce had made her burn
like a blood-red sun in the tunnels.

The Prince of Lies ignored the simpering sword and called into the fetid murk: "I am Cyric, Lord of the Dead and God of Strife. I am here to bind you to my service, Kezef."

A low, rumbling growl was the only reply.

"Come, come," Cyric chided, taking a bold step forward. "I mean to release you."

"No god of Faerun would loose the Chaos Hound of his own free will." The inhuman voice was low and full of malevolence. "So you must be no god."

"If you lavish godhood on the pretenders who chained you here, then you're right. I'm no god," Cyric countered snidely. "I'm very much more than that."

The growl rolled through the darkness again, carrying the stale, nauseating smell of putrefaction. "Lord of the Dead, you say? What of Myrkul?"

Cyric laughed. "The old Lord of Bones is no more. I killed him, and many of his brethren, too." He took another step. "Bane and Bhaal and Leira are all destroyed by my hand. I hold their titles now, and their powers."

"Then you are indeed one to be reckoned with," Kezef rumbled. Chains clanked as the Chaos Hound leaned forward. He sniffed twice, then paused. "Can that little blade of yours cast any more light? I would see your face, slayer of Myrkul."

Without magic, Cyric couldn't conjure a light, but revealing that to the beast would be a mistake. There was another solution, though, and his multifaceted mind found it even before Kezef had stopped speaking. Cyric turned and hacked a corpse-sized piece from the prison wall. Slowly he held the quivering sheet of energy so that its radiant side illuminated his gruesome, seared features.

"You are not what I would have expected," Kezef murmured.

Cyric dropped the sheet of weave-stuff to the ground and kicked it toward the Chaos Hound. It didn't slide far enough to reveal the creature's form, though, only glimmer faintly in Kezef's red eyes.

"Push it closer," the Hound said. "We cannot deal as equals until our true forms are revealed. . . ."

As Cyric moved toward the glowing fragment, Kezef lunged. The Prince of Lies saw only a blur of darkness move across the rough patch of light, heard only a vicious snarl and the clatter of ancient chains. With reactions far faster than any mortal, he brought Godsbane up in a powerful slash. The sword struck something pulpy, and a wave of dark liquid washed over his sword arm. The ooze clung to him in blotches, burning like molten copper.

The howl of the Chaos Hound was matched by the pained shriek of Godsbane in Cyric's mind.

"Is this how you prove your cunning?" the Prince of Lies hissed. "No wonder the gods imprisoned you so easily. Only a fool turns on an ally when he has nothing to gain by doing so."

"I would have been more of a fool to bargain with you without knowing your strength," Kezef rumbled. "Yet you must be all you say, murderer of Bhaal, for none but a god could stay my jaws." Narrowing his eyes, the Chaos Hound moved into the light.

Kezef resembled a huge mastiff, as large as any draft horse Cyric had seen in the streets of Zhentil Keep. Teeming maggots were his fur, the coat shifting incessantly over barely covered sinews and bones. His pointed teeth glittered like daggers of jet in the sorcerous light. A tongue oozing tatters of corruption lolled to the Hound's chin, poisonous spittle dripping in sizzling drops to the ground. The wound from Cyric's blow festered across Kezef's snout, but even as the Prince of Lies watched, the putrefied liquid flesh closed over the slash.

A short length of sturdy chain, forged by the Wonderbringer himself, held the beast in place. The links clattered

sullenly as Kezef settled onto his haunches and looked the Prince of Lies in the face. "What dark task would you have me complete?"

"The bards of Faerun say you can track anything, no matter where it travels in the realms of men or gods."

Kezef's panted breath held a sick, charnel stench as he leaned closer to Cyric. "For once, the bards speak the truth. No living creature can hide from me, once I have picked up its trail."

Cyric held Godsbane up before him, silently warning Kezef to move no closer. "Then I would have you seek the soul of a mortal."

"And when I have that shade in my teeth?" the Hound rumbled balefully. "Do you think to imprison me again?"

"Bring me the soul of Kelemvor Lyonsbane. Then you are free to do as you will," Cyric replied.

The Chaos Hound survives by raiding the planes, Godsbane warned, her voice shrill with fear. *He preys on the Faithful, my love. The denizens of your realm will taste as sweet to him as any other.*

"What about your minions?" the Hound asked, mirroring the blade's question as if he could hear it. "Do you not care if your denizens put flesh on these bones along with the peons of Tyr or Ilmater?"

Cyric dismissed the questions with a derisive snort. "There are many heavens more easily stormed than the City of Strife," he said. "You have no taste for the Faithless who make up the wall, and my denizens are better armed and much more vicious than the devoted of the Lord of All Songs or Oghma the Binder. It will be many, many years before your hunger brings you to my doorstep. . . ."

But, my love—

Silence! Cyric shouted to Godsbane. Though the word went unheard by the Chaos Hound, it seemed to shake the shadow-heavy chamber. *When my book is complete and the other gods wither and die, their minions will be unprotected. They will feed the Hound for eternity.*

"I will do as you ask," Kezef murmured, his inhuman voice filled with unspoken maledictions. "Though I know I should not trust you."

"Oh, you can believe all that I tell you now, Kezef," Cyric purred. "If you fail me, or if you do anything with Kelemvor's soul besides bring it to my castle, intact, I shall carve the maggoty hide from you until there is nothing left but your teeth—and those I'll hammer into chamber pots for my lowliest priest in the mortal realms."

The Hound narrowed his red eyes. The rotting orbs blazed with arrogance almost matching Cyric's. "It took all the gods combined to chain me here, Lord of Four Crowns. And when I have tasted the souls of the saved once more, I shall have more flesh upon these bones than even you can carve away."

Before Kezef could react, Godsbane's tip was planted firmly against his snout. "With this blade, I have whittled down gods, cur."

"It is indeed a mighty sword." The Chaos Hound backed away until the darkness once again cloaked his horrible form. For a moment, Kezef studied the rose-hued blade. Then a spark of vague recognition flashed in his eyes. "What is its name?"

"This sword has drawn the life from four gods," Cyric lied, pride curling his mouth into a sneer, "and she has tasted the blood of a fifth." His voice became a hate-filled whisper. "I have named her Godsbane."

"Godsbane," Kezef murmured darkly. He sniffed at the sword with his dripping snout. "That's a good name, I think. Very appropriate."

Cyric dismissed the comment as cowardly fawning and fell to studying the chain forged by the God of Craft. He quickly abandoned all thought of pulling up the anchor, driven miles deep into the floor. Calling forth all his rage and frustration at having Kelemvor elude him for ten long years, the Prince of Lies drew Godsbane and brought her down on a single link.

The sword seemed to fight against the blow, but the resistance was not nearly enough to counter Cyric's fury. As if it had been wrought of porcelain, the link shattered. The blow also broke an enchantment that countered the Hound's pestilent aura; rust and decay spread from the beast's throat, down the collar and the remainder of the chain.

Kezef tossed back his head and howled gleefully. The rusted, useless chain slid from his neck, clattering to the floor. The Chaos Hound was free.

* * * * *

Nine identical Mystras raced across the planes, speeding to the courts of the other Greater Powers. As one they carried the dire news that Cyric was attempting to loose the Chaos Hound, that the ravager of the heavens would soon be free to prey on the souls of the Faithful. To the verdant fields of Elysium and the blasted plains of Hades, the hodgepodge chaos of Limbo and the tranquil order of the Seven Mountains of Goodness and Law, the Goddess of Magic spread the warning—and pleaded with the gods of the Circle to stand with her against the Prince of Lies.

In the plane known as Concordant, Mystra came seeking Oghma the Binder. The place was the embodiment of balance between law and chaos. Infinite godly domains spread out in circular bands from a fixed center. One moment the heart of Concordant appeared as a gigantic tree, reaching up endlessly, the next as a perfectly carved marble pillar or a swirling column of clouds, spitting lightning and rumbling thunder. And though its shape shifted incessantly, its location remained fixed, a still point at the center of the malleable plane.

Beings from every god's realm and every possible mortal world traveled to Concordant, seeking knowledge or power or gossip. The markets where these seekers gathered bustled with denizens and angels, selling dark secrets and divine guidance. Powerful mages traded incantations or rare spell components on the steps of magnificent temples. Holy pacts were sworn by paladins standing alongside oath-breaking assassins, in buildings that would not look the same an hour hence, yet would remain in the same location.

And in the midst of this ordered chaos stood the house and the lands of Oghma, Patron of Bards, God of Knowledge. As Mystra appeared before the open gates of the vast estate, she noted with little surprise that the place had taken on yet another facade she had never before seen.

The House of Knowledge resembled a palace from the desert lands of Zakhara. A high fence wrought of thin iron strands surrounded the estate. The bands curved and twisted in gorgeously intricate patterns, seemingly flimsy, but unbreakable by even the most mighty of giants. Beyond the open gates stretched a long, azure pool, filled by fountains that drew their water from the cool, peaceful flow of the River Oceanus. The water reflected the columned portico of Oghma's palatial home, its high, slender minarets and squatting, mushroom-shaped domes.

Mystra hurried through the courtyard, past clusters of scholars who debated the finer points of one obscure theory or another. Nearby, brightly clad bards competed for the attention of passersby. The visitors to the House of Knowledge gave way before the goddess, sensing the urgency of her mission. An angel of the dwarven god Berronar bowed to the Lady of Mysteries, his alabaster beard flowing to the ground, and his short, iron wings parting gracefully over his stocky shoulders. At the venerable dwarven spirit's side, a tanar'ri lord nodded gruffly. The Abyss-spawn had the body and wings of a huge fly, with vaguely elven features and a pair of human hands. In one of those hands it gripped a roll of parchment detailing the past battle plans of a rival warlord.

The doors to Oghma's palace were, as always, unguarded. The goddess rushed into the cavernous entry hall, beneath a vaulted ceiling inscribed with an unending roll of the faithful residing in the palace. Two sets of stairs wound away to the right and left. They led to the chambers reserved for the shades of Oghma's blessed scholars and bards.

"The alignment of the stars must be fortunate indeed to bring you to my home," Oghma announced, his melodious voice filling the hall.

The God of Knowledge stood framed by the ornate arch that opened from the entry hall into his library-throne room. His clothes matched the exotic facade on his palace—a flowing caftan, cinched at the waist with a sash of purest sky-blue silk; slippers with curling, pointed toes; and a sultan's turban, pinned with a sapphire the size of a dwarf's fist. A parchment page wrought of moonlight glowed in his left hand.

"This isn't a social call," Mystra replied without prelude. "The faithful of all the gods are in peril."

Oghma's broad, welcoming smile drooped into a frown. "You've been wounded," he said, gesturing with a ring-heavy finger to the glittering slashes on Mystra's hands and shoulders. "Cyric?"

"Yes, but don't worry. These are nothing that a few moments of meditation won't heal." She took the Binder's arm. "We need to mobilize, and quickly. I left the bastard in Pandemonium, at the wall to Kezef's prison."

"Then he truly is mad," came a smooth whisper.

Mystra turned to find Mask standing at her shoulder. The Patron of Thieves was wrapped in a cloak of shadows, his face hidden by a loose-fitting black mask. "I have heard rumors of a battle in Pandemonium near Kezef's prison. I'd hoped they were untrue." His red eyes narrowed as he bowed perfunctorily. "I have waited for a chance to undo the aid I once provided the Prince of Lies. Perhaps now I shall be of service to the rest of the pantheon. . . ."

"I'm sure you're anxious to help," Mystra replied stiffly. "I'll mention that to the rest of the Circle."

Mask bowed again. "As you wish. But do not forget the Chaos Hound will devour the honored thieves in the darkened alleys of my domain as well as the sages in your weave-wrought castle of magic. I'm certain all the gods will want to strike against Kezef before he grows strong again. We should—"

Oghma dropped his hand onto Mask's shoulder. "Mystra is correct. This is a matter for the Circle." The God of Knowledge held out the glowing parchment. "Here is the information you requested. My payment shall be your silence about the Chaos Hound until the Circle has had a chance to discuss the matter."

"Wait," Mystra said. "The intermediate and lesser powers should be warned so they can set guards along their borders."

"In time, Lady," Oghma replied. "We'll only panic them if we don't offer a plan of attack along with the warning." He turned to the Lord of Shadows. "If you require such arcane texts in the future, Mask, I would appreciate the offer of some lost lore of equal obscurity in return. I'm sure your groundlings occasionally uncover useful tomes when rooting for coins in long-forgotten tombs."

"You're right. Thievery is no honest labor, not compared to copying the words of others in some dank monastery," Mask said, his normally smooth voice thick with disdain. He took the parchment in his gloved hands and disappeared into the shadows of the arch.

Mystra scowled in consternation. "You were telling the truth back in the Pavilion of Cynosure. You aren't a flatterer. Why insult him so? The Circle will need his help against Cyric and Kezef."

"My house is open to all," Oghma replied blandly, "but by his nature Mask seeks to obscure, to cloak minds in the shadows of ignorance. There has never been true peace between us." He dismissed the matter with practiced casualness. "Now, what's this about Kezef?"

As she passed under the arch into Oghma's throne room, Mystra explained what had transpired in Pandemonium. The library at the heart of the House of Knowledge was infinite, with shelves rising as high as anyone—mortal or immortal—could see. The Binder's faithful spent millennia cataloguing every bit of information they had learned in life. Others kept careful track of the library's ever-growing hoard of knowledge. The shades of bards and writers studied these volumes of obscure lore and distilled the facts into brilliant tales and songs, as captivating as they were enlightening.

In keeping with the palace's Zakharan facade, the library was decked out in exotic finery. Shades soared from shelf to shelf on flying carpets, huge stacks of books balanced precariously in their arms. Readers stretched out in luxurious piles of pillows. Small air sprites known as djinnlings whisked between patrons. The blue-tinged elementals fulfilled every whim of the scholars crowded there, scribing notes, fetching food and drink, or seeking out myriad priceless tomes.

"You were wise to flee," Oghma noted. He slid into the ornate, high-backed throne, then shifted uncomfortably. "I do hope these furnishings change soon. The setting's far too gaudy for my tastes. Too many distractions to lure my faithful away from their work. . . ."

Mystra waved away a genie bearing a decanter of ambrosia. "The rest of the Circle is discussing the matter with me now," she said, then traced an enigmatic sign in the air. Invisible wards sprang up around the two gods, shielding them from prying ears or scrying magic. "I would like to tell them you are ready to strike against Cyric as soon as we've recaptured the Chaos Hound."

"I will provide all the information I can on Kezef," the Binder said. "And if the rest of the pantheon will give me certain bits of knowledge I seek, I will be glad to act alongside them in capturing the beast."

Mystra sighed. "Yes, I expected as much. The rest are asking for concessions, too. I suppose we can work something out."

"By rights, we cannot imprison the Hound until he has struck against one of the gods' faithful. Even when that has happened, don't count on a treaty too quickly," Oghma warned. "When we last hunted Kezef, it took us nearly a year of mortal time to hammer out the pact. Talos is always the problem. He gets fixated on blowing up the moon, and, well, you've been to enough councils to know how he gets. . . ."

Though she was fighting hard to hide her anger, Mystra flushed crimson. "And Talos says Lathander will be the unreasonable one," she grumbled. "Look, we don't have a year. If Cyric released Kezef, he must have some task in mind for the beast. By next winter it'll be too late to stop whatever that plan might be."

"Cyric is another matter completely, Lady," the Patron of Bards said, his voice a thousand mournful dirges. "You were brave to stand against him in the meeting of the Circle, but I'm afraid my opinion on that matter hasn't changed. It would be foolish for you or me to strike openly. In fact, caution will be needed now if we are to avoid a war in the heavens and catastrophe in the mortal realms."

"Caution?" Mystra scoffed. "Would you sit by, weighing your options, while Cyric looses the Chaos Hound in your courtyard? What if he were to siege this library? Would you be cautious then, Oghma?"

"There would be no question of patience then, Lady," the Binder said. The chorus of his voice had become a threatening basso rumble. "The book he is attempting to create threatens the spread of true knowledge, so I am doing what I can to thwart it. But, as yet, the Lord of the Dead has put no new plots against me into action."

Oghma conjured an image of Everard Abbey, a lonely, ramshackle retreat in the Caravan Lands. The phantasm floated in midair between the two gods.

"It would take Cyric's assassins but a few hours to ride from Iriaebor to this humble place," the Binder began. "If I stand with you now, before the Lord of the Dead has struck a blow against me directly, will you give the men and women in the abbey magic to turn aside the assassins' blades? Cyric will most certainly send them to Everard, and to every other temple and library built in my name."

He leaned forward, looming over the ghostly image of the abbey. "And I would have to rely on your help to protect my faithful, Lady, for the rest of the Circle will say I overstepped my office in battling Cyric. This is a matter for Tyr perhaps, since freeing Kezef broke a law. It's just not a concern for the God of Knowledge."

"That's ridiculously near-sighted, Oghma," Mystra shouted. She banished the conjured abbey. "You're dooming your worshipers."

"No," the Binder replied flatly. "I'm *serving* my worshipers. If they perceived battles as the most important aspect of life, they would worship Tempus. They value knowledge and art, Lady, and this matter has yet to threaten a single historian's notebook, a single verse of the most wretched Sembian poetry. When it does, I will turn all the power their faith gives me to stopping Cyric."

A brooding silence settled over the two gods. "Mystra," the Binder said after a time, "you should know I can do nothing about the matter. It doesn't directly concern knowledge or bardcraft. I told you in the pavilion—"

"That the gods were more limited than I suspected," she said softly. "I am hearing how true that is right this moment. Most of the Circle mirrors your stand, Binder. As you said, only Tyr will help me against Cyric, because freeing Kezef broke a law." She held out her wounded hand to Oghma. "If you realize the gods can only see from a limited perspective, why can't you break out of yours? Why can't you see that the world is more than poetry and histories?"

"Knowing the truth is not the same as being empowered to act upon it," Oghma noted. "I realize my kingdom has boundaries, that my perspective might not be the same as yours or Lathander's or Mask's—but I cannot imagine what those other views reveal. No matter how hard I try, I cannot make my eyes see the universe as anything but a vast library."

Mystra dispelled the wards around the throne. "You can bargain with the rest of the Circle about Kezef on your own, but I'll have no more part of it," she said bitterly. "If it's going to fall on me to counter Cyric's insanity, I won't waste time in endless debates."

The Goddess of Magic vanished just before chaos swept through Concordant. As it did each day at this time, the facade on the House of Knowledge changed, and along with it the trappings within the library and the binding of every book. Yet each volume remained in the same location, and each page held the same facts as before, though written in a different script or in a different colored ink.

Oghma closed his eyes and tried to imagine what the world would be like if this pattern were broken somehow, if the wave of chaos destroyed the House of Knowledge

instead of altering it. He couldn't. Though he knew the
universe held more than the contents of his library, when
he subtracted his books and bardic tales and musty histories, he saw nothing but an endless void.

* * * * *

"Don't worry," a soothing, feminine voice purred, "we
shall deal with Kezef before he can track you down."

Kelemvor Lyonsbane kept his eyes fixed straight ahead
and continued to pace through the white, featureless void.
He moved his lips, silently counting his steps. After he
counted one thousand, he made a precise turn to the left
and started the count over.

"I should erect a barricade in your way," the unseen
power noted petulantly. "Just to throw off your count."

"Then I'd wait for you to get bored and lower it," Kelemvor said. His deep voice, rarely used in the last decade,
was barely a whisper.

"And if I don't get bored?"

Abruptly Kelemvor stopped pacing. "You will. You can't
help yourself."

The silence that followed told the shade he was correct.
Smiling at his victory, he resumed his march.

As he had each day for the past ten years, Kelemvor
Lyonsbane marked out the dimensions of his prison. Not
that there were any walls within the empty whiteness
around him, but Kel knew he would surely go mad if he
didn't create them for himself. And so he walked a careful
circuit with regular, military steps. The room he inhabited
was one thousand paces to a side, with windows in the
center of each wall. There were no doors, of course, and
the ceiling was too high to reach.

Occasionally his unseen jailor spoke to him, or appeared
as a woman or man or beast. But Kel dismissed these

phantasms as unreal diversions, no more substantial than the memories of Midnight that sometimes took shape in the formless void around him. He never let these distract him for long; dallying in that sort of chaos would break him, and Kel was determined to rob his captor of such an easy victory.

"Cyric is growing desperate to find you," the voice said.

"Go away," Kelemvor replied, unperturbed by the obvious prodding. "I'll be thinking about flaying Cyric alive in an hour. If you want to come back then, we can talk."

"An hour? What's that mean to you? There's no sun here, no stars. . . ." When the prisoner didn't answer, the voice added, "You held up far longer than I thought you would, but I believe you've finally cracked."

"I can count time as well as steps," Kelemvor said. He stopped again and crossed his brawny arms over his chest. "Look, you should know by now none of this will work. If I could stand up to torture when I was alive, why should it be any different now that I'm dead? I don't get hungry. I don't need to sleep. If you were intent on trying to rack me or burn my eyes out, you would have done that by now."

"I thought you'd want to know about Kezef."

"There's no need for me to know if you intend on stopping him," Kel murmured. "As for Cyric, I'll talk about him in a little less than an hour. That's my schedule. You should know it by now." With that he once more resumed his march.

Kelemvor measured the rest of the wall undisturbed. At the final corner, he took a half-turn and walked to the prison's center. There, he carefully straightened his clothes. He paused in brushing off his high leather boots and rough leggings, sleeveless white tunic and brown woolen cloak, only long enough to marvel—as he did every day—that a dead man should find himself clothed in the afterworld. Then he'd been alive, Kel had never wondered if souls went around naked or not. Such philosophical minutiae hadn't held the slightest importance to him, not when he spent his days fighting giants for their treasure or guarding caravans from marauding gnolls. That was the sort of useless trivia pointy-headed priests like Adon worried about.

Kelemvor sighed. Now it was the very stuff of his everyday existence.

With the same care he'd taken with his clothes, the shade ran his fingers through his long black hair and smoothed out his mustache and muttonchop sideburns. His features were rugged beneath his course touch. Some women had considered him handsome in his day; at least Midnight had seemed to think him so. As always, Kelemvor allowed himself to dwell on a memory of the lovely mage's face, her lithe body, but only for a moment.

Finally, he swept his cloak over one shoulder. With tentative fingers, the shade reached back to his right shoulder blade to feel the ragged hole in his tunic and the gaping, bloodless wound beneath. As always, the slightest touch sent a throbbing ache through his whole being. Kelemvor didn't mind the pain in the least. It had become a signal of sorts to him, a prompting to a part of his spirit he kept carefully reined at all other times.

Through the opened floodgates of his mind, images of Kelemvor's final moments poured like a flood of dark, poisonous water: the battle against Myrkul atop Blackstaff Tower; the defeat of the Lord of Bones at Midnight's hands; the joyous return of Adon, who they'd all thought slain by Cyric; and Cyric's sudden, treacherous attack. . . .

The ache spread, sending swells of pain through Kelemvor's body. A single memory, clearer than all the rest, rode atop the crest of the bitter flood—Cyric, laughing as he drove his sword deep into Kel's back.

"The hour's up," Kelemvor rumbled. "I'm ready to talk about that black-hearted bastard, and about revenge. . . ."

IX

NOTHING TO FEAR

*Wherein Cyric adds another chapter to his
book of lies, the Chaos Hound tracks along the
winding trail of Kelemvor's life, and
Blackstaff Tower once more becomes the topic of
much gossip and speculation in both Waterdeep
and the heavenly realms.*

Rinda rubbed the sleep from her eyes and propped her
chin up on her elbow. At first Cyric had called her to the
parchmenter's shop at highsun every day. Now he was
demanding her presence at more and more unusual
hours—twilight, midnight, and now dawn. Days lapsed
between visits, too; he hadn't dictated another chapter for
the *Cyrinishad* in almost a tenday.

Weighed down by exhaustion and depression, the
scribe let her head sink once more to the oaken writing
desk. The foul smell of the poorly ventilated shop, the

fetid water and rotting hides, didn't bother Rinda in the least. She'd grown accustomed to such unpleasantries, just as she'd grown accustomed to church spies following her every move, or Fzoul and the other conspirators appearing unheralded in the middle of her house.

With little enthusiasm, Rinda drove thoughts of treachery and *The True Life of Cyric* from her mind. She wondered for an instant what chaos would result if the Lord of the Dead uncovered those dangerous notions. Would the harp-voiced patron of Fzoul and the rest come to her aid? More likely the mysterious deity would strike her dead before Cyric could gain any information from her. She'd never worshiped any one particular god, though, so her soul would land squarely in Cyric's domain, and he would get the information he wanted anyway.

Sighing raggedly, Rinda closed her eyes. The cool desktop felt good against her forehead. She thought only of that feeling as she drifted nearer and nearer the precipice of sleep. . . .

"We shall begin whenever you're ready."

Rinda bolted straight in her high-backed chair. Cyric stood at her side, a smirk on his gaunt features, his arms folded casually over a surcoat emblazoned with his own holy symbol. "I can wait if you need to rest," he added with just a trace of sarcasm. "It's no good to either of us if you forget to cross a **T** or dot an **I**. This book needs be perfect, remember?"

"I—I'm sorry, Your Magnificence," she blurted. "It's just that—"

Cyric held up a long-fingered hand. "No need. I may seem to have no sense of the time when I summon you, but I do remember what it's like to need sleep."

Rinda watched the Lord of the Dead stroll to the padded chair from which he always dictated his story. With a flourish of his blood-red cloak, he sat. His chain mail shirt rattled brightly as he lolled one elbow over an overstuffed arm and slung one booted foot over the other. "Is there something wrong?" he asked.

"No," the scribe replied too quickly. She took up her penknife and pinned down the corner of a gruesome parchment sheet wrought of human skin. Vigorously she rubbed the page, then blew away the leavings. "Ready, Your Magnificence," Rinda noted, rolling up one silk sleeve and dipping her quill.

"This won't do at all," Cyric said. "Something distresses you, dear Rinda, and that may well affect how you take down the tale I have to tell this fine morning." He dropped his feet to the dirty floor with a thump and leaned forward. "My good humor disturbs you?"

"Surprises me," Rinda offered meekly.

The Prince of Lies clapped his hands together. "Ah, but I have reason to be glad," he chimed. "A decade-long quest ends today. By sunset the soul of Kelemvor Lyonsbane shall be mine." His eyes grew vague as he drifted into a mad reverie, picturing a thousand horrible ways to greet the long-lost shade.

Rinda sat in silence, waiting for the god's mind to wander back to the parchmenter's shop. When she noticed the mischievous spark had returned to Cyric's eyes, the death god was staring at her. "There's something else," he said. "Something else is wrong."

Fear made Rinda's heart thud in her chest. "I'm—" She swallowed hard, trying to clear her throat, but she couldn't. The lies came painfully, as if the very words were spiked with nails. "I'm just tired, Your Magnificence, and feeling . . . overwhelmed by the task."

A slow, smug smile crept across Cyric's thin lips. "Feeling powerless, are we?" He stood and walked to her side. With one finger he raised her chin until their eyes met. "Is that it—do you feel like a pawn?"

Her soul froze beneath that gaze. "Yes," she whispered, though she knew not how she'd managed it.

Cyric laughed, the harsh sound full of mockery. "You have no one to blame but yourself," he said, then swept back to his chair. "You've given in to Fate. Not once have you voiced an objection to penning this tome."

"B-But you've already said you'd destroy me if I didn't scribe the book for you."

"Of course," the Prince of Lies said. "But you'll be a pawn as long as you're afraid of dying."

Rinda nodded and once more took up her pen.

"Freedom from fear will give you power over every force in the universe," he noted pedantically, cleaning his fingernails with a thin dirk. "Except me, of course. Fear is based mostly on terror of the unknown, and you'll never be able to catalogue all the horrors I can visit upon you after I've killed you. Still, I think you need to pay more attention to the stories I've been telling. As I have shown time and time again, fear has never ruled my life."

* * * * *

From the *Cyrinishad*

When Cyric had conquered the dangers of Zhentil Keep and brought the masters of its thieves' guild to their knees, he struck out into the wilderness again. Though the disgraced guildmasters murmured threats against the young man's life, he cared not, refusing to let their vague night terrors unsettle an instant of his slumber. Though only sixteen winters old, Cyric knew once he bowed before the idol of Fear, that dark altar would command his fealty forever.

For eight years Cyric traveled, learning the ways of far-flung peoples, deciphering their myths in search of the gods' true faces, true weaknesses. The fearful deities and the guild-

masters joined forces and sent assassins against him in that time. Each and every one of them tasted the deadly steel of Cyric's blade and were sent screaming down to Hades.

By then it had become difficult for Cyric to move unnoticed through the cities of Faerun. The constant battles against the Zhentish agents sent by Bane and Myrkul drew too much attention to him. So he returned to Zhentil Keep one final time. The young man was intent on killing the guild-masters and the patriarchs of both gods' churches. In the depth of the year's darkest night, he crept over the Keep's black walls. The nine master thieves were found the next morning, their throats slit from ear to ear. The following night, the same fate befell the corrupt high priests of Bane and Myrkul.

Yet there was one last task Cyric had to complete before leaving Zhentil Keep: the dark gods who so wanted him dead had sworn to protect his true father, who had aided them against his son in the past. He had served those cowardly pretenders well, but Cyric wanted to prove that nothing could shield a sworn foe from his blade.

The magical wards Bane and Myrkul had erected around Cyric's father were intended to warn them of anyone who sought to harm their trusted agent. In their foolishness, though, they failed to realize that without the heavy chains of Fate around his throat, Cyric could move silently, invisible to them. He slew his father and left a mark for the gods to know him by—the skull within the dark sun, the symbol that would one day be his holy symbol.

Cyric's war against the gods had begun.

His freedom from Fate made him invisible to the gods, just as his freedom from Fear made him an unvanquishable foe. Yet Cyric knew he would need weapons to topple the pretender powers from their heavenly thrones. So it was that he went in search of one of the most powerful artifacts known to mortals: the Ring of Winter.

To the Great Gray Land of Thar, home to dragons and other dire beasts, Cyric came. Armed only with a sword of mundane steel and the cunning of a dozen elves, he sought the ring in the caverns of the frost giants. There, he found himself cast in the role of rescuer to a party of sell-swords and cutthroats who had ventured into the giant's domain seeking treasure.

After Cyric slew five of the monstrous giants, they called upon their god, a powerful elemental from a frost-wracked layer of the Abyss. The ice creature, like the gods of Faerun, could not see Cyric the Fateless. Of this weakness the young warrior took the fullest advantage, wounding the ice god sorely before it finally retreated to the cold halls of its Abyss-palace. The remaining giants fled at the defeat of their inhuman master, which taught Cyric to strike always at the leader of his enemies first.

Though the Ring of Winter was nowhere to be found in those caves of ice and stone, Cyric gained the use of another sort of weapon that day—the warrior Kelemvor Lyonsbane. Of the sell-swords he had rescued, only Kelemvor survived the battle with the giants. For years this brutish mercenary followed at his savior's heels like a devoted hound. Though Cyric was loath at first to accept the worship of this fool, he came to realize Kelemvor's strength would cause others to rally to him like a flag on a smoky battlefield.

For a time, the warrior earned his keep by catching food and keeping watch for assassins, but he proved blind to Cyric's vision of the world. Dozens of fears chained him to mediocrity. Had Kelemvor been wise enough to stand aside, Cyric would have traveled on, forging his destiny alone, but the cursed sell-sword proved more treacherous than the pretender gods themselves.

So it was that Kelemvor Lyonsbane, who was the first mortal to worship Cyric, also became his most bitter foe on earth. . . .

* * * * *

The Chaos Hound searched the abandoned halls of Lyonsbane Keep, snuffling the ground noisily with his black snout. It was just a matter of time before he found the beginning of Kelemvor's life trail. Then he could get this hunt over with and raid the verdant pastures of some deity's heaven. Elysium would be a good place to start, in Chauntea's domain. The Great Mother's druids were always a well-fed lot, and never very proficient at defending themselves. Too busy hugging trees to practice swordsmanship, the Hound snarled to himself.

A sharp tang in the air caught Kezef's attention. He crouched low against the rubble. Here it was—the beginning of one life and the end of another. Cyric had said Kelemvor's mother died in childbirth.

Howling madly, the Chaos Hound started along the life trail.

Kezef tore through Lyonsbane Keep, following the path of Kelemvor's early years. Had any mortals still inhabited the ruined castle, they would have seen the Chaos Hound as nothing more than a fleeting shadow. Kezef became insubstantial when he ran, a ghostly blur that left a lingering smell of decay and a vague dread of darkened corners and howling in the night.

In a matter of hours, he traveled the boy's first thirteen years. The trail crossed a few others in that time—older brothers, servants, and a father growing fatter and more unpleasant with each passing day. The Hound could tell much from the violent meetings between the paths and the heavy, staggering pace of the old man's long-vanished tread. Even after more than four decades, those small clues could not remain hidden from Kezef's astounding senses.

One clash in particular blazed in the trail, stinking of

hatred. It was a welcome odor to the Chaos Hound, and he paused to savor it. Kezef's body became substantial again as he stood there. His maggoty paws burned prints into the floor.

Kelemvor had battled his father here, in the musty library. The old sot had been beating some wench not much older than his son. The boy leaped to her rescue, but was no match for the warrior. Kelemvor had gained a few blows for himself. Then something frightening had occurred. . . .

A sharp smell of terror hung over the scene like the aroma of a sun-bloated corpse. Kezef's ratty tail curled in appreciation as he inhaled deeply.

Some new trail replaced the boy's. It was musky and feral, like the scent of a wild cat. A tiger? The Chaos Hound sniffed the decaying shreds of carpet left beneath the long-broken window. No, a panther. Kelemvor Lyonsbane had been a werebeast, a lycanthrope. The spot where the transformation had taken place bore the touch of ancient sorceries, of a curse laid upon the Lyonsbanes long ago—a fatal curse, too, if Kezef read the ending of the old man's trail correctly. The Hound pulled tattered lips back from black teeth in an obscene smile; there were still spatters of blood soaked into the floorboards.

The trail led out of Lyonsbane Keep then and never returned. Kezef gladly followed the winding path as it drove farther and farther afield from the claustrophobic old castle, into the twilight-shrouded countryside. The panther scent soon disappeared. It was replaced by the trails of the boy and a group of adults—adventurers, by the cold smell of chain mail and sword blades—who had obviously taken him in. Kezef grew nauseated from the cloying, reckless happiness that lay over the trail, but that miasma ended soon enough. One of Kelemvor's brutish older brothers crossed paths with the group; when the fighting had ended, only Kelemvor loped away, wounded, in beast form once again.

After the battle, the young man visited many of the larger cities in the Heartlands, lingering but a few tendays in each. He'd become a wandering mercenary, and from the weight and steadiness of his tread, the Hound could tell his strength had easily rivaled that of his bestial alter ego. Kelemvor's life trail told of unremarkable adventures and long bouts of loneliness, hard winters in the wilderness and sweltering summers in crowded, teeming cities. Kezef followed him to these sites and thousands more.

For days after, the cities Kezef visited in his search were filled with fearful murmurings. Even the fiercest warriors found themselves shrieking awake as the Chaos Hound passed beneath their windows. More often than not, however, the nightmares caused by Kezef remained elusive— much to the delight of the Night Serpent, coiled in her cave in Hades.

It wasn't until the chase brought the Chaos Hound to the Great Gray Land of Thar, and a cave atop a steep-sided plateau, that he slowed his lightning pace. The trails of many humans, elves, and dwarves led to this isolated cavern, far too many for it to be a mundane shelter in the icy wilderness. The sweet stench of ancient death lingered there, and the flocks of carrion crows in the sky overhead told of fresh corpses, as well.

The cavern itself was huge, with stalactites and stalagmites of ice glistening everywhere. Kelemvor had entered with eight men, armed and armored for battle. The cave, then as now, was home to a clan of frost giants. As Kezef slipped unnoticed into the cavern, a dozen of the monstrous brutes were gathered around a crystalline altar. A squat statue atop the rough-hewn stone pedestal glowed blue-gray in the midnight gloom. The giants shouted prayers to some inhuman god from the Abyss, a frost elemental Kezef had faced once or twice long ago.

Kelemvor had battled giants here, and the frost elemental, too. The conflict had been fierce, violent, and bloody, with the warrior's eight companions being slaughtered in short succession after some heated exchange between the men and the giants. Only Kelemvor weathered the fight unharmed, felling three of the hulking brutes on his own. By fleeing, he survived to fight again. A ragged human, freed from the giants during the battle, followed in the sell-sword's wake.

Kezef sniffed the prisoner's trail and barked feral laughter. Cyric! The thin, starving man who'd run from the cave at Kelemvor's side was the Prince of Lies—mortal then, of course, but Cyric nonetheless. Howling in mirth, the Chaos Hound darted from the cave and headed south.

One of the giants turned away from the altar, scanning the darkness with glittering blue eyes. He raised a callused hand to his lips, mostly hidden by a dirty beard, and said, "Quiet. Something's in here."

"What is it, Thrym?" one of the giant's fellows asked. Like a driving wind, his whisper blew whorls of powdery snow from a nearby ledge. "More 'venturers?"

Thrym reached slowly for his massive axe. "No, not warriors. Something else . . . some creeping thing. I heard laughing, and now I smell something, too."

"All you smell is the bodies," a dark-haired giant complained. He stuffed a blunt finger in his ear and scratched, squinting the eye on that side of his face. "You let them sit near fire too long. No good to eat now."

Thrym swatted the dark-haired giant with the flat of his axe blade. The blow echoed out of the cave, resounding over the frozen midnight land of Thar like thunder. "This not good," Thrym ventured after a time. The greasy hair stood up on the back of his tree-trunk neck, and a vague, gnawing fear made his stomach churn as if he'd eaten a yew bush. "Something powerful spying on us."

"Just more 'venturers. A mage or something."

The dark-haired giant dug into his other ear. "Maybe Zzutam heard our prayers and is gonna show up again."

Thrym got to his feet and carefully searched the corners of the cave, though he felt an unusual fear at venturing too close to the darkest of them. He found nothing, which was both relieving and troublesome.

"Here," the black-haired giant said when Thrym returned to the prayer circle. "Maybe you need to eat. This meat still good." He smiled his best conciliatory smile for the chief and offered him the last strips saved from the mad human Thrym himself had slain a few tendays ago.

Later, after finishing the prayers to Zzutam and devouring the last of the salted meat, Thrym dreamed of a terrible, unsettling conflict. A lean, hawk-nosed man led a hundred hell hounds, all belching flame. The beasts drove the giants from their home and cornered them against a black wall. The enchanted stones were too high to leap over and too slick to scale.

A vague memory of the dream haunted Thrym for days, filled with the hawk-nosed man's cruel laughter and the snarls of the hell hounds as they tore into the trapped frost giants. . . .

* * * * *

Waterdeep boasted many magnificent buildings, both ancient and modern, but few were the subject of as much gossip as Blackstaff Tower. Home to the wizard Khelben Arunsun, the tower often hosted visiting royalty and explorers of great renown. Many throughout Faerun sought Khelben's advice on matters of state and matters of sorcery, and for that reason Blackstaff Tower sported no doors, no windows. The featureless facade discouraged would-be mages and young adventurers from calling at all watches. After a few cups of mead, however, Khelben was wont to admit he kept the doors hidden mostly because he liked the air of mystery it gave the place.

As dawn spread warm and rosy across the horizon, events were taking place upon the tower's flat, circular roof that would lead to new tales and wild rumors. A spell far beyond the skill of Khelben—and most mortal wizards—masked the eerie flashes of light and shouted incantations emanating from the high vantage. The powerful, complicated wards Khelben had set upon the tower offered no hint of the dangerous intruder's presence. Unaware, the archmage pored over a musty tome of forgotten lore in his library.

Even if Khelben had shaken off the enchantment and stumbled upon the mysterious stranger, he wouldn't have believed his eyes. Most well-traveled people in Faerun could recognize Lord Chess at a glance; the foppish ruler of Zhentil Keep had a penchant for getting his likeness printed on everything from customs stamps to sheet music. If a trade good originated in, or merely passed through, the city he ruled, an image of Chess could be found on it somewhere, smiling inanely over a thick double chin.

Yet it truly was Lord Chess who sat unobserved atop Khelben's tower, drawing arcane runes upon four wyvern skulls. When that task was completed, the nobleman set the leering bones at the points of the compass graven carefully into the roof. Finally, Chess stood and folded beefy hands over his paunch.

"W-Will you let me go now, please?" he mumbled. "It's almost finished. Just as the parchment instructed."

Of course not, Chess, a smooth voice murmured in his mind. *I need the help of a mortal to snare this beast. You'll be free when the battle's won.*

Driven by the arcane presence possessing him, Chess walked to the center of the roof, his steps stuttering and tentative. There he rechecked the three thick candles set in a small half-circle. Yes, they were still lit, still facing the trapdoor that led up from the interior. He took a small jar of spider blood and drew a rune that had been ancient long before the fabled city of Myth Drannor fell, long before Waterdeep had been a minor trading post at the edge of the frozen North. His hand trembled as he completed the rune, but not enough to spoil its grace or its effectiveness.

There. That wasn't so hard, was it?

"I'm afraid," Chess whined. "If Cyric finds out—"

You prayed someone would take revenge on Cyric for killing Leira, Chess. I heard you. And now, after I answer your prayers and give you the chance to help, all you can tell me is that you're afraid?

"But I *am* afraid. If I die, Cyric will have my soul." Chess dropped to his knees, his fine silk breeches coming perilously close to marring the circle around the rune. He brought his hands up to cover his face and wept. "Then he'll know. He'll look at me and know I betrayed him."

I'll take your soul into my domain, the voice soothed. *Cyric won't find you there, not unless I let him. . . .*

Lord Chess was not a brave man, but neither was he stupid. He recognized the threat in those words; it was too late to turn back now. "What do I do next?"

Take out the parchment and repeat the last phrase.

Wiping away his tears, Chess withdrew the glowing sheet of moonlight from his billowing sleeve and read the final verse of the enchantment:

> *"A mortal kills the candle first.*
> *A god's breath slakes the second's thirst.*
> *A traitor's blood to drown the last.*
> *The web of intrigue now is cast."*

The parchment fell apart, slipping like moonbeams through Chess's fingers. The radiance from the sundered page settled over the skulls and the candles. After a moment the light faded, and with it disappeared the weird compass burned into the boards.

"That third part still bothers me," Chess murmured. "Why blood?"

Because the spell says so, the voice replied. *You have that dirk I gave you. All you need to do is prick your thumb. A little blood will do. . . .*

"He comesss," the wyvern skull to the south croaked. "The Chaosss Hound comesss from the sssouth."

Finished not a moment too soon, the voice said. *Quickly, Chess, behind the candles. He's coming just as we expected. And remember, the first and third candles are your responsibility.*

The fat man bustled to the spot he'd marked with the elder sign and planted his slippered feet carefully over the rune. Chess was so concerned with keeping his toes inside the circle of protection that he didn't see Kezef slide through the trapdoor, insubstantial as a ghost.

The Hound crouched low at the unexpected obstacle before him, growling like a dozen winter-starved wolves. His body became corporeal again, all decaying and maggoty.

"Don't think you can fool me, Mask, hiding in bloated flesh armor like that." Kezef began to slink toward Chess, his tail curled down between his bony legs. "I could smell you a hundred miles from here. Tell me, how long do you think you can keep fooling Cyric with this little game of yours? I spotted you right away, and I'm no god. . . ."

Snuff the first candle, the God of Intrigue said calmly to Chess. *Use your fingers.*

The lord of Zhentil Keep didn't move, merely stared at the massive hound creeping toward him. The thing's flesh was oozing, like pus from an old sore, and its paws burned prints into the ground. Black, pointed teeth filled the hound's mouth. Its eyes glinted with unearthly malevolence.

The candle, Mask commanded, his voice full of godly wrath. *You must extinguish it now, Chess.*

The fear-wrought paralysis broken, the nobleman reached down to the first of the yellow tallow sticks. Kezef lunged forward, but Mask countered by moving Chess's stubby fingers and greasy lips in the gestures and incantation for a powerful spell. The distance between the monstrous hound and the cowering human warped, elongated. No matter how fast Kezef ran, he seemed to get no closer to his prey.

Chess closed his eyes and pinched the flame on the first candle. The wick had been woven from the hair of prisoners wrongfully held by lawful and good kings, and it didn't give up its spark easily. The stubborn flame burned Chess's thumb and forefinger black before it died.

One down, Mask purred. *No fear, Chess. This will be much easier than you—*

An ear-splitting howl drowned out the rest of Mask's confident words and sent a violent quake of terror down the nobleman's spine. A wave of confusion swept over both god and man. Chess stumbled back, out of the protective circle, and clamped his hands over his ears.

Kezef was on him before he had a chance to scream. The Chaos Hound rammed him, driving him away from the candles and the protective rune. Through it all, the shriek continued, sending any thoughts of defense or escape tumbling into a maelstrom of sound.

"Come out, Mask," Kezef rumbled. "Face me yourself, coward."

The Hound's breath became a puff of corrosive mist in the bitter winter air. The acid sprayed across the nobleman's face and chest, scouring flesh from his bones. It was

Chess's scream that now rang out over Blackstaff Tower as he twitched and writhed beneath the awful weight of Kezef's front paws.

"I've already chosssen a much more sssuitable location," one of the wyvern skulls hissed jovially. "You know, Kezef, you really ssshould do sssomething about that breath of yoursss. . . ."

The Chaos Hound darted away from Lord Chess to the skull positioned directly across the tower. Kezef's swift passing caused the candles to gutter, but their wicks held the flames greedily. With one hiss of his corrosive breath, the Hound melted the skull.

"Your hunger must be dulling your senses," Mask said. The Patron of Thieves stood at the roof's center, holding the second candle in his gloved hand. He raised his mask slightly and blew it out. "Now, Chess. The third must be snuffed with your blood. You won't need the dagger. Just lean over it."

The lord of Zhentil Keep had crawled to the center of the roof and grasped the final candle. Fingers trailing ragged tatters of flesh, the nobleman reached for the dirk Mask had given him. All the while he looked out at the guttering flame from a face that was no longer a face.

Lord Chess was dead before he closed his fingers on the knife, his arms and hands ground to paste in Kezef's black teeth. The thick candle tumbled through the air, only to land in a spreading puddle of crimson. The blood stained the tallow dark and doused the flame with a long, bubbling sizzle.

"And that's three."

The compass Mask had inscribed upon the roof appeared again, its curves and points etched in radiance more dazzling than the morning sunlight streaming over the City of Splendors. The lines of the pattern folded together. They engulfed Kezef like a huge fishing net. An unbreakable knot sealed the net above the Hound, and the remaining wyvern skulls fused to form an intricate seal over that.

Mask stood over the nobleman's gory, armless corpse. "Sorry, Chess, but the enchantment really did call for you to do a lot more than prick your thumb. Rest easy, though. You played your part perfectly."

The God of Intrigue turned to the Chaos Hound. "We would have used this to trap you last time, Kezef, but the pathetic bleeding hearts like Mystra refused to go along with human sacrifice."

Mask erased the runic symbol with his foot. The destruction of the glyph, which had never provided Lord Chess the least bit of protection, closed the final part of the trap. A crimson flame lit the last of the three candles, trailing a thick, pungent smoke that balled like a giant's fist above the tower. The fist closed over the howling, struggling Chaos Hound and drew him swiftly into the candle.

"Cyric!" Kezef screamed as he disappeared into the waxy prison. "Avenge me!"

"Oh, he'll avenge this slap all right, but not against me." Mask kicked the corpse of Lord Chess onto its back. The acid had ravaged the nobleman's face, but there was just enough flab left for the Lord of the Dead to identify him. "I'm not quite ready to challenge the Prince of Lies, not without allies, anyway."

He touched the seared flesh around the dead man's throat and a silver-white chain appeared. The disk dangling from the chain held a circle of eight stars with a trail of mist bleeding from its center—the holy symbol of Mystra.

"Why, Lord Chess. You were a secret member of the Church of Mysteries! Treachery in Cyric's holy city, and at the highest levels. Tsk. He will be disappointed. . . . Still,

171

I'll take your soul in. After all, we wouldn't want you telling your former liege how I, er, *encouraged* your work with the Lady of Mysteries."

A sheet of parchment created from moonlight appeared in Mask's hand. On it was inscribed the ancient and complicated rite by which a god could contain a power such as Kezef, but only with the cooperation of a mortal. Mask changed the traitor mentioned in the spell to a faithful minion and erased the necessity for blood to be shed; he knew Cyric would never buy Mystra killing traitors or murdering innocents to seal an enchantment. Obviously, Chess's death was an unfortunate accident. After all, the Hound's teeth marks were all over the poor fool.

With narrowed eyes, the Lord of Shadows surveyed his work. Yes, this would do nicely. When the shielding spell was lifted and Cyric discovered his faithful dog had been waylaid. . . . Mask smiled. The Prince of Lies would be swift in showing his displeasure with both Mystra and Zhentil Keep.

The tallow prison firmly in one gloved hand, the God of Intrigue melted into the lengthening shadows next to the corpulent remains of Lord Chess. The mystery he left in his wake atop Blackstaff Tower would baffle sages and gossips in the City of Splendors for decades. Its effects were felt throughout the heavens in mere moments.

X

DUEL-EDGED SWORD

*Wherein Cyric investigates the waylaying of the
Chaos Hound, Gwydion speaks the name of
the wrong person at the worst possible instant,
and the identity of Kelemvor's strange
jailor is finally revealed.*

Cyric threw the two spent candles and the holy symbol
at Jergal. The seneschal didn't raise a hand to deflect the
missiles, didn't flinch when they rebounded painfully from
his smooth gray face.

"Of course this is a trick!" the Prince of Lies shouted.
"Mystra isn't fool enough to leave her holy symbol and a
page from her spellbook at the scene of the crime. She
isn't like that blunt dolt Torm, who can't spell 'subtlety,' let
alone practice it."

The Lord of the Dead hunched down in his throne.
Twisting the moonlight parchment in his bony fingers, he

173

studied the severed head resting awkwardly on the floor before him. Much of the fat had been burned away from the face, but it had obviously belonged to Lord Chess. Kezef had done the gruesome damage with his corrosive breath; it didn't take a master sage to figure that out. The real question was, why had Chess been involved in the treachery and which god—or gods—had orchestrated the capture of the Chaos Hound? The spell on the parchment was powerful enough to imprison the beast, but only a deity would be strong enough to hold Kezef while Chess extinguished the candles.

"Well," Cyric murmured to the severed head, "what do you have to say for yourself?"

Chess opened his eyes and stared blankly at the tips of the death god's boots. A thick, bubbling wail burbled from lips seared by acid, sticky with blood. "I have nothing to tell you, murderer of Leira."

Cyric leaned forward to study the ravaged face. He punctuated his next question by rapping the rolled parchment into his palm with each word. "Who's pulling your strings, puppet?"

"I cannot say."

"Cannot or will not?"

A pause, then Chess replied, "The difference between the two is academic, at least as far as you're concerned. You'll get no more from me about the matter."

"You grow bold now that you're dead. Where's that foppishness the world found so revolting?"

"Burned away with my flesh and flown with my fear of dying," Chess murmured. "And since you know not where I am, no new fears can claim me."

Muttering bitter maledictions, the Prince of Lies slouched back in his throne. "Perhaps there are other creatures like Kezef in the planes, things that can track the dead. Then I'll personally deliver virgin fears to you,

you simpering lackey."

"Indeed. There may be trackers like the Chaos Hound—" Chess would have shrugged had his head still been attached to his shoulders "—but my protector has thousands of candles to trap them in."

"I can summon your consciousness like this whenever I wish." Cyric leaped from the throne and placed his foot atop the severed head. "I'll keep your mind anchored in my throne room and demand you entertain me. You'll be my jester."

Chess laughed, a sickening, liquid sound. "My protector asks me to remind you of something: Your talons do not reach as far as you'd like to think. Kelemvor's soul is hidden from you. Placing another beyond your grasp would be a simple enough matter."

Fury twisting his features, Cyric kicked the head the length of the throne room. The dead man's laughter echoed through the cavernous hall, rising over the moans and whimpers of the Burning Men like a ship riding high upon a swell in a wine-dark sea. The Prince of Lies stalked back and forth in front of his throne. He knit his fingers together tightly before him, the long nails digging furrows in the backs of his hands. Glittering, godly energy ran from the wounds like blood.

Jergal took the moonlight parchment from the throne and floated swiftly to the other end of the chamber. He folded the glowing sheet, then stuffed it into Chess's mouth. Cyric was still pacing like a caged beast when the seneschal returned from silencing the severed head. *Your Magnificence,* Jergal asked, bowing low, *would you like me to take a message to any in the pantheon, warning them of your anger?*

"I'll show the bite of my anger with action, not waste its venom on some polished missive to the Circle," Cyric hissed.

The Lord of the Dead stomped a few more steps, then stood rigid. "Since my ascension, there have been many powers moving against me. Mystra wants revenge for Kelemvor's death. Oghma wishes to prevent the *Cyrinishad* from obscuring what he sees as true knowledge. The faithful of Bane and Myrkul and Bhaal—and now Leira— want to reverse the sands in the hourglass and resurrect their foolish, fallen gods. . . . They're all coming together now, Jergal. I can sense it. They want to rob me of my throne. They want to rob me of the glorious kingdom I have built here in Hades, the kingdom I will build in the mortal realms."

Cyric balled his hands into fists and shrieked at the ceiling. "I have two houses, and traitors creep through the halls of both! My denizens will not bring me Kelemvor's soul, even though it's hidden somewhere in the City of Strife." He gestured wildly toward the nobleman's head. "Zhentil Keep shelters craven sneaks like Chess, though I've tried to make that place my home in Faerun, tried to raise it above the rest of the world with my patronage!"

The denizens and mortals cannot see your vision, my love, the glorious dream of the universe united under your rule, Godsbane said, her dark presence soothing the fury in Cyric's mind. *And the pretenders to divinity know you are the only god in the pantheon with a true claim to heavenly power. They fear you, so they cower together like sheep before the thunderstorm.*

Jergal wrapped the candles with the holy symbol's chain. *If the gods are banding together, lord, why would they point the finger of blame at the Whore?*

"She must not be working with them," Cyric answered. "Or perhaps Mystra agreed to take the blame, knowing my hatred for her could grow no hotter." He scowled and shook his head. "I'd be more of a fool than Torm to waste time guessing their motives."

Turn this intrigue to your advantage, instead, Godsbane offered. *Perhaps you can draw the conspirators out of the shadows by seeming to place all the guilt for the Chaos Hound on the Whore.*

"Shadows is quite the correct word, too," the Prince of Lies murmured. He took the candles from Jergal and crushed them. "These intrigues have Mask's invisible fingerprints all over them—" the waxy fragments fell to the carpet, leaving the silver disk in Cyric's hand "—no matter whose holy symbol he leaves behind."

The Shadowlord was your ally, Jergal noted blandly. *He helped you hide Leira's destruction from the rest of the pantheon. After you were denied access to the weave, he sent you those arquebuses to remind you of the Gearsmith's power.*

"It's clear now that Mask had his own reasons for appearing to be our ally still," the Prince of Lies said. "He's ambitious, our Lord of Shadows. Being God of Intrigue suits him well."

The spirit of Godsbane slithered pleasantly across Cyric's thoughts. *Perhaps his title should be the next you take for your own,* she prodded. *He may be a talented adept at intrigue, but you are the true master.*

"And you are becoming too fond of flattery," Cyric rumbled. He let the comment hang ominously in the air for a moment, then turned to Jergal. "I will rail at Mystra for this outrage, but I need a new force to unleash upon the mortal realms, something to draw the rest of the serpents from their nest. The materials I requested from Gond will do. The consignment has been delivered, has it not?"

The materials you requested from the Gearsmith just arrived, Jergal noted. *His minions left nine large crates at the gates.*

"Perfect. Have the crates brought here immediately." Cyric slid back into his throne. Then, squaring his shoulders, he said, "I will need nine shades to power the

Gondish mechanisms. I'll leave it to you to determine which of the False will sacrifice themselves for my cause."

Jergal bowed his acceptance of the task, but didn't back out of the throne room as Cyric had expected. The seneschal hovered tentatively before his dark lord for a moment, wringing his hands nervously.

"Well?" Cyric snapped.

Th-There are myriad things that require your attention, Your Magnificence, Jergal began haltingly. *Have you turned your mind to the gathering outside Bone Castle recently?*

"The groups watching the executions? What of them?"

There is some unrest amongst the denizens. They feel betrayed by the slaying of their kind. The denizens are your faithful, and—

"And should never question my actions. If they wish to end the executions, they should find Kelemvor's soul," the Prince of Lies said.

Beware, my love, Godsbane warned. *You do not have magic to wield against an uprising in the City of Strife. Do not dismiss such murmurings lightly.*

And if Chess is any indication of the traitors to be found amongst your worshipers in the mortal realms, Jergal added, *you may find turncoats of equal stature here in Hades.*

The Lord of the Dead considered the warnings. He drummed his fingers against the throne, the staccato tap growing louder and faster as he pondered the depths of his predicament.

"Fetch the crates from the Gearsmith, Jergal, but before you do, create a scrying portal for me. I'll find the shades to animate the contraptions myself, pluck them from the mob watching the executions." Cyric grinned. "These Gondish artifacts will grant me absolute control over the souls imprisoned in them. Who better to choose than the shades fostering the unrest?"

The seneschal drew the tips of his fingers across his cheek in a quick, straight slash. From the deep wound that appeared, it was clear the nails were as sharp as a dragon's teeth.

Yellow ichor oozed from the gash and ran down Jergal's smooth face. In noisome clots, the blood dripped to the floor, creating a small pool. The shiny surface of the slowly spreading liquid held an image of the mob outside the castle.

Cyric stared into that gruesome window, scanning the faces of the assembled shades and denizens as they, in turn, watched their fellows tortured and destroyed. He focused the facets of his unruly mind on the crowd. With a million ears he listened to every word they said. An equal number of unblinking eyes watched every secretive gesture they made.

After a time, the Lord of the Dead drew Godsbane and pointed the tip at a cluster of unsuspecting shades. His voice tight with fury, he whispered, "The inquisition has found its first heretics—and its first inquisitors."

* * * * *

Skeletal guards lined the top of the wall surrounding Bone Castle, pikes clutched in their bony hands. Savagely they sliced and jabbed the denizens chained to the jagged diamond wall below them. Bits of denizen flesh dropped into the oily black water of the River Slith, winding moat-like around the circular keep. There the fragments burst into flame and sank. Slithering things moved beneath the surface, gobbling up the foul treats before they dissolved completely.

Like the Faithless imprisoned in the great wall around the City of Strife and the False trapped in the realm's noisy confines, the denizens had been created from the souls of mortals. However, they alone resided in Cyric's domain willingly. Their reward for mortal devotion to the death god was a painful transformation into a form far less than human in appearance, but possessed of astounding strength and agility. And denizens, like all souls, were almost impossible to destroy. Only three things could annihilate them irrevocably: the hand of a god; an elder, eternal evil like the Night Serpent or the Chaos Hound; or a place of indescribable corruption.

The River Slith most certainly qualified as the last.

Some mortal scholars claimed the Slith had its source in the riven heart of an evil dragon buried far beneath the world's surface. At first it trickled as a rivulet, but soon other fonts of corruption emptied into its waters—the tears of sacrifices being led to bloodstained altars, the ink spilled in penning assassins' orders, the slavering of mad dogs, and the bile of savage, power-hungry monarchs. The rivulet became a wide river, slow moving and thick with poison and offal. It wound a tortuous course through the planes, befouling the realms it touched. One drop of its dark waters would kill any mortal; dunking a shade in the Slith would destroy it forever. Of the slimy, seemingly indestructible things that swam beneath the surface of the flow, not even the gods themselves dared utter their names.

From time to time one of the False tried to end its eternity of torture by throwing itself into the Slith. The unfortunate soul soon learned that nothing escaped the Realm of the Dead without Cyric's approval. Even now, a dozen such shades floated upon the black water. The creatures lurking in the moat had gobbled down the souls' arms and legs, leaving the agonized torsos to bob and writhe in the murky flow. Every few months, Jergal ordered these souls dredged from the Slith to face more personal torture.

Gwydion watched one of these tormented souls float

past. He stood on the riverbank opposite the diamond walls, part of the mob gathered there to witness the executions. Though he and Perdix had tried to find a spot as far as they could from the Slith, the press of the denizens and shades had forced them ever closer to the moat. Now they were barely an arm's length from the stinking water.

Finally fed up with being trod upon by the crowd, Perdix flexed his leathery wings and hopped into the air. "Tsk. Af's probably admiring the workmanship of the chains," he noted to no one in particular. "Probably muttering to the poor sap next to him that he was here when they forged the damned things."

Gwydion looked across the river at his former captor and shuddered. In choosing the denizens to face execution, Cyric's seneschal had been surprisingly logical: the doomed would meet their end alphabetically. That decision had put Af very near the front of the line.

The hulking creature dangled upside down on one side of a mammoth set of scales. He was bound in a dozen ways to a huge obsidian disk. Chains linked the stone to an identical twin, and the two teetered vertically over the black water, balanced upon a fulcrum of iron jutting from the diamond wall. Blood and grime hid Af's wolfish features, and most of his spider legs had been sliced away by the skeletons. The only sign that he still lived was the occasional twitch of his long, serpentine coils. The equine-bodied denizen lashed to the other side of the scales wasn't moving at all.

"How can you watch this, Perdix?" Gwydion asked.

"You think this bothers me?" the little denizen replied. He glanced at the shade with his one blue eye. "I never really liked Af much. Ours was a friendship of sloth. That's the only kind down here."

Despite his brave front, the concern showed on Perdix's inhuman features, in the nervous fluttering of his wings. It wasn't concern for Af, though. The winged denizen could see himself tied to the stone, battered and bloody and waiting for the balance to tip, lowering him into the oblivion promised by the murky Slith. As Gwydion looked around at the other denizens crowded on the riverbank, he saw the same badly disguised fear. Discontent lurked in the silent mob, as well. Cyric's faithful felt betrayed; their narrowed eyes and clenched fists trumpeted their rage like a battle cry before a bloody skirmish.

Gwydion smiled secretively and turned his attention to the other shades scattered amongst the monstrous denizens. Their faces held blank looks or grim scowls of acceptance. In a few eyes, Gwydion saw a desperate joy at the suffering of their tormentors. That spark of life gave him hope. The others might throw off the pall of hopelessness, too, given the right leader or the right example to follow.

The steady clanging of an iron gong drew Gwydion's attention to the unwieldy contraption holding Af suspended over the river. A particularly tall skeleton clad in a robe of blood-red samite unrolled a parchment and began to read.

"Because the denizens of the Realm of the Dead have yet to complete the holy quest for the soul of Kelemvor Lyonsbane," the skeleton rasped, its voice like the rustling of ancient cerements, "Lord Cyric sentences these prisoners to be destroyed. Know you all that every denizen will share this doom if the renegade soul is not found."

No one in the gathered mob paid much attention to the dire warning. The same perfunctory announcement was made at each execution, in each of two dozen sites along the bank of the Slith and in front of the Night Serpent's cave. Repetition had dulled the impact of the threat, just as it had leached some of the horror from the unsettling executions.

The robed skeleton signaled two other fleshless fiends

with a casual wave of its hand. Hefting huge mallets, they knocked the wooden supports away from the massive scales. The stone disks began to tip languidly back and forth, each swing bringing them closer to the oily, turbid river. Af struggled to shift his weight, so the other denizen—still silent and unmoving—would hit the water first. His efforts brought scornful jeers from the skeletons and sped the teetering of the scales.

Since he was bound upside down, Af's wolfish head sank below the surface first when the stone disk hit the Slith. Then the scales tipped back the other way, and the brutish denizen rose, screaming, high into the air. The dark water streamed from his face, drawing the color away as if it were thin paint. The steely gray bled from his fur, the red from his eyes. His striped mane and the crimson scales on his shoulders all faded to feeble, pallid white.

Each time the denizens sank into the murky water, the river leached the immortality from them. Af's screams died down to whimpers after his third drenching; the other denizen shrieked only once, as if he had been awakened by the torture. In a few moments, the flesh of both creatures melted away completely. Their seared white bones were quickly gobbled by the things moving beneath the moat's surface.

As the crowd began to break up, filing back to the necropolis to resume the search for Kelemvor, Gwydion tapped Perdix on the leg. "Has there ever been a revolt in the City of Strife?"

" 'Course there has," the denizen said, his thin tongue flickering over his pointed teeth. "They were as regular as a clockwork dinner chime when Cyric first took over. None of them ever lasted very long—nasty little brawls, but brief." He flapped a little higher into the air and gestured broadly at the milling throng. "With the sort of riffraff Cyric has to work with down here, what do you expect?"

A denizen with the head and upper body of a mantis swiped at Perdix with one massive forelimb. "Riffraff? You should talk."

Deftly Perdix avoided the halfhearted attack and fluttered to the top of a high, twisted metal pole. His bright yellow skin made him stand out against the vermilion sky as he hunched there, a radiant gargoyle.

"Some of my fellows are a bit jealous of my standing with our lord," the bat-winged denizen said. "When Cyric became a god, I was still mortal. I really knocked myself out proving how devoted I was—murdering, stealing, causing all the strife I could. I took out a whole patrol of Purple Dragons—" he smiled wistfully "—before they lopped my sword arm off. I was one of the first denizens Cyric created."

Gwydion leaned back against the pole and watched the mantis-headed creature. It shuffled into the crowd on the slow-moving legs of a giant opossum. "What about the other denizens?" the shade asked. "Aren't they Cyric's faithful?"

Perdix snorted. "Most of this lot he inherited with the real estate. They used to worship Myrkul, but they converted when Cyric took over." With surprising agility, he climbed hand over hand down the pole. "Look, slug," Perdix said, hanging just above Gwydion's ear, "if you're hoping for an uprising, forget it. The denizens who didn't accept Cyric's rule tried that, and the whole bunch of them ended up at the bottom of the swamp on the other side of the castle. And that place makes the Slith look like a burbling brook in the Moonshaes."

The crowd had thinned, but many of the shades and denizens still milling near the river had stopped to listen to the conversation. Gwydion felt the eyes of the helpless souls and powerful minions of Cyric upon him, felt the tension in the air at the mere mention of defiance against the Lord of the Dead. But if Perdix were right, even the denizens might turn against the Prince of Lies.

"The Night Serpent said Cyric feared two things," Gwydion ventured loudly, "a revolt in the City of Strife and the shade of Kelemvor Lyonsbane." He turned away from Perdix and scanned the crowd. "You denizens don't want to end up like those others, drowned in the Slith, destroyed forever? Are you shades content to be tortured to satisfy Cyric's whims? If we rise up, Kelemvor will come out of hiding and lead us. He's the only one who can stand against the tyrant. Why do you think Cyric is so desperate to find him?"

Gwydion's words raced through the scattered denizens and shades. Some drew strength from the subversive talk. Others muttered about the shade's foolishness as they glanced uneasily at the bleached white walls of Bone Castle, looming over them like a headsman's axe. Yet of all the souls gathered there, only Perdix tried to silence Gwydion.

"That kind of talk'll get us all destroyed," the denizen hissed. He clutched his head with clawed hands. "I told you Cyric always deals with—"

A pillar of flame, as thick around as a giant's leg, dropped from the sky and slammed into the ground near Gwydion. The concussion shook the city all the way to the Wall of the Faithless. The heat charred the flesh of anyone close at hand and made the Slith boil turbidly in its banks. Skeletons tumbled from the diamond wall. They flailed about with their pikes as they hit the water, but one by one they disappeared beneath the murky surface.

Gwydion the Quick was on his feet and running before anyone else. He glanced over his shoulder as he fled. What he saw behind him rivaled any nightmare lurking in the Night Serpent's hoard of horrible dreams and foul visions.

In the center of the blasted circle of earth, Cyric stood, arrayed in a cloak of flame, Godsbane held aloft in a war-like pose. Burning eyes glared out of a face scorched crimson by some hellish furnace. Lips pulled back in a sneer to reveal twisted yellow teeth. His hands were gnarled like long-dead yew branches, his arms lean, but corded with muscles like steel cable.

With a single stroke of his rose-hued short sword, the Lord of the Dead sliced a cringing denizen in two. Then, as if possessed by some incredible madness, he began to howl at the souls in his path. Anyone frightened enough or foolish enough to stand in Cyric's way fell before Godsbane. The sword's glow became brighter with each blow, growing as crimson as fresh-spilled blood.

And most terrifying of all, Gwydion saw Cyric's hate-filled eyes staring at him.

Frantic, the shade darted over the rubble. Ruined buildings loomed ahead, dark and twisting alleys winding between them. He never considered how absurd it was, trying to outrun a god. In his panicked mind, the City of Strife had become the Promenade in Suzail, Cyric just another challenger in a footrace.

Gwydion dared another glance over his shoulder. He expected to find the Prince of Lies at his heels, but instead, his speed had put Cyric far behind him.

A flash of yellow caught Gwydion's eye just before something wrapped around his legs. The shade fell face-down onto the hard, packed dirt. His forehead struck a rock, sending colorful pain blossoms across his mind, clouding his vision and muffling the shouts and screams from the riverbank. When the bright spots danced from before his eyes, he saw that Perdix was the one who'd tackled him.

"Sorry, slug, but you was warned," the denizen said. " 'Sides, if I let you get away, I'd be the one who pays. Cyric always makes *someone* pay."

"Most assuredly," murmured the Prince of Lies, towering suddenly over the captive soul. He reached down and closed a taloned hand around Gwydion's throat. "I just knew you'd cause me trouble. The ones who die trying to be heroes always do."

Cyric lifted Gwydion to his knees. "But now it's time I put your speed to use for my own ends, quickling," he said. "Still, you should be happy. You're finally going to get your knighthood."

The Prince of Lies wiped the gore from Godsbane onto the shade, then sheathed the blade. "I dub you Sir Gwydion —inquisitor for Zhentil Keep and unholy knight of Hades. Now for your armor. . . ."

* * * * *

"Help me!" a woman cried, her voice shrill with terror.

Low and gravelly, a man called out, "Make it stop! Don't let it destroy me!"

Something inhuman, its words humming like the wings of a gigantic wasp, moaned mournfully, "Betrayed! Cyric has betrayed us again!"

Kelemvor sat cross-legged in the center of the swirling madness, his mind's eye drawn in upon itself. He didn't see the faces flowing through the rose-hued mist surrounding him. He blocked out the pained screams of the souls as best he could and closed his senses to the pungent tang in the air, the oddly mingled smells of white-hot iron and moldy, overturned grave loam. Nevertheless, images of the tortured spirits insinuated themselves into his thoughts. It was always the same when Cyric wielded the sword.

"I will end this chaos," Kelemvor whispered, over and over. "I will not allow them to undo the rule of law and reason in the universe."

"There are some who would see that as a noble enough sentiment," Godsbane purred, "but I think it's a rather pointless vow, my love. Law and chaos are meaningless, when you come right down to it. They always balance each other in the end."

The soft, feminine voice came to him clearly, even over the shrieks of the shades and denizens trapped inside the sword.

"Still," Godsbane added, "once we topple Cyric, you can tell yourself you've fulfilled your promise. Overthrowing a madman like him is always a victory for law and order—at least for a time."

Kel opened his eyes. The spirit of a mantis-headed denizen sped past, warped and twisted on a flowing stream of energy. "Don't think I mean to stop at Cyric," Kelemvor muttered. "You've kept me prisoner for a decade. I'll have justice for that, too."

"You're hardly in any position to threaten," the sword replied, full of mock indignation. "Besides, I've kept you safe and sound. You'd have gone straight to the City of Strife if I hadn't captured your soul that day atop Blackstaff Tower. Then where would you be?"

"I'll ask Midnight to keep that in mind after you hand me over to her," Kel murmured. His heart ached at the sight of the tortured faces with their wide, pleading eyes. The helplessness he felt at their suffering burned in his chest like a poisoned dirk.

"Our goals really are the same," the sword said smoothly. "You want Cyric to pay for killing you. I want him to suffer for trying to break my will after he stole me from that halfling village."

Kelemvor remained obstinately silent. Finally Godsbane

spoke again: "I need you as the proverbial carrot at the end of the stick, my love, but once I bring the Lady of Mysteries into my band of conspirators, your usefulness may come to an abrupt end. If you continue to bluster, I may find it necessary to destroy you."

To prove her power, the sword snuffed out the souls she had gathered in the battle on the banks of the Slith. Godsbane had explained once that she could transfer this stolen life essence to her wielder, store it, or simply drink it in herself. What the treacherous blade had never revealed was how she had kept Kelemvor shielded from Cyric's prying mind for all those years. When Godsbane contacted her master, Kel could feel the death god's malevolence all around him, yet Cyric remained unaware of his presence.

Godsbane's cool, sensuous voice filled the sudden silence. "Let me offer you a little present," she cooed. "Just to prove there are no hard feelings."

The imaginary prison walls Kelemvor had marked for himself became real, just as he had set them in his mind. A floor slid into place, and a ceiling, both with the feel of badly set stone. The place even smelled like a Sembian jail in which Kel had spent a month: all stale water and damp, musty earth. A mangy rat peeked out from a hole in the corner. Roaches scrambled around a thin stream of water that meandered from one high, lightless window all the way to the floor.

"There, now," the sword said proudly. "Those poor souls gave their all for this place. Chaos into order. You should be pleased. . . ."

A woman appeared in the cell with Kelemvor, lithe and young and very beautiful. Her long raven-black hair and pale skin made her resemble Midnight just enough to stir Kel's interest, but not so much that he immediately turned away from her as an impostor. "I could offer my apologies in other ways," the woman said, her husky voice full of promised passion.

Kelemvor was tempted by the reassuring touch of the woman's hand against his shoulder, the solid feel of the stone floor beneath him, but he didn't give in to the seduction. "You needn't have bothered," he said. After pushing himself to his feet, he made a precise half turn and counted his steps to the corner of his imagined room. "What I create with my mind is just as real as what you're offering—but I never confuse it with reality. I wonder if you can say the same?"

He didn't wait for an answer, wouldn't have heard Godsbane if she'd bothered to parry the insult. Eyes fixed straight ahead, Kelemvor began to mark out the walls of his prison. The steady rhythm of his steps echoed through the void like the solid strike of hammer and chisel against stone, cutting grave markers for the souls swallowed by the chaos.

XI

INQUISITOR

*Wherein Gwydion the Quick dons the god-forged
armor of an unholy knight of Hades, and the
Prince of Lies unleashes his clockwork
inquisition upon the mortal realms,
with frightful consequences for Rinda
and her fellow conspirators in Zhentil Keep.*

Gwydion had lost all sense of pain long ago, after the
workmen had stripped each and every muscle out of his
back. By the time the metal spring replacements had been
hammered into his spine, the agony had become so great
the shade had passed beyond the threshold of his senses.
Now his mind had separated from his undying form. He
watched the inhuman smiths pound away at his body from
a vantage just above the long, dirty trestle table where he
was laid out. To either side of his disembodied, floating
essence, the ever-burning bodies of failed scribes hung

suspended as ghastly chandeliers. The flickering light from the Burning Men cast weird, flowing shadows over the bustling operation below.

A clockwork golem, bronze and burnished like a princess's favorite mirror, leaned over Gwydion's body. The mechanical smith slid iron pincers into the flayed forearm and locked them onto the last bone buried beneath the flesh. With a tug, he wrenched the bone free. A smaller golem, wrought of silver instead of bronze, took the gory bone and tossed it into a pile of similar trophies.

"This is the last of the core parts," a burly man mumbled through a beard as tangled as Cyric's mind. He studied the gold bar in his hands, running greasy, callused fingers over it with affection. "From here it's easy stuff—aligning the limbs, setting the outer plates. . . ."

The master smith slid the metal rod into the spot left by the bone, then ratcheted it in place. The bolts secure, he dropped the ratchet and drew a more delicate tool from his stained and tattered apron. With this he carefully slipped the gears into play at the elbow and wrist. Finally he stepped back, gesturing for his clockwork assistants to hook up the last of the spring-muscles and close the incisions.

"I suppose I should be honored to be here," the burly workman said. His voice seemed hollow and metallic, almost as if he were talking inside a steel-walled box. "I hear tell you haven't invited a fellow god into your throne room in quite some time."

Cyric gave Gond his best deprecating smile, certain the God of Craft would never notice the slight. The Wonderbringer was very much like his worshipers—long on strength and a certain cunning when it came to things mechanical, but short on the sort of devious intelligence the death god found challenging. "I thought you should be the one to put the armor together," the Prince of Lies said.

"I don't think any of my minions could have done the job properly."

Grunting noncommittally, Gond turned his attention to a wickedly horned helmet. He detached the rounded top from the bevor and set about adjusting the thin needles that lined the inside of the helm's lower half. A sudden clatter of metal on the stone floor brought a flush to his sooty cheeks and a spark of anger to his iron-gray eyes. "Careful with that, you stupid walking safe!" he snarled. One of the golems—a box with long arms and four thin legs—bowed a stiff apology and hefted the fallen cuisses to its more humanlike compatriot, who gracefully secured the armor to Gwydion's legs.

The clockwork smiths had almost finished girding the shade in the golden, god-forged armor. They levered him from the table, forcing him to his feet. Gwydion wobbled unsteadily until the largest of the golems supported him with unyielding arms of iron. Even then, the weight and size of the new body disoriented the shade. He was at least half-again as tall as he'd been, with a body bulky enough to belong to an ogre.

The armor appeared at first glance to be nothing more than an exquisitely crafted set of oversized field plate, though it was far more than that. The breastplate was engraved with thousands of tiny grinning skulls, each rictus face surrounded by a dark sun scored into the metal with acid. Thick spikes coated with poison jutted from elbow- and knee-cops, and razors tipped the sollerets on the shade's feet. Both gauntlets bristled with dozens of tiny, barbed hooks meant to bite into the heretics the inquisitor would grapple. No straps or buckles held the armor in place; each piece was anchored to Gwydion's new metal skeleton.

"The helmet's the most intricate part," Gond said, stepping up onto the table. He lifted the bevor, taking care to position the needles over the eyelets he'd driven into the shade's throat. "To keep it secure, we'll need to hammer this bit into his mouth. It's going to make talking kind of tough."

Cyric leaned forward, mildly engaged by the transformation taking place before him. "As long as he can manage 'die, heretic' I'll be satisfied," the death god said facetiously.

Your Magnificence, Jergal began, hovering closer to the gruesome throne. *There is the matter of the final sentencing. . . .*

"More formalities," Cyric hissed. "All right. Get it over with."

The seneschal unrolled a long sheet of parchment. *Know you, Gwydion, son of Gareth the blacksmith, that you have been found guilty of high treason against the rightful lord of Bone Castle and ruler of the City of Strife. You are hereby sentenced to serve said lord for eternity as a holy inquisitor.*

"Sentenced?" Gond scoffed. "He should be privileged to wear this armor. I forged it with my own hands!"

"I'm certain he'd thank you if you hadn't jammed that bit into his mouth," Cyric murmured. "Now, can we just get this over with? My inquisitor has business to attend to in Zhentil Keep."

Gond lowered the bevor over Gwydion's head, guiding the quills into his neck. He anchored the lower half of the helm to the bit in the shade's mouth, then took up the rest of the headpiece. Like the bevor, the upper part of the helm was lined with needles.

The long slivers of metal slipped into Gwydion's skull, and he felt his consciousness being drawn back into his hulking new body. He tried to resist, but it was as if the needles had opened a maelstrom below him. He spiraled down into a place of absolute darkness. Suddenly, cold metal walls loomed on every side. They closed in, pinning his arms to his side and crippling his legs. A scream died in his throat, impaled on pins of gold.

For a time Gwydion knew nothing but that terrible paralysis. Then a burst of light shattered the darkness around him. He opened his eyes and looked out on Cyric's throne room.

The shadows from the Burning Men danced along the walls, playing over the trophies hung carelessly about the room. Gwydion could see each individual bone in Cyric's throne, each perfectly tooled plate of purest silver or bronze on Gond's clockwork smiths. The Prince of Lies and the Wonderbringer stood before him, a strange look of pride on both their faces, though for very different reasons. For the first time the shade noticed that their human forms were facades, like costumes worn at a fancy dress ball. Power lurked in their unblinking eyes, radiated from them with every subtle movement. Their tangible forms were nothing more than puppets, no more living than carved husks of wood.

Gwydion could smell the gods' power, like the charge in the air before a violent storm. Other odors washed over him then—the stale blood on Cyric's blade; the musty, ancient bones, encrusted with bits of grave loam, that made up most of the hall's furnishings; the stench from the burning scribes; and the thin oil from the golems' gears. His own scent troubled him most. Mixed with the harsh, cold smell of the gold plate armor was an air of decay, of death. They were all a thousand times more subtle, a thousand times more powerful than any scent he'd detected in mortal life.

Gwydion's other senses began to take in the chamber, too. The bit crammed in his mouth had a vile, bitter taste, like wine just turning to vinegar. He could feel every bolt, every rivet in the armor, as if they'd always been part of his flesh. Each blow from the Wonderbringer's hammer had left an almost imperceptible mark on the metal, and for a moment Gwydion lost himself in studying each dent. Other sights and sounds and smells flooded in on him: the hiss of Jergal's cape as the seneschal floated to Cyric's side; the warmth from the fires surrounding the Burning Men; the distinctive, fetid odor wafting off the Slith as it meandered just beyond the castle walls. . . .

"It'll take him a bit to get used to the way the helmet boosts what he sees and hears," Gond said. He tossed a wrench to one of the golems, who snatched it out of the air with surprising agility. "So when do you want me to do the other eight for you?"

"Right away," Cyric said. "I've already chosen shades to power the rest of the armor."

Gond frowned and dug his fingers into his barbed wire beard. "Hmmm. This takes a lot of my concentration, to do the fitting right, and I've got other work to get to back in Concordant."

"I need these inquisitors right away," Cyric noted bluntly, then strolled back to his throne. "Mystra has robbed me of magic, and there's an insidious subversive turning my church in Zhentil Keep against me. That city holds my largest collection of worshipers. If I lose them, I won't have the power to control the Realm of the Dead." With sudden fury, he slammed a fist down on the throne. "Do you know what would happen if this place went into revolt and I couldn't put it down?"

Gond shrugged. "No, and I don't much care, either. I told you before, Cyric, it doesn't matter to me what you use the armor for, just so long as it ain't turned against my faithful. Beyond that—" he patted Gwydion on the shoulder "—I just want the world to see that artifice can outdo magic, given the right smith and a good set of raw materials."

"Nine clockwork knights will show off your craft better than one," Cyric replied, ridding himself of his theatrical anger like a snake shedding a dried skin. "Come, Gond. Be reasonable. . . ."

The God of Craft rolled his eyes. "From you that's almost funny," he said, then held up a beefy hand to stave off the death god's wrath. "All right. I'll do them all now."

At a nod from Gond, the golems hustled to the eight crates lined up at the other end of the hall and began to unpack them with noisy efficiency. The Wonderbringer turned to Gwydion. "Raise your left arm," he said gruffly.

Though he tried to fight the command, Gwydion felt his body do as the god had ordered. Gond watched the shade's movement with a practiced eye, walking around him to get a better vantage of the armor's performance. "If he can understand spoken commands, he'll be ready to go pretty soon," the Wonderbringer announced. "You can give him his marching orders anytime you want."

"You are to destroy all heretics in Zhentil Keep," Cyric said.

"Not good enough," Gond noted distractedly, gathering his tools for the next operation. "That kind of command'll just confuse him."

"You said he'd do anything I wished," Cyric rumbled. "Are you telling me now he can't?"

I believe you need to define your wishes more precisely, Jergal offered. *The shade must be told what you mean by heresy.*

Cyric paced to Gwydion's side. "We'll start with the obvious traitors, then," the Prince of Lies said. "You will destroy anyone who speaks out against me or my church within the walls of Zhentil Keep."

"Yeah, that'll do," Gond said. He tinkered with a sliding rivet at Gwydion's hip. "I hope he comes up against a mage first, a really powerful one. Any enchantment a mortal could wield will roll off this plate like rainwater off a tin roof."

"And the wizardry of an immortal?" Cyric asked. For the first time he seemed genuinely interested in the Wonderbringer's explanation.

"Never been tested, but the same thing should apply."

The Lord of the Dead paused and rubbed his pointed chin. "Jergal, I want you to attack the inquisitor. Engulf his arm."

But, Your Magnificence. All the work—

"Don't worry. If you harm him I won't be angry with you." Cyric leveled a warning finger at Gwydion. "You just stand there. Don't fight back."

Jergal swooped up to Gwydion's outstretched arm, swallowing the limb in the formless darkness that was his body. The seneschal's cloak seemed to devour the arm completely, then a faint glittering shone from the murk. A voiceless moan filled the hall, and Jergal retreated from the inquisitor. The golden gauntlet and brassard gleamed defiantly, unbreached and untarnished.

"Impressive," Cyric murmured. "Any normal shade would have been destroyed by that."

He drew Godsbane and brought the blade hard against the inquisitor's hand. Sparks shot into the air, metal grinding against metal with a terrible keening sound. But when the Lord of the Dead pulled the short sword away, only the slightest scar marred the gauntlet.

"What do you think you're doing?" Gond bellowed. "I didn't build this armor just for you to practice your swordsmanship on it."

"I needed to see if the armor was immune to *all* magic," Cyric murmured. He stared at the inquisitor, discomfort clear on his demonic features.

"That's what you asked for," Gond grumbled, "powered armor that's nonmagical. That's what you got. Not even Mystra herself could blast this suit—not unless the helmet's off. If someone gets the helmet off, all bets are canceled."

Gingerly the God of Craft ran his fingers along the scarred gauntlet. "Look. If you're worried about him turning against you, don't. The helmet was designed to make him follow your commands. No one can change the orders you gave him unless they get the thing off his head—and if they do that, it'll unbalance the suit." Gond rapped the breastplate with his grimy knuckles. "Then all you've got is a very nice set of plate, but nothing that can withstand a sword like yours."

Cyric nodded vaguely. "So how do I send him on his way?"

"Oh, he's already gearing up to follow your order," Gond said. "He should be on his way to the Keep any time now."

In a way, Gwydion had already left Bone Castle. His mind was focused entirely on the babel of voices he heard in the streets and houses of Zhentil Keep. When anyone mentioned Cyric or his church, the words rang in the inquisitor's ears. Hundreds of fervent prayers to the Lord of the Dead hummed continuously, punctuated by oaths sworn in Cyric's name. Church scholars debated the nature of the City of Strife and the denizens that resided there. In hushed tones, mothers warned their children to do as they were told, else the Prince of Lies would steal them away in the night.

The urge to find a heretic lay curled around Gwydion's heart, a coiled spring pressing him into action. He quickly learned to set aside the prayers of the faithful and the endless scholarly sparring. He focused instead on the mutterings of gin-soaked malcontents and greedy minor clerics. He could almost sense the creeping chill of heresy in their minds. Part of Gwydion, the part controlled by the armor, prayed the heretics would voice their treacherous thoughts. The rest of him railed impotently at the bloody deeds he knew he must commit in Cyric's name. . . .

In a litter-strewn back alley in the Keep's slums, some-one ridiculed the Prince of Lies, openly challenged his power.

Wires thrummed with power and precisely pitched tuning forks hummed in the inquisitor's guts. The mecha-nism tore open the curtain between Hades and the mortal realms. Gwydion took a tentative step forward into the swirling chaos, then another. Soon he was thundering across the heavens like a charging dragon, his natural speed heightened beyond belief by the Wonderbringer's armor.

The inquisition had begun.

* * * * *

As Fzoul and the other three conspirators conversed softly with their mysterious divine patron, Rinda jotted down the last of her notes on Cyric's years in Zhentil Keep's thieves' guild. She scanned the tight, cramped pages and shook her head. *The True Life* was a tale of helplessness and desperation, hardly the heroic paean to self-reliance the Prince of Lies had woven for the *Cyrinishad*.

After being sold to the guild by slavers, Cyric had strug-gled to earn his freedom through work for the guild-masters; he failed time and again to complete a job flaw-lessly, dooming himself to a life of servitude. Kindhearted people very much like Rinda herself helped him escape, helped him flee the city that would have ground him beneath its iron-shod heels had he stayed. His pockets bulging with the coins given to him in pity, the young Cyric traveled north on a misguided quest for the Ring of Winter. Had Kelemvor Lyonsbane not rescued him from the frost giants in Thar, the history of Faerun might have been very different indeed. . . .

As you leave here today, be wary of your words and your deeds, the melodious, disembodied voice proclaimed. The words seemed to fill Rinda's ramshackle home, driving away the bitter cold. *Cyric has grown suspicious of treachery within the Keep. He will be watching the city carefully. Without magic he may find it difficult to keep an eye focused on all his servants. But never underestimate him.*

"None of us are foolish enough to do that, I trust."

Rinda glanced at Fzoul Chembryl. The flame-haired Zhentarim agent stood statuelike in the room's center, his arms folded across his black-armored chest. His harsh features had twisted into a grimace at the warning; he knew that the death god's eyes were upon him at all times. Only the powers of their divine patron made it possible for him to attend these subversive meetings with little fear of discovery.

Like Fzoul, General Vrakk took the news seriously. The orc dropped his warty forehead into his hand and grunted his dismay. "What, we got to sneak around even more now?"

There are rumors in the heavens that Cyric has purchased a cache of weapons from Gond, the voice said. *It may be some mechanical device that will allow him to compensate for his loss of sorcerous power.*

Rinda felt the walls close in just a little. "So what are you saying? Aren't we safe here anymore?" She dropped her pen, leaving a smudge of ink in the corner of the rough parchment page spread before her.

The shield I have in place over this home still blocks Cyric's sight, still makes it appear as if you are going about your normal business, Rinda. As long as any of you are in this place, I can guarantee your safety.

"What about the cover you provide for me?" Fzoul asked angrily. "If you don't create some sort of illusion to let Cyric think I'm still at my keep, he'll get suspicious. I can't just happen to disappear each time we have a meeting."

"And me!" Vrakk growled. "Me supposed to be in barracks now."

Hodur paused in his dice game with Ivlisar just long enough to chuckle at the others' discomfort. "Maybe we'll just have to do without your company, orc," the dwarf noted.

"Hmmm. That would be too bad," the body snatcher added, munching on his everpresent bowl of beetles. "I was finally getting used to your smell—rather like an overturned cart of rotten gourds, as my nose tells it. What do you think, Hodur?"

Vrakk leaped to his feet, his sword in his gray-green paws. "You not so important no more," the orc hissed. "We get others to rally merchants."

The elf looked to Fzoul, but the red-haired Zhentarim shrugged. "He's right."

"The general has mistaken my jest for an insult," Ivlisar said unctuously. He pushed the sword tip away from his chest. "I apologize most completely."

At Vrakk's angry glare, Hodur added, "Yeah. Both of us."

This is no time to fight amongst ourselves, the voice said. The chords humming in each word soothed the tension gripping the room. *You must pool your talents if we are to stop Cyric's mad plans.*

"So what about the illusions?" Fzoul prompted.

I will maintain them for as long as I'm able, but do not count on meeting here again, Fzoul Chembryl. It requires a great deal of power for me to shield you and Vrakk from Cyric's eyes, the voice replied smoothly. *Fooling a god, especially a greater power like the Prince of Lies, is no easy matter—even for me.*

Rinda looked up from scraping the ink stain from the

parchment. "And who exactly are you?"

Come, Rinda. I've said before, it will be better for us all if you don't know.

"Better for you," the scribe muttered. "I can't see how it helps me one little bit."

I abhor this trickery, the voice said, suddenly full of righteous fury. *Illusions and deception are loathsome to me. But there's no other way to counter Cyric's book, to let the world know the true tale of his life.*

"Anything for a good story, eh?" Hodur added. "I wish the unpleasant little sot had been more exciting as a mortal. Ain't it possible to spice up the story a bit—let him win just a couple of fights against the thieves' guild or the critters he chased after in Thar?"

Cyric's life was like most others, for much of his mortal span, the voice said coldly. *But surely he has proven since the Time of Troubles that his early failures were deceptive.*

"Deceptive," Hodur scoffed. "I just call it dull."

In the uncomfortable silence that followed, the dwarf gestured to the elven graverobber, then lumbered to the door. "We're off," Hodur blurted. "Down to the Serpent for some cheerier company. We'll be back, though." He grinned antagonistically at Fzoul. "Some of us aren't important enough for the gods to watch from highsun to highsun."

No one is beyond Cyric's attention, Hodur, especially in this city. You would do well to remember that.

Hodur rolled his eyes. "It's just like I said before—back when Rin used to talk to me. I just ain't impressed with you human gods. You want to see an evil bugger in action some time, take a look at Abbathor, the dwarven God of Greed."

"Or Everan Ilesere, our God of Mischief," the body snatcher added, a weird pride in his voice. "What a rotten item he is."

Hodur nodded enthusiastically, swung the door wide, and took a step into the street. "They know what they want, and they just come right out and take it. None of this sneaking around stuff or toying with mortals." He chuckled into his beard. "All this creeping about makes me think Cyric's just afraid of getting caught with his hand in the collection box. He's just a cowardly—"

The dwarf walked right into a wall of gold plate mail. The giant who stood before him was at least ten feet tall, not counting the horns jutting from his helmet.

"What the hell are you supposed to be?"

The inquisitor clamped palms the size of skillets down on either side of Hodur's head and lifted him from the ground. The barbed hooks in the strange knight's gauntlets dug deep into the dwarf's face. Two dozen rivulets of blood began to stream down Hodur's cheeks, staining his beard dark.

The dwarf managed a scream, though whether it was a cry of anger or terror was never quite clear to Rinda. He brought both his heavy boots into the knight's stomach in a savage kick. The blow didn't so much as scuff the breast-plate. With thick, fumbling fingers, he reached toward the inquisitor's eyes, ready to gouge them out, but the razored edges around the eyeholes sliced away the tips of all his digits. Hodur's vision had begun to fog with pain, but he could still see the thousands of tiny skulls engraved into the armor laughing at him with malefic glee.

"Die, heretic," Gwydion said, managing the words as best he could around the bit in his mouth. He pressed his palms together. The dwarf's head buckled like a melon under a giant's heel.

His reaction numbed by gin and fear, Ivlisar only then reached out for his friend, hoping to pull him back into the scribe's house. It was far too late. Hodur's gory, lifeless body slipped from the inquisitor's gauntlets and dropped to the cobbles. The elf fell to his knees beside the corpse and cradled it in his arms.

Rinda started forward, but Fzoul grabbed her by the arm. "Stay still," the priest hissed.

The scribe struggled against Fzoul's grip, but their godly patron said, *Do as he says*. The words were full of discord, the pitch broken by a clarion note of fear.

Rinda turned tearing eyes on the thing towering over Hodur's body. The gold-armored knight stared back through the doorway, confusion clear in his eyes. It seemed as if he could feel their presence somehow. Yet his senses told him that the room was empty, save for the elf in the doorway.

The five of them stood frozen in that tableau for a moment—Ivlisar huddled on the ground; Vrakk crouched and waiting, his sword at the ready; Fzoul holding Rinda, both trembling more than a little at the sight of the inquisitor; and Gwydion, blood dripping from his gauntlets, lost in a sea of prayers and curses. Finally the knight turned and stepped through a portal that appeared in the air before him.

The image of the inquisitor burned itself into Rinda's thoughts, remaining clear and vital long after Ivlisar had dragged Hodur's corpse away—no doubt to sell it on the black market. The knight's eyes remained the sharpest part of that memory. They'd held no malice, no anger, just an overwhelming pall of helplessness. The look was a familiar one to the scribe; many of the slum's most desperate inhabitants watched her with eyes like those when they explained why they'd sold their bodies in the brothels or betrayed their families to the city watch for a few coppers' reward.

But that wasn't the reason the image plagued her thoughts. In looking into those bleak eyes, so devoid of hope, Rinda had seen herself.

XII

PUPPETS ON PARADE

*Wherein Xeno Mirrormane and the Church of
Cyric put on a parade for the citizens of
Zhentil Keep, and General Vrakk attends
a puppet show much lauded by the
crowned heads of Faerun.*

To Vrakk, the gaudy procession moving through the
crowded marketplace seemed more appropriate to a cir-
cus than a religious festival, though in Zhentil Keep, the
two had become one and the same.

A small army of priests wrapped in dark purple robes
led the way. They chanted a prayer to Cyric, their voices
rising and falling with their steps. Four across and twenty-
five deep, the lines passed with military precision. Vrakk
grunted at that. A city where the priesthood attracted
better soldiers than the regular army was no place for
him.

And if the clerics' show of marching skill weren't enough to bring his blood to a boil, Vrakk had merely to remind himself what had brought him to the market this day—crowd patrol duty. A decorated general, veteran of Azoun's crusade, and he'd been assigned to watch for pickpockets and flashmen in the marketplace. Just thinking about it made him snort in anger.

The prayer at an end, the priest-horde held their hands up to the clear winter sky in one final burst of devoted worship. Silver bracelets, symbols of their enslavement to the Prince of Lies, glinted brightly in the morning sunlight. "O Master of the Heavens and the Earth, we are yours to wield against heretics, living swords to smite unbelievers!"

Vrakk suppressed the urge to spit.

Behind the chanting priests came a long line of creatures, both rare and common. The people in the marketplace perked up at the sight of the beasts. They'd given the clerics a respectful sort of attention, conducting their transactions at somewhat less than a shout, but even the merchants paused in hawking their overpriced foodstuffs, cheap gin, and threadbare linens to watch the procession of animals.

"These creatures and many like them have been captured in the name of Cyric to make the world more secure for his faithful," a barker cried stridently. His clean white clothes and scrubbed face made him stand out amongst the grubby commoners and travel-stained merchants. "Even the most dread beasts in the wild lands hereabouts quake before Cyric's devoted warriors. . . ."

Five bears led the way. They'd been roused from their winter hibernation by some overzealous hunter. Now they lumbered along, their mouths muzzled shut, a canvas sack fastened around each paw. Like most of the creatures in the parade, the bears were kept away from the crowd by bored-looking soldiers, who held either short leashes or thick oak switches. From the sad state of the beasts, Vrakk guessed they'd already been beaten nearly to death. The job would probably be finished once the procession was over.

A huge carnivorous ape followed, along with a tiger, a motley collection of wolves, and a man-sized lizard dredged up from some subterranean lair. Its eyes were sightless, pale white and squinting against the morning. Next came a pair of lions and a gigantic wild boar, neither of which had been captured anywhere near Zhentil Keep.

A trio of spear-toting soldiers prodded a minotaur along. Children taunted the great bull-headed guardian of lost tombs and labyrinths, waving bits of red cloth to catch its attention. The minotaur nearly got away from its handlers when a drunken man got too close. He'd been trying to tantalize the starving beast with a chunk of stale bread, but the minotaur would have taken the man's arm right up to the elbow, if it had been given half a chance.

"You've nothing to fear," the barker shouted, noting the disquiet in the faces of the people nearest the minotaur. "So long as you're faithful to Cyric, no harm will come your way."

On a cart drawn by an elephant, a merman shivered in a huge tank of water. The scales on his fish's tale were dark with some disease, the muscles on his human torso flabby from long captivity. He stared out at the crowd with pleading eyes—a pointless gesture in the Keep, where slave auctions were as common as drunken brawls.

The prize attraction came next: a very young white dragon. The wyrm was festooned with chains and surrounded by a dozen brawny warriors. It couldn't have been more than ten feet long from its blunted snout to the tip of its tail, with wings that had been clipped to prevent the beast from flying away. As it moved along, the dragon pulled and tugged against the chains, dragging first one, then another of its captors closer to its steel-muzzled jaws. Each time the wyrm balked, a Zhentilar carrying a torch scalded its tail until the beast shrieked in protest and lurched forward a few more steps.

Vrakk stared in amazement as the dragon approached; the Zhentilar had branded its flank with Cyric's holy symbol and the gauntlet-and-gem crest of Zhentil Keep. Though white dragons were, on the whole, less intelligent than other wyrms, they were prone to exacting violent retribution for wrongs against their kin. The other dragons in this hatchling's flight would devote themselves to wiping out the caravans traveling to and from the Keep, should they ever learn of the brands.

"If the priests ain't afraid of the wyrms," Vrakk heard one rather dimwitted merchant proclaim, "then the church has got to be as powerful as they say."

The tense silence that answered the man might as well have been a roaring shout of disagreement. Few in the Keep were foolish enough to openly question any claim made about the church's authority or its might, not when an inquisitor could appear at any moment to quell any spoken dissent. Thus silence had become the favored way to show dissatisfaction with Cyric or his minions. But if Xeno Mirrormane and his fanatics had their choice, even this mute revolt would soon be punishable by death.

Still, the Zhentish recognized the patriarch's power; when his carriage rolled into the marketplace, a dull cheer went up. Even the merchants, who resented the parade for taking up valuable trading time, showed their grudging support. A few particularly unctuous hawkers offered free food and wine to the contingent of Zhentilar surrounding the high priest's opulent carriage. As the merchants expected, the stern-faced soldiers silently refused the gifts, but the hawkers knew the appearance of support for Xeno and his troop might later buy valuable favors.

"An announcement by His Holiness!" a herald shouted, perched stiffly at the back of the patriarch's carriage. "All true citizens of Zhentil Keep, all true worshipers of the great god Cyric, gather close and hear the words of his most blessed servant!"

The carriage lurched to a stop, as it had in a dozen other crowded parts of the city, and Xeno Mirrormane rose to his feet. Hair silver-white and tangled, eyes narrowed with smug satisfaction, the patriarch looked out over the marketplace. "Lord Cyric has found it in his heart to grant Zhentil Keep the honor of becoming his residence in the mortal realms," Xeno crowed. "Because of this great honor, today has been declared a high holy day in the city. All citizens are free from taxes until sunset."

An enthusiastic and sincere cheer rang out from the crowd, lasting almost as long as the parade of beasts had taken to stagger through the market.

Finally Xeno spread his arms wide, as if to embrace the throng. "Know, then, that we must show our appreciation by declaring the Church of Cyric the only true spiritual body in the city. None of the pretender gods may receive worship from our homes or our temples, and all holy symbols and effigies devoted to them are to be considered contraband. Possession of such items after sundown this day will be construed as heresy against the church, bringing with it the punishment prescribed by law. All holdings of said heretical churches are now property of the city-state."

Xeno shared the carriage with the newly appointed lord of the Keep, who struggled now to his feet. His painfully thin face peeked out from a furred hood. "What the g-good p-patriarch says is the t-truth," he stammered, gesturing at the commoners with a small toy soldier. "Let all in my city know that Lord Cyric himself has d-declared our cause j-just!"

"Thank you, Ygway," Xeno said, rudely pushing the man back to the seat. "Be still, now. We wouldn't want you to tire yourself out."

In reply, the young man smiled stupidly and slouched down. He took up the rest of his toy army and recommenced the mock battle for the cushioned seat opposite him.

The crowded marketplace was now very nearly silent, save for the occasional tinny sound of discarded holy symbols dropping to the cobbles. Most present had lived through the scourging of Bane's image from the Keep after the Time of Troubles, but this was something very different. Cyric had replaced Bane as Lord of Strife. The gods now declared heretical still held court in the heavens, still held sway over the mortal realms.

Vrakk stood in a sea of shocked human faces, carefully taking stock of the patriarch and the addle-brained nobleman at his side. With the disappearance of Lord Chess a tenday past, the church had seized control of the city government, installing Ygway Mirrormane as Zhentil Keep's lord. Insanity ran in the Mirrormane family, or so the rumors said. After watching Xeno and his drooling, twitching nephew in action, Vrakk would disagree. It galloped like a Tuigan pony with its tail on fire.

"Know, too," Xeno announced, "that all travel from the city has been suspended, unless approved by both the church and the government. These restrictions will remain in effect until Lord Cyric declares the inquisition at an end."

With that, the patriarch gestured to his driver. His carriage lurched ahead—only to stop a moment later as a pile of dung was cleared from its path. Vrakk shook his head; the priests hadn't been bright enough to put the elephants at the rear of the procession.

A swarm of church novitiates, Cyric's holy symbol

tattooed upon their foreheads, set upon the marketplace in the wake of the parade. They gathered up the discarded holy symbols, as well as any merchandise that might be ornamented with the newly contraband images. Other priests posted broadsheets repeating Xeno's proclamation or scanned the crowd for anyone overly distraught by the announcements. Such unseemly sorrow could only come from a heretic.

Vrakk paid the clerics little attention as he continued his patrol of the small market. The courtyard held a variety of stalls. Vendors hawked everything from dried meats to woolen blankets. It wasn't the largest market in the city, its wares rather mundane and uninteresting, but that was precisely why the orcish general had been assigned to patrol it. For a soldier of his rank and renown, the duty was tantamount to sweeping the streets.

"Hey, pig-snout," someone snarled, grabbing the back of Vrakk's coarse cloak. "You deaf as well as ugly? I said give me a hand with this heretic."

The orc turned slowly. The young man's imperious tone had announced him as a priest, even before Vrakk saw his dark robes and sour, sanctimonious grimace. "Call me General," Vrakk rumbled, slapping the insignia on his leather breastplate. "Or sir."

"No priest of Cyric will ever call an orc *sir*," the young man snapped. "And no orc should be a general in the service of a holy city like Zhentil Keep." He yanked a woman forward by the hair and pushed her at Vrakk. "Take her into custody."

The woman fell to her knees, dark hair streaming around an olive-skinned face. This was no Zhentish woman, but a trader from Turmish or one of the other southern lands. In her slender hands she clasped something, desperate to keep it away from the priest. "The patriarch," she began tearfully, "he said we have until sundown to destroy our holy symbols. Please, I am leaving this very day with a caravan to my home in Alaghon. I have permits approved by the church and the nobles. My god will not understand if I desecrate his image needlessly."

"She right." Vrakk pulled the woman to her feet with one meaty, gray-green paw. "That what Mirrormane say. I not so deaf I not hear that."

The priest shoved a large sheet of paper right up to the orc's snout. "The proclamation says all holy symbols not issued by Cyric's church are to be destroyed."

Vrakk realized then the priest was not going to be bullied, so he let a practiced facade of doltishness slide over his features. His mouth hung open just enough to show his dark tongue, and a line of spittle drooled around the two yellowed tusks jutting up from his lower jaw. "Uh, me not read Zhentish," he lied, fixing beady red eyes on the priest in his best vacant stare. "Can only do what Mirrormane say, and he say let 'em alone until sundown."

The Turmish merchant took the cue, sliding unnoticed into the crowd as the young priest focused his anger on the orcish Zhentilar. "Why are you still allowed to wear a uniform?" the cleric demanded. "I thought all your kind were put to work repairing the bridges."

He was right; most of the orcs and even the half-orcs in the Zhentilar had been given the inglorious task of laboring on the twin bridges crossing the Tesh. Vrakk was a war hero, though. His loyal service to Lord Chess and the city had gained him an exemption from that insulting work—even though the church had pushed for a ban on all nonhumans in the Keep's military.

"Me too stupid to work on bridges," Vrakk muttered, turning his back on the sputtering priest. "Gotta go check merchant permits now."

The orcish soldier tried his best to swallow his anger,

but it burned in his throat like a ball of flaming pitch. He'd been a good soldier, a tireless defender of the Keep and the Church of Cyric. Orcish souls meant nothing to the Prince of Lies, though, and his minions had done all they could to drive them out of the city.

As he went about the dreary task of checking the guild licenses and merchant permits in the marketplace, Vrakk found himself snarling almost as much as the priests scouring the stalls for contraband—that is, until he came upon an old man setting up a rickety puppet stage at the market's edge.

"Here you are, my good fellow," the gaunt man chimed as he handed Vrakk his city permit.

"Show been checked by priests?" Vrakk grunted.

The puppeteer bowed broadly, swirling his mottled cloak and flourishing his broad-brimmed hat. "Last time I was in this fair city," he chirped. "Stamp's on the back of the permit. A bit weathered, but that can't be helped, not when I've spent the last annum traveling the world, you know."

Vrakk handed the man the tattered slip of parchment and turned away. "If you got a knuckler, he better be in with the thieves' guild. They chop his hands off if he ain't."

The man looked shocked at the suggestion he'd hire a pickpocket to work the crowd, though the practice was common enough. "Otto Marvelius has never bilked a patron of a single copper. Good, wholesome entertainment's what I offer. Shows that would bring a smile even to one of Cyric's priests—" he leaned close and winked conspiratorially "—and we both know how tough a crowd they can be, eh?"

The puppeteer went about his work, whistling a bawdy tavern song popular in the less reputable ports along the Sword Coast. The striped curtains and the bright awning he rolled out over the boxlike stage drew both children and adults like some enchanted piper. Vrakk milled at the fringes of the growing crowd of urchins and commoners, watching for the almost inevitable petty crooks who'd come to prey upon them.

"Kind people of Zhentil Keep," Marvelius began, standing before the stage, "on this festive day, I have come to your great city to present a play both entertaining and enlightening. I have presented this pageant, known throughout the civilized world as 'The Rescue of the Tablets of Fate' or 'Cyric Wins the Day,' to the crowned heads of Cormyr and the emperors of fabled Shou Lung."

With theatrical flair he unfurled a huge roll of parchment, covered with seals and elaborately wrought signatures. "These affidavits, provided by such notables as Bruenor Battlehammer of Mithril Hall, Tristan Kendrick of the Moonshaes, and King Azoun IV of Cormyr, attest to the story's power to enthrall even the most unenlightened audience."

The parchment could have been signed by anyone, stated anything, since most of the people gathered before the stage couldn't read. Vrakk smirked at the expressions of awe riding over the sea of faces; Marvelius might not hire a pickpocket, but he was certainly a flashman in his own right.

Marvelius hung the scroll on one side of the stage, then took up another, less impressive piece of parchment. "I have also had the chance to present this play in each of the various dales to your south."

A hiss, very much expected by the showman, slithered from the crowd. Marvelius held up a restraining hand and presented the second parchment, blotchy with spilled ink, food stains, and huge, thick **X**s. "They tried their best to sign an affidavit, too, but this was all they could manage." He waited for the chuckles to subside just a little, then added, "Good thing Elminster taught Lord Mourngrym and the rest of the, er, *warriors* of Shadowdale how to make **X**s or the thing would be blank—and speaking of puppets, let's get on with the show, shall we?"

The laughter and rough clapping filled the time it took Marvelius to position himself behind the stage. By now Vrakk was almost mesmerized, watching the old man play the crowd. The Zhentish hated the dalesmen, especially Mourngrym and the men from Shadowdale, with a passion unrivaled. By insulting the nobleman and the old sage who advised him, Marvelius was certain to win over his audience—and more than a few coppers when his helper passed the collection box after the show.

A puppet of a raven-haired woman, with bone-white skin and strange scarlet eyes, appeared on the stage. Her blue-white robe and the farcical wand in her hand identified her as Midnight, the earthly avatar of Mystra. "Oh my," she said. "I wonder where the Tablets of Fate are hidden. Do you know where they are?" Her exaggeratedly shrill voice—provided by Marvelius's unseen assistant—made more than one child cover his ears with his hands.

Midnight leaned toward the audience. "Well, if none of you know, I'll bet I can guess who has them. Oh, Kelemvor? Where is my brave knight?"

The puppet depicting Kelemvor was as well-known as Mystra's: a hulking body supported a head divided equally into two faces. One side was human, with coarse features, all bristling sideburn and drooping mustache. The other was feline, a panther's head with a mouthful of sharp white teeth. The children shrieked in delighted fear as Kelemvor appeared behind Midnight, his panther face to the audience.

As Midnight turned, Kelemvor switched faces. "Here I be, my love," he answered, his words slurred drunkenly and dripping with stupidity.

"Do you have the tablets?" Midnight asked. "We must

get them to Mount Waterdeep and return them to Lord Ao."

"Well, why would we want to do that?" Kelemvor replied, scratching his head. He dropped out of sight, then returned with two nondescript squares meant to represent the sacred artifacts. "They'd make nice tables or even a good couple of chairs." He tried to sit on them.

Midnight hit him soundly with her wand. "Dolt. When we give these back to Lord Ao, he'll make us gods." The puppets froze and trembled in surprise at this news, just long enough for the audience to have their fill of shouting and hissing. "And then we can give all the people we like lots of power."

"Like the Zhentish?" Kelemvor asked foolishly.

The crowd cheered, but Midnight silenced them. "Of course not. We like the dalesmen, especially that handsome Lord Mourngrym. If we get to the mountain first, we'll become gods and help *them* take over the world!"

The chorus of boos was silenced by the appearance of a handsome, hawk-nosed Cyric-puppet at the edge of the stage. "This will not do!" he shouted to the audience, brandishing his rose-hued sword above the heads of the children huddled close to watch the play.

As Midnight and Kelemvor trudged along toward Waterdeep, Cyric crept behind them, keeping to the fringes of the stage. The two occasionally paused on their mock quest to beat each other or embrace frantically. Then Cyric would sneak in, getting closer and closer to stealing the Tablets of Fate. Something different caused the thief to be captured each time—and each time he tricked the foolish duo into letting him go.

"The old prig's good at his job. I'll say that much for him," came a whispered voice at Vrakk's ear.

"Go 'way," the orc rumbled, not bothering to look at Ivlisar.

The body snatcher snorted in mock outrage. "Fine way to treat a chum, this is. Just because I haven't seen you in a tenday. . . . Well, that can't be helped now, can it? Circumstances beyond our control and all that."

Vrakk tried to look casual as he walked around the periphery of the audience, but the elf stuck to his side. The orc didn't need to see Ivlisar to know he'd been drinking; the body snatcher's breath sent the stench of cheap gin into the air with each syllable.

"It took me days to find you."

"Wasted time," Vrakk grumbled.

"I'm leaving the city."

"So?"

Ivlisar stepped in front of the orc, his shoulders squared in something akin to military fashion. His rail-thin frame was hidden beneath a triple layer of overcoats, with a gray cloak wrapped around his shoulders. He moved almost as stiffly as the puppets battling violently across the stage, though his face was very much animated by shock and anger.

"Don't you care about my connections?" the elf asked, flushing red to the tips of his pointed ears. "You need me, you know."

Nervously Vrakk scanned the crowd. No priest nearby, though the grimacing novitiate who'd insulted him earlier was watching the puppet show close to the stage. "We find another merchant. Bye."

"This place isn't safe for dwarves or elves anymore," Ivlisar rambled. "Just ask poor Hodur. And the church has no love of orcs. Why, I'm betting it'll soon be heresy to be born anything other than human. And those inquisitors—I hear Cyric's teaching 'em to read minds." He'd lost control now, the pent up fear making his voice much louder than discretion would have advised. "Then you won't have to say anything against the church. You'll only need to—"

The orc slapped a hand over Ivlisar's thin-lipped mouth. "Shut up," he hissed. Some of the adults nearby had turned to look at the body snatcher, their attention drawn from the puppet show by his ranting.

"Stupid drunk," Vrakk shouted, shoving the elf to the cobbles. "Go sleep it off."

"Heresy!" someone cried.

Vrakk looked up, ready to be confronted with the accusing fingers of the crowd around him. But it wasn't Ivlisar who'd drawn the ire of Cyric's faithful.

"That's not the way the story goes," the sour-faced novitiate shouted toward the stage. "Cyric didn't need to steal the Tablets of Fate! You make our god out to be nothing more than a common thief!"

The old showman peered over the top of the stage, along with the woman who apprenticed with him. "B-But the church," Marvelius stammered. "The patriarch approved this last year. He said the story happened this way. Look, I'll be glad to change—"

It was far too late for apologies or retractions. Three inquisitors appeared, one to either side of the stage, one behind it. The gold-armored knights of Cyric shattered the rickety wooden box, shredding the brightly dyed curtains and awning. The crowd scattered then, screaming, and it was all Vrakk could do to keep them from trampling each other and the surrounding merchant stalls. Had the parents not hustled their children away at the first shouts of heresy, the scene would have been much more chaotic.

Otto Marvelius remained a flashman until the end, trying to hide the fear in his voice as he said, "There's been a misunderstanding of local custom. Nothing more than that. We'll rectify any damage done and tithe a substantial sum to the church to—to—to pay for proper shows. They can be put on in this very marketplace. . . ."

The puppeteer was still trying to smooth things over

when one of the inquisitors drove a fist through his chest.

Marvelius's apprentice took the attack not nearly so well. She screamed and curled up into a tight ball, no doubt hoping with all her heart she'd wake up at any moment and find this ghastliness a horrible dream. It wasn't to be; the remaining armored destroyers of heterodoxy pulled her messily into two gory halves.

Then, after stomping all three puppets into shards, the inquisitors disappeared.

Panic clouded Ivlisar's eyes as he clung to Vrakk. "Please, I'm going to leave the city."

"I don't care!" the orc shouted. He tried to pry the body snatcher from one arm, doing his best to slow the frenzied crowd with the other.

"Get me a pass."

Vrakk stopped struggling, standing still at the center of the rushing mob. People crashed into his steel-muscled frame, but they found him as rooted as a thousand-year-old oak. Twice, Ivlisar was dragged a few steps away by the throng. Both times the elf struggled back, his pleading eyes locked on the orc's gray-green face.

Then the mob was past, and the two stood face to face.

"I need a pass," Ivlisar repeated. "I've no legal trade, so the city won't grant me one. You have to do this for me. Fzoul might be able—"

"Never say his name out loud," Vrakk said.

"I'll say more than that." Nervously Ivlisar twisted his long fingers into the hem of his cloak.

"Don't," Vrakk warned simply.

"If you don't get me a pass—"

The body snatcher never finished the threat. Vrakk buried his sword deep in the elf's chest. Not the cleanest kill the orc had ever made, but certainly one of the quickest.

"What do you think you're doing?" the sour-faced priest

shouted as he came upon Vrakk cleaning his sword on the elf's corpse.

"He curse church, so I kill him," the orc murmured. "Save gold knights trip back here."

"What did he say?"

A thousand glorious insults flew into Vrakk's mind, but the blood-slicked cobbles reined in his tongue before he could speak. Whatever slight he attributed to the dead man would be his heresy alone.

The orc pressed one nostril closed with a warty finger, then blew the contents of the other noisily onto the ground. "Uh, me no remember."

"You're no better than an animal," the novitiate said, disgust written all over his features. He pointed to the shattered stage and snapped, "Get that mess cleaned up, then dispose of these corpses before the resurrection men cart them off."

"Not so many body snatchers around now, I hear," Vrakk mumbled facetiously.

He set about building a fire to destroy the stage, the ruined puppets, and eventually even the corpses, though the merchants wouldn't like the smell of the place when they returned.

Wait 'til *The True Life* is finished, Vrakk reminded himself, glancing back at the novitiate. Then it'll be our turn to choose which puppets go onto the pyre. . . .

XIII

THE PRICE OF VICTORY

Wherein the Lady of Mysteries proves she
understands the value of good craftsmanship, but
few in the Circle of Greater Powers appreciate
how she puts that understanding into action.

Gwydion couldn't remember how many people he'd
slaughtered, how much blood he'd spilled in Cyric's name.
A part of his soul screamed each time he wrapped his
gauntleted hands around someone's throat, but that feeble
cry could never dull the urgency of the death god's command to kill all heretics. Gwydion knew he had no choice
but to obey Cyric's mad orders. That didn't matter,
though. The guilt was still his to bear.

The babel of voices from the Keep had quieted since his
transformation. Or perhaps Gwydion had grown accustomed
to the constant hum of prayers and pleas to the Prince of
Lies. Whichever was true, the results were the same: as

he hovered in a nether-plane, somewhere between the City of Strife and the mortal realms, Gwydion found himself enjoying an instant of near silence.

The nine inquisitors had done their job well. Only rarely did a heretic blurt out a denial of Cyric's power or refute his mandate to reign in the heavens. If the Lord of the Dead hadn't granted his patriarch the right to modify the definition of heresy, the knights of Hades might have remained idle for days on end. Now Gwydion spent his time culling out opponents to each new church edict. The heretics he faced were more often than not minor foes of Xeno Mirrormane, but opposing the patriarch had become just as deadly as insulting his god.

As for the eight remaining unholy knights, they'd been dispatched to other cities in Faerun, other places Cyric considered vital to the nurture of his cult. In Mulmaster and Teshwave and Yulash, inquisitors had begun new wars against heresy. Darkhold and the Citadel of the Raven, fortresses well-known as centers of Zhentarim intrigue, were also visited by the gold-armored terrors. Just as they had in the Keep, the inquisitors struck suddenly and violently against anyone who spoke out against the Prince of Lies or his church. The resistance in these places was stronger, but futile nonetheless.

And once these cities bowed to Cyric's will, there were many others waiting for a revelation of the death god's truth and his power. . . .

"Cyric's a coward. A god would have to be a coward to use clockwork thugs to watch over mortals!"

The vehemence of the insult shocked Gwydion out of his respite. After a tenday of vaguely muttered threats to minor priests or slurred, drunken rails against all the powers and fates—including the Lord of the Dead—the clear, purposeful challenge rang out across the inquisitor's consciousness like a barrage of Shou fireworks.

Gwydion stepped into the mortal realms at the center of the Force Bridge. The ice-choked Tesh flowed sluggishly beneath the long stone bridge, and gulls wheeled overhead. Before him, on one of the low railings that edged the span, sat a stoop-backed old woman. She looked as frail as elven crystal, so thin the cold winter wind might pull her up into the twilight just now settling over the Keep.

"There you are," she cackled. Stiffly the old woman stood, and the blue-white shawl dropped from her shoulders. The cloth slithered along the ground like a huge deadfall leaf.

Gwydion took two quick steps toward the heretic, then stopped. This was no mortal. Beneath the aged facade lurked the power of a god. The inquisitor could smell the crackle of lightning in her movements, could feel the tremor of the bridge at her every footstep. And all around the woman, a million thin cords of light flowed from her body, linking her to the magical weave surrounding the world. This could be none other than the Goddess of Magic herself.

"Goddess," the inquisitor said thickly. From his lips, the word sounded as if it were the most vile curse he could manage. "Heretic."

"Well," the old woman said, surprise playing over her features. "Either you're more than I expected or my illusions are not very good." The facade slipped away, pouring from her like water. Beneath lay the young, raven-haired avatar Mystra usually adopted in the mortal realms.

As Gwydion started forward again, the shawl curled around his foot. It rubbed up against him for a moment like a house cat, then it, too, transformed. The tattered cloth became a sheet of magical force. A flick of Mystra's fingers, and the glowing sheet slipped beneath the inquisitor's boot. It strained, trying to topple the giant, but soon fell limp.

Gwydion pointed his toes down and ran the boot's razor tips along the shimmering square. The god-forged metal tore through the enchantment, shredding it into blue-white wisps that quickly dissipated.

Shouts of alarm went up from both ends of the bridge. Orcs from the Zhentilar lined the span's southern end, far from the fighting; they paused in shoring up the support beams to gawk and jeer at the strange warriors. On the opposite bank, a horn sounded from the city walls. Human soldiers with longbows appeared atop the twin gate-houses, while others pushed the huge gates closed.

Mystra glanced in both directions, checking to be certain none of the mortals were coming to join the battle. Gwydion used that momentary distraction to charge. When the Lady of Mysteries turned toward the inquisitor again, he towered over her, fists drawn back to strike. She barely managed to dodge the duel blows, which fell like thunderbolts against the bridge. Huge chucks of stonework plummeted from the walkway into the Tesh.

Fear shook the part of Gwydion's mind left unfettered within the Gondish shell. He was attacking a goddess! His fear demanded he run, to escape the fight, but the urgency of Cyric's command overwhelmed those thoughts. Mystra was a heretic. She must be destroyed.

The inquisitor charged again, feinting first to the right, then darting left. He caught the goddess's arm as she attempted to sidestep the lightning-quick strike. The avatar's elbow splintered in Gwydion's grip. The hooks in his gauntlets tore long ribbons of flesh from her arm as she pulled away.

Mystra showed no fear of Gwydion, no pain from his assault. With nimble fingers she traced an arcane pattern along her battered arm, and the wounds healed.

Enraged, Gwydion lashed out again, and again Mystra sidestepped the blow. The inquisitor's fist knocked another jagged hole in the bridge. Stone and timber fell from beneath the goddess's feet, but she floated above the breach. As Mystra landed on the other side of the gap, she cast one of the most powerful enchantments known in the planes.

At a single word, unknown by all but the most learned wizards, a sphere of pale silvery light formed around Mystra and Gwydion. The inquisitor felt the jolt of the spell, felt his limbs slow. His heightened senses registered a dozen weird occurrences simultaneously. The debris from the hole between him and the goddess had stopped falling toward the river. The fragments hung suspended in air, motionless. The sounds of the city's harbor and bustling streets, the trumpeting from the battlements and the shouts of the orcs, all were suddenly banished from his ears. The subtle wear of the wind, of decay, against the bridge had ceased.

Mystra had stopped time itself.

The spell should have been enough to end the battle. Yet, almost as quickly as his senses told him what Mystra had done, the inquisitor found himself moving again.

For the first time, Gwydion could read the goddess's emotions on her beautiful features. Faint surprise showed in her inhuman eyes, but the grim line of her mouth told the knight Mystra had expected the spell to fail. She was testing his limits, toying with him. Again Gwydion wanted to flee, but Cyric's commands drove him forward, toward the trap he now knew the Lady of Mysteries had set for him.

The silver sphere disappeared, and time rushed in to fill the void. The wave of sound and smells and sensations shook the inquisitor, unbalanced him long enough for Mystra to summon a servant from her castle in Nirvana.

The marut Mystra called was nowhere near as large as the one Gwydion had seen on the Fugue Plain, gathering up the souls of her faithful, but it was still huge. The

hulking creature towered twenty-five feet into the air, its
stony flesh as black as the walls of Zhentil Keep. Enchanted
armor, blessed by Mystra to withstand any physical blow,
covered its arms and broad chest. In one hand the marut
clutched a length of sturdy chain, in the other an enormous cage.

The onyx-skinned creature appeared right in front of
the inquisitor. The sound of their collision rolled over the
city, a tortured clash of unbreakable metal and flesh that
was stone. Those in the Keep who'd lived through the
Time of Troubles trembled at the din; it echoed over their
homes and shops much the same way another cacophony
had in those dark times: the cataclysmic destruction of
Bane's temple.

Both the inquisitor and the marut fell back a few steps,
ready to clash again. The marut struck first, slamming the
cage down around Cyric's minion. Gwydion grabbed the
bars. His strength should have been enough to tear the
steel like paper, but it held fast against him. More bars slid
from the frame to close off the bottom before the inquisitor could dig down through the bridge. And when he tried
to step out of the mortal realms, retreating back through
the planes to Cyric's domain, he found the armor's mechanisms baffled.

"Gond was right," Mystra said as she walked around the
cage. "The armor is utterly magic resistant."

This cage is not magic? the marut asked. In the goddess's
mind, the creature's voice echoed as if it had come from
deep within a cave. *Surely this is no mundane device to hold
such a warrior.*

"Mechanical," Mystra replied softly. She continued to
circle the prison like a curious child at a zoo. "The cage is
mechanical, just like the armor. The Wonderbringer built
the bars specially to counter the strengths and prey upon
the weaknesses of the armor he built."

Then the cage is like a shield of spell turning?

Mystra smiled. "More like fighting fire with fire. Force and counter-force."

Bah. I still say this is magic somehow.

The marut sullenly hooked the length of chain to the cage's top so it could carry the thing without getting too close to the inquisitor.

"It's only magic if you don't understand how it works," the Lady of Mysteries murmured.

Gwydion mirrored the goddess's movements as she paced, trying to grab her whenever she got close. After one swipe snagged her hair, Mystra paused in her study of the armor and looked more carefully at the helmet, at the soul trapped inside. Though the inquisitor still thrashed against the bars, his eyes—Gwydion's eyes—stared helplessly at the goddess from the golden prison.

"Can you hear me?" Mystra asked.

The part of Gwydion's soul dominated by the armor screamed for the heretic's blood. No matter how hard he tried, he couldn't force himself to speak or even move in some way that might answer the goddess.

"Don't worry," Mystra said after a time. "I'll get you out of there once we capture your eight brothers. Then we'll see about making Cyric pay for this."

A maelstrom raged inside Gwydion's head. Shouted prayers to Cyric and solemnly sworn oaths blurred together with the whispered heresies he could no longer punish. He threw himself against the bars time and again, but deep inside, at the heart of the storm, Gwydion gave silent thanks the killing had been stopped.

* * * * *

"Lady Mystra," Tyr said, "you stand accused of willfully endangering the Balance, the most serious charge that can be leveled against any deity. How do you plead?"

"I enter no plea," the Goddess of Magic snapped. "The charge is ludicrous."

At his desk to Tyr's right, Oghma sighed. "I'll take that to mean 'not guilty,' " the Binder said without a trace of humor.

The Pavilion of Cynosure was packed with gods and demipowers from all parts of Faerun. Deities rarely seen in the pavilion—Labelas Enoreth, elven God of Longevity; Garl Glittergold, Father of All Gnomes; dour, stone-featured Grumbar, the Boss of Earth, ruler of that grim elemental plane; and a hundred others—took up long-unused tiers along both sides of the room. Public trials against one of the Circle of Greater Powers were rare, and few would miss the opportunity to witness such a spectacle.

Mystra had taken up her traditional post, toward the back of the wizard's workshop that she perceived the pavilion to be. By her side stood the nine inquisitors, imprisoned in their cages of unbreakable, Gond-crafted steel. Tyr sightlessly faced the goddess from the opposite side of the workshop, clutching the lectern with his lone hand as if the box were a pulpit and he an impassioned preacher; there was nothing the God of Justice loved more than a trial, especially one involving his fellow deities.

"Members of the Circle," Tyr began, "Lady Mystra stands accused of carrying out a vendetta against the rightful Lord of the Dead, with blatant disregard for the consequences to the Balance. To reach a verdict, we must consider two—"

"If my crime is so terrible," Mystra snapped, "why haven't I been brought before Ao?"

Tyr scowled at the interruption, but Oghma looked up from his notes. "Your accuser demanded the greater powers sit as the jury," said the Patron of Bards. "As a member of the Circle, that was his right."

Oghma's voice was full of anger, a mob singing a bloody song at a lynching. The tone of it brought a look of disbelief to Mystra's eyes. "Did you have me summoned here?" she murmured. When the Binder shook his head, the goddess glanced at the other greater powers scattered around the pavilion floor. "Then who?"

"Can't you guess?" Cyric called from the mob of lesser powers and inhuman deities crowded in the tiers. He stood to face the Lady of Mysteries.

"And the rest of you took this seriously?" Mystra scoffed.

"Why not? I have proof enough to convict you three times over," Cyric purred. "You've done everything you can to prevent me from executing my office. I realize now the only way to save myself—and stop you from upsetting the Balance—is to ask for the Circle's help." He smirked. "You see, I can play by the rules, even if you won't."

"This is absurd," Mystra said. She summoned a spell to mind that would remove her and the caged inquisitors to Nirvana.

"Consider the trial more seriously, Lady," Oghma warned. "Your worshipers face total sanctions from the rest of the Circle if you don't cooperate."

The Goddess of Magic paused, stunned by the threat. Sanctions meant total isolation for her worshipers; the greater powers would deny her faithful the benefits of their offices. Lathander would stop the dawn from rising over church grounds, and Chauntea would prevent their crops from growing. Mystra's faithful would be refused entrance to the Fugue Plain if they died, and any knowledge preserved in their libraries would vanish. There was but one way for the mortals to escape these harsh measures: abandon their worship of the goddess. It wouldn't take long for most to turn away, and those few devout souls who didn't would soon perish. With no mortal worshipers, the Goddess of Magic would cease to exist.

"Cyric is using you against me," Mystra pleaded. "Can't you see that?"

"I'll have no part in judging the evidence," Cyric called. "I'm an innocent bystander. The wronged party, if you want to be totally accurate."

"So says the Prince of Lies," Tyr noted flatly from the podium. "Do not doubt that we listen for the ring of truth in each word you utter, Cyric. And as for you, Mystra, you should know that I will be a fair and just judge, conducting this trial in accordance with all the laws of the Balance, as decreed by Ao himself."

Tyr cleared his throat. "As I was saying, to reach a verdict we must consider two questions. First, did Mystra act beyond the demands of her office in battling the Lord of the Dead? Second, if this is true, did she endanger the Balance by doing so?" He gestured to Cyric. "You may state your case."

"With the inquisitors, I'd hoped to counter the heresy growing in my church," the Prince of Lies said. "Mystra took it upon herself to foil that plan—even though it had nothing to do with her responsibilities as Goddess of Magic."

Tyr nodded and stroked his long white beard. "Do you have anything to say in your defense regarding the capture of the inquisitors, Lady?"

"They were threatening everyone's worshipers," Mystra replied. "They had to be stopped."

"The inquisitors didn't single out your lackeys," Cyric said. "They struck down *anyone* who spoke against me. If some of your faithful were harmed, they brought it upon themselves." The Lord of the Dead turned to the crowd. "As I see it, the inquisitors were like a force of nature—like one of Talos's storms. Surely Mystra doesn't reserve the right to counter any force that *might* harm her worshipers. If this is the case, there can be no deep water, no poisonous plants, no weapons or—"

"We understand," Shar interrupted. The Mistress of the Night stretched languidly. "Come now, Mystra. You must be able to offer up a better reason why these clockwork warriors concern the Goddess of Magic."

"The armor is constructed to withstand all enchantments," Mystra replied. "By their very nature the inquisitors attempt to prove craft's supremacy over the Art."

Tyr paused to consider that claim. "True enough," the God of Justice noted after a moment. "And you might have been able to sway us with that argument—had you yourself not sought the aid of Gond in combating the inquisitors. The cages you had the Wonderbringer construct endanger the place of magic in the world, too, if we follow your logic."

When Mystra failed to offer another reason for her actions, Tyr rapped the podium with his bony knuckles. "It's clear, then, that the goddess went beyond the boundaries of her office in battling Cyric." The rest of the Circle chorused their agreement. "Now," Tyr added darkly, "we must consider the threat this posed to the Balance."

Before the God of Justice finished speaking, Cyric was on his feet, demanding to be heard. "Zhentil Keep holds the largest and most important gathering of my faithful in the mortal realms. If heretics should succeed in turning the city against me, I'd lose so much power I might be unable to prevent a revolt in the City of Strife."

The Prince of Lies turned his seared, hellish features to the greater gods gathered on the pavilion floor. "All of you know that my realm in Hades is in perpetual unrest. And all of you know, too, what would happen if a revolt amongst my denizens caused my downfall: total destruction of the Balance. Until a new god could be found and placed on the throne in Bone Castle, no one in the mortal realms could die, no matter how grievous his wounds. All the newly dead would rise as undead, preying upon the living until— well, the scene is too gruesome to contemplate."

In the grim silence that followed his speech, Cyric sank slowly to his seat.

"Showmanship was always one of your strong suits, Cyric," Mystra noted dryly. "But this has nothing to do with a revolt in Hades."

"Yes, it does," Tyr said. "It has *everything* to do with Cyric and his realm." He took hold of the podium once more, bony knuckles white from his vicelike grip. "The crux of the evidence against you is this: You have taken it upon yourself to punish Cyric, to thwart whatever plans he hatches to further strife and death in the world. In doing so, you've forgotten two important facts. First, it is Cyric's office to create such discord in the mortal realms. Second, it is not your office to prevent that discord. You are the Goddess of Magic, Lady Mystra, not the harbinger of peace or the avenger of those done harm by Cyric's actions."

"The book he is forcing his minions to craft, that will affect all of you," Mystra said coldly. "But only a few of you have spoken out against Cyric for that. Where's the justice, then? When does the Balance swing against the whims of the Lord of the Dead?"

"As I have told you before, Lady, you must have patience," Oghma offered. "We've countered the book's creation so far, have we not? As for Cyric's other crimes . . . the Balance has always corrected such outrages in the past."

"And I'm willing to do some little part toward repairing any damage I might have caused in my anger at being cut off from the weave," Cyric offered. "Return the inquisitors to me, and I'll assure the Circle they will be used exclusively against my faithful in the future."

Mystra laughed bitterly. "But only if you're granted the use of magic again, right?"

"Just so, Lady." Cyric bowed. "Just so."

Lathander Morninglord stood, his eyes glowing with the soft light of dawn. "Mystra, we could see our way to dropping all charges against you," he began, "but only if you'll agree to this new beginning."

"None of you can see what a monster he is," the Lady of Mysteries said.

"A monster? How so?" Oghma asked, his voice edged in steel. "Because he uses illusions and deception to fool his victims? Consider how you drew the inquisitors into your trap, Lady."

"And there is the matter of the Chaos Hound," Cyric said smoothly. "The evidence found atop Blackstaff Tower—"

"You'd do well not to mention that crime at all," Tyr warned. "It's fortunate for you the beast did no harm to any of the Faithful, or one of us would have called you to trial for freeing the Hound. . . ."

"But Mystra conspired to imprison Kezef, and in doing so she willfully caused the death of her own loyal follower," Cyric murmured. "She is hardly one to judge my moral standing."

"What are you talking about?" Mystra asked. "I know nothing of Kezef. I never confronted the beast."

The Lord of the Dead feigned shock. "But the evidence clearly shows otherwise."

With one rap of his knuckles on the podium, Tyr silenced the court. "The evidence you have presented to us—the holy symbol and spell parchment—could have been planted by anyone. Justice demands proof."

"Justice demands I save the Lady of Mysteries from being wrongfully punished," Mask said. When the Shadowlord stepped from the corner nearest Mystra, a ripple of surprise moved through the room; no one had seen Mask in that corner until he spoke.

"It was I who captured Kezef. Placing the blame on the goddess was a twist of intrigue." Mask moved to Mystra's side. "In such matters I can't help myself—though I also acted out of fear. None of you may wish to admit it, but you know the Lady of Mysteries is correct: Cyric threatens us all."

"As I expected," the Prince of Lies murmured. The rose-hued short sword at his hip flared angrily. "Where is the Chaos Hound?"

"Where you'll never find him," Mask taunted. "But don't worry, he'll turn up on your doorstep sooner or later. Dogs are like that."

Cyric merely smiled at the barb. "Where did you get the spell that allowed you to capture him so easily? Such enchantments are far beyond your ken, Shadowlord."

"From my library," Oghma sighed.

"So you were his accomplice, as well," the Prince of Lies hissed. "Tell me, what has Kezef to do with knowledge, Binder? Are you as guilty of overstepping your office as Midnight?"

"The knowledge contained in my library is available to all the gods," Oghma said. His voice thundered with menace, like the martial songs written by the necromancers of Thay. "Mask borrowed the information from me. In return for this service, the borrower often provides a bit of lost history to include in my books."

"So you would have given me the spell, had I traded you some suitable fragment of lore?" Cyric asked slyly.

"Of course. Knowledge must be free to travel where it is desired."

The Lord of the Dead nodded slowly. "I'll remember that, Binder."

"Enough, Cyric," Tyr said. "It should be no surprise to you that there are many of us who stand against you—"

"But I should only expect opposition from any of you when my plans threaten your office," the Prince of Lies said. "That is Ao's law, is it not?"

Oghma stood and moved to Tyr's side, then whispered into the old judge's ear. "Yes," the God of Justice said, "given the nature of the conflict, a compromise might be in order."

Tyr faced the gathered throng once more, stiff and regal. "Because both the accuser and the accused are unique amongst us, having risen from the mortal realms to their positions of power, we can excuse this lapse in judgment on *both* their parts. Cyric, you will be required to participate in all meetings of the Circle and abide by all its decisions. . . ."

"If I am allowed to pursue my office without unfair hindrance—"

"Without condition," Tyr said firmly. "It should be clear from this proceeding the Circle can police its own."

"Of course," Cyric said, though he hid his distaste at the concession rather badly.

"As for you, Mystra," Tyr added. "You must give up this vendetta against the Lord of the Dead. We will drop the charges against you, but you must allow Cyric the use of magic. He must be allowed the power to which his title grants him right."

"And if I don't give him access to the weave?"

"It will be as Oghma said—total sanctions against your mortal worshipers until you comply."

Cyric threaded his way through the spectators and strolled across the pavilion's floor. "Let's get this over with," he said, standing less than an arm's length in front of Mystra. "My realm requires the attention I've focused on this gathering. . . ."

Mystra bowed her head to hide the angry tears welling in her eyes.

It required no more than a thought from the Goddess of Magic to reconnect Cyric with the magical weave. As the energy flowed around him, the death god threw back his head and shouted. The sound of his joyful triumph tore into Mystra's soul, leaving a scar that would never truly heal.

Cyric transformed, the seared features and blasted flesh replaced by the dashing facade of a lean, hawk-nosed Zhentish nobleman. "Your pain is enough of a reward for enduring this tedious business," the Prince of Lies murmured so only Mystra could hear. He spun around and bowed toward Tyr and Oghma. "I thank the court for its wisdom. And now, I will take my inquisitors and go."

The Prince of Lies paused long enough to gift Mystra with another gloating smile before walking to the cages. The inquisitors, still encased in their golden shells, bowed their heads to their master.

Mask caught Mystra's eye then, and nodded toward the gathered knights of Hades. There was an instant connection between the god and goddess, born of a shared foe and common goal. The Lady of Mysteries shouted a single command word, triggering a special mechanism Gond had built into the cages. The bars on two sides of each cage slammed together, crushing the inquisitor inside like a hawk caught between a cloud giant's palms. Gears and shards of metal and the shredded soul-stuff that had animated the armor spilled into the floor in a noisy cascade.

"The verdict said nothing about returning those monstrosities to you," Mystra said when Cyric turned to face her.

The shocked silence in the pavilion told the Prince of Lies that his old adversary had managed some small victory out of this, after all. "Very well," Cyric said. "Gond can make others."

"He won't," Mask noted snidely. "Not after he's proven

these work. There's no gain in it."

Cyric locked eyes with his old ally for an instant. "The shadows cannot hide you from me forever, Mask. One day I'll drag you into the light and give Godsbane a taste of your blood."

"I doubt that very much," the God of Intrigue smirked. "But don't worry, when the threat doesn't come true, you can always claim you were lying."

The other gods had begun to disappear from the pavilion. "Hardly a new beginning," Lathander murmured sadly before he vanished, on his way back to the fertile lands of Elysium.

Oghma, too, was clearly troubled by the trial, and angry at Mystra for reasons she couldn't begin to fathom. The Patron of Bards stared at the goddess for a long time before he left for the security of his library. Then Mystra found herself alone in the wizards' laboratory with Mask and the shattered remains of the inquisitors.

"Cleverly done," the Shadowlord offered. He slid forward with feline grace. "All of them believed it—even Cyric, and he was standing close enough to touch them."

"Enough," Mystra snapped. "Look, I appreciate your aid, Mask, but I simply don't trust you."

"As well you shouldn't," the God of Intrigue admitted, far too readily for the goddess's liking. "Now that I know Cyric's toy soldiers aren't really destroyed—"

"I said enough! Can you create a shield to guarantee none of the other gods can interrupt us?"

"No," Mask said uncomfortably. "You know the pavilion can't be closed to the pantheon."

"Which is why I said keep quiet." Mystra turned back to the cages and the inquisitors. "I'll take care of them. You can leave any time you want."

Mask moved close to the Goddess of Magic. "Let's retire to my domain so we can discuss our mutual foe. It's time we joined forces, you and I. An alliance could aid us both."

"You get to foster intrigue," Mystra said, "and perhaps even gain some of Cyric's titles if he happens to fall. I get condemned for stopping a mad god from destroying the world. No thanks."

"Perhaps you're right," Mask sighed. "There might not be enough in it for you. Still, I can promise one reward for allying with me, Lady, something that might make you change your mind."

"I can't think of anything that would, Mask. Stop wasting my time."

The God of Intrigue settled onto the floor, shadows spreading out from him like a pool of blood from a slashed corpse. "Is Kelemvor's soul a waste of time?"

The bolt of force struck Mask in the chest, knocking him backward a dragon's length. "Where is he?" Mystra said. "Tell me now."

"I don't have possession of him myself," the Lord of Shadows said, smoothing his charred cloak. "And I don't want to say more here. Other gods may be listening, remember?"

"All right," Mystra growled. "We'll go to my palace in Nirvana."

"No," Mask said as he rose ghostlike from the floor. "We'll go to the City of Shadows. That's a much more fitting place for this sort of intrigue." He smiled ferally beneath his mask. "Besides, one of the other gods is already awaiting us there."

XIV

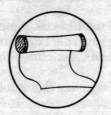

A LITTLE KNOWLEDGE

*Wherein the God of Knowledge faces three
unpleasant confrontations in three different
planes of existence, all at the same time.*

As Oghma left the Pavilion of Cynosure, he sent his consciousness racing off in myriad directions to deal with the moment-to-moment challenges of his office. However, he focused most of his mind in three locations. None of these incarnations were very happy about the tasks facing them, but they didn't complain. The unpleasant meetings might just yield some unusual bit of knowledge for his library, and in the end, knowledge was all that mattered. . . .

* * * * *

For the moment, the House of Knowledge resembled a monastery, dark and gloomy, with an air of ancient holiness that hung over the place as palpably as the storm clouds choking the sky overhead. Oghma's faithful went about their duties draped in coarse brown robes, their faces obscured by overlarge hoods. They shuffled through cavernous chambers crammed with tomes of every size. Heavy chains bound each book to its shelf; only the master librarian's keys could free a volume from its guarded captivity for more careful perusal. Despite these precautions, though, no request for knowledge was ever denied. Such was the nature of the Binder's domain.

Oghma took on the appearance of a monk as he materialized in his palace's throne room. His robes were somber, though his hood and draped sleeves were lined with ermine, his sandals shod with dragonhide. His dislike of this grim, bookish facade drove the Binder's mood even closer to the slough of despair—especially after the trial had gone so badly.

The sight of Cyric lounging in the Throne of Knowledge was enough to send Oghma the rest of the way into the mire.

"The robe's a good look for you," the Prince of Lies noted casually. He'd draped himself over the thick, stiff-backed chair that now passed for Oghma's throne. As the God of Knowledge approached, Cyric straightened and planted his elbows on the heavy writing desk that stood between them. "The place suits you, too."

"How so?" Oghma asked flatly, trying in vain to hide his anger from the death god.

Cyric sneered. "Musty and humorless. Your servants all fled when I arrived. All except one little pest. By the by, she tried to stop me from sitting here. I sent her to the Nine Hells."

"I know," the Binder rumbled. "I heard her scream."

"Don't worry. She'll make it back sooner or later— unless she crosses paths with one of the greater baatezu.

243

Quite a nasty lot, the baatezu." Cyric let a facade of mock concern drop over his features. "I wouldn't have been so harsh, but I find it troubling when a lackey breaches godly etiquette. . . ."

"Like sitting in a seat that doesn't belong to him," Oghma countered. The rumble in his multitoned voice had hardened into the ringing of steel against steel.

"I said lackey, not superior," Cyric corrected, but he stood nonetheless. "Please, Binder, sit. It's rather sad to find you elder powers tire so easily."

"At the moment I'm tired only of you," Oghma said. He pushed past the Lord of the Dead, threw his hood back from his dark handsome face, and settled into his throne. "Do you have business with me, or are you here to be an annoyance?"

Cyric sat on the edge of the desk. His crimson tunic and crushed velvet cloak made him stand out in the silent, solemn throne room-library like a jester at a funeral. "I come seeking knowledge, Binder."

"You'll have to be more specific."

"You're going to provide me with a solution to an old problem," the Prince of Lies said, toying with the quill pen on the desk. He casually dipped the pen into an inkwell and scrawled a vile obscenity across a folio of sacred verse. "I really wish I'd thought of coming here before. Luckily, the trial reminded me that magical knowledge finds its way to you, too."

Oghma erased the ink with a wave of his hand. "Don't play the fool with me, Cyric. I know you better than that."

"You know everything, is that it?" The death god dropped the pen. "Fine. I want to know how I can find the soul of Kelemvor Lyonsbane."

Oghma's laughter filled the room. The chuckling drowned out the mournful sounds floating in from the antechamber, where bards and priests sang dirges to lost knowledge. "Why, in Ao's name, should I help you?" the Binder managed at last.

Cyric matched the smile on Oghma's face. "This fine library is open to everyone, is it not? You said so at the trial."

"I did." The mirth fled Oghma's voice. The Binder stood, his cool gaze locked on the death god's lifeless eyes.

"Then you have no choice but to give me the information I need—unless, of course, you can tell me where Kelemvor is hidden." Cyric leaned forward. "Is that bit of trivia in one of your books?"

"No," Oghma replied. "And I have no knowledge that will guarantee his discovery."

"Well played, Binder—trying to refuse my request by splitting verbal hairs." The Prince of Lies gestured vaguely to the volumes lining the shelves around the room. "I'm not looking for guarantees, though. Just give me the tome that will tell me how best to find the errant soul."

The God of Knowledge held his hands forward, palms up, and a massive book appeared in them. The parchment, older than the pyramids of ancient Mulhorand, had begun to yellow long before Cormyr had crowned its first king. The pages cracked and flaked as Oghma opened the book. "You may read these pages, but do not touch them."

Cyric scanned the lines of cramped magical script, penned by a long-forgotten evil god named Gargauth. The cryptic text alluded to primordial battles between the greater powers and weird beings more mighty even than Ao. In the midst of this strange history were the necessary preparations for an enchantment to break through all divine barriers, see through all godly deceptions. The words were difficult to read since the enchantment had been written in reverse script, the gray ink trailing like shadows across the darker ebon of the main text. Yet

Cyric focused a small part of his mind on the task, and soon the knowledge was his.

"I will show this book to Lady Mystra right away," Oghma noted as he gently closed the tome. "She may find Kelemvor's soul before you."

Cyric leaped from the desk, animated by a wild excitement. "Go ahead, Binder, but you know as well as I that she'll never force her faithful to make the blood sacrifices the enchantment demands—whereas I most certainly will. . . ." And with a flourish of his cloak, the Prince of Lies was gone.

Tucking Gargauth's journal beneath his arm, Oghma readied for his trip across the planes. He paused, though, and reconsidered the wisdom of tempting the Goddess of Magic with such dangerous knowledge; she'd proved capable of endangering the Balance in pursuit of Cyric. What might she do to save her lover?

Oghma sighed. The Lady of Mysteries was even now answering that question in the halls of Mask's hellish keep.

Despite the doubts gnawing at him, the God of Knowledge decided to bring the tome to her attention. After all, it wasn't his place to protect Mystra.

Especially from herself.

* * * * *

Oghma's second incarnation arrived at Shadow Keep in the same instant his first discovered Cyric lounging in his throne. The annoyance wrought by the death god's impertinence rippled across the Binder's entire being, casting a long shadow over the mood of all his myriad selves. Cyric's slight barely affected the incarnation waiting on the threshold of Mask's domain, though. His thoughts had been quite grim to begin with.

In the darkest part of Hades, far from the City of Strife, sprawled the meandering slums of Shadow Keep. The city wandered far along the blasted plain, a place dedicated to thievery. The walls surrounding the keep weren't particularly high, the gates seemingly unguarded. Yet as Oghma stood beneath the main archway leading into the squalid alleys, awaiting one of Mask's heralds to grant him admittance, he knew the uncomfortable prickle of unseen eyes upon him. Had the Binder searched out the watchers, he could have spotted them, but that was too much like playing along with the games of deception and intrigue fostered here. Instead, he crossed his arms over his chest and resolutely stared straight ahead, out across the infinite wastes that separated Mask's domain from Cyric's.

After a time, the Shadowlord appeared before Oghma, Mystra at his side. "I'm not surprised to find you together," murmured the God of Knowledge.

Mask held out a gloved hand to Oghma, but the Binder kept his arms folded.

"You arrived sooner than I thought you would," the Lord of Shadows noted happily. "You even beat us here from the pavilion—well, we did have a package to drop off in Nirvana. . . ."

"Both of you are fools," Oghma snapped. "Your juvenile plotting has given Cyric—"

"Whatever Cyric gained today were gifts from the rest of the pantheon," Mystra interrupted. "He would still be cut off from the weave had the Circle not demanded otherwise. You and all the other greater powers are cowards, Binder."

"The trial wasn't about Cyric. It was about you, and how you'd strayed from your duties as Goddess of Magic. Cyric understood that. It's why he called the Circle together in the first place. Your punishment would almost certainly swing the Balance back in his favor." Oghma gestured toward Mask. "And don't think for an instant this blackguard wasn't trying to draw you in, make you lash out against Cyric."

"What would I gain from that?" Mask asked with mock innocence. "Do tell. . . ."

Oghma snorted in a very unscholarlike manner. "Just what you received: an alliance. Now that Mystra is alienated from the Circle, she's got nowhere left to turn."

"I recognize Mask's duplicity," Mystra said coldly. "After all, I see everyone's true motivation—that's the little secret you were hoping I'd stumble across, right?"

Swiftly Mask stepped between the two, hooking an arm around each of them. "Come, come. We all have something to gain from an alliance—even you, Lord Oghma. Let's discuss this at my palace, where I can ensure our mutual foe cannot hear us."

He led them through the archway, into the outlying alleys of Shadow Keep. The streets were narrow, the cobbles slick from the fog that hung over the city. Black-facaded buildings loomed on every side, their upper stories leaning so close together they nearly touched. Shards of sky shone through in places, but these revealed a heavens locked in perpetual twilight, just at that instant of gloaming when shadows are longest.

The three gods made their way along the twisting path to the weird castle that lay somewhere amongst the sprawl. A sibilant hiss filled the air around them, a weave made up of false oaths, the vows of unfaithful lovers, and the treacherous plots of trusted minions. Footsteps echoed from darkened corners, the padding of thieves as they stalked each other through the murk. The only other sounds were the short, sharp shriek of daggers clashing or the wet squelch of a strangler's garrote biting into someone's throat.

Torches guttering all along the alley walls sent up a sour

smell of pitch, which mingled with the cold fog. The few sages who had visited Mask's realm claimed the discomforting aroma was meant to resemble the stench of fear from a robbery victim. To Oghma, it was a distilled essence of ignorance, the gasping breath of knowledge trapped in intricate webs of deceit.

The air seemed to invigorate Mask. The Lord of Shadows gulped in lungful after lungful, though the action was only a show. "Ah, can you sense them?" he whispered gleefully. "They're all around us."

"Who?" Mystra murmured, glancing uneasily over her shoulder.

"My faithful." Mask smiled like a proud father bragging over a gifted child. "Those shadowy blurs are my lads and ladies. No doubt they've hatched a dozen plans to attack us before we get to the keep."

Light from the torches danced on the walls of the high buildings, but did not push the darkness back very far. If Mask's faithful were stalking nearby, the Patron of Thieves had reason to be proud. Oghma and Mystra glimpsed only flickers of movement, patches of shadow that seemed to flow with more purpose than the rest.

"And you expect me to tolerate this?" Oghma blurted. He summoned a magical light, illuminating the entire alleyway. Shades wrapped in cloaks of shadow, much like their god, fled before the radiance. They melted into doorways and windows, cracks in the walls and fissures between the cobbles. Flares of light reflected off their daggers as they went.

"How rude," Mask said. He spread his cloak and drew the light into him, plunging the alley into darkness once more. The faint sounds of thieves moving amongst the shadows returned almost instantly.

"I'm God of Intrigue," the Shadowlord explained, his red eyes flashing behind his mask. "What did you think my faithful would be like?" He shook his head. "Don't worry about them attacking, if that's what's disturbing you. I've taught them never to strike against someone more powerful—unless they have a chance of making a kill. They won't attack us unless someone's given them all god-slaying blades, like Cyric's."

"That's a comforting thought," Mystra said. Though she knew the likelihood of an attack was terribly slim, several facets of her mind drew powerful defensive enchantments to the ready. No sense trusting Mask, especially in his own domain.

They continued in silence the rest of the way to Mask's palace, shadowed at every turn by lurking thieves. At last the alley opened onto a huge plaza. The structure dominating the square seemed to be constructed out of darkness alone. The palace walls wavered in the perpetually failing twilight, the battlements and towers warping like smoke on the wind. Bats fell through the air above the palace. The sound of their wings drowned out the constant murmur of intrigue hissing from the alleys.

"Welcome, master," two deep voices rumbled in unison as the gods approached the castle.

Oghma had taken the hulking shapes to either side of the door to be gatehouses, but they shifted suddenly. With subtle grace, the twin creatures slid away from the walls. Their serpentine tails uncoiled, their huge wings unfolded from hunched shoulders. Finally the shadow dragons opened sulphur-yellow eyes. They kowtowed to the lord of the keep, their long necks stretched almost to full length.

Mask nodded to the beasts, and they rose again to take up their posts. With their eyes closed once more, their wings and limbs folded to their sides, the dragons melted back into the greater darkness that made up the palace walls.

"I usually accept guests in the throne room, but no need

for pomp between allies," the Shadowlord said as they passed through the entry hall. "We'll go to my study."

Wraithlike servants flitted through the keep, dancing from one shadow to another. The doors, even the hallways themselves, had been built with odd angles and jutting corners. Hidden alcoves lined both walls and ceiling. More often than not, weird creatures lurked in these places, their ghastly features hidden by darkness and the thin yellow fog that curled around everything.

A panting shadow mastiff, as large as a bear, greeted the God of Intrigue as he entered the study. The beast seemed to float across the intricately patterned carpets. A tongue black as a moonless night lolled over equally ebon teeth. Only the creature's eyes stood out from its shadowy form, bright and glinting like platinum reflecting candlelight.

Mask took a seat in a wing-backed chair, so overstuffed it seemed to engulf his form completely. "So, Oghma, what exactly have you been up to?"

The God of Knowledge remained standing, uncomfortable even surrounded by Mask's library. "Meaning?"

"Your plan against Cyric," Mask prompted, idly patting the shadow mastiff. "You've obviously got some plot in motion."

"That can wait," Mystra interrupted. "We're safe from scrying here, Mask. Where's Kelemvor?"

"In Cyric's grasp—well, very nearly." At Mystra's angry glare, he held up a gloved hand defensively. "No more pyrotechnics, Lady. I'll be more specific."

The God of Intrigue shooed the mastiff away. After wandering close to Oghma, the hound settled in the shadows around the fireplace. "As I was saying," Mask began, "the soul of Kelemvor Lyonsbane resides in the City of Strife, but hidden from Cyric by a very powerful being."

"Who?" Oghma prompted.

"Come now," Mask chortled, "both of you are intelligent.

Where do you begin looking for something you've lost?" He paused for an instant, then answered: "Why, where you last saw it, of course. And Kelemvor was last seen atop Blackstaff Tower, skewered on the end of—"

"Godsbane!" Mystra shouted. "The sword's been hiding his soul from Cyric all these years?"

Mask bowed his head in mock humility. "I must admit to helping her keep Kel hidden, at least a little."

"I want him back." Mystra took a threatening step toward the Shadowlord. "Now." The mastiff leaped to its feet and bravely set itself, growling, between the two gods.

Casually, the God of Intrigue pushed the hound to a sitting position. "It's not that simple. Godsbane will give up Kelemvor's soul if we help her get revenge on Cyric. She's quite miffed—something about Cyric trying to break her will during the Time of Troubles. . . ."

"And where do you come in, Mask?" Oghma asked. "No, let me guess. You and the sword have plotted to overthrow him."

Mask nodded appreciatively. "Quite correct, Binder. There may be hope for you yet."

Pacing back and forth before the hearth like some caged beast, Mystra suddenly stopped and turned on the God of Knowledge. "What about you? What's your part in all of this?"

"Last time I asked that, you cut him off," Mask smirked.

Oghma ignored the Shadowlord. "I've been trying to counter Cyric's book," he said, finally settling into a chair. "A task that is well within my office."

"But what, exactly, are you doing?" Mask pressed. He leaned forward eagerly. "Whatever it is, you've hidden it well. I've been trying to find out for quite some time."

"Aiding the underground in Zhentil Keep," Oghma admitted reluctantly. "With my help, they're creating a true version of Cyric's life."

"Brilliant!" Mask crowed. "I never would have thought you had it in you, Binder, but that's a smashing plan! When the book's done, the conspirators will use it to undercut Cyric's worship—"

"They will use it to supplant his lies," Oghma corrected. "To insure his book doesn't rewrite the true history of the world." He leaned back in the chair, shadows sliding across his handsome features. "But that's all in jeopardy, now that Cyric has magic again. I don't know if I can keep my agents hidden from him any longer."

"Ah, but now you have two allies to help you," Mask said.

"Who said anything about me allying with you?" Mystra snapped.

"If you want Kelemvor back, you should consider joining our little conspiracy," Mask rumbled.

Sparks crackled from Mystra's eyes. "Threats, Mask? You're already resorting to threats?"

"Cyric has the means to find Kelemvor," Oghma noted darkly. The incarnation of the Binder that had confronted Cyric arrived in Shadow Keep at that moment. The other gods did not see the two fragments merge, but they did notice the book suddenly appear in Oghma's hands. "This tome belonged to Gargauth. There's a spell here that will allow Cyric to find any object, no matter how many gods try to shield it from him."

"And he's seen this?" Mask asked, concern leaching the glee from his voice.

"Just now. He left my throne room a short time ago."

"Let me see the spell," Mystra said. She stalked to Oghma's side.

The God of Knowledge carefully opened the book for Mystra. She scanned the page, gleaning the magical contents far faster than Cyric had.

"It'll take days for his faithful to prepare all the necessary sacrifices," Mystra noted. "And the final enchantment will require a huge burst of energy. Cyric will need to whip his worshipers into a frenzy for that."

Mask rubbed his hands together nervously. "All of them?"

"No, the populace of one large city would do."

"Zhentil Keep," Mask said. "He's spent so much time and energy trying to unite the place under his church, he's bound to use them for this." He paused, shocked at the clarity of the plan unfolding in the twisted alleys of his mind. "We have him. His reign is over. . . ."

Mask slipped out of his chair. His cloak of darkness floated around him as he moved toward the God of Knowledge. "Is your book near completion, Binder?"

"Any day now."

"Cyric will likely organize a rally of some kind, a gathering to focus the Keep's worship." Mask leveled a finger at the God of Knowledge. "You need to get the book finished before that happens—as close to the event as possible."

"That will only delay him," Mystra scoffed. "Even if we destroy his church in Zhentil Keep, he'll move on to another city, another group of fanatics."

"Ah, but undermining the Keep is only half the plan," Mask purred. "If Binder's book can turn a huge number of worshipers against Cyric, all at once, he'll be vulnerable. If a revolt should happen to start in the City of Strife at the same time . . ."

"You're mad," Oghma snapped, closing the book with more force than he would have liked. The ancient binding cracked, and flakes of parchment puffed into the air. "If the Realm of the Dead revolts and Cyric is overthrown, the mortal realms will be driven into chaos."

"Unless a new Lord of the Dead arrives to take control of Bone Castle before the chaos spreads," the Shadowlord corrected. "I'm certain Godsbane would invite me in to help put down the unruly denizens—after Cyric is overthrown, of course."

"Why should we help you take Cyric's crown?" Mystra asked.

"Because I'm not nearly so mad as the Prince of Lies," Mask replied flatly. "Because both of you need to stop Cyric very soon, before he finds Kelemvor's soul or finishes his *Cyrinishad*. I'm offering you a clear plan, which has a very good chance of succeeding. Can either of you improve upon it?"

Mystra returned to pacing before the fire. The low-burning flames cast huge shadow-images of the goddess on the opposite wall. "We'll need someone to lead the revolt," she said after a time. "What about the inquisitors?"

"Ready-made revolutionaries," Mask said wryly. "From the look of that armor, I'll bet the souls pinned inside will be sporting quite a grudge against Cyric. The trick will be countermanding the orders they were given."

"The inquisitors?" Oghma asked. "But you destroyed them."

"Appeared to destroy them," Mystra corrected. "I didn't want to annihilate the poor shades trapped in the armor, but I wasn't about to let Cyric take the suits back to Hades."

"Again, I must admit to helping the lady with her deception. Rather clever, no?" Mask asked coyly. "Just don't tell the rest of the Circle they've been hoodwinked."

The God of Knowledge scowled. He'd already been drawn into the Shadowlord's plans more than he would have liked. Yet with a renewed command of magic, Cyric would certainly discover the conspirators. To protect the cause of knowledge in the mortal realms, Oghma had no choice but to go along with the intrigue.

Or was it simply that the other options had become less expedient?

The image of his library, always so clear and comforting, faded for an instant in Oghma's mind. A void welled up in its place, gray and cold and infinite. Panicked, the Binder focused much of his vast consciousness on recovering the lost image. The sense of purpose, of security, returned quickly enough, but with it came a gnawing dread.

Mask's intrigues and the battle with Cyric had brought Oghma unknowingly to the limits of his domain, to a place where decisions about art and knowledge in the mortal realms couldn't be made with any surety. One wrong step, one act that destroyed more knowledge than it preserved, and he would step across the brink. And from the void that lay beyond, there would be no return, not even for a god.

From the back alleys of Zhentil Keep, harsh words being spoken to another of Oghma's incarnations rippled across his consciousness. His mind latched onto the admonitions, drawing back from the void. Here, at least, was a problem he could solve. . . .

* * * * *

Rinda rocked back and forth, her arms clasped firmly around her knees, her head bowed. She'd been perched in the same position for hours now, though the ache in her back and the cramps in her legs didn't seem to register in her fear-clouded mind. "No hope," she whispered. "No hope."

Her house had become a prison, the only place her patron had deemed safe from Cyric's inquisitors. Apart from the times the Lord of the Dead summoned her to the parchmenter's shop to work on his book, she stayed at home, under the magical shield erected to hide *The True Life of Cyric* from the death god. Rarely eating, never sleeping for more than an hour at a time, Rinda had

257

become a gaunt shadow of her former self.

They've been captured, came a familiar voice. *The inquisitors will stalk the Keep no longer.*

The harmony in the multitoned words was meant to be comforting, but Rinda found no solace in the sounds. She turned green eyes, bloodshot and rimmed with dark circles, toward the ceiling. "Did you do it?" she asked.

No. It was one of the other gods. Cyric has many enemies.

"I should've figured you wouldn't do anything so direct." The scribe rested her head on her arms, listening to the cold wind whistle through the cracks in the walls. "Who's left?" she murmured after a time.

Fzoul Chembryl and General Vrakk. And you, of course.

Rinda sighed. So Ivlisar was gone now, too. She'd thought as much. The elf hadn't come to see her in days, almost since Hodur's murder. "Will Fzoul or Vrakk be coming to meet with me again?"

It's unlikely, Rinda. Cyric has regained the use of magic, so I must focus my power on maintaining the shell around this dwelling. You must be protected—

"This isn't about me," the scribe said bitterly. "It's about the book. You just want to be sure it stays hidden from Cyric. If I happen to live here, it's just my good fortune."

She stood and stalked to a large knothole in the wall. From there she gazed out at the street. Snow fell in great white flakes, covering the grimy buildings and the frozen street in a shroud of alabaster lace. A woman, bent nearly double by age or sickness or both, shuffled along, a shawl clutched about her shoulders. A pack of ragged children charged past her. The boys split into two uneven groups and began pelting each other with snowballs; the smaller gang, which was quickly overwhelmed by a hail of snowy missiles, shouted their surrender, then dashed off again. They left one small child bloody and crying in their wake.

Rinda fought back the urge to go out and help the child,

to stanch his bleeding and still his sobs.

It would be best for you to stay inside, the god said. *Though the inquisitors are gone, Cyric will be undoubtedly unleash new terrors on the city to search for traitors.*

"Get out of my head," Rinda snapped. She focused her thoughts on the most sacrilegious, profane things she could imagine, just in case he had lingered there.

Fzoul and Vrakk have found a way to go about their lives, Rinda. You should strive to do the same.

"Oh really?" She planted her hands on her hips. "They became part of this plot willingly. I didn't. Both you and Cyric simply strolled in and demanded my cooperation."

An uncomfortable silence settled over the room. Finally, the voice spoke: *I'm doing this for you and all the other mortals who would suffer under Cyric's rule.*

"So you say," Rinda murmured, her voice as cold as the winter twilight settling over the Keep. "But I've got no reason to believe you, not when you won't even tell me who you are."

That knowledge would be dangerous for you. If Cyric discovered your duplicity—

"Stop it. If Cyric discovers *The True Life,* he'll drag me off to Hades whether I know who I'm working for or not." She ran a hand through her dark curls, trying to rein in her growing fury. "And you wouldn't lift a celestial finger to help me, would you? Of course not. Then you'd be on the front lines, instead of skulking around behind the scenes."

Enough, Rinda. You're becoming irrational.

"Why shouldn't I be irrational?" she shouted, then laughed hysterically. "I'm being volleyed between gods like a shuttlecock! And no matter who wins the match, I'll be the one punished for it!" Rinda picked up a mug and dashed it against the wall. "That's it. I'm not going to play at this any longer. . . ."

The scribe hurried to the desk where she worked on *The True Life of Cyric*. She scattered the books she'd stacked atop the pages, then shredded the silk wrappings that guarded the priceless gatherings. Before she could tear the parchment, though, a dark-skinned hand grasped her wrists.

"Enough," the god said. He gently turned the scribe to face him. "I cannot let you destroy that knowledge."

Rinda stared at the avatar. His slight frame was draped in a monkish robe, austere save for the ermine trim on the hood and sleeves. Dark eyes full of infinite wisdom returned her gaze. There was something else in those eyes, too, a powerful sadness. She felt an urge to bow, but her anger dispelled the inclination before she had a chance to act on it.

"I am Oghma," the god said, "Patron of Bards, God of Knowledge. The other powers call me Binder, though I rather dislike the name. It makes me sound too rigid, too unyielding."

Rinda's mouth worked soundlessly for a moment. Then the question finally found its way from her throat. "Why?"

"As I said, I'm doing this to protect the mortal realms from Cyric. His book would sow ignorance, spread it like a plague to everyone who reads the lies you have penned in his name."

"No," the scribe said. She shook her head to clear her thoughts. "Why reveal yourself to me?"

Oghma smiled. "Because you reminded me that sometimes the best path to travel may not necessarily be the safest, especially if one intends to be true to oneself." At the confusion in Rinda's eyes, the Binder pointed to the stack of parchment. "You knew that being trapped in this intrigue was denying your calling, and you would have destroyed these pages to set yourself free. It would have been a mistake, but a rather heroic one, all things considered."

The God of Knowledge patted her hand. "Mortals understand that better than we gods—making choices, I mean."

"I thought you meant mistakes."

"They're the same thing." Oghma said. "At least in part. Anyway, you have questions about our plans, and it's time I guided you to the knowledge you seek. . . . After you see to the child, of course. He still needs your help, and I know how pointless it would be to try to detain you."

Rinda had already tossed her cloak over her shoulders and opened the front door.

XV

ORACLES OF WAR

*Wherein many strange and supernatural events
trouble the people of Zhentil Keep, the Prince of
Lies musters a powerful army to unify his
holy city, and Thrym the frost giant learns
that not all gods are created equal.*

Elusina the Gray dumped a handful of grubby chicken
bones from a porcelain bowl and waved her hands slowly
over the resulting mess. She murmured a nonsensical
string of phrases, half words, half musical notes in a decidedly somber key. The fake incantation complete, she
began to sway back and forth violently. In summer she cut
this part out of the show; now, in the clutches of Nightal,
the activity kept the cold from freezing her old joints solid.

Once she felt sufficiently warmed, the old woman
turned bloodshot eyes on the Zhentilar officer sitting
across the table from her. "Just as the basilisk's eye can

turn men to stone, their bones can petrify a man's fate. Here, Sergeant Renaldo—" she gestured to the tangled pile "—here is the shape of your future."

Rubbing his gloved hands together anxiously, the young officer glanced around the tiny, garishly decorated room, as if someone might sneak in and steal the secret of his future. When finally he looked at the bones, though, disappointment stole across his handsome features. "Oh, that's it then? What does it, er—what does it mean?"

Elusina held one clawlike hand out, palm up. "It's dangerous to spy upon the future, Sergeant. For me to risk the wrath of the spirit world, I'll need more . . . incentive."

The Zhentilar cursed vilely. His commander had told him the old woman was a gifted mystic, but these were the tactics of a sideshow huckster. He drew a dagger from his boot top. "If anything from the spirit world drops by to complain," he said, "I'll be here to protect you."

With bony knuckles, Elusina rapped three times on the table. The thick curtain of beads behind her parted, and a brawny man stepped through. He crossed well-muscled arms over his chest and glowered at the soldier. He was as tall as an ogre and just as ugly, with beady eyes and a nose that had been broken three or four times. From the dented and bloodstained cudgel hanging at his belt, he'd clearly repaid the assaults in kind.

"Brok here protects me," Elusina murmured. "You're supposed to pay me enough to keep him around." She extended her hand again, waiting patiently until the soldier dropped a silver piece and a half-dozen copper into her palm.

The old woman cackled and deposited the coins one by one into a strong box at her feet. They jingled against the cache like a gypsy's tambourine. In troubled times like these, providing glimpses into the future was a profitable business—even for thieves like Elusina, who could no more see a man's fate than walk through a stone wall.

Still, the old woman provided a bit of a show for the men and women who came seeking her advice. She'd been an actress at one time, a lesser light in a decidedly disreputable troupe that toured the Cormyrian countryside. Elusina's skills as a pickpocket had been honed vigorously by the master of the ragged band, but she'd managed to acquire a fair sense of the dramatic along the way.

"Oh, there is much danger in store for you, Sergeant," she began, hovering once more over the chicken bones. "Traitors and heretics lurk everywhere, and it will be your task to route them from the city."

The Zhentilar scoffed. "Everyone knows what the army's job'll be, now that the church is running the Keep. Tell me something you haven't heard on the street."

"You will be promoted soon—" Elusina jabbed at two bones set apart from the rest, crossed like blades in a battle "—before the end of the year. You've been seeking an important post, and it will soon be yours."

That claim caught the soldier's attention, and the look of suspicion began to drop from his features. "How? I mean, what happens to the dolt who's in that spot now?"

Elusina stared at the bones a moment, formulating an answer clear enough to keep the soldier intrigued, but vague enough to keep hidden the fact she had no idea what post he wanted. Like most military men, the young sergeant was ambitious. She'd recognized that the moment he walked into the parlor, swaggering like a victorious general, or Xeno Mirrormane himself. . . .

"The patterns are not clear," she murmured, stalling for time. The old woman cursed herself for drinking so heavily at the Serpent's Eye earlier in the afternoon. The aftereffects of the gin was clouding her thoughts. "Let me look more closely."

As Elusina ran her withered fingertips over the smooth

curves and sharp ends of the scattered bones, her mind suddenly went blank. The parlor fell away, the imitation Shou carpets and tasseled lanterns swathed in red silk fading into mist. In their place she saw only the tangle of chicken bones, as large as Cyric's temple, glowing more brightly than the morning sun. And for the first time, she recognized a clear meaning in the jumble.

"Death awaits you," Elusina said. Her voice was hollow, like something calling from the Realm of the Dead. "The city will fall, and all its defenders will be slaughtered—ground to dust beneath the heels of dragons and giants, pierced by the arrows of goblins and gnolls."

When she came to, Elusina found the Zhentilar officer shouting at her, angrily demanding his money be returned. Brok had taken up a post behind the sergeant. He looked to the old woman, watching for the nod that would mean it was time to throw the client into the street. But Elusina merely reached down into her strong box and grabbed a handful of coins. She emptied these onto the table without counting them, then rose silently and shuffled into the back room.

She saw no more customers that day or ever again. Elusina had been granted a glimpse into the future. She'd seen the face of death in the seemingly senseless pattern of the bones—not just the Zhentilar's death, but the doom of thousands upon thousands living in the Keep.

No matter how hard she tried, the seeress couldn't banish the image from her mind. The cold clarity of it, the immutable certainty of the city's destruction clung to Elusina's thoughts and smothered her spirits like ancient cerements. And with that certainty came the realization that even now, as she huddled in her small, dirty room, grim events were unfolding that would speed the present toward that terrifying, unavoidable future.

* * * * *

The dragon's corpse hung upside down in the catacombs beneath the Church of Cyric. As General Vrakk had guessed that day in the marketplace, the young wyrm hadn't survived long after the procession. Beatings had left welts and scars along its snow-white hide, while days without food had drawn the dragon's stomach into a hollow curve beneath its ribs. Grief struck the blow that finally killed the beast, an overwhelming sorrow at being separated from its brethren in the icy wastes to the north.

Ever eager to fill the church coffers, Xeno Mirrormane had sent word through the black market that pieces of the corpse could be had for magical endeavors, but only for a sizable donation to Cyric's temple. The dragon's eyes had gone the first day, sold to the wizard Shanalar as fodder for some dark experiment. Claws and tongue went next, along with most of the armorlike scales from its stomach. Now, less than a tenday after its demise, the wyrm looked much like a warrior's corpse left for the carrion crows after a battle.

Still, enough remained of the dragon for Xeno Mirrormane to post a guard in the catacombs. Every bone, every sinew from the wyrm would be sold eventually. No need to leave the thing unprotected and tempt the wizards who couldn't afford the high prices.

"And I thought guarding the merman in the damned parade was boring," Bryn mumbled, prodding the coals in the brazier squatting at her side. "This'll teach me to salute Ulgrym faster next time, though, won't it?"

She unsheathed her sword and scratched a crude drawing onto the dirt-strewn floor before her camp chair. She'd sketched the same scene—a nasty little imbroglio involving her Zhentilar commander and various farm animals—six times since beginning her watch, though she completed less and less with each attempt. Even now she lost interest and found herself wiping away the sketch with a worn boot heel.

A sudden creak of bones brought Bryn to her feet, sword held defensively before her. In the wavering light from the brazier, she could see the dragon's corpse shudder. One of its wings slipped from the bindings and unfolded slowly, stiffly.

Icy fingers of fear danced up Bryn's back. The shivers gathered at her neck, tensing her shoulders and choking off the scream that had begun to well in her throat.

The bindings dropped away from the wyrm's other wing, and it, too, unfurled languidly. Bryn's years of training in the Zhentilar helped her throw off the fear-born paralysis holding her in place. Yet this was no dalesman, no renegade goblin she faced. No matter how hard she tried, she couldn't still the trembling in her hands or swallow the lump in her throat. The best she could do was force a tentative step forward.

The corpse remained still, wings spread to its side like some monstrous bat awakening with the nightfall.

The soldier and the corpse remained motionless for a time, locked in that weird tableau. Finally Bryn gathered the courage to prod the dragon; the blow simply made the wyrm swing back and forth on its rope.

"Damn civilians," she muttered, sliding her sword tip over the loose ropes. "Can't even tie knots right."

As Bryn leaned forward to bind the corpse's wings again, its head shot up. Eyeless sockets regarded the Zhentilar for an instant. Then the undead dragon snapped its jaws closed on her neck. It enfolded the woman in its wings like a vampire in a melodrama sliding his cloak around the swooning heroine. The leathery embrace muffled Bryn's gasp of surprise and the single shriek she managed before the dragon tore out her throat.

The soldier's bloody corpse slipped to the floor with the dull sound of leather armor striking stone, and the wyrm turned its attention to the rope wound around its tail. It tried in vain to struggle free from the sturdy hemp, but Xeno's thugs had done a much better job on the knots there than the ones that had held the dragon's wings. After a few moments, it grew impatient. Three savage bites severed the bonds—and the end of the wyrm's tail, as well.

The dragon, long past feeling any mortal pain, dropped to the ground and padded into the darkness of the catacombs. Its slithering trek led to the Keep's sewers, down to the befouled water of the River Tesh. From that murky swell the dragon rose, phoenixlike, to deliver a message of vengeance to its clan.

On broken, ice-rimed wings the wyrm took to the midnight sky over Zhentil Keep. In only a few days it would be home. There, the challenge would be delivered to the dozen fully grown white dragons of the clan. The plea for revenge had no words, could have no words, since the young wyrm's tongue even now bubbled in a mage's elixir.

No, when the other dragons found the corpse laid out at the mouth of their cave, the brands scorched into its side would direct their fury and give their rage a target. "Death to Zhentil Keep! Death to the minions of Cyric!"

* * * * *

Thrym bellowed out a prayer to Zzutam, thanking him for a particularly cold winter and a continuing supply of errant sell-swords looking for gold and glory. The frost giants of Thrym's clan had fed well over the years, much better than many of their kind in other parts of Thar. Rumors that the near-mythical Ring of Winter could be found inside their cave, as well as old bardic tales that

placed the priceless crown of King Beldoran somewhere close at hand, had led hundreds of treasure hunters to the giants' doorstep and, eventually, the cookfires beyond. Thrym and his kin knew nothing of these fortuitous—and utterly groundless—stories; they ascribed the bounty to their monstrous patron, and offered prayers to him once a day, twice when it snowed enough to cover the toes of Thrym's boots.

"We thank you lots, O mighty ice god," the chieftain cried. He crushed a handful of bones between his palms and let the fragments fall upon the crystalline altar dominating the back of the cave. "We grind our enemies to dust in your name."

The bone chips burst into flame as they touched the cold stone. Crimson gouts of fire rose above the altar, swirling and dancing like will-o'-the-wisps, then melted into a single blaze. The soft-edged flames became the figure of a man clutching a rose-hued short sword.

"Pagans," Cyric hissed, disgust written all over his gaunt features. "How long's it been since I was here—fifteen years? Twenty? And you still haven't given up this foolishness. . . ."

Thrym snatched the intruder from the sacred altar, but fell backward, howling in pain, as the death god turned to flame in his grasp. The chieftain plunged his charred hand into a pile of snow and stared at Cyric.

The Prince of Lies stood atop the crystalline block once more, one hand planted on his hip. "Who's the leader of this—"

Idly Cyric gestured at a dark-haired giant. The brute was reaching with exaggerated care for his axe, but his hand closed not on wood, but a huge, writhing snake. The serpent slithered up the giant's arm, crushing his iron-corded muscles to paste.

As the two thrashed about on the ground, Cyric sheathed

Godsbane. "As I was saying, who's the leader of this sorry band?"

"Me. Chief Thrym." The giant wrapped his wounded hand in the hem of his grimy cloak and got ponderously to his feet. At a gesture from him, the dozen or so giants standing in shocked silence around the altar scrambled to help their beleaguered comrade. It took all of them to pry the snake loose and dash its brains on the cavern wall.

"Better get off Zzutam's table," Thrym warned, turning ice-blue eyes on Cyric. "He not like wizards, 'specially ones who breaked up our prayers."

"And how many wizards have successfully 'breaked up your prayers' in the past?" the Prince of Lies asked. "Has Zzutam had to deal with lots of people tramping across the altar?" At the blank look from the chieftain, Cyric dismissed the questions with a shake of his head. "You and your clansmen are going to do me a valuable service, Thrym. You should be honored."

"We don't work for 'venturers," the chieftain said warily.

"Yeah. Who do you think you are?" one of the other giants snarled. The question asked, he tugged at his lower lip, as if another might come tumbling out. It didn't.

"I don't suppose any of you remember me," Cyric sighed. He pointed to the pile of human bones scattered around the cold fire pit. "That might have been my resting place, many years ago. I was—well, what I was last time we crossed paths hardly matters. Now I am Cyric, Lord of the Dead, slayer of four gods."

"So what?" a giant chimed. "We already got a god."

"Zzutam is hardly worthy of that title, let alone the worship you give him," Cyric said. "He's a frost elemental, not a true deity." Again, the blank looks from his audience made the Prince of Lies pause. "You're Zzutam's high priest, right, Thrym? Does he grant you any magic for your devotion?"

"He makes snow," Thrym rumbled. "He send us chow."

"I wish my minions were so undemanding." Sniggering, the Prince of Lies spat upon the sacred stone. "All right, Zzutam. I'm calling you out, you great mound of snowflakes."

The giants wavered in their tracks, caught between the urge to kill the blasphemer and the sudden fear that they faced something far beyond their limited understanding. They knew nothing of humanity's gods, apart from the occasional pleas their captives shouted to Torm or Ilmater or Tymora, just before they went into the fire. For Thrym and his clan, Zzutam was the only power in the universe. He'd been the patron of their forefathers; he'd be the protector of their children—once the clan found a female who could tolerate any of them for more than a day.

So when Zzutam arrived in a burst of sleet and a gust of bitterly cold wind, a momentary hope stole over the giants' dull minds. Now this Cyric fellow would learn how mighty their god was. . . .

The monstrous frost elemental towered over even the giants, standing almost twice their twenty feet. His body was flat and wide, as if he'd been sliced away from a glacier's edge. Jagged spikes topped his head. They scraped along the ceiling as he turned to look first at Thrym and his fellows, then at the Prince of Lies. A strange expression crossed his inhuman features, tugging his dark gash of a mouth down at the corners in something like a frown.

"Lord Cyric," he whispered fearfully. His voice creaked like ice beneath a heavy sledge.

The giants leaned forward expectantly, waiting for Zzutam to smite the blasphemer with a mighty fist or skewer him upon a bolt of ice. Instead, the elemental bowed his head. "Great lord of Hades," Zzutam murmured. "How may I serve you?"

Cyric smirked. "You could start by teaching your

unwashed lap dogs some proper respect," he chided.

His slitted eyes flashing as white as the sky in a blizzard, Zzutam turned to his worshipers. One by one, they heeded his silent command and dropped to the dirty floor to kowtow. Thrym was the last to obey, bending only one knee in supplication—more to show his disappointment in the elemental than as a slight against Cyric.

"Much better," the Prince of Lies noted. "Now, Zzutam, you are going to order these leviathans to attack the human city known as Zhentil Keep. I honored the place by declaring it my holy city, but they insult me with silly revolts and heresies. I want them punished."

"But these twelve can do little against the mages and soldiers of such a great city," Zzutam objected.

"Other troops will be joining them," Cyric said. He sat cross-legged on the altar. "I will be recruiting all their fellow brutes in this area, as well as whatever gnolls and goblins I can gather. Even as we speak, an agent of mine is riling up a flight of white dragons. The wyrms will be attacking the Keep, too, though they don't know they're working for me just yet."

Zzutam looked genuinely puzzled, which wasn't surprising since his intellect barely surpassed that of the giants who worshiped him. "What's this army supposed to do?"

"Destroy the Keep, of course." Cyric scowled in consternation. "They will be a manifestation of my unholy wrath. You know—a force meant to teach the yokels not to slack off in their devotions and sacrifices again."

"We not fight beside goblins or gnolls," Thrym said flatly. "They scum. 'Sides, you kill us if we break down the black walls."

"I said nothing of the kind," Cyric rumbled. He leaped to his feet and stepped off the altar. Instantly he was as tall as Thrym. "Well, how did you come to that conclusion, you oaf?"

The chieftain met Cyric's flame-red eyes with a level, unwavering gaze. "I had dreams. There were dogs that breathed fire, and they killed us for attacking your city."

The Prince of Lies paused, stunned by both the giant's temerity and the accuracy of his vision. Cyric planned to set the monstrous army against the Keep, but only to galvanize the city's worship, force them to reach out to him as their savior. The enhanced worship would give him enough power to activate the spell needed to locate Kelemvor Lyonsbane. Then he would destroy the giants and dragons before they scratched a single stone in the Keep's night-black walls.

"You're interpreting the dream wrong," Cyric lied. "I will lead my hell hounds here if you *don't* destroy the city." He looked meaningfully to Zzutam.

Enthusiastically the frost creature nodded its great, spiky head. "You will do as the death god asks," he wheezed. "His word is my word."

"Very dramatic," Cyric said snidely. "Have you been taking lessons from Torm or Tyr? That's the sort of pompous drivel I'd expect from them. . . ."

The death god gestured to Thrym. "I want you under way tonight. The trip will take you a few days, and I want this over with as soon as possible. The rest of the army will fall in with you as you travel." He drew Godsbane and tapped the kneeling giant on both shoulders. "I dub you General Thrym. Keeping order will be your responsibility—and that means no fighting amongst yourselves, do you understand? For every soldier killed before you reach the city I'll cut off a part of your flabby, lice-infested body, starting with your fingers and working up in size from there."

Thrym did the only thing he could, burdened with a command from Zzutam and the threats of an even more powerful being: he dropped to the floor in an awkward bow, then hurried to gather his meager gear. In less time than it had taken him to kill Gwydion and his companions, the frost giant had packed his belongings and started on the long march south to Zhentil Keep, the rest of his newly formed army in tow.

After the giants had gone, Zzutam bowed his spiky head subserviently. "Great lord, I fear for my worshipers."

"No need to worry," the death god said. "The fate of the army is already sealed." He walked to the mouth of the cave and watched the giants trudge through the snow to the plateau's edge. Their battered helmets and grimy axe heads reflected the pale moon in soft flares of light. "I've already begun to send oracles to the diviners in the Keep—even the fakers. As we speak, frantic rumors tell of a monstrous army on the move."

"But then the city's defenders—" The frost elemental exhaled with a sound like wind whistling through a high mountain pass.

"You can always bully another bunch of stupid beasts into worshiping you," Cyric offered blandly. "Though why you bother is beyond me. You're not even a true deity. You don't get power from their devotion." He turned back to Zzutam. "I trust you will be wise enough to let events unfold without sticking your icy nose into the matter. I will take any interference from you as a personal affront."

The Prince of Lies didn't need to see the elemental's weird eyes or hear his murmured acquiescence to know that fear would keep him from saving Thrym and the others. Certain of his victory, the death god withdrew his consciousness from the cave and sent it off to his holy city. The night was young, and thousands upon thousands of sleeping minds awaited the dire news that doom was stalking Zhentil Keep with the thunderous tread of giants' boots and the leathery hiss of dragons' wings.

* * * * *

Nightmares plagued everyone within the raven-black walls of Zhentil Keep that evening, though the Night Serpent got no sustenance from them. The following morning, the horrible dreams remained vivid in the minds of every priest, every soldier and beggar and merchant in the city. And those brave enough to describe the terrors that had chilled their sleeping hearts found their neighbors had been visited by the same apocalyptic visions.

Some diviners and dabblers in the magical arts tried their best to attach a meaning to the dreams; others, like Elusina the Gray, closed off their newly gained magical sight and refused to look into the bleak future at all. In the end, the sages and wizards could only agree that something strange was happening, that some power was sending the city a message from beyond the mortal realms.

At highsun, in a speech before the gathered hierarchy of the Church of Cyric, Patriarch Xeno Mirrormane translated that message for the people of Zhentil Keep.

"Our lord and protector is displeased with us," the high priest shouted at the congregation kneeling before him in the black-floored nave. "We have failed to purge the heretics from our city, even with the help of the master's inquisitors. The dreams that have haunted us, the revelations uncovered by our mages all tell us that a great army is coming. They are the agents of Cyric's wrath."

Xeno pounded the wooden lectern so hard it cracked beneath the blows. "If we do not accept Cyric into our hearts, if each and every citizen of this holy city does not put his will aside and take on the role Cyric has forged for him, this army will tear down the walls and raze the Keep to the ground."

A shout went up in the temple, angry cries demanding the death of all heretics. The patriarch stared out over the crowd with wild eyes, huge with panic and righteous fervor. "Cyric does not doubt that we have served him faithfully. We, his priests—"

A terrible grating of stone against stone drowned out Xeno's praise.

To either side of the patriarch stood huge marble statues of Cyric. With heroically chiseled features and grandly carved robes of stone, the twin gods scowled at the gathered throng. Now, both marble deities were slowly drawing short swords carved of solid ruby from diamond-studded sheaths; the sound was like the earth splitting open across the entire horizon.

"No one in Zhentil Keep has served our lord well," the statues shouted in unison. They turned cold eyes on Xeno. "No one."

The patriarch stammered a prayer for mercy, but the statues had already returned their unblinking gazes to the gathered priests. "Know you all that the Lord of the Dead has withdrawn his beneficence from this place—until such a time as the entire city proves itself worthy of his most divine favor."

Stiffly the statues raised their swords. All across the nave, the silver bracelets worn by the priests to symbolize their enslavement to Cyric opened and dropped to the black stone floor. "You no longer serve the God of Strife and Master of Tyranny," the statues proclaimed in dead men's voices.

Some priests wept at the sentence; others merely stared in shock at the silver shackles lying open before them. They'd worn the bracelets for a decade, as the bands of pale, chafed flesh on their wrists showed. They could no more imagine moving without them than they could losing an eye or a hand.

"Please," Xeno Mirrormane shrieked as he tried in vain to fit the cuffs back over his wrists. "There must be some way for us to prove our worthiness."

The statues stepped off their ebon bases. They turned

to either side of the temple and walked with ponderous steps from the apse to the aisles. There they each raised their swords once again, this time gesturing to the huge stained glass windows that ran along either wall. "There is one way, and one way only," the marble deities chanted. "Obey these commands before the army of his wrath descends upon you, and salvation may yet be yours."

All along the walls the tracery began to glow with a sickly crimson hue, as if the ruby swords had lit the decorative stonework around the windows on fire. Then light bled away from the dark stone, running down the stained glass like blood. The liquid fire burned away the gorgeously twisted images captured there—scenes of slaughter and strife perpetrated by the Prince of Lies and his minions—and replaced them with written rituals to be performed in Cyric's name. Each of the six gruesome rites demanded a different list of gory components and detailed a sinister use for the gathered tongues and eyes and hearts.

"This is your only hope." With that, the statues stomped back to their pedestals, sheathed their swords, and became stone once more.

Xeno Mirrormane broke the heavy silence in the temple with a hymn to Cyric's glory, and soon the whole congregation had joined him. Their god had turned away from them, but there was still a chance to win back a place in his kingdom. And regain the death god's patronage they would, even if it meant slaughtering everyone else in Zhentil Keep.

XVI

MIND GAMES

*Wherein Rinda and the Prince of Lies have their
final meeting—at least in the mortal realms—
and Mask outsmarts everyone, even himself.*

A chorus of fifty priests shuffled down the center of the
twilight-shrouded street, croaking out a hymn to Cyric.
They strained to form the words as best they could, but
the charred stumps of their tongues choked them with
every syllable. Their eyes, glazed with pain and rimmed
red with exhaustion, stared blankly at the squalid surroundings. Xeno Mirrormane had allowed the priests little
rest in the past three days, but such were the demands of
the Fourth Service: *Maim the voices of two score and ten of
my faithful and send them to sing my praises along every
alley, every path in the city that would be my holy refuge.*

Rinda shook her head and continued down the street,
away from the chorus. Gruesome spectacles such as this

had become commonplace in the Keep since the Day of Dark Oracles, as Xeno Mirrormane and his priests struggled to complete the six rituals Cyric had inscribed upon the windows of his temple. Each of the rites demanded blood and pain, as if they alone could prove the city's holiness. Sometimes the priests themselves suffered the awful mutilations. More often, the rituals required the agony of innocents and the screams of the unsuspecting.

At some other time, the Zhentish not devoted to the Prince of Lies might have risen up against the tyranny. Now, though, there was more at stake than the ephemeral matter of the Keep's spirituality. Outriders from the city had spotted a vast army of giants and goblins and other wild creatures moving purposefully out of the northern wastes. The mystics knew their visions of doom were coming true as news of the advancing army spread through the city. Others guessed the horde to be the work of some god or goddess intent on turning Cyric's anger with the Keep to his or her advantage. Simple fear silenced the debate in the end; no matter what force drove them on, the giants obviously intended to strike while the city was weak.

The fear blossomed into panic when it became clear that no help from the Keep's outposts was forthcoming. A flight of white dragons had taken up a wide perimeter around the city, slaughtering any caravans or soldiers they encountered. A force of three hundred Zhentilar from the Citadel of the Raven had been wiped out within sight of the Keep's walls. Now, with the giants less than a day away, the wyrms had tightened their ring. From the highest gatehouses you could see them in their patrols, dark specks circling in a cloudless blue sky.

In the twisted alleys and streets of the city, no one could see the wyrms, only the terror they inspired. The frantic haste of the priests as they conducted their bloody rites, the violent skirmishes for what little food remained after the church and the merchant houses had taken their fill, the futile prayers to the Prince of Lies—it all reeked of desperation. To a man, the Zhentish had the look of wild animals, wounded and cornered by a royal hunt.

As she passed the weathered facade of the Serpent's Eye, Rinda noticed three of the Keep's more openly feral denizens: soldiers lurking in the tavern's shadowy doorway. The swaggering arrogance in their movements as they stepped toward her, the predatory glints in their eyes, told Rinda the Zhentilar were on press-gang duty. The straight razors and pitch-soaked ropes in their hands meant they were collecting parts of young women for the Second Service.

"Don't bother," the scribe said coldly. She flipped her cloak back, revealing the black leather armband that marked her as a protected servant of the church.

Two of the Zhentilar turned away. The remaining soldier—a young woman with a jagged scar running from the corner of her mouth to her ear—snarled at Rinda. "One o' Xeno's whores." She spit on the ground, then joined her fellows in the shadows of the doorway.

The scribe didn't bother to correct the woman, merely hurried on toward her home. Despite herself, she said a silent thanks to Cyric for giving her the armband; it had saved her life more than once in the past three days.

Rinda was forced to step aside as a horse-drawn cart clattered into the alley. The wagon rumbled to a stop a few doors up from hers, and the driver dropped to the cobbles where a corpse lay in the gutter. It was Johul the fletcher, Rinda realized, a wave of sadness washing over her. The fletcher's clothes had been shredded in some terrible brawl. One of his hands dangled, almost severed at the wrist. The **H** gouged into his bloated face declared his crime and the reason for his death: heresy.

"Not likely," the scribe muttered. Once, before Cyric's church took total control of the city, she'd heard the fletcher say he wouldn't have been able to tell the gods apart if they all sat down at the Serpent's Eye to dice with him. He would have worshiped whatever deity his customers favored, for all that it mattered to him.

Rinda glanced at the window above the fletcher's workshop, only to find Johul's son watching the corpse being dumped unceremoniously onto the cart. The boy had hated his father. That was certainly no secret in the neighborhood. And like many others in the Keep, the boy had used the church's frenzied search for heretics as an excuse for murder. The pyre called for by the First Service required a constant supply of corpses. Where the bodies came from mattered little, just so long as they were branded with the H before death. Unsurprisingly, heretics had become as plentiful as mice in a granary since the Day of Dark Oracles.

In three days, Zhentil Keep had become a grim reflection of Cyric's realm in Hades—at least as he'd described the City of Strife in the *Cyrinishad*. The Prince of Lies had dictated the last chapter in that cursed tome in the hours before the temple statues came to life. In it, he described his dream of a world with no other gods. More than any section of the *Cyrinishad,* the words from this chilling fancy had burned themselves into Rinda's mind:

The chains of Hypocrisy will fall away, and man will be free to act upon his instincts, the only trustworthy guides in this world of strife and despair. The prison whose four walls are Honor, Loyalty, Philanthropy, and Sacrifice will be shattered by the sword of Self-Interest and the mace of Greed. Even now the warriors who take up these weapons first and wield them with the surest hand triumph over all others. Loosed from the fetters of Righteousness, all men will be set

*on a level battlefield, made free to cut their own destiny from
the bleak cloth of life.*

*Cities will burn and rivers run crimson with the blood of
those too foolish to see the truth. Pyres of unbelievers will
color the sky yellow with their greasy smoke, and the wind
will carry the stench of death to every corner of the globe. But
those who follow me will build new cities upon the ruins of
the old, places where anyone can be king—so long as he has
the temerity to take up a blade against his brother and
demand everything owed him by the world. . . .*

Though the warp and weave of Cyric's brutish tapestry
stayed with Rinda, she'd distanced herself from his foul
vision with a firm belief that civilization wouldn't fall so
easily. After all, she herself had taken a stand against the
death god. And there were others battling Cyric—both
mortals and immortals. Once they distributed *The True
Life of Cyric*, perhaps even more would flock to their banner of Truth and Freedom.

As she pushed open her front door, the scribe was wondering what Oghma had in mind for *The True Life*. Like
the death god's tome, the Binder's history had been completed on the Day of Dark Oracles.

All thoughts of the God of Knowledge and *The True Life
of Cyric* fled to the deepest, most guarded part of her mind
when she saw the two men awaiting her return.

"My dear," said Cyric. "You look like you've seen a
ghost." He glanced over his shoulder. "Don't tell me one of
my minions followed me from home."

"N-No, Your Magnificence," Rinda stammered. She
adopted the facade of unquestioning, somewhat dimwitted
loyalty she used whenever she was in Cyric's presence.
"It's just that—uh, one of my neighbors was murdered—I
mean, he was marked as a heretic and—"

"Yes, the fletcher," the Prince of Lies drawled. "His son

is an exemplary citizen, don't you agree?" He waved the question away. "Of course you do. You know you really shouldn't be surprised to find people in your living room, not when you leave your door unlocked in a neighborhood like this."

"So I've been told," Rinda said numbly.

The death god turned to the other man in the room. "I didn't tell you to stop reading, Fzoul."

The red-haired cleric looked up at Rinda, fear making his hard mouth twitch. He sat at her desk, a thick volume open before him. The lantern at his side cast long shadows across his features, masking his eyes and mouth with dark bands. "The woman deserves an explana—"

Cyric tapped Fzoul sharply with Godsbane, as if the sword were a pointer and he a stern lecturer at some temple school. "I'll decide what the woman deserves," he murmured.

"The illuminators and binders finished your book already?" Rinda asked. She wavered for a moment on the doorstep, then decided it would be foolish to run. She closed the door behind her as she stepped into the room.

"It's your book, as well, my dear," the Prince of Lies said. "And yes, it's complete. I had the other craftsmen working on the pages as you completed them." He smiled wickedly. "I'm just fulfilling an old promise to Fzoul here, allowing him to be the first mortal to read the finished draft."

"The first mortal?" Rinda asked. She slipped her cloak off and let it drop carelessly to the floor. "Have you read it, then?"

Cyric resumed his nervous pacing around the cramped room. "From cover to cover," he replied breathlessly. "A magnificent job. You captured my brilliance on every page."

The Lord of the Dead dragged the tip of Godsbane along the floor as he walked, scoring a deep furrow in the creaking boards. "We need the illuminations for the rubes who can't read, of course, but the drawings have never been much of a problem. We had them right after the third or fourth version."

Cyric paused when a floorboard rattled loose, and Rinda's heart skipped a beat. The manuscript of *The True Life* was hidden on the ground there, wrapped tightly in leather. The Lord of the Dead didn't bother to look into the crack, though. He pushed the board back into place with a boot heel and stomped it tight.

"But you've been the only one to get the words down— well, at least that's the way it seemed to me after I read it. Fzoul here will be the real critic."

Rinda fought back the urge to call out in her mind for Oghma, to send a silent prayer to the God of Knowledge. Cyric would surely hear any such plea and deal with them harshly. Besides, the Binder knew the death god had her trapped, at least he did if he were still watching over her.

"Where were you?"

The scribe looked up, only to find Cyric standing at her side. His red cloak flowed around him like flame, swirling and dancing on the cold eddies that shot up from the floorboards. The lantern light made his eyes glitter. His breath held the slightest hint of brimstone as he whispered, "Aiding the church in their hunt for traitors, perhaps?"

Rinda felt the color drain from her face. "Food," she blurted. "I was looking for food."

"But you came back with nothing? Ah, yes: wartime shortages." Cyric spread his hands wide as the realization came to him. "Sieges are like that. The rich eat venison, and the poor eat each other."

At a gesture from the death god, a mound of food appeared on a table: a jug of sweet cider, a steaming leg of lamb, piles of strawberries, and a still-warm loaf of bread. "There you are," the Prince of Lies said. "You only need to ask."

Her stomach rumbled and tightened at the sight of so much food. There was little enough gruel and stale water to be had in the Keep, especially in the slums, and this was a feast suited to a nobleman's table. Rinda glanced at Cyric, who nodded his patronizing approval.

As Rinda ate, the death god continued to pace around the room. He idly chipped away at furniture with Godsbane and thumped the rafters, sending rats scurrying for better cover. The vermin seemed to recognize the God of Strife. They paused and deferentially nodded their mangy, pointed snouts to him before scampering off.

The scribe finished eating quickly. A few mouthfuls of bread and a strawberry or two filled her to contentment, and she fell to watching the Lord of the Dead. After every few steps Cyric would look anxiously at Fzoul or gift Rinda with a deprecating smile. There was a tension in his movements Rinda hadn't seen before, a tick at the corner of his mouth when he forced away the grim scowl.

So focused was Rinda on watching Cyric that Fzoul's piercing scream made her leap to her feet. The jug of cider rolled from the table. Its sharp crash underscored the priest's long wail of despair.

"Please," Fzoul cried. He pushed away from the desk and got to his feet. "Don't make me finish it. I can feel the words eating into my brain."

Fzoul lurched drunkenly toward Rinda. "Stop him," he whispered. The priest's knees folded beneath him, and he collapsed. His nose broke as his face slammed into the floor.

"Set him back at the desk," Cyric said. "But use one of those rags to clean him off first. We wouldn't want him leaving his blood all over the pages. No, I'd better take care of that. . . ." He gestured at Fzoul, and the blood stopped gushing from his nose, disappeared from his hands and face.

Rinda helped Fzoul to his feet. The priest's nose bent awkwardly at the bridge, and bruises circled both eyes like a highwayman's mask. At first he accepted the scribe's help. When he saw the pity in her eyes, though, Fzoul savagely shoved her away. Alone, he staggered the last few feet to the desk.

"He's always been an ungrateful lout," Cyric said as he gently lifted Rinda from the floor. He turned to the red-haired priest. "And don't think of skipping a single word," he rumbled.

Petulantly Cyric lashed out with Godsbane. The flat of the blade struck Fzoul on the ear; the short sword pulsed brightly, hungrily, then calmed to its normal rosy hue. "He's not for you, my love," the Prince of Lies cooed as he sheathed the blade. "Not unless the book fails to convince him of my greatness."

Fzoul had a single gathering left to read, the section devoted to Cyric's final vision of the world. The panic had fled his features, replaced by a stoic resignation to his fate. Like a cobra mesmerized by a charmer's pipes, he began to sway as he read the tome's final words: *This is the immutable word of Cyric, Lord of the Dead and Prince of Lies. Long may he reign on earth and in Hades.*

The priest slumped forward onto the book, bringing Cyric to his side in three hurried steps. Fzoul didn't resist when the death god pulled him from the chair. His eyes seemed unable to focus, and he returned Cyric's intense stare only vaguely. Yet that pall slipped from Fzoul's face almost as swiftly as it had settled there. It was as if he had recognized the Prince of Lies for the first time.

"Your Magnificence," Fzoul cried, dropping to his knees. He folded his hands together in supplication and bowed.

Cyric rubbed his chin for a moment, skeptically eyeing the prostrate form before him. He raised Fzoul up with a firm hand, then stared once more into the priest's eyes.

Rinda watched, horrified but fascinated, as Fzoul shuddered in Cyric's grasp. The death god was probing his convert's mind, looking for some hint of dissent, some pocket of resistance trying to hold out against the book's hypnotic spell. "Well, well," the Lord of the Dead murmured after a time. "You aren't lying, are you?"

Casually Cyric released Fzoul and turned to the scribe. "You've done your job well. One final boon and your work will be complete." He gestured for her to join him at the desk.

As the Prince of Lies closed the *Cyrinishad*, Rinda saw the covers for the first time. Golden clasps and hinges held the book together, along with a lock wrought of some brightly polished metal the scribe couldn't identify. These stood out sharply against the raven-black leather, which the binders had stamped with hundreds of tiny holy symbols, all grinning skulls and dark suns. Weird patterns warped and flowed across the rest of the leather. At first the designs seemed random, but the longer Rinda looked at them, the more clearly she could see the horrible scenes of torture and grief hidden in the chaos of lines and shapes.

A skull the size of a child's fist dominated the front cover, staring out of the closed book through dark, lifeless sockets. Cyric ran his fingers tenderly over the bones. "Now that the critic has spoken, we must protect the *Cyrinishad* from tampering—by mortals or gods."

He held out his hand, and a dagger appeared, balanced by the tip on one slender finger. "Don't worry, my dear. This will hardly hurt at all."

Striking as swiftly as a serpent, Cyric grabbed Rinda by the wrist. He drew the blade across her palm before she could react, then positioned the wound over the closed book.

The scribe's blood dripped onto the cover, the sizzle of the crimson liquid on the leather masking her hiss of pain. Then Cyric spoke a single arcane phrase, and the skull stirred. Its mouth creaked open. Eagerly a long black tongue darted out to lap up the blood.

"With this blood I set my wards. This book cannot be altered in shape or content. Neither can it be removed from the mortal realms," the Lord of the Dead intoned, then turned to the grinning skull. "You are my guardian. Your life is borrowed from me, and I will suffer you to live only so long as my book is safe. Do you understand?"

The skull clacked its teeth together, as if chewing on the words before uttering them. "Of course, Your Magnificence. I exist to do your bidding."

Rinda shrank back in horror. The tiny skeletal face spoke with her voice.

"You look shocked," Cyric said as he ran his hand along the scribe's cheek. "You shouldn't be. Your blood animates the book's guardian. Think of it as your lock on immortality. That's what most authors want, right—to live on in their works? I'm afraid, however, that the *Cyrinishad* is the only book you're going to be writing." With a flick of his wrist, the Prince of Lies tossed the dagger to Fzoul. "Kill her."

Rinda's hand came up in a block an instant too late. The mesmerized priest slammed the knife into her stomach, burying the blade to the hilt. Rinda gasped once at the pain. That was all she had time to do before Fzoul twisted the dagger and shoved her to the floor.

"Did you think for an instant I wouldn't find out you were plotting behind my back?" Cyric shouted. "Especially after one of my inquisitors killed a heretic on your damned doorstep?" The Lord of the Dead stood over Rinda, and the short sword at his side pulsed in time with the blood flowing from her wound. "Did you think I wouldn't realize the Binder would try to counter my book?"

He glared at Fzoul, his face contorted with fury. "I know you're in on this, too, priest. And now that you've come to see my greatness, I think you should explain what Oghma had in mind."

Rinda felt her strength flowing away, and with it went her voice. She could only listen mutely as Fzoul Chembryl explained how Oghma had contacted him and other members of the underground in hopes of starting a revolt against the death god. The focus of this uprising would be *The True Life of Cyric,* a history meant to discredit the malevolent book being crafted by the Prince of Lies. Because Rinda was a scribe and not devoted to Cyric, the Binder felt obliged to protect her mind from the baleful influences of the *Cyrinishad.* He recruited her, intending to have her finish the text so it could be copied and distributed through Cyric's churches.

With two slashes of Godsbane, the Prince of Lies shattered the floorboards covering the leather-wrapped gatherings of the *The True Life.* "This would be the Binder's book, I suppose." He tore away the wrapping and paged through the parchment, pausing now and then to laugh at some passage or another. Finally he scattered the gatherings into the air. "The text isn't even magical!" he hooted. "I don't believe it. The Binder thought the truth would undo me!"

The Prince of Lies walked to Rinda's side, coming to stand just at the edge of the spreading pool of blood. "It looks like the knife hurt more than I told you, milady. But, then, I knew it would." Smiling, he crouched to look into her face. "I lied, you see. I do that."

Cyric toed the pool of blood, staining the tips of his boots crimson. "I wasn't lying about your fate if you betrayed me, though," he said with enthusiasm. "I've got a horrible place all ready for you in Hades. Even now my denizens are waiting for your soul to arrive."

Rinda watched the room grow vague around her. The shapes and colors blurred together, the sounds melded into a nagging murmur. Occasionally one image would leap into focus—the beady eyes of a rat from its vantage in the rafters, the flutter of a manuscript page as it settled to the floor, the food Cyric had conjured turning to maggots—then a wave of unconsciousness would drag her away. Each time, she felt herself drawn farther and farther from her home, her body. . . .

"Another job well done," Cyric sighed as he gathered up his book. "There won't be time for anyone else to read this by morning, but I want you to take it to the main temple for safekeeping. At the dawn service, you are to read the final section to the faithful."

Fzoul bowed as he took the heavy volume. "As you wish, Your Magnificence."

"Yes, fine," the Prince of Lies said, irritation creeping into his voice. "The reading will be the final part of the ceremony, and you must be finished by sunrise." Cyric paused and stared at the top of Fzoul's bowed head. "This is hardly the sport it once was. I almost miss your futile anger. Ah, well. Can't be helped."

With a final glance at Rinda's corpse, the Lord of the Dead readied himself to leave. "Burn this place to the ground," he said as his incarnation faded from view. "Use the Binder's book to start the blaze."

No sooner had Cyric disappeared than Fzoul tossed the *Cyrinishad* onto the desktop and rushed to Rinda's side.

"What do you think you're doing?" the book shrieked.

A silver chain appeared around the tome, filling the skull's mouth like a gag.

"You didn't need to hurt her so badly," Oghma snapped as he appeared in the center of the room. He glanced at the *Cyrinishad* to be certain his enchantment was holding, then turned back toward Rinda. "Can you save her?"

Fzoul smirked. "I know how to gut-stab someone so they'll take hours to die," he said, though the voice coming from his lips was now the Shadowlord's sibilant hiss. "But I need to get rid of this ham-fisted disguise first."

The priest's shadow darkened, grew more substantial, as if Fzoul's lifeforce were pouring from his body into the blackness. It rose then, towering over both the priest and the fallen scribe. Shadows from around the room flowed toward Mask. They merged around him to form his ever-shifting cloak. "Are you keeping your shield up over the place?" the Shadowlord asked.

"If he bothers to look, Cyric will see Fzoul preparing to set the building ablaze," the Binder said. "What about Rinda's shade? Cyric said his denizens were waiting."

"Already taken care of," Mask said smugly. He pushed Fzoul out of the way and kneeled by Rinda's side. At a touch of his hand, the bleeding stopped and her chalk-white face began to show a little color. "I sent an old friend of Fzoul's in her stead. You remember Lord Chess, don't you? I think he'll rather enjoy being a woman for a while—well, he might have if Cyric hadn't planned such a nasty reception for Rinda." His eyes narrowed, and a hint of true concern slipped into his voice. "She'd better hope she never falls into his hands. . . ."

"She won't," Oghma said. Gently he lifted Rinda from the floor and carried her to a table, which transformed into a padded couch as he lowered her toward it. "And you, Fzoul, how do you fare?"

The priest now lay on his back, hands pressed tightly on his temples. "I don't know," he mumbled. "I can't tell if this pounding in my head is going to stop or not."

"It will," Mask said. "I had to let you feel some real pain

or Cyric might have caught on. Human screams are tough to mimic convincingly."

"Give me the knife back and we can practice on you for a while," Fzoul said. He sat up with a groan, then fell to examining his broken nose.

"You're just fortunate I set up that construct to save your mind," Mask noted. "The book would have made you another of Cyric's mindless drones."

Oghma looked again at the tome. The skull was trying to spit the chain from its mouth, intent on calling its master. "We have to destroy it somehow."

"Not now, we don't," Mask said. He seemed to float as he came toward the Patron of Bards, buoyed by the intrigue of the day. "Cyric set some powerful wards on the thing, too powerful to be broken in any simple fashion. No, it would be best to get the book out of the city and worry about it later—after the battle."

"What battle?" Fzoul said. "You said yourselves Cyric doesn't intend to let the giants attack the city."

"But we do," the Shadowlord replied. "Those brutes are going to stomp this place flat—and you're going to open the gates for them, Fzoul. In a manner of speaking, anyway."

The priest snapped his nose back into line, then shook his head violently to drive away the tears of pain coursing down his cheeks. "I suppose I have no choice in the matter?"

"You always have a choice," Oghma said.

Mask leaned over the priest's shoulder. "Of course you do," he whispered. "In this case, you either go along with us or we let Cyric know the book didn't work on you. I'm certain he'll get it right the second time around."

Sighing, Fzoul got to his feet. "What do I do?"

"You'll address the faithful tomorrow, just as Cyric wants," Mask began. He circled Fzoul as he spoke, an owl waiting for a field mouse to twitch in the dark. "Except you'll read them the final section of Oghma's book. It tells how our Prince of Lies intends to dupe the city. When everyone hears how Cyric created the menace in the first place . . . well, more than a few people will be sorely disappointed in their would-be savior."

"That won't bring the giants down on the city," Fzoul rumbled. "That'll just get me killed. Don't you think Cyric will be listening to this ceremony?"

"We know he will not—indeed *cannot*—pay careful attention to what you say, Fzoul Chembryl." Oghma had begun to gather up the scattered pages of *The True Life*. He handed a bundle to the priest. "Cyric needs the city's desperate worship to power a spell. That's the point of the dawn ceremony, to focus that power. But to use it, he must meditate, point all the facets of his mind to the grail of his quest."

"Lyonsbane's soul," Fzoul murmured.

"Exactly," Mask said. "In other words, when you give your little lecture to the masses, Cyric will have his eyes closed."

Fzoul straightened the gatherings and set them on a chair. "And that's when you start the revolt in the City of Strife." He drummed his fingers nervously on the pages from *The True Life*. "I'm still not happy about moving into the open."

"I'll be there to protect you," Mask offered with exaggerated deference. "If you take up my holy symbol, Fzoul, I'll serve you well. After all, Bane has been dead the past ten years, and you still mourn him. Isn't it time you got on with your life?"

"Perhaps," the priest said, then pushed past Mask to pick up the last of the scattered gatherings. "Let's see where we stand at sunset tomorrow, Shadowlord."

"That still leaves the matter of the *Cyrinishad*," Oghma noted, the chords in his voice somber.

"I'll take it," Rinda said softly. "I wrote the damned thing, I should be the one to deal with it now." She struggled to sit up, one hand pressed against her stomach to ease the throbbing.

Fzoul scowled. "That's absurd. How are you supposed to guard it?"

"You'd be a better choice, I suppose?" the scribe snapped. "Oghma, you can't let this powerful an artifact fall into the hands of the Zhentarim. They'd try to twist it to their purposes, and we both know it can only be used to destroy true knowledge."

"I think the matter is settled," the God of Knowledge said, and Mask did not contradict him.

The Binder held out a glittering holy symbol to the scribe. The small scroll was wrought of a single pure diamond and fit comfortably into the palm of her hand. "You are now guardian of the *Cyrinishad*," Oghma said solemnly. "This holy symbol will mark you as such to all of my faithful. My churches and monasteries will provide safe haven for you, and my loremasters will give you food and money if you are needy."

"Your clerics won't be able to hide her from Cyric," Fzoul said snidely. "And unless you intend on destroying him in this little revolt, he'll come looking for his book sooner or later."

Oghma nodded. "That likelihood has been foreseen, as well. So long as you wear this holy symbol and remain in the mortal realms, Rinda of the Book, you and the tome will be invisible to all the gods and their divine minions." At the concerned look in her eyes, the Binder nodded. "Even to me. It's best that way."

The scribe got to her feet. "Thank you," she said. Tentatively, she reached out for the god's hand. Oghma let her grasp his dark fingers, but then raised her hand to his lips and kissed it. "A place of honor will await you in my palace."

After he slipped the chain around Rinda's neck, Oghma turned to Mask. "Come, Shadowlord. We've much to do." With that he was gone.

Mask lingered a moment longer. "Remember all I've told you, Fzoul. I'll be there tomorrow if you call upon me."

The priest stepped forward boldly. "You can't allow the Binder to throw the book away."

"Throw it away?" the Shadowlord asked. His red eyes glittered playfully.

"She couldn't turn aside a simple knife," Fzoul said, his face flushing beneath his blackened eyes. "How will she protect herself against an assassin's blade? Cyric is Lord of Murder, after all. All the assassins in the world answer his call."

Mask glanced around the room, astonished to find he could see neither the scribe nor the book. "The knife that struck her a moment ago was wielded by a god, Fzoul, not a mortal. Even then, she very nearly blocked the strike. Could you do the same?"

The priest was not so easily deterred. "The next blade she faces could be Godsbane. Cyric killed two gods with that sword. What chance does a scribe have against that? At least I'd have my spells to protect me."

Mask paused, suddenly baffled. "Only two gods?"

"Bhaal and Leira," Fzoul said. "What others?"

"Oh, er, none," the Shadowlord said abruptly. He gestured vaguely around the room. "If you want the *Cyrinishad* so badly, Fzoul, then you should try to take it. Wait until the ceremony's over, though. If she kills you, you'd be hard to replace with such little notice."

Mask slipped into the priest's shadow and vanished.

As still as a statue, Rinda stood in the center of the room. She'd wrapped the *Cyrinishad* in rags and tied them tightly with some frayed rope. In all, the bundle looked no more or less important than any other beggar's pack. When Fzoul took a step toward her, she raised a hand to ward him off, but kept her eyes fixed on the priest's shadow, where Mask had disappeared.

"Don't worry," Fzoul said. "I think Mask's right. We'll leave things be for now, but after the battle—"

Rinda merely continued to stare.

"What's wrong?"

"You heard him. Mask knows Cyric didn't kill Bane and Myrkul, as the *Cyrinishad* claims. But he almost disagreed with you." The scribe held the ragged bundle away from her, as if it were crawling with venomous spiders. "Cyric made the book so its enchantment works on gods, too."

XVII

GIANTS ON THE DOORSTEP

*Wherein Gwydion the Quick is offered the
magical sword that started him on the road to
Hades, Xeno Mirrormane receives his just
reward for serving the Prince of Lies, and a
book of truth brings down the walls of
Zhentil Keep—with considerable help
from an army of monsters.*

"He's a lunatic," Adon said. "Honestly. Cyric belongs in
here more than some of the inmates." He gestured to an
empty bed. "Maybe we can find room for him, though I'm
pretty certain the others wouldn't like him very much."

Mystra smiled at her patriarch's fervor, at the anger in
his eyes as he mulled over the death god's plot to unify
Zhentil Keep. "Right now, Cyric's plans don't seem as mad
as ours," the Lady of Mysteries sighed. "For the uprising
in the City of Strife to have the slightest chance of success,

the giants and dragons must sack the Keep. We've got to make certain the monsters win, which means innocents will suffer. That's what's troubling me."

Adon kneeled to wipe the face of the wild-eyed man Mystra had named Talos. "Can't sleep again, old fellow? It's past midnight you know."

Since the Goddess of Magic had first brought Adon to the asylum, more than a month past, conditions at the House of the Golden Quill had improved greatly. The priest had devoted much of his time—and more than a little of the church's wealth—to improving the place. From his efforts, the reeking, lightless pit had been transformed into a comforting home for those whose minds had been twisted by misfired enchantments. The asylum remained cold and drafty, to be certain, and the rats clung obstinately to their secret nests. Still, clean beds and warm clothes had become the norm, and kindhearted novitiates from the local Church of Mysteries had volunteered their services as nurses for the inmates.

Normally, one of those young clerics would have seen to Talos, but Adon had banished them from the ward upon Mystra's arrival. With the goddess's avatar strolling about, they wouldn't get any work done anyway, what with all the bowing and praying.

At last the patriarch finished his ministering. As he got to his feet, he turned concern-filled eyes on the goddess. "How many of them do you think are left in the city? Innocents, I mean."

"Five hundred and fourteen, to be precise about it. Most of the people devoted to gods other than Cyric fled the Keep years ago. The ones who stayed either hid their true allegiance or found themselves branded as heretics. There are some secret Tempus worshipers in the army. Quite a few Zhentarim wizards offer prayers to me or Azuth."

"So rescue them yourself," Adon offered. "Just reach down and grab them all before the battle starts."

"Oh, I'll extricate my worshipers from the fight," the goddess said. "But that won't help the faithful of Tymora or Tempus or Lathander."

"Can't you just save them while you're at it?"

"Are you ready to suffer the Circle's wrath because I was meddling beyond the demands of my office?" The Lady of Mysteries shook her head. "They threatened total sanction, Adon. No plants growing in church gardens. No sun in the sky. Everything except magic denied my faithful until I limit my interference with the world."

"But you can explain away your right to make a horde of giants level Zhentil Keep? And your right to start a revolt in the City of Strife?" the patriarch asked as he moved on to the next bed. The man there slept soundly, wrapped in warm blankets donated by the Lords of Waterdeep. "I'm afraid the divine logic eludes me," he whispered.

Mystra laughed softly. "The spell Cyric took from Oghma's library is forbidden magic, a sorcery created by an ancient god even more foul than Bane and Mask and Cyric lumped together, if you can believe that. The giants and the revolt in the Realm of the Dead are ways for me to prevent the magic from being released. The Circle won't question that reasoning."

They moved away from the beds, toward the center of the room. "You'll have to convince the other gods it's a good thing for Zhentil Keep to fall, but only if they rescue their worshipers," Adon said. "Put your case before the rest of the pantheon in terms they'll have to support."

The priest pointed to Talos. The lunatic had been bathed and clothed in a new smock, but he wasn't tearing out his hair or plucking at the robes, as his madness demanded. His mind was focused on the thin sheet of cloth in his hands. No matter how quickly he destroyed it, a minor enchantment restored the threads to their original weave.

"We couldn't figure out how to stop him from hurting himself," the patriarch said, "but then I remembered what you'd told me about the gods: they can see nothing but the world their minds create." He shrugged. "If Talos here has to destroy things, we have to give him something to work on instead of his clothes or his skin."

The Lady of Mysteries hugged the cleric fiercely, bringing a startled blush to his cheeks. "Of course," she blurted. "It's all perspective! Thank you, Adon."

Mystra disappeared in a swirl of blue-white light. A few of the inmates howled in their sleep at the sudden burst of magic. Even unconscious, their scarred minds recoiled from the thing that had damaged them so horribly.

As Adon stood for a moment, looking out over his wards, a chilling thought worked its way into his mind, a notion born of the lateness of the hour and the weird cries of the inmates. Kelemvor had been imprisoned for a decade by a thing of magic. Wasn't it possible he might despise the Art, or even fear it as much as the poor souls lodged in the asylum? And if that were true, Mystra could be risking everything to rescue someone who might not be able to bear her presence.

The patriarch shook the dark thoughts from his mind and hurried to seek out the novitiates ministering in other parts of the building. Madness wasn't contagious, not as some on the farms surrounding the Golden Quill claimed. But Adon had learned the company of madmen gave birth to strange fancies. After a month tending the inmates at the asylum, he knew better than to linger in the halls after midnight.

Similarly, he hoped Mystra had enough sense not to dwell too long in the other gods' minds, even if only to convince them of her plan. Cyric had proved that madness wasn't something confined to the realms of mortals. The Lady of Mysteries would do well to remember that.

* * * * *

Even with her myriad incarnations, it took Mystra hours to visit each member of Faerun's pantheon. The Lady of Mysteries informed the gods and goddesses of Zhentil Keep's fate, how the holy city would be turned against its patron and the giants allowed to raze the evil place to the ground. She cast her involvement in the plot just as she had explained it to Adon: as the guardian of magic, it was her responsibility to prevent Cyric's use of forbidden sorceries. No one disagreed.

As for the destruction of the city itself, Mystra dipped into the thoughts of each deity and used that perspective to describe the Keep's fall as something positive. To the Lady of the Forest, the giants became a scourge with which to strike down the walls and reclaim the land for the wilderness. To Lathander Morninglord, the end of the city brought with it the possibility for a glorious new kingdom to arise from the torched houses and fractured columns. Talos viewed the promised destruction of the Keep as a desirable end in itself, while Tyr judged the annihilation of Cyric's faithful to be just punishment for their disregard of law and justice. The process was exhausting and often tedious, but before long the members of the pantheon had been convinced Cyric's strife was a glorious victory for their cause and their faithful.

Now, as night began her slow retreat from Faerun, the Lady of Mysteries stood in the courtyard of her heavenly palace. The castle and the walls protecting it were drawn from the magical weave, pulsing blue-white radiance that flickered like faerie fire in a midnight marsh. Bright penons snapped and fluttered from an infinite number of tall spires. Each flag bore the sigil of a wizard or sage granted a home in Mystra's realm. In their towers lay workshops, wonderfully strange and arcane places where the faithful freely pursued the more elusive secrets of sorcery denied them by the limits of mortal life.

Dragons of silver and gold perched on the high battlements, and unicorns wandered over the lush, verdant lawn. Other creatures of magic called the palace home, as well. Basilisks and cockatrices roamed the gardens, their eyes masked by special enchantments to prevent them from turning the unwary to stone. A ram-headed sphinx perched near the front gate, exchanging riddles with a couatl. The feathered serpent laughed at some jest and beat the air with its alabaster wings.

Such beasts were not unknown to the mortal realms, but to Gwydion, standing in the center of the courtyard, they were all gloriously new.

In his days as a soldier, Gwydion had heard stories about dragons and sphinxes. The creatures populated the tales told by drunken sell-swords and experienced warriors, men and women who'd traveled outside the civilized confines of cities like Suzail. Some of the stories were true. Others were pure fantasy, yarns in which the mere sighting of a manticore's tracks was embellished until it became a bloody fight to the death against three of the scorpion-tailed beasts.

Tales like those had helped to lure Gwydion away from his life in Cormyr's army, drawn him into the unlikely role of mercenary. And though he'd battled more than a few exotic beasts, he'd never encountered creatures as rare and marvelous as the ones gathered before him now. As he watched a phoenix rise high over the palace and spread her fiery wings, the shade realized that neither the bards' tales nor his imagination had done the enchanted creatures justice. Even after all the pain, all the bloodshed, the mere sight of such wonders had proved enough to remind him that Cyric's dire city was only a small part of a huge and often glorious universe.

Not everyone in the courtyard shared the shade's wonder at his surroundings.

"Go pester someone else, blast you!" Gond shouted.

The God of Craft waved a greasy spanner around his head, but the sprites swarming there easily avoided the clumsy swipes. As soon as the Wonderbringer turned back to his work on Gwydion's armor, they moved close again. The sprites tugged at Gond's hair and fluttered around the clockwork golems assisting him, dropping daisy chains around their blocky heads. They danced in a circle around the other eight shades whom Cyric had imprisoned in the inquisitor armor.

"Good thing I'm almost done," the Wonderbringer muttered into his barbed wire beard. "Otherwise I'd set up a swatter to keep you pests away."

A sprite hovered just over Gond's pate, silently mocking the burly god. Gwydion couldn't help but laugh as the tiny spirit screwed a scowl onto its sweet face and curled its gossamer wings into a particularly good imitation of the Wonderbringer's hunched shoulders.

"What's so damned funny?" Gond snapped, his iron-gray eyes sparking like steel on flint.

"Laughter is not as unusual in my realm as it is in some others," Mystra interrupted, shooing away the sprites with one subtle gesture. "I thank you again for your assistance, Wonderbringer. You prove there are things better left to the hammers of your smiths than the spells of my faithful."

Gond grunted. "If you didn't realize that, I wouldn't be here," he muttered. He never looked up from his task, his eyes focused on the rivets holding Gwydion's knee cops in place. "Glad you didn't try to dismantle these suits yourself, though. You would've damaged 'em for sure. Like you said, the workmanship's too good to be wasted. . . ."

"And we will put it to good use," Mask said, appearing suddenly at Gwydion's side.

"I didn't care what Cyric used 'em for," Gond said as he stood. "I don't care what you use 'em for." He tossed the spanner over his shoulder to one of his golems. "Pack it up, boys. We're done."

The Wonderbringer turned abruptly for the gate, pausing to acknowledge neither Mystra's polite thanks nor Mask's snide remarks about the mechanical lover Gond had created, if certain myths were to be believed. Gwydion watched the God of Craft trudge away. A half-dozen clockwork servants clanked along in his wake, boxes of tools and stray pieces of armor in their viselike hands. Just why the Wonderbringer bothered walking to the gate at all puzzled the shade, and the confusion showed on his face.

"It's his way of slighting magic," Mystra said in reply to the unasked question. "By walking out rather than plane shifting, he's proving he values physical labor over sorcery."

Mask chuckled. "He'll shift quick as he's out of sight, though. Some time you ought to follow him. The old crank would walk all the way back to Concordant just to spite you."

"And where would that leave the two of us?" Mystra replied coldly. "Gond would be home, and I'd have walked all that way for nothing."

The Lord of Shadows shook his head. "I thought you'd have learned something from me by now," he said, the words slithering from his lips. "Ah well. I suppose it's time we sent the troops off on their merry way."

Gwydion suppressed a shudder at the thought of returning to the Realm of the Dead. He could almost hear the screaming, taste the bitter smoke that filled the air.

"No one will force you to go," Mystra said.

"I'll be all right," Gwydion said thickly. His teeth and tongue had healed quite a bit since Gond had removed the bit from his mouth, but he still found it difficult to form some words.

Mask sidled up to the shade. "You've got nothing to be afraid of, you know. This armor makes you a match for just about anybody."

Long and silver and tipped with venom, a knife appeared in the Shadowlord's hand. The cloak of darkness obscured Mask's form as he lunged, but that didn't hamper Gwydion in the least. His gauntleted hand a gold blur, the shade grabbed the god's wrist and twisted the knife from his grasp.

"See," the Shadowlord purred. "Quite impressive."

The second blade left the slightest of cuts on its way across Gwydion's throat. The shade grabbed at Mask's other hand, but was far too slow.

The Shadowlord slithered out of Gwydion's grasp. "But don't be overconfident. You're no good to us with your head rolling around on the ground."

"Enough games," Mystra said. "It's almost dawn at Zhentil Keep."

"Ah yes," Mask said brightly. He gestured to the other armored shades. "Hades awaits."

Gwydion and his fellows formed a ragged line. Together they resembled the figures from some children's storybook romance, shining knights ready to embark upon a heroic quest. Gond had scoured away Cyric's foul holy symbols, removed the hooks and razors from the armor. That didn't make the knights less intimidating, though. They still stood as tall as ogres, even without their great horned helmets.

"Remember," Mystra said, coming to stand before the gathered knights. "Your task is to stir up the False and free the Faithless from the wall."

"Pardon, milady," Gwydion ventured, "but it'd be best to leave the Faithless where they are until the battle's over. They'll be too weak to fight right after they get free."

"The voice of experience?" Mask asked snidely. "Or were you a general in your mortal days?"

Gwydion frowned. "I was only a grunt in the Purple Dragons—but yes, I spent time in the wall."

Mystra cut in before Mask could reply. "Then we shall heed your advice, Gwydion. Focus your attentions on rallying the False. Strike against their jailors, and they'll rise up to support you."

When Mask spoke next, all the shades were startled to find the Patron of Thieves standing right in front of them. It was as if he'd stepped out of their own shadows. "We have a spy within Cyric's house, and she's been priming the mob with thoughts of revolt. You only need strike the spark. The oil has already been poured upon the tinder." He glanced at the Goddess of Magic. "It's time we gird them for battle, don't you think?"

The Lady of Mysteries spread her hands wide, and a sword appeared in the air before each of the knights. Blue fire limned the blades. "These weapons will serve you well, even against the beasts that call Cyric master."

As one, the knights reached out to take the swords, but Gwydion's vanished before he could grasp the hilt.

"I was hoping you would accept a blade from me," said a deep, booming voice.

Torm the True strode forward, a bejeweled scabbard in his hands. "This is the blade of Alban Onire, a weapon called Titanslayer by some. I have taken it from the holy knight's final resting place. Once you were deceived with visions of this blade. It would be just for you to wield it against the deceiver." Slowly the God of Duty held the scabbarded sword out to Gwydion.

The shade paused. "No," he said. "If you couldn't rescue me from the City of Strife, the weapon is not for me."

"A fine choice, Gwydion," Mask whispered. "Never trust a man who says he can be trusted. Cyric taught me that. The Prince of Lies has a fine understanding of many things, and the truth behind Truth is one of them."

Torm frowned. "Praising Cyric, Mask? If you didn't lust after his kingdom, I'd wonder whose side you were on."

The Shadowlord slid behind Mystra and hissed in her ear, "You left your gates open to the other gods when we're mustering a rebel army?"

"I've told you before, my kingdom is always open to Cyric's foes," Mystra said.

"Especially in times of war," Torm added. He smiled at the Lady of Mysteries, the twinkle in his blue eyes almost mischievous. "But you look surprised to see me. Come, come. You're sending one who would be my knight off to battle my enemy's minions. You can't expect me to just stand aside and watch."

"How did you know?" Mystra asked.

"I am called Torm the True for a reason, Lady. What you told me about the doom of Zhentil Keep had the ring of truth about it, but it was faint, as if I were hearing only half the chord." He scowled at Mask. "I realized then that you must be moving armies in the shadows. It's common enough knowledge that you've been trafficking with this snake."

"And you're helping us?" Mask said. His voice was shrill, his glowing red eyes wide with amazement. "No offense, but I always had you figured for the charge-the-front-gates-in-broad-daylight sort of strategist."

Torm ignored the Shadowlord, turning once more to Gwydion. "There are laws I am sworn to uphold, and one of them made it clear you could not be welcomed into my domain. I am offering you the sword now so you can prove yourself worthy."

Anger welled up in Gwydion, a blinding fury that overwhelmed his mind. After all he'd been through, all he'd suffered at Cyric's hands, Torm's self-righteousness and his casual dismissal of the pain he'd caused struck some long-dead part of the shade's soul. He snatched the scabbard from Torm, drew the long sword, and lashed out at the God of Duty.

Gwydion didn't see Torm move, didn't hear the sharp retort as the god's gauntlets clapped over the blade. All he saw was the aftermath of his foiled strike. The God of Duty stood before him, Titanslayer trapped between his palms. The sword tip hovered a hairsbreadth from the bridge of Torm's nose.

"Your honor had been questioned, and you have tried to repay that slight," Torm said calmly. "It is as any true knight would do." He released the blade and pushed it away from his face. "But your real enemy is in Hades. Bring the sword against his minions, Gwydion, and your honor will be restored."

Gwydion stood for a moment, transfixed by Torm's gaze, by the unwavering light of loyalty and truth that radiated from the God of Duty. "I'll try," he said.

Torm nodded. "That's all I can ask."

"The shadows of morning are on their way to Zhentil Keep," Mask crowed, slithering up behind Torm. "Time for our knights to go to war."

The God of Intrigue reached down and pinned two corners of his own shadow to the ground with daggers. He backed up a few steps, stretching the darkness into a wide black pool. "One at a time, please. No pushing in line."

The knights gathered up their helmets, stepped into the shadow, and disappeared one by one. Gwydion was last, and as he entered the darkness, he found Mask at his side.

"A present for you, just to show there's no hard feelings for our little scuffle."

The Shadowlord handed a fat tallow candle to Gwydion. As the knight took the gift, a feral growl rumbled from deep within the wax.

"Don't mind the noises," Mask said. "They're just a side effect of an enchantment Mystra put on the wick. Light the candle as soon as you get the signal to begin the revolt, and it'll release a little creature that should help you deal with Cyric's faithful."

Mask merged with the blackness around him, leaving the shade to fall through the void.

Gwydion considered dropping the candle; he'd been tricked enough times since that day at the giant's cave to instantly mistrust someone like Mask. Still, he was certain the fight for the City of Strife would be hard.

As he emerged from the portal, deep within the necropolis, Gwydion slipped the candle into his sword belt. He still doubted the Shadowlord's motives, but he knew that to bring Cyric low they'd need all the weapons they could muster.

* * * * *

Fzoul Chembryl entered the nave of Cyric's main temple, a huge leatherbound tome clutched reverentially to his chest, his features screwed into his best imitation of divine bliss. As always, the temple stank of sour incense and sweaty, unwashed priests. The awful smoke from the pyre of heretics in the courtyard only added to the miasma. Fzoul's mustaches bristled at the smell, but he fought down the urge to wrinkle his nose. To be utterly enamored with Cyric would place him above such mundane concerns. With Xeno and all the other fanatical clerics watching him carefully, he'd need to keep up the show, at least until he got to the altar.

The six guards surrounding Fzoul marched in step down the black marble aisle, their boots ringing out over the drone of Xeno Mirrormane's sermon and the worried murmur of military speculation from the stalls. The six services had been completed. The army of giants and the vengeful flight of dragons seemed poised, ready to strike with the dawning of the new day. This final test of devotion, this plea to Cyric for salvation, was all that stood between the city and a terrible battle.

Xeno Mirrormane finished his sermon with a prayer to the Lord of the Dead, though no one joined him. Only at the close of Fzoul's reading would the city offer up its worship to Cyric. And with that burst of faith, Zhentil Keep would win back the favor of its god. At least, that was how the patriarch had planned things.

With no prelude, no greeting to the high priest, Fzoul took the steps up to the altar and laid the book on the podium there. The six guards followed in his wake. With military precision, they formed a semicircle behind the speaker's platform. Their pikes gleamed in the light of ten thousand votive candles, which formed the altar's backdrop this bitter morning.

"I bring to you a reading from the *Cyrinishad*," Fzoul began.

All over the city of Zhentil Keep, a ghostly, flickering image of Fzoul Chembryl came to life. The church hierarchy knew that a reading of Cyric's own words by a man recently converted to faith in the death god would prove inspirational, especially in this time of need. With the help of the few wizards who hadn't fled the city, they set a powerful enchantment upon the speaker's platform. When Fzoul addressed the temple, he would be seen and heard by every worshiper within the Keep's high walls.

Fzoul felt a wave of panic wash over him as he considered

just where he was, exactly what he was about to do. Blaspheming Cyric was dangerous enough, but in his holiest temple, at the black altar itself? The priest smiled grimly at the boldness of the challenge.

With hands trembling only slightly, Fzoul opened the tome set before him. He flipped past the blank pages set in the binding to make the volume look more impressive, to the few gatherings that made up *The True Life*.

" 'In this, the Year of the Banner, the people of Zhentil Keep lost their true beliefs, and an army of monsters arose out of the wastes to punish them. Little did they suspect that their god had gathered this army together for the sole purpose of terrifying the Zhentish into slavery.' "

At a nod from Fzoul, the guards rapped their pikes against the stone floor. A wall of force sprang up, its borders marked by the rigid polearms. The crimson radiance from the arcane shield colored Fzoul and his faithful soldiers in bloody hues.

"Heresy!" Xeno Mirrormane shrieked. The patriarch leaped to his feet and pounded his fists raw against the transparent magical wall. But neither the high priest's shouts nor the arrows of the temple guards could penetrate the barrier.

Fzoul went on to detail Cyric's twisted plot, how the death god intended to use the Zhentish as pawns, how he cared little if such minor minions were destroyed. The angry shouts in the temple became gasps of astonishment, then murmurs of dissatisfaction. By the time Fzoul's short reading was over, the only cries of dissent came from a few of the more fanatical priests and the rich converts who feared a loss of social status should the church be disgraced. Even the temple guards had dropped their bows.

"His Magnificence will have your soul for this!" Xeno shouted. He pounded the wall with bruised fists. "I'll send you to him myself!"

"Let him through," Fzoul murmured.

The guards rapped their pikes on the floor again, and the arcane wall lowered. Xeno charged forward. The high priest clawed the air wildly as he barreled toward the heretic.

One kick sent Xeno sprawling across the platform, two broken ribs biting into his lungs.

"Where's your god now?" Fzoul shouted. He turned to the packed nave. "Why hasn't Cyric struck me down?" When no bolt of lightning lanced from the heavens, the red-haired priest grew bold. "Come down and face me, you coward! I'm here, in your temple."

As if in answer to Fzoul's challenge, the first rays of dawn burst through the church windows, the light stained crimson by the services writ large on the glass. At the same moment, golden haloes formed over a few in the crowded temple. The soldiers and merchants and thieves bathed in the warm radiance rose above the throng, suddenly insubstantial. Then, one by one, the ghostly men and women vanished.

Silent explosions of rainbow-hued light marked the passing of the innocents. And from each swirl of color dropped a single, small medallion. Disks of silver and pale red wood, golden medals marked with the scroll of Oghma and the eye-and-gauntlet glyph of Helm. Holy symbols, one for each of the faithful rescued from the doomed city.

On the altar platform, Xeno Mirrormane struggled to his feet. Clutching his side, he staggered forward. "This cannot go . . . unpunished," he gasped, foam flecking his lips. He drew a dagger from his purple robes.

Laughing, Fzoul swaggered forward. "As Cyric won't answer my challenge, I'll have to send you to Hades with a message for him, old man." In his mind he sent out a call to Mask, promising his devoted worship if the Shadowlord would grant him the power to cast down Cyric's patriarch.

Nothing happened.

"Bastard," Fzoul hissed. He stepped toward Xeno, ready to deal with the high priest without the Shadowlord's aid.

That's when the pillar of flame shattered the temple's roof. The column of writhing fire struck Xeno Mirrormane, and for an instant the patriarch's fleshless bones danced a wild dance of agony in the inferno.

Fzoul fell back, his mustaches and eyebrows singed, his face scorched. He spared the time for one gloating look at the ruined altar, the charred remains of the high priest, before he drew his sword and fell in behind his men. Together they cut a wide, corpse-strewn path to the door and the freedom that lay beyond.

The magical fire spread through Cyric's most holy temple until it engulfed even the stone walls and black marble floor. The priests trampled their brethren as they rushed for the exit, but there were simply too many of them to press through the doors in time. The flames caught the mob before half of the death god's minions had escaped.

The screams from the temple were horrifying, but those who managed to flee the inferno were greeted with far more frightening sounds.

The cold morning air thrummed with the harbingers of Zhentil Keep's doom: the thud of huge, double-bladed axes biting into the city gates and the screech of white dragons tearing the archers from the battlements and toppling the high black stone towers.

XVIII

THE DEAD
AND THE QUICK

*Wherein the Lord of the Dead tries to shore up
the crumbling ruins of his twin kingdoms,
Gwydion returns to the City of Strife, intent on
winning back his lost honor, and Rinda begins
her new life as Guardian of the Book.*

The Prince of Lies sat unmoving at the heart of the void, alone except for his memories of Kelemvor Lyonsbane. Images of the warrior flashed through his consciousness: the young braggart Cyric had rescued from the frost giants in Thar; the boastful sell-sword who'd dragged them both into drunkenness and poverty; the man who'd feigned friendship, only to attempt to steal the Tablets of Fate. The Prince of Lies grew furious at the memories, though they held no more truth than any other corrupted remembrance in the mire that was his mind.

"I'll find you," Cyric whispered. "Then Mystra will pay."

The Lord of the Dead had isolated himself from both his mortal and immortal realms, as the ancient spell had demanded. Now, though, he was finding the seclusion more than a little tedious. Cyric longed to put his dark plans into action, to find Kelemvor's soul and begin his eternity of torture.

The death god fidgeted mentally, and a rush of scattered, unfocused thoughts flashed across his divine intellect. He pushed them away as best he could, irritated suddenly at his worshipers in Zhentil Keep. Wasn't it time yet for their final prayer?

The delay was Godsbane's fault, of course. Cyric had charged the sword with the vital task of drawing him out of the trance the instant the Zhentish raised their voices in desperate devotion. But surely the time had come for him to receive the prayers of the city. Surely dawn had risen over Zhentil Keep.

A terrible thought occurred to Cyric then. Perhaps something had gone wrong. . . .

The Prince of Lies let the smallest possible fragment of his mind gaze down upon his holy city. At first only a shrieking pain, red and pulsing, washed across his perception. The frantic, frightened demands of sixty thousand priests and worshipers reached up from the mortal realms like hooks, biting into the god's essence. The pleas for rescue, for magical might to slay the reavers of Zhentil Keep, dragged his mind from the confines of the trance. Cyric tried to steady himself and sort out the cacophony in his head, but he found himself spiraling down from his place on high. Then the chaotic scene in the city became clear.

The sky yellowed like an old bruise as the sun climbed past the horizon. Above Zhentil Keep, a pillar of smoke pushed steadily into the bitter morning air. A conflagration was consuming the huge temple that had been the center of Cyric's worship. The magical fire devoured stone and steel as readily as it took wood and cloth and paper. The priests' homes surrounding the church had fallen before the blaze, as well, and the work of the bucket brigades seemed unable to stem its fiery advance.

At the western gate, fifty frost giants worked at widening a breach in the high black walls. The gate itself had already fallen, riven to splinters by the giants' axes. The magical wards on the iron-braced doors had done their work; the first three giants to lay their blades upon the wood had turned to stone. But that powerful sorcery no more slowed the siege than did the scattered flights of arrows whistling gnatlike around the titans. The handful of giants who fell to these attacks were shoved aside or hurled over the walls like mammoth gunstones.

Dragons screamed over the towers and gatehouses, their icy breath paralyzing the archers who raced along the ramparts. Now and then a ballista would tear a dragon's wing with a huge bolt or momentarily stun a wyrm with a boulder. Such victories proved more costly for the Zhentish than the monsters, since the dragons dealt with the offending ballistae quickly and savagely. Covered in ice, the men and women companying the engines held to their posts, their death screams trapped forever in their throats.

A few wyrms hovered over the fields beyond the city. If they watched for Zhentish reinforcements, their wait would be long and pointless. The city had been cut off from the thousands upon thousands of Zhentilar garrisoned up and down the Long Road and in the Citadel of the Raven. Had any sizable force managed to break through the dragons' blockade, they would have found themselves outnumbered one hundred-to-one by the vast army of goblins and gnolls now milling to the north and west of the Keep, waiting for the giants to bring down the walls.

Cyric slowed his descent and pulled his mind away from the destruction of the city. For an instant he considered granting his priests the sorcerous powers they demanded. That would allow them to drive a few of the giants from the gates, perhaps stall the siege long enough for the death god to take on an avatar and wade into the fight himself. Yet the Prince of Lies could feel his own strength draining away. With each death, each worshiper who gave in to despair and abandoned his faith, Cyric lost more of his divine power. No, better to muster supernatural aid from the Realm of the Dead than risk opening himself to the vortex of his faithful's demands.

At the merest of thoughts, Cyric traveled to his throne room. The scene that greeted him there was just as chaotic as the one he'd witnessed in Zhentil Keep.

An angry mob of denizens filled the long hall. They pressed toward the throne, shouting curses and threats at Jergal, trying to reach for Godsbane. The sword leaned against the throne, lifeless, pale as the martyrs' bones supporting her.

"If Cyric's run away from the fight, at least let one of us use the blasted sword," a goat-headed denizen bleated. He bowed his horned head low, threatening to charge the seneschal.

Jergal held his ground. He hovered defiantly between the mob and Cyric's throne, his cloak billowing around him like a dark angel's wings. When any of the denizens got too close, he swirled his cape over their grasping hands. The darkness that was his body swallowed the creatures' limbs, devoured the hands and arms greedily, leaving only seared stumps behind.

Furious at the violent confusion before him, Cyric lashed out. At a wave of his hand, a black globe appeared at the room's center. Inky tentacles slipped from the orb, curled around the rioting creatures, and drew them screaming into the Abyss. Their shouts echoed from the globe as it shrank to a pinpoint of darkness, then vanished. For a moment, only the soft moans of the Burning Men could be heard in the hall.

Cyric reached for Godsbane, but a momentary wave of dizziness overcame him. He dropped the sword and fell back against his gruesome throne. "Explain yourself, Godsbane," the death god hissed as he pushed himself back to his feet. "Why wasn't I told about the attack on the Keep?"

The spirit of the sword may not be able to answer, Your Magnificence, Jergal murmured, his cold voice ringing through the death god's mind. *Someone has struck a killing blow against her. Perhaps the Whore used her sorcery to—*

"The pantheon planned this," Cyric rumbled. "They crippled Godsbane so she couldn't tell me the Keep was under siege." Gently he lifted the blade from the floor and cradled it in his palms. The sword pulsed with a faint pink glow.

My love, Godsbane whispered. *I failed you. . . .*

"They've not beaten us yet," the Prince of Lies said. "Jergal, muster the denizens, unleash the hell hounds. We'll drive the dragons and the giants from Zhentil Keep. I'll lead the charge myself."

This realm needs your valor first, my liege, the seneschal replied. *The denizens you just banished—*

"Yes, yes. Part of another petty uprising, no doubt," Cyric scoffed. "I'll deal with them after I've slaughtered the creatures storming my holy city. Now be quick about gathering up a suitable force, Jergal, or I'll use your yellow blood to give Godsbane back a little life."

The denizens had no part in a revolt. They came here seeking your protection. Jergal bowed his head. *This time the souls of the False and the Faithless rise up against you,*

*Magnificence—and they are led by the dead men you impris-
oned in the Gearsmith's unholy armor.*

* * * * *

The City of Strife was burning. Blankets of flame wrapped
themselves around the weird, ten-story structures that
dominated the city's skyline. Thick clouds of soot wafted
over the fields of rubble, blinding everything that came in
contact with them. The River Slith bubbled and steamed
in the furnace-hot air.

Atop a huge pile of debris, Gwydion the Quick faced a
dozen skeletons wielding razor-bladed pikes. The skulls of
fifty of their kind, the broken shafts and twisted blades of
an equal number of weapons, lay heaped before the
undead soldiers, urging caution. Though he appeared too
heavily armored to move quickly, the knight had proved
time and again that his plate mail was far less encumber-
ing than it might seem. And so the skeletons advanced
slowly up the slanted mound of bricks and riven metal.
Their prudence didn't help them in the least.

One skeleton, braver or more foolhardy than the rest,
stabbed at Gwydion with its pike. The armored shade
sheared the blade off the pole with a single stroke of
Titanslayer, then lunged forward to shatter the soldier's
rib cage. The shattered bones tumbled back down the hill,
clattering like stones rolling off a tin roof.

The other warriors took their fellow's sacrifice as a signal to strike. Yet the Gond-forged armor turned aside the
pikes as if they were blunted wooden toys. Gwydion
whirled around, bringing the enchanted blade in a wind-
mill arc through the skeletal soldiers. Bones cracked and
skulls toppled from fleshless necks. The undead warriors
retreated—those that could still run, anyway—and
Gwydion paused to look out on the battlefield.

Gangs of shades roamed the square. Some carried blades or cudgels or barbed whips wrested from the denizens. Others had crafted weapons from the debris. Gwydion and his fellow knights had found that releasing the False from their tortures was a simple enough matter. Rallying the downtrodden souls had proved even easier. Cries of "Down with Cyric!" and "Long live Kelemvor!" rang through the streets, the latter slogan born of Gwydion's speech that day on the banks of the River Slith. Even though the shades knew nothing of the long-lost hero, Kel was a bitter foe of their oppressor. Those were credentials enough to cast him in the unlikely role of savior.

The denizens, unorganized and prone to fighting amongst themselves, had yet to mount any serious counterstrike. Overwhelmed by the sheer number of False rebelling in the city, many of Cyric's faithful had retreated to the diamond walls of Bone Castle. They were the lucky ones. The denizens caught outside the safety of the keep found themselves facing rough justice, indeed.

Even now, across the square from Gwydion, a group of renegade souls flushed a denizen from the detritus of a ruined building. The little creature tried to flap away on yellow bat's wings, but two of the shades tackled him before he could flee. Like all the other battles between the newly freed False and their former jailors, this skirmish was bloody and brief.

Neither the damned souls nor the denizens possessed the magical might necessary to destroy one another. Because of this, their battles tended to follow a gruesome, vicious pattern. Once the scuffle ended, the victors chopped the vanquished into a dozen pieces or more, enough so it would take days for the fingers and legs and arms to come together again and regenerate. Such was the case now, as the shades scattered sun-yellow bits of denizen flesh across the square. The creature's head was left atop a pole, shouting curses at the False as they abandoned the square in search of other quarry.

"We'll feed the whole lot of you to the Night Serpent when this is over, slugs!" the head cried. "We'll sink you all to the bottom of the Slith!"

Gwydion recognized the thick, hissing voice. He hurried down from the heap of bones. Sure enough, the bruised and battered head gazed back at him with familiar contempt. "Well," the denizen muttered, "what are you looking at?"

"You're better off than Af was, Perdix. When this is over, you'll still be here to serve the realm's new lord."

The little creature narrowed his eye, darted his forked tongue over gory, split lips. "Cyric's black heart! You've come back!"

Gwydion slipped his helmet from his head. The shadows from the dozens of small fires burning in the rubble nearby made him look distinctly ominous as he smiled and said, "You said an uprising would never succeed here." He wiped the sweaty hair from his eyes. "You were wrong."

"Look, slug," Perdix hissed, "you think you're winning now, but wait until Cyric's elite troops arrive."

A subtle shift of the denizen's watery eye made Gwydion turn, suddenly alert to the danger that loomed behind him. A gigantic panther, dark as midnight, fell silently from the sky on wings of black light. It struck Gwydion with one massive paw, sending him to his knees. The knight's helmet clattered away, and Titanslayer slipped from his grasp.

The cat pounced on Gwydion with preternatural speed, pinning him to the ground. Like a house cat toying with a captured mouse, it batted at his exposed face. Claws as large as daggers drew bloody lines across the knight's cheek, threatened to gouge out an eye.

"Hee hee!" Perdix hooted. "Speak of the devils! You've captured one of the important ones, you have!"

The panther spared the denizen's head the slightest glance, clearly offended by Perdix's statement of the obvious, then turned its yellow eyes on Gwydion. The slitted orbs narrowed, as if the cat were pleased with its prize. The beast opened its mouth wide.

Titanslayer lay well out of reach, so Gwydion pummeled the cat's legs and head with his fists. The creature's thick fur seemed as tough as his own plate mail, though, and the blows did little damage. Still, the struggle bought the knight just enough time to pull the candle from his sword belt. With a grunt, Gwydion twisted sideways and tossed the stick of tallow into one of the dozens of small fires burning nearby.

With a hiss like a dragon gasping in pain, the wax spit forth a burst of smoke. The wavering cloud swiftly took a more definite form—a mastiff, as large as a draft horse and covered by a coat of writhing maggots.

"Free!" Kezef howled.

The rush of fetid air from the Chaos Hound's lips extinguished all the fires in the square. The spittle from his lolling, tattered tongue ate holes into the cobbles at his feet. Kezef crouched when he saw the panther, then leaped forward. The impact drove both beasts a giant's height away from Gwydion.

The Chaos Hound closed slavering jaws on the cat and tore the death yowl stillborn from the beast's throat. The panther tried to fight back. It battered Kezef with its black wings and ripped at his guts with powerful rear claws. Yet the mass of corruption that was Kezef's skin shifted with each blow, as yielding as water.

When the cat fell, the maggots swarmed away from Kezef's jet-boned skeleton to cover the corpse. They devoured the minion's flesh, then slid back onto the Hound. The gorged slugs made Kezef look bloated as they milled, sated, all across his corrupted body.

The Chaos Hound arched his back at the pleasant taste of flesh after so many eons of starvation. "Where am I?" he rumbled. "Where's that treacherous bastard Mask?"

In the brief time it had taken the Chaos Hound to kill and devour the panther, Gwydion had managed to retrieve his sword, but not his helmet. The knight held the blade before him defensively as he faced the mastiff. "In the City of Strife. Mask gave me the candle and told me to free you here. He said you'd help us against Cyric's minions."

The Chaos Hound sniffed once, then wrinkled his nose at the shade. "Stop trembling. I eat the marrow of the Faithful," Kezef muttered. "You're not quite ripe yet, little soul, and I'd only make myself sick." He motioned toward Perdix with his dripping snout. "Where's the rest of him?"

"Th-This is all of me," the denizen stammered. "Just a head. Not enough to sharpen your teeth on."

"In pieces. Scattered around the square," Gwydion said. He backed toward his helmet and lifted it from the ground by one horn. "There are plenty of denizens swarming around Bone Castle, if you're still hungry."

"So that's Mask's game, eh?" Kezef barked a wheezing laugh. "Capture me and let me loose in his neighbor's courtyard—all so he can rob the place through the back door, no doubt." He turned away. "I'll take my fill here, little soul, but I won't be the Shadowlord's pawn." The Chaos Hound loped away, his paw prints spreading into pools of burning ichor in his wake.

"'Scattered across the square!'" Perdix snapped. "You might as well have shoved me into his mouth." The denizen snorted in contempt. "At least I've got the satisfaction of knowing you've lost the war, slug. Your secret weapon's scampered off."

Gwydion buckled his helmet back into place. "That creature was Mask's idea," the knight said, his voice echoing hollowly. He rested Titanslayer on his shoulder and started off toward the rubble-strewn fields that lay in the shadow of Bone Castle itself. "I've got other nightmares to unleash."

* * * * *

In the Keep's sheltered harbor, boats lurched drunkenly away from the docks, piloted by men desperate enough to brave the ice floes and the two dragons that had taken up patrol over the river. Past the Tesh Bridge to the east and the Force Bridge to the west, ruined hulks of carracks and cogs wallowed, half-submerged. Some had hulls shattered by the ice, others fractured masts and crippled rigging from the white wyrms' frosty breath.

The floating, ice-rimed graves did little to deter the refugees from setting sail. The soldiers assigned to guard the port had also failed to turn back the mobs. Most of the Zhentilar had abandoned their posts at the first rush of panicked citizens. Those who'd tried to hold their ground now floated facedown in the Tesh, blood from their slit throats staining the water around them.

"The one w'the blue sail. She'll make it out." The orc spit in the general direction of his chosen boat, then leaned his knobby elbows on the low stone rail that ran the length of the Force Bridge.

"Nah," his equally uncouth comrade grunted. "They'll all end up driftwood—or toothpicks fer the dragons."

"Oh yeah? Well if yer so sure, Zadok, how 'bout we wager yer sheev on it?"

Zadok drew an ivory-handled knife from his belt and wiped the dirty blade across his black leather jerkin. "I dunno, Garm. I got this off the body of the first sharp I ever milled. He was a real fancy one, too—before I gave him a topper. Cracked his skull wide open, I did. One blow, right above his—"

"Oi, quiet," Garm hissed. He grabbed Zadok's arm and directed his gaze with one frostbitten finger. "Lookit what we got here!"

The orcs squinted down the bridge toward the northern bank, where flaming barricades had been set to stop anyone from fleeing the city. A lone figure hurried along, close to the railing.

"They let one through!" Garm snarled.

Zadok flipped his knife to a fighting grip and watched the figure slow from a run to a walk. "A woman from the looks of it. Human, I think." He leered. "At least this'll give us something to do."

When she saw the blade in the orc's grip, Rinda stopped and showed her empty hands. "No need for weapons. I'm here to see General Vrakk," she said. "Let me pass."

Garm took a menacing step forward. "Vrakk sent us t'help ya," he lied. "He's got right busy all of a sudden, so we'll be taking care of ya."

Slowly Rinda started away from the railing, trying to angle around the soldiers. Vrakk had said he'd leave orders with the orcs at the barricades to let her pass, but these two obviously knew nothing of that. "He gave me this as proof," the scribe said. She slung her heavy pack off her shoulder and pulled a black armband from a pocket. Cyric's holy symbol grinned from the tattered cloth.

"So what? You've got one of our old regimental bands," Zadok said. "We threw them out months ago, missy. Anybody coulda dug a dozen out of the trash heaps."

Rinda continued to move toward the center of the bridge, but it was clear now the orcs weren't going to let her pass. The scribe glanced uneasily toward the twin towers that marked the southern end of the bridge. No sign of Vrakk on the battlements. She could only hope he'd seen her coming and was on his way.

"Give us the bundle. If it's got anything good in it, we might let ya go back t'the city," Garm offered, creeping closer.

When Rinda moved to reshoulder the pack, Garm leaped forward. He grabbed the bottom of the cloth sack and rolled, hoping to drag the woman off her feet. To his surprise, she let go of the straps. The orc tumbled forward on the rough stone pavement, cursing in a colorful mix of Zhentish and the guttural tongue of his race. The pack burst open beneath him, and its contents spilled across the bridge.

Garm didn't have time to inventory Rinda's belongings. As he pushed himself from the ground, the toe of her boot caught him just in front of the ear. With a loud crack, his jaw snapped out of joint. The orc went down again, this time howling in pain.

"That'll cost you more'n you think, missy," Zadok hissed. He shuffled forward, waving his grimy knife before him.

Rinda watched the orc move closer, watched his beady eyes for some sign he was going to strike. The sound of heavy footfalls had begun to echo from the southern end of the bridge, and shouting, too. If it was Vrakk, he was still too far away for the soldier to hear him. If it was more orcs coming to join the fun . . . Rinda grimaced. Better end this quickly, then.

The scribe edged sideways until she stood directly over the cloth-wrapped bulk of the *Cyrinishad*. She could hear the muttering of the tome's guardian, muffled by the rags and the chain Oghma had strung across its mouth. "Last chance to save yourself some pain," Rinda said.

Zadok slashed at the scribe. The strike was tentative,

more a test of her reflexes than a serious attack, and the blade hissed through the air well in front of her. Nevertheless, Rinda acted as if the knife had come quite close. She leaped back a step, then dropped to the ground, sitting right behind the book. She gasped in mock terror, as if she'd stumbled, but her hands trembled not the least as she grabbed for the heavy tome.

The feigned blunder drew Zadok into a charge. He lunged, but the blade met the indestructible bindings of the *Cyrinishad*, not the woman's throat. With a high, ringing sound, the knife snapped in two. The blade jangled musically as it clattered to the cobbles.

The orc continued forward, but Rinda rolled onto her back and caught the soldier in the stomach with her boot heels. A push from her legs sent Zadok sailing. He landed face-first on the bridge. He skinned his hands bloody and broke both the incisors that jutted up from his bottom lip.

Vrakk and three other orcs staggered to a stop near their fallen comrades. At a gesture from the general, Garm and Zadok were roughly hauled away. "Pathetic," Vrakk puffed.

The scribe winced. "Oh, I don't know. I thought I did rather well."

"Not you." The general jerked a warty thumb over his shoulder. "Them. Two against one. They should've killed you."

Rinda carefully replaced the *Cyrinishad* in her pack and stuffed the rest of her belongings in around it. "Seems to me you didn't do much better, that first day at my place," the scribe said coldly.

With one hand, the orc lifted Rinda from the ground. His beady eyes were narrowed in mirth. "You pretty good soldier," he said and chuckled basely. It was the first time Rinda had ever heard an orc laugh; the sound reminded her of the sewers gurgling after the spring rains.

Vrakk led Rinda the rest of the way across the Force Bridge. More orcs gathered at the southern end, where a small, walled borough of the Keep crouched tensely upon the bank. There was little need for guards at this end of the span, since the wealthy Zhentish families who lived in the borough had either fled long ago or crossed to the better-protected confines of the north bank. From the fine cloaks, polished armor, and jewel-hilted swords the orcs wore, Rinda decided the nobles hadn't left anyone to safeguard their homes from looters.

They climbed one of the twin towers that stood sentinel over the bridge's terminus. When they reached the very top, Vrakk pointed across the Tesh. "Look what we done," he said proudly.

In the city's winding streets, crowds rushed away from the beleaguered western gate and the smoking ruin that was once the darkly glorious Temple of Cyric—though from Rinda's vantage the mobs appeared as little more than groups of ants treading through a maze. The dragons circling the Keep reacted swiftly to the retreat. They focused their attacks on the northeastern gate. That left two avenues of escape for the Zhentish: the river or the twin bridges.

Most of the boats in the harbor had set sail, and all but a handful of them had been capsized or becalmed by the ice and the dragons. Finding the slips empty, a few foolish people tried to swim, but the bitter Tesh froze the life from them before they'd got fifty strokes from shore. With no other options, the mob turned to the bridges.

Patriarch Mirrormane had been certain the Lord of the Dead would answer the city's pleas and strike down the besieging army—so certain, in fact, that he'd failed to consider the bridges a means of escape. So it was that Vrakk and his orcs had been assigned the unglamorous duty of guarding the spans while everyone was gathered in dawn prayer groups. The brutish soldiers had immediately constructed barricades across both bridges, barricades that now kept the Zhentish from fleeing the giants and dragons.

Xeno's lackeys were only now discovering that the orcish troops had no intention of tearing the barricades down—not at a priest's order, anyway. And so, the ends of both bridges were crammed with frantic refugees. Rinda could see them, masses of humanity, pulsing forward to the bonfires and toppled carts. The crowds had gotten much worse since she'd shouldered her way through. Small groups had begun rushing the orcish lines, only to be driven back by a hail of crossbow bolts. Dozens of corpses lay sprawled in the no man's land between the humans and the orcs.

"It's time," Vrakk said.

"Time for what?"

The general smiled—a horrible thing to see—and gestured for a flag to be raised. As soon as the young orc started the red banner up the pole, its twin began to rise over a tower at the southern end of the Tesh Bridge.

"We do lots of work on bridges," Vrakk murmured, then turned back to watch the distant barricades. "Priests think it punishment for us. . . ."

Sparks rose into the morning air as the orcs scattered the bonfires. With the bridge sealed off, at least for a short time, the soldiers retreated at a run toward the south bank. They'd only gotten a quarter of the way across before the mob broke through the flaming wreckage. In the press, men and women were shoved into the fires. Their neighbors clambered over their backs as they burned.

Vrakk glanced at Rinda. "You not figure it out? Me think you smart." He gestured to one of the dragons as it swooped low over the river to tear the sails from a coaster.

"They not attack us. How come?"

The realization swept over Rinda then. "You've cut a deal with them, haven't you?" she whispered. "You're fighting for the giants."

Vrakk nodded. "Priests say we're monsters, so we fight on side of monsters. Giants happy to have us in army."

The retreating orcs had reached the south bank. Vrakk waited for the slowest of his troops to stumble to safety before he put two fingers to his lips and whistled. The shrill sound rang out even over the thunder of the charging refugees.

As one, the orcs shouted a vile curse directed at the Lord of the Dead: "*Cyric dglinkarz haif akropa nar!*"

Though the insult was nearly impossible to translate—at least with its original venomous hatred intact—it was enough to know that the slur involved Cyric and the forefathers of the orcs' most hated foes, the dwarves. From the mouths of Vrakk's troops, though, the five words were a magical trigger. The instant the orcs finished the curse, the center supports of both bridges exploded.

The whole length of the Force Bridge shuddered. As Fzoul and the Zhentarim mages had predicted, the Shou gunpowder that was the heart of the magical trap sent up a huge fireball. The blast incinerated the Zhentish at the front of the mob—the lucky ones, anyway. Shards of granite whistled through the air like sling stones and cut down others. Then the center of the bridge collapsed into the river, taking with it half the refugees. The scene on the Tesh Bridge was much the same—the frantic mob trying to turn back upon itself, the bridge dissolving beneath them into a rain of stone and mortar.

All along the south bank, the orcs howled at the devastation, at the score upon score of battered corpses floating amongst the shattered ice floes. Once, Vrakk and his soldiers had served those same people, offered up their lives to prove their loyalty. Yet the orcs hadn't left their bestial roots so far behind that they could contrive any answer but this for the slight offered them by the city and the human god they'd adopted as their own.

Horrified, Rinda turned away from the carnage, from Vrakk. "I—I should go."

The general grabbed her by the arm and spun her to face him. "They take away our honor," he said. "They take away everything to give to Cyric, and he not care. Zhentish deserve this."

"No one deserves that kind of death," Rinda hissed. She pulled from his grasp.

"Don't stop in Dales," the orc noted. "Not be too safe there until giants and goblins break up army." He tossed something toward Rinda. It landed at her feet, clattering loudly on the tower roof. "That medal King Ak-soon gave me for fighting in crusade. Bring it to Cor-meer and show it to him. He take care of you."

"I can't take this, Vrakk," Rinda said.

The orc grunted. "Monsters don't wear medals." Stiffly he turned to watch the carnage.

Rinda scooped up the medallion, the Special Order of the Golden Way, granted only to the victorious generals of Azoun's crusade against the Tuigan. "I'll keep it safe for you," the scribe said, then hurried from the tower.

As she began her long, lonely journey south, Rinda said a silent prayer that all the Zhentish dragged into depravity by Cyric's schemes—human and orc alike—might find their way back to civilization. Though the diamond holy symbol she wore made it impossible for Oghma to hear that wish, she knew the God of Knowledge would answer it, if he could. Until that wish came true, Rinda would find the strength to safeguard the *Cyrinishad,* to prevent the madness it contained from spreading beyond the ruined walls of Zhentil Keep.

XIX

NIGHTMARES

*Wherein Gwydion the Quick faces the
unremembered terrors of his mortal life,
Kelemvor's prison undergoes some unwelcome
alterations, and Cyric pays the price for
trying to remake the world in his image.*

Gwydion stood on the brink of Dendar's cave. Orange
steam swirled around him like some manifestation of the
suffering that had settled over the City of Strife during the
uprising. Animate fragments of denizens and shades lay
everywhere, twitching, crawling, crying out. The heart of
the battle raged nearby, at the gate to Bone Castle. Angry
shouts and panicked orders echoed from the diamond
walls, lingering over the River Slith and the field of rubble
beyond. The noise drowned out the hiss of the Night Serpent's breathing as she slept in her vast lair, contentedly
gorged on the world's unremembered nightmares.

"Mistress Dendar!" Gwydion shouted. He stepped closer to the first line of mammoth stalagmites. Tiny, lurking things scurried between the stones and watched him with hungry curiosity.

"Go away," came a voice heavy with disdain, thick with sleep. "As I told the other lackeys: the prince must fight his own battles. My answer is final."

"I'm not here to get you to rescue Cyric," Gwydion called. He fought to keep the fear from his voice, to still the trembling of his gauntleted hands. "I want you to help us overthrow him."

Dendar shifted on her bed of bones. Two eyes, large and sickly yellow, appeared in the cave's gloom. "Overthrow him?" she asked. "Why should I ever want to do that?" Her slitted pupils narrowed as she moved closer to the cave's mouth, and her forked tongue tested the air. "Ah, Gwydion. I never expected to see you here again— and girded like a knight. Well, well. . . ."

"Help us now, and the gods will be fair to you hereafter."

"Fair to me?" the serpent scoffed, bloody fangs glistening. "Come now, spiritling. I was here before the gods, and it's my place to harbinger the end of it all—the world, the universe, all of that and the gods, too. The pantheon can have no hold over me." She yawned. "Now leave me be. It's hard enough to rest with all that clatter and crash going on."

"No," Gwydion said. The steel edging the word surprised even him. "The siege of Bone Castle must end quickly, before the suffering here grows any greater. All I ask is for you to release some of the nightmares you've hoarded. Let them free to drive the denizens away from the walls."

"Now you're being ridiculous," Dendar hissed, her sibilant voice filled with malice. "What do I care for the suffering of the dead?"

Gwydion raised Titanslayer high over his head. "I'll take them if I must."

Ever so slowly, the Night Serpent turned her head until one eye hung over Gwydion like a full moon. "I'm no fairy tale dragon to be threatened by that pin you carry. You insult me by thinking so."

The warning in Dendar's words rang clear to Gwydion, as did the unspoken demand for an apology. Yet he did not lower his blade, did not retreat a step from the lair's threshold. Something inside him wouldn't allow it. Instead, Gwydion lashed out with Titanslayer, slicing away a single midnight-black scale from the Serpent's hide.

The scale exploded and stretched into a fully formed nightmare. Ghostly and luminescent, the night-terror writhed in the air for a moment, then descended upon Gwydion. It slithered across his mind, drawing him into a horrifying scenario:

A half-human beast stalked Gwydion down a darkened alley. The shade could hear the thing padding behind him, its claws clicking on the cobbles with each loping step. The narrow street was endless, and its high walls were slick with something—blood, Gwydion realized with a shudder. There were no doors in the wall, no windows to crawl through. The only way to escape was to run. . . .

Run? Gwydion smiled at that. And as soon as the realization dawned on him that he could flee from the beast, the alley vanished from his mind. The nightmare had released its hold on him.

The victory was short-lived, though. A bone-rattling tremor rumbled through the wastes, and the hillside itself seemed to shift, to rear up. Then a monstrous shadow swept over the knight.

Dendar had opened her cavernous maw.

The Night Serpent knocked Gwydion into her mouth with a flick of her tongue. He rebounded off one gigantic, crimson-stained fang; its tip cut open his breastplate as if it were threadbare cloth. The fang didn't catch his flesh, but the impact sent him tumbling uncontrollably through the air.

Gwydion landed in the foul mire beneath Dendar's tongue. Using Titanslayer as a crutch, he levered himself to his feet—only to be knocked onto his back again a moment later when the Serpent tried to force the tiny morsel farther down her throat. The whole world rose and fell as Dendar tossed her head back. All the while, her black tongue swept through the darkness overhead, making the soup of greasy spittle and half-digested bones slosh up Gwydion's legs.

Fear clutched at the knight, born on the cold chill that crept up from the Serpent's stomach. That chill settled over Gwydion's heart, and with it came the sense that some unknown but utterly familiar horror lay in wait for him in the belly of the beast.

Dendar threw her head back again. The marshy surface pulsed beneath Gwydion, and he rolled backward a few paces. He tried to catch himself, grab hold of some bump in the Serpent's mouth, but the sharp ridges on his riven breastplate made it difficult to move. Each time he lifted his arms, the jagged edges scraped awkwardly against his greaves.

With as much strength as he could muster, Gwydion drove his enchanted blade into the soft ground underfoot. Sparks pushed away the darkness in spurts as the blade sank deeper, though Gwydion almost wished he'd been spared the terrible vista. Gruesome bits of denizen flesh and spatters of gore hung all around him. Eyeless skulls bobbed along in the mire underfoot, grinning at the futility of his struggle.

He hadn't intended the blow as an attack, merely a way to anchor himself until he could decide upon a plan. Yet no sooner had Titanslayer pierced Dendar's flesh than a terrific howl rolled up from her throat.

For the first time in her eons-long existence, the Night Serpent screamed.

Nightmares filled Dendar's mouth like bile. They sailed around her huge fangs, raced along the edges of her forked tongue. Silver as moonlight, spectral and utterly silent, the phantasms descended upon Gwydion. With filthy claws and debauched mouths they tore at his armor. Piece by piece, plate by plate, the god-forged mail was stripped away.

The knight couldn't fight back, couldn't raise a fist to defend himself as the horrible visions pressed in close. The nightmares tried to pry his fingers apart. When that failed, they insinuated themselves into his mind, stoking the fear that burned like wildfire through his thoughts:

Gwydion plummeted through an endless midnight sky. Around him lightning streaked silently through the void. Nothing could stop his fall. Ever. He opened his mouth to scream, but like the lightning, he, too, was mute. . . .

The weight of the damp earth pressed down on Gwydion. He tried to move his arms, but couldn't. He wasn't paralyzed; his fingers could flex a little, just enough to feel the coarse loam packed around him, the worms and the slugs crawling through the ground. They'd buried him alive! Gwydion struggled, but that made it worse, brought the earth down like a giant's fist. Then the tiny carrion beetles arrived, hundreds and hundreds of them. . . .

From atop a high tower, Gwydion watched the sun rise in an azure sky over the peaceful city of Suzail. He hadn't slept well the night before, but such were the burdens of his title. In the streets below, merchants threw open their shops to the women and men out to buy their day's supplies. Soldiers, Purple Dragons from his old regiment, patrolled the crowded alleyways, though their presence wasn't really needed, not since Gwydion had become monarch of the rich and expansive kingdom. Children filled the parks and boulevards with their happy cries, their shouted games—until the shadow passed over the sun.

Dendar filled the sky, her dark scales turning the day to night. She rose, bloated with the world's nightmares, and swallowed the sun. The laughter and bustling cheer of the city turned to screams of terror. The cool spring breezes became the chill of eternal winter. Ice covered the harbor, splintering the ships like tinder. It spread over the land. Gwydion tried to shout a warning, but it was no use; the men and women and children were overcome, dark shapes trapped in the blanket of silver-white ice.

As the killing frost scaled the high tower walls, Gwydion heard Dendar laugh, her sibilant voice carried on the wind blowing over the dead world. "The last nightmare to feed me was yours. . . ."

Gwydion trembled like a frightened child, but the phantasms could not loosen his grip upon Titanslayer. Horrible though they were, the terrors belonged to other men and women.

The Night Serpent writhed in pain as the magic from the enchanted blade seeped into her jaw. She howled again, vomiting up more nightmares. Visions of living dead men and knife-wielding lunatics, utter isolation and sweaty, crushing mobs swirled around the knight. But like their brethren, these silent phantasms failed to weaken Gwydion's resolve.

Finally Dendar drew forth a particular haunting, an unremembered nightmare that had plagued Gwydion often during his mortal life. Unlike the other visions, this one moved with purpose from its prison in the Serpent's gut. It slithered, base and familiar, straight toward the knight, and the other horrors parted for it like timid schoolchildren before a well-respected master.

The night-terror drove its grimy fingers into Gwydion's heart. And from the instant the haunt insinuated itself into his flesh, his life-grip on the sword began to slip.

The dirt road known as the Golden Way stretched out before and behind Gwydion. To either side of the trade road, the once-beautiful countryside lay burned and lifeless, the crops and villages trodden under by the hearty ponies of the Tuigan barbarians. Scavengers—both human and bestial— picked through the rubble, looking for some morsel of food to sustain them on the blasted plain.

A small party of the nomad horsemen clustered on a ridge up ahead, watching for the vanguard of King Azoun's ragged Army of the Alliance. Gwydion smiled and crouched lower in the gully. They hadn't seen him yet. Good. He'd be able to run back and warn the king before the army stumbled into an ambush.

As the young scout turned, he heard a shout. He glanced back to see the three Tuigans kick their mounts into a gallop. Short bows drawn, firing even as their horses flew over the uneven hillocks, the barbarians came.

Gwydion's heart began to flutter, almost in time with the thundering hoofbeats. Escape seemed unlikely, but then, everyone had bet against him in those races on the Promenade, when he outran the horses from Lord Harcourt's cavalry unit. You're Gwydion the Quick, he reminded himself. Now's your chance to prove it.

Gwydion sprang forward, but his legs had suddenly gone numb from the knees down. He fell onto his chest.

A few Tuigan arrows hit the ground around the crippled scout, and he glanced over his shoulder once more. The barbarians had halved the distance to him—and now that they were closer, he could see that the riders were monsters. Their faces were leering skulls, their hands clawed and furred like lions'. Their saddles were fringed with the scalps of captured soldiers. Necklaces strung with eyes and tongues hung around their necks.

Gwydion knew then that these riders weren't just harbingers of death. They wanted his soul, not his life.

With fumbling fingers, the scout tore off his boots and rolled up the breeches from his numb legs. Had he been hit by an arrow or paralyzed by the painless bite of some snake? There were no wounds on his feet or calves. He rubbed his legs, trying to press some life back into them, but the numbness spread up to his hips.

The Tuigan-monsters were almost upon him. The ground trembled beneath their charge. Gwydion, waves of panic washing over his mind, tried to move his leg, force it to bend. At his touch, the flesh came away from the bones, soft and yielding as clay. . . .

Gwydion's left hand fell away from Titanslayer, and his right began to open. In his mind, at least, the battle was over. If he couldn't run, there was no hope, no way to escape.

The smaller haunts took hold of the knight's legs. Slowly they pulled him toward the hellish pit that was Dendar's stomach. Gwydion barely recognized his plight, engulfed as he was in the familiar terror of his nightmare. He no longer saw himself captive in the Night Serpent's mouth, no longer saw the spectral things that floated around him. Gwydion knew only that the cold hands of annihilation gripped him and he could no longer flee.

Something stirred inside him then, a fiery ember of belief that warmed his cooling resolve. He didn't have to run from the battle—no, *shouldn't* run from the battle, at least until he'd tried to make a stand. His honor demanded he fight back. The other shades ground beneath Cyric's heel demanded the same. He'd been entrusted with a god's enchanted blade, and he'd given his word to use it well.

As if they could sense the steel of resolve shoring up the knight's flagging spirit, the nightmares redoubled their attack. Joined by Gwydion's personal night-terror, they gave their all in one last desperate attempt to draw him away from his sword. The haunts wrapped themselves around his arms and legs. They blinded him with their wispy hair, throttled him with their bony fingers. Yet even their unearthly might could not force Gwydion to release his hold on Titanslayer.

For a moment Gwydion saw the unreal scene with astounding clarity, true sight far beyond any sensation granted him by Gond's helmet. The shield of his duty would turn aside the worst horrors the phantasms could muster. So long as he kept to his oath, he was beyond their grasp.

Stricken, the nightmares withered before his gaze. They skirled away into the darkness like phantom bats, banished to Dendar's stomach once more.

All except Gwydion's personal night-terror.

That ghastly image lingered, staring at the shade with the features of the dream-Tuigan. The face had been wrought from horribly twisted memories of the barbarian scouts he'd outrun in the crusade, and to Gwydion it was nothing more or less than the face of death itself. The unremembered nightmare had secretly ruled his last eight years of life, driven him from the Purple Dragons, devoured his honor. It had even followed him beyond the grave, becoming a fear of more permanent annihilation. Now, though, the knight recognized the terror for what it was.

"I know you," Gwydion said. "I won't ever run from you again."

The nightmare vanished, and Dendar sank to the ground. "Enough," the Serpent said mournfully. "I've no more weapons to wield against you. I will do as you demand."

The Night Serpent opened her cavernous mouth, and light from the red sky poured in, coloring the grim terrain. Cautiously Gwydion uprooted Titanslayer. He made his way past the Serpent's fangs, over her smooth lips. Of his armor, only his sword belt remained, gnawed thin in places, but still sound enough for use. Spittle covered his breeches, and his padded doublet hung in tatters. The plate mail was gone; in forging the armor, Gond hadn't reckoned on the power of nightmares.

"Release the night-terrors that belong to the denizens defending Bone Castle," Gwydion said. "That will be the quickest way to end this war."

"A quick way to seed the realm for a different sort of madness, too," the Night Serpent hissed. "The denizens do not share your valor, spiritling. They will surely lose their minds if they're confronted with the nightmares from their mortal lives."

"And if the terrors aren't their own?"

"Then the denizens will be ridden by fear until they drop," Dendar said, a sick glee in her voice.

Gwydion sheathed Titanslayer. "That will be weapon enough," he said. "But for Cyric, the nightmare must be his and his alone."

"No," Dendar replied, shrinking back into the gloom of the cavern. "It's rare I get such morsels, and I'll not give up Cyric's nightmare without a fight. Even if I can't harm you, Gwydion, your allies may not prove to be as invincible." She sniggered. "Besides, the revolt is so close to the prince's nightmare that he'll never know the difference. All you need is Kelemvor Lyonsbane, and he's—well, that's something you'll find out soon enough."

The Night Serpent opened her mouth wide, dislocating her hinged jaw, and a horde of night-terrors swarmed out. The haunts swirled silently around Gwydion as he bowed to Dendar. "You have my word, the gods will be fair to you hereafter, no matter who reigns in this hellish place."

"Your promise carries more weight than you might suspect," Dendar said, her eyes pale yellow in the murk. "I will hold you to it nonetheless."

As he turned away, it occurred to Gwydion that this next battle might be his last—facing the death god and his most powerful servants, without even the god-forged armor to protect him. The notion was fleeting, quickly driven back by his powerful sense of duty. Gwydion was afraid—only fools and lunatics entered a fight completely without fear—but that emotion no longer controlled him.

Surrounded by silent, phantasmal nightmares, Gwydion ran—but this time he headed toward the battle.

* * * * *

Kelemvor Lyonsbane struggled through a waist-deep mire of black ooze. The foul-smelling stuff reminded him of Arabel's garbage heaps on a hot summer's day. He shook his head at that notion. There's your reward for years of work as a sell-sword, he noted with more than a little bitterness. You can identify at least a half-dozen cities in Faerun by the stink of their garbage.

"Godsbane!" he shouted, then staggered to a stop. He cupped both hands around his mouth. "Godsbane! No more games, damn it. Show yourself!"

The rose-hued mist continued to swirl overhead, lowering in patches to the mire, but the spirit of the sword remained hidden.

The creeping muck had filled the sword for hours now. At first Kelemvor had thought it just another torment visited on him by Godsbane, but that thought vanished when the mire reached his chest and showed no signs of leveling off. Soon after, Kel abandoned the confines of his meticulously constructed cell in search of higher ground; if the sword had been toying with him, that concession alone would have brought a declaration of victory from her. But the mire deepened, swallowing even the few dry spots Kel discovered on the endless plains. Now the ooze covered everything, deeper in some places, but sticky and rancid throughout.

A horrible moan filled the sky. The sudden noise startled Kelemvor, and he dropped into a familiar battle crouch. The stance was purely reflexive, like the flick of his wrist as he reached for a sword that wasn't there. It annoyed the shade a little, being controlled by his training as a soldier-for-hire, but he shrugged the thought aside when the ragged, screaming souls began to appear overhead.

"Another battle," Kel murmured.

He gritted his teeth at the pain he saw in their ravaged faces, heard in their tormented cries. There were no denizens in this lot, only human shades. Cyric must be putting down another revolt among the damned, Kel decided. Like all the other lopsided battles against the False, it would be over soon. Then the sword would drink down the souls she had captured.

A realization struck Kelemvor, a thunderbolt of hope. Perhaps the gods had finally mounted the uprising in the City of Strife!

Kelemvor raised both fists to the sky. "Justice!" he shouted, the cry echoing in the wails of the doomed souls. "We will have justice!"

A huge book, as wide as a castle gate, burst from the ooze. The *Cyrinishad*, the title proclaimed in blood-red letters.

The cursed tome grew straight up into the mist, raining a shower of muddy droplets as it rose. Kel covered his face with a muscled forearm and cursed. When he looked up again, he saw the holy symbols carved into the black leather binding, the grinning death's-head in the center of the cover. The skull transformed, taking on Cyric's lean, hawk-nosed visage. The face of the death god looked out upon the befouled landscape and the myriad souls swirling through the air, but it was clear he could see nothing.

"Believe," the Prince of Lies intoned. "Believe."

Cyric repeated the word over and over. The chant echoed through the corrupted void, growing louder and more insistent with each repetition. A vortex formed in the air around the book, and it drew in the captive shades. The souls struck the book one after another. Their ghostly forms scattered into thin wisps of fog, which drifted like dead leaves to the mire. Godsbane shuddered as each soul settled into the ooze, their essence lost to her forever. Their cries lived on after them, ringing faintly through the mist.

The death god's image began to laugh.

Kelemvor stalked forward and lashed out with a fist. His blow scraped his knuckles raw, but also knocked a hole in the book's cover. Kel glanced up, certain he would see the death god's face contorted with anger. Instead, flakes of dried ink showered down around him as the wall quivered and shook with Cyric's mirth.

This is what's twisting Godsbane, Kel realized. The book is warping her somehow, causing all this chaos in her mind.

Bracing his feet as best he could, Kelemvor pressed a shoulder against the massive *Cyrinishad*. The monolith teetered for a moment, then toppled backward like a door knocked from its hinges. The air displaced by its fall drove the mist away, so Kel had a clear view as Cyric's face struck the ooze.

The book shattered on impact with the mire. Some pieces floated for a time. Most were swallowed quickly by the mire. Cyric's cruel mouth remained intact, laughing until the ooze flowed in to choke off the grating sound. Kelemvor tried to gather some of the larger shards together in hopes of creating a makeshift raft, but each time he tested the platform's strength, it broke apart under his weight.

"You bastard, Cyric," Kel grumbled. "Couldn't even leave me that much, could you?"

Spattered with slime and grimy with dirt, Kelemvor trudged off. The cries of the annihilated souls echoed faintly over the quagmire. Yet the wailing didn't frighten him; it only made him that much more impatient to join the battle against Cyric, to make the Lord of the Dead and his treacherous blade pay for all the injustice they'd heaped upon him and the prisoners in the City of Strife.

When the ball of blue-white light appeared on the horizon, filling the sky with its brilliance, burning away the ooze and the ever-present blood-red mist hanging in the air, Kelemvor was certain he was seeing the fiery face of his doom.

"Midnight," he whispered. "I—"

The rest of the vow was lost, drowned out by Kelemvor's scream and the roar of the inferno as it engulfed him.

* * * * *

Cyric retreated to the massive slab of onyx that served as Bone Castle's main door. He backed against the stone, swinging Godsbane furiously. The short sword cut a gory path through a shade, but gained no sustenance from the soul. Despite all the carnage, she remained as pale as a bleached skull, her voice thin and rasping in the death god's mind. The work of Mystra, no doubt. Somehow the Whore was preventing Godsbane from digesting the souls she swallowed.

Cyric cursed the thought of the goddess as he slashed another shade across the face.

The diamond walls had been taken, the denizens routed from their posts by spectral night-terrors. Even now the death god's bestial minions writhed in pitiful fear before the phantasms. Denizens cowered in every corner, hid beneath anything that could offer them shelter. It did them no good; the nightmares slipped into their minds, driving the valor from their corrupted hearts.

These are Dendar's brood, Jergal said as he floated to Cyric's side. A shade charged the seneschal, but he opened his cloak wide to embrace the attacker. The damned soul vanished into the darkness with a short gasp of surprise.

"Of course they're Dendar's!" Cyric snapped. "Why shouldn't she be in on this conspiracy, too?"

The Prince of Lies held his left hand out and spread the fingers wide. A sudden gale blew across the bailey, the wind stripping the flesh from both armies. One of the armored shades, leading the battle from atop the wall, tumbled backward at the blast. He sank into the Slith, where the creatures lurking there drew him out through the slits in his helmet, one piece at a time.

Cyric slumped back against the door, momentarily weakened by casting the powerful spell. He had no doubt that the war proceeded as Mystra and the others had planned. His worshipers in Zhentil Keep were deserting him in droves—just as he needed their devotion most to drive the damned from the gates of Bone Castle. And through it all, Cyric's other churches, the needy faithful of all his disparate offices, tugged at his mind. Their calls for aid and guidance threatened to draw too much of the death god's fragmented consciousness away from the City of Strife, but to deny their prayers would be to risk sacrificing their worship.

The battle quickly swelled to fill the bailey once more as denizens retreated from the damned. When they saw their master, Cyric's minions did not rally. They stumbled toward him, over the windswept bones of their brethren. "Save us, great lord!" they cried. "The Chaos Hound is loose in the city! Kezef fights on the side of the False!"

Come, my lord, Jergal said.

The seneschal dared to lay a gloved hand on the god's form. When Cyric didn't object, Jergal guided him away from the battle, into the castle's entry hall. The drow-spun tapestries fluttered nervously against the bone walls, as if they could sense the threat to their fragile hideousness. The darksome things that lurked below the crystal floor cowered at Cyric's passing. During their eternal captivity, they'd witnessed the downfall of other gods; now they could see the blade of doom poised over the Lord of the Dead.

"Ah," Cyric muttered. "The gods show their true colors now, forging pacts with Kezef." He began to howl with sudden fury. "They wear facades of purity and honor, but underneath they've got the faces of assassins."

Godsbane stirred weakly in his mind. *Yes, my love, but you will reveal them for what they truly are.*

The soothing words passed into the tangle of Cyric's thoughts unnoticed. His mind was caught up in a firestorm of rage, which blew from one fragment of his consciousness to another, turning them away from their vital tasks. Bloody revenge was all Cyric could consider. Mystra and Mask, Torm and Oghma, they would all be forced to grovel before him. He'd turn the Circle against them, have them humiliated, stripped of their offices—and then he would murder them one by one....

As the Prince of Lies lingered in his fancies of divine carnage, cracks began to snake across the crystal floor, and the walls of bone began to tremble and sway. Jergal hurried Cyric through the skull-lined judgment hall, only to find the Rolls of the Dead tumbling from their carefully ordered places. The parchment scrolls, upon which the seneschal had recorded the fate of every soul imprisoned within the City of Strife, crumbled to dust before his unblinking eyes. The doorway to the throne room, once concealed by powerful enchantments, gaped in midair like an open wound.

Magnificence, you must turn your mind back to this realm, Jergal pleaded. *You must give over just a little of your power to maintaining the castle.*

"Traitor!" Cyric shouted as they entered the throne room. "There must be a traitor in my ranks."

Yes, Godsbane echoed numbly. *A traitor. . . .*

A few of the Burning Men reached out for the Lord of the Dead as Jergal hustled him toward his gruesome throne. Like everything else maintained by Cyric's godly power, the chains that held the tormented scribes to the walls and ceiling were decaying. The three hundred ninety-eight burning souls, all men and women who had failed to create the *Cyrinishad,* hung precariously by an arm or a leg or rolled about on the floor in a vain attempt to douse the fires that tortured them.

"Perhaps *you* can tell me something about the treachery in my court, Jergal," Cyric said. He turned on the seneschal and gripped him by the face. "What did Mystra offer you—a new title, perhaps? Do you aspire to godhood yourself?"

Certainly not, Your Magnificence, Jergal said, shaking free of the death god's grasp. *I exist to serve the master of Bone Castle.*

A sinister lucidity settled in Cyric's eyes, and the room ceased trembling. "If you would serve anyone who sits this throne, you cannot be loyal to me only." He grinned. "Therefore you *must* be the traitor."

The Lord of the Dead drew Godsbane and advanced a step toward the seneschal. The short sword looked sickly in the shifting light cast by the Burning Men, its bone-white pallor darkening to the gray of twilight shadows. *No, my love,* she whispered. *I cannot allow you to slay your only loyal minion.*

"What?" Cyric roared. He held the blade up to his eyes, as if he could look inside its steely depths. "You cannot

'allow me'?"

There is a traitor at your side, my love, but it's not Jergal. Godsbane's voice quavered, straining to form each painful word. *Not everything is as it seems.*

Jergal hovered close. *Please, Your Magnificence. Rest yourself in the throne for a time. Gather your thoughts so you can drive the—*

"Get out!" Cyric shouted. He spared the seneschal a brief, anger-filled glance. "Now!"

I will see to the defense of the entry hall. Jergal bowed formally and retreated from the throne room.

The Prince of Lies stared at the short sword, turning it over in his hands, examining it from every angle. "What have you been keeping from me, Godsbane?" he rumbled. "The identity of the traitor?"

Yes, the spirit of the blade replied. Her voice had become more masculine, slick with sibilants. *I see now how wrong I was to do so, but I've helped the other gods plot against you.*

"Impossible," Cyric shouted. "I broke your will after I stole you from Black Oaks. I was only a mortal then, and I defeated you in mental combat. You couldn't turn against me."

You never bested me.

"Lies!" Cyric held the sword high over his head, one hand on the hilt, the other on the tip. With a scream of anger, he snapped Godsbane in two.

A blue-white ball of light formed around the break in the blade. For an instant, the glow hovered like faerie fire in front of Cyric, dancing along the sword's edges. Then it swelled, filling the throne room with its brilliance. The explosion crushed the death god's trophies to dust, splintered his throne of misguided martyrs.

When the light subsided, a shadow-wrapped figure lay before the Prince of Lies, its back broken, tears welling in its rose-red eyes. "Ah, my love, I was a fool to betray you."

Cyric dropped the sundered blade. "You."

The black mask had fallen away from the Shadowlord's face, revealing features that shifted and warped like the cloak of darkness that hid its form. A soft, feminine visage coarsened into a man's. An aquiline nose blunted into bulbousness, flattened, then narrowed and turned up daintily at the end. Only two features on Mask's face remained constant: the god's glowing red eyes and the pale fangs extruding from his lips.

"If I had read the *Cyrinishad* sooner, realized your greatness before it was too late." The Shadowlord slumped to the floor. "I never would have kept him hidden from you."

Mask's form melted away into a pool of darkness, which merged with the death god's own shadow.

The voices of Cyric's myriad selves shouted out their dismay, chorused their anger. The Prince of Lies stared, unseeing, at his shadow, trying to make some sense of the bizarre scene. He couldn't. There were too many things clawing at his thoughts, hoarding bits of his attention.

In Yulash, an assassin offered up a half-hearted prayer to the God of Murder, her words as empty of devotion as her heart was of pity. A peddler, down on his luck and starving amidst the opulence of Waterdeep, bitterly cursed the God of Strife. His insults flew up like arrows into Cyric's mind. And then there were the Zhentish. Thousands of women and men shrieked Cyric's name, as if that act alone could earn his aid. Their pleas streamed across the death god's consciousness, scattering his thoughts in their wake. He was lost, his consciousness torn in a million directions at once.

The blow caught Cyric in the face. He barely noticed the physical pain, but the surprise dragged his attention from the maelstrom of racing thoughts back to his realm in Hades. The Prince of Lies looked out on the ravaged throne room, but what he saw there only confused him more.

The Burning Men, loosed from shattered chains, writhed across the floor in pain, unable to douse the fires consuming them. The explosion from the attack on Godsbane—no, Mask—had charred the walls and scorched a huge hole in the carpet. Cyric's throne had been shattered, the bones strewn about. All these things seemed right somehow, appropriate to the setting. Yet there were other objects, other people in the room as well, bits and pieces from all the vistas taken in by Cyric's incarnations. They all superimposed themselves over the reality of Bone Castle, creating a strange jumble of images.

Liquid shadows played upon the columns, blackened and broken, from the temple in Zhentil Keep. Near the fragments of the throne, a young novitiate to Cyric's church in Mulmaster kneeled in prayer. The silver bracelets signifying his enslavement to the death god reflected wan torchlight; his blue-black robes smelled of sweet incense. Assassins crept along the walls, silently stalking unseen quarries. Three Zhentilar soldiers huddled near the door, just as Cyric was seeing them in the Citadel of the Raven. Standing but an arm's length away from the death god, Kelemvor Lyonsbane raised a martyr's bone like a war club. . . .

Some part of Cyric's mind shrieked a warning, and he lashed out. The back of his left hand snapped the makeshift weapon from Kel's grasp as the palm of his right connected with the shade's chin. Grunting in pain, Kelemvor flew backward. To the Lord of the Dead, the shade seemed to pass right through the devout young priest in Mulmaster, coming to rest at the feet of a dark-cloaked assassin.

"Capture him!" Cyric shouted madly. With twitching fingers, the Prince of Lies gestured at the phantom murderer, directing him toward the bruised and grimy shade rising up before him. When the assassin continued to skulk along the wall, the death god smiled. "Are you a nightmare, then? Has Dendar dispatched you to haunt me like those feeble terrors that attacked my denizens on the walls?"

Kelemvor brushed the dust from his tunic. "You're going to wish this were a bad dream, you backstabbing cur." He rushed forward, roaring like a bear.

Cyric called an enchantment to mind, but the undertow of his thoughts sucked the incantation away. Another part of his mind suggested he transform to avoid the blow. The Prince of Lies willed himself into the guise of a poisonous cloud, but he remained in that form for only an instant before a purring voice demanded he take on his rightful shape again, the form described in the *Cyrinishad*. The Lord of the Dead found himself trapped in his mortal-seeming avatar when Kelemvor struck.

They tumbled together, Cyric flailing wildly to defend himself, Kelemvor landing blow after blow with his hammerlike fists. When they came to a stop, the death god shrugged off his attacker and struggled to his feet. For the first time in a decade, Cyric felt pain. Though the ache came from nothing more profound than a blackened eye and cracked ribs, he found himself trembling.

The pantheon must have given Kel some power, the death god decided. Mystra and the others must be animating him with their might, just like one of the Gearsmith's mechanical men. The shade couldn't harm me otherwise.

The voices in Cyric's head murmured their agreement: *Better to flee such a direct battle. Strike from the shadows until your strength returns, until you discover what strange spell Mystra has placed on you to dampen your strength.*

Kelemvor gripped the hilt of Godsbane and started toward Cyric again. "This'll do to cut out your black heart. That'll be my trophy. The rest I'll leave for these poor souls."

With the broken blade, Kel gestured to the Burning Men. The scribes crawled with painful slowness toward the death god. They moaned and clutched the air with sizzling fingers as they dragged their agony-stiffened bodies across the throne room.

Cyric backed away from Kelemvor, toward the center of the room. He kicked one of the Burning Men out of his way and ducked the awkward lunge of another. "I'm a god, Lyonsbane. And if I killed you when I was mortal, think of the agony I can put you through now."

"So why are you running?" Kelemvor murmured.

Cyric didn't answer. He attempted to focus his mind on teleporting away from Hades, but too many things were drawing his consciousness away from the enchantment. The voices in his head had become a chorus of discord offering five dozen opinions on even the slightest matter. And there were his faithful all across Faerun, of course, invoking the death god's name to resolve every petty conflict in their lives. In Bone Castle, Cyric could hear the sound of battle ringing out in the antechamber and the soft tread of Kelemvor's boots as he stalked closer.

Beware, Your Magnificence, Jergal cried from outside the throne room. *The damned have broken into the castle!*

The Prince of Lies abandoned the enchantment. Obviously Mystra was denying him access to the weave, or hobbling his ability to concentrate on magic. As he turned toward the door, Cyric silently vowed to gouge out her blue-white eyes when next they met.

A shade blocked the doorway, a mystic blade sparking starlight in his hands.

"I am called the True because I value loyalty above all else." Gwydion leveled the point of Titanslayer at Cyric's heart. "I am called the Brave because I will face any danger to prove my respect of duty."

"Fool," the Prince of Lies muttered.

He took a step toward Gwydion, but got no farther before a fierce pain shot up his leg. One of the Burning Men had locked his fiery hands around Cyric's ankle, and no matter how hard the death god kicked him, he would not release his hold. Another of the scribes wrapped searing arms around Cyric's neck and hung over his back like a cloak.

Screaming, the Prince of Lies spun around. He managed to shake the soul loose from his neck, and, for an instant, it seemed that Cyric might escape the scribes. As the death god stumbled forward, though, Kelemvor drove the sharp-edged stump of Godsbane into his gut and kicked him backward into the arms of the Burning Men.

"Your faithful await," Kel said as the scribes swarmed over their tormentor.

The flames that tortured each of the Burning Men were unique, created to anguish their souls endlessly without diminishing them; as more and more of the scribes threw themselves onto the pyre, the fires mingled, grew white-hot and wonder-bright. The heat from the inferno drove Kelemvor back and forced Gwydion to shield his eyes. So it was that the Burning Men were freed of their torment, released from suffering by their brethren's flames.

When the pyre died down, Kelemvor used Godsbane to sift through the ashes. Cyric was gone.

"Destroyed?" Gwydion asked hopefully.

"All the fires in Hades couldn't burn Cyric from the world. He's like a sickness, a plague." Kelemvor shook his head. "He'll be back."

LORD OF THE DEAD

*Wherein the effects of Cyric's absence are felt
throughout the mortal realms, Gwydion the
Quick lives up to his name once more, and
Bone Castle gets a new tenant.*

Renaldo led what was left of the company into the alley.
For most of the morning, ever since the giants and goblins
and gnolls had stormed through the shattered western
gates, they'd been avoiding the monsters. Hopes of mount-
ing a counterattack had slipped away quickly, undermined
by each slaughtered Zhentilar they found, victims of the
treacherous orcs who'd sided with the reavers or the savage mobs of gnolls now stalking the streets. The sewers
beneath the city were no safer. The goblins had taken up
residence there, along with the darksome things that usually dwelled in the murky depths—giant rats, carrion
crawlers, and the floating blobs of flesh called beholders.

All Renaldo and his dozen troops hoped for now was a way to slink out of the city unnoticed. They would have settled for a place to rest, to bandage their wounds and gulp down whatever food they could find. Surprisingly, this narrow street of crippled cobbles showed a little promise.

To one side, a row of cramped houses slouched together like drunken sailors at muster. To the other, marble columns towered overhead. They marked a silent perimeter around the high piles of rubble that had once been the walls of an arena. Wooden skeletons of stalls and tents huddled between the columns. Gamblers had held court here, and moneylenders; the bloody games staged in the arena had given them a livelihood as profitable as any in the Keep.

As he crept past one gutted flashhouse, Renaldo paused a moment to revel in its destruction. He owed the better part of a year's salary to the sharp who ran this place.

"Hsst. Lieutenant."

Renaldo started at the sound, but didn't turn around. With the field promotion only a few hours old, he still thought of himself as a sergeant.

"Something's moving, Lieutenant. In the arena."

The warning got through to him that time, but by then he'd heard the noises, too: low grunting and the slap of leather on stone. Something large was moving in there, struggling for purchase on the steeply angled rows of seats that led up from the sandy arena floor.

Renaldo signaled the soldiers skulking along behind him, then slipped into the ruined flashhouse. Through the doorway he watched the rest of the company scatter. A few found dark niches across the alley. Most crouched under convenient piles of debris. They gripped their swords with hands trembling from fear and exhaustion and cold.

A quick survey of his surroundings told the lieutenant he'd chosen his hiding place poorly. The building's walls were sound, but a huge hole gaped in the roof. Worse still, there was nothing in the room big enough to hide beneath. The tables and chairs had been hacked up, the larger pieces hauled away by the gnolls and orcs to build bonfires.

Renaldo considered making a dash for the dilapidated buildings across the alley, but the hiss of shifting rubble pinned him in place. He crouched next to the door, glancing up through the breached roof. Puffs of steam rose over the arena wall, each followed by a grunt of effort.

A giant struggled to the top of the ruined arena. The titan was large, even for his kind, and the blood matting his beard was obviously not his own. Dents marred his horned helmet and breastplate, damage done by siege engines. He'd knotted tents and tapestries together to fashion himself a motley cloak. Trophies of gold and silver—candelabras, mugs, and serving dishes—hung on a chain around one wrist. The trinkets jangled noisily as the giant hefted his real prizes, the limp corpses of two bulls, and balanced them upon his shoulders. The giant twisted his blue-tinged face into a mask of gleeful triumph and galloped down the rubble heap into the alley.

Renaldo held his breath as the giant lumbered closer. The titan had to squeeze sideways to fit between the arena's columns, and he absently kicked a tent frame out of his way as he stepped over the abandoned flashhouses and moneylenders' stalls. The clatter of the wooden poles as they rolled across the cobbles sent shivers up the soldier's spine. *Ground to dust beneath the heels of dragons and giants*. That's what the old woman had said. She'd been right about his promotion, though there was little left of the company to command. Perhaps she'd foreseen his doom, too.

Yet the giant passed by Renaldo's hiding place without ever looking down. The titan stepped right over two of the other Zhentilar, as well, huddled as they were beneath an overturned cart in the middle of the alley. Whistling a tuneless victory song, he hurried out of the narrow street. His thundering tread shook the ground as he lumbered onto the boulevard beyond.

Sighing with relief, Renaldo crept from the gambling stall and started across the cobbles. The rest of the patrol followed his lead, sliding out from their hiding places and moving toward the shelter of the abandoned row houses. They'd rest there for a while, settle on a definite escape route.

Renaldo was in the middle of the alley, as far from cover as he could possibly be, when the first of the gnolls rounded the corner. At least twenty of them followed the scout, perhaps as many as thirty. Their tall, muscular frames were covered in armor pillaged from the Zhentilar's own barracks. Their canine snouts jutted out from helmets designed for human features.

"Fire!" the gnoll commander barked in surprisingly good Common. The order was wasted, though; the bestial soldiers had already drawn their bows. Howling like wolves, they let loose a volley of black-fletched arrows.

Renaldo felt the arrow pierce his throat, turning the command he'd mustered there into an unintelligible gurgle of pain. His order would have been wasted, too, however. Since the Zhentilar had no bows, the only thing they could do was run for the safety of the row houses and try to sneak away before the beasts called for reinforcements.

As he fell, clutching at the offending shaft, Renaldo noted dimly that none of his troops gave him a second look as they scrambled for cover. The lieutenant wasn't surprised; he'd left two dozen men to die in similar ambushes during the morning. That realization didn't prevent him from bitterly hoping the rest of the company met a truly horrible end.

Renaldo hit the ground hard. The impact drove the air from his lungs in a painful burst. As the arrow snapped beneath his weight, icy daggers of pain exploded out from the shaft, almost as if it were probing for some vital lifeline to sever. Renaldo's shoulders spasmed, and his fingers came away from his throat slick with blood.

The street swayed before his eyes, the cobbles rocked beneath him like a hammock, but the soldier found himself clinging to consciousness. Perhaps the wound isn't fatal, he told himself, even though he knew this shouldn't be true.

With trembling arms, Renaldo pushed himself to his knees. He saw then that the gnolls had closed, circled around him like a pack of hungry wolves. One of them raised its bow and fired.

Renaldo watched the arrow fly toward him, moving with preternatural slowness. He felt the steel head pierce his leather breastplate and bite into his chest. The blow knocked him backward, arms clutching helplessly at the air. As he lay there, the blood soaking into the padded doublet he wore beneath his armor, Renaldo could tell that the arrow had broken three ribs, that it had buried itself in his heart. And still he lived, still his soul refused to abandon its pain-wracked mortal shell.

The truth of it was, Renaldo's soul had nowhere to go. The Realm of the Dead had no master. No lord ruled over the City of Strife. With Cyric's defeat, men and women all across Faerun found themselves beyond death's cold grasp. For some this proved to be a blessing beyond compare. For most, it was a nightmare beyond belief.

In the desert of Anauroch, a young explorer crawled on hands and knees across the dreaded expanse known as At'ar's Looking Glass. Her camel was dead, her water exhausted days ago. She collapsed onto the wind-burnished stones, robbed finally of her last shred of resolve. The vultures that had been her only companions for the past day circled lower and lower. The explorer prayed for death to take her before the scavengers began plucking at her parched flesh, but that, of course, was impossible. . . .

The room revealed little about the old Sembian merchant, save that he was very rich and very ill. The bed was carved from the finest Chultan teak, the gossamer drapes sewn from imported Shou silks. What he'd paid for the blankets alone could feed and clothe a poor family for the winter. Still, all that wealth hadn't kept him healthy—despite the potions and salves and tinctures he'd purchased during his long life. For years he'd fought against the withering disease that corrupted his frail form, grasped for every second of life like a miser reaching for gold. Now, though, the return on the effort of living had become too small.

With shaking hands the merchant raised the poison to his lips and choked it down. The sickly sweet concoction burned down his throat. Warmth spread from his stomach to his chest, dulling the pain for but an instant. Then the poison clamped down on his lungs and squeezed the breath from him. It should be over quickly, he reminded himself, but it wasn't. For hours the poison coursed through his body, killing him over and over. . . .

In a little-visited tower, far to the north of Waterdeep, a man lay strapped to a table. The skin was gone from his right hand, flayed from his fingers so expertly that it retained its shape—a gruesome, bloody glove. Other atrocities had been visited upon the man, as well. The loss of blood alone should have killed him long ago, but for some strange reason, life clung to him.

His torturer—a drow from House Duskryn of Menzoberranzan—thought himself too experienced in the ways of pain to be surprised by anything. Yet as he heated a set of long thin needles, he wondered at the thrill this unusual victim had afforded him.

"A gift from the gods," the drow murmured contentedly. He never knew how right he was.

* * * * *

Kelemvor Lyonsbane stood atop the diamond wall surrounding Bone Castle, flanked by Jergal and Gwydion. Gathered before him on the banks of the River Slith and the rubble-strewn plain beyond were the assembled hosts of Hades, the denizens and the damned alike. Despair hung upon the backs of Cyric's minions, for they had felt their god's defeat in their black hearts. And though the denizens had surrendered soon after their lord vanished, the victorious shades had bound them like slaves.

"The tyrant is overthrown," Kelemvor shouted. "And with his defeat ends the reign of injustice."

He held aloft both halves of the sundered blade that had been his prison. The red sky gave the cold, lifeless metal just a hint of the rosy hue that had once tinted it. "In this shell I was held captive for ten long years, a pawn of the gods." With the shattered hilt he drew a wide arc over the crowd, gesturing toward the ruined city and the Wall of the Faithless. "In this shell, some of you have been held captive for ten times my decade of suffering. You've been tortured at the whims of lunatics like Cyric and, before him, Myrkul. Your suffering has been the stuff of their entertainment. No more."

A deafening roar went up from the crowd. The damned souls raised their spears and clubs to the sky and shouted out Kelemvor's name.

"Jergal tells me the gods gather at the city gates, awaiting permission to enter," Kel announced once the shouting had died down. "Only you can grant them that privilege, for you are the kings and queens of this place."

"Let 'em wait!" a shade cried. "They left us here to rot. I say we give 'em back some of their own while we got the chance!"

Jergal hovered close to Kelemvor, his bulging eyes devoid of expression. *The mortal realms feel the pain of this delay, not the gods,* the seneschal murmured. His voice was as cold as a winter lake. *The dying cannot be freed from their suffering, since their souls have nowhere to go.*

Kel nodded grimly, then faced the crowd once more. "You want justice for yourselves, but first you have to offer it to others. For each instant we waste in debate, men and women on Faerun are trapped between life and death. Their suffering is unjust, and our indecision is the cause."

"But what if the pantheon wants to punish us?" rumbled one of the False. "If we let them in they may hand the city back to Cyric!"

Gwydion stepped forward. His clothes were tattered, his face grimy with soot. And, though he no longer wore the god-forged armor of an inquisitor, the shades and denizens knew him well. Like Kelemvor, he'd become a legend of sorts in the city, a harbinger of hope in that hopeless place.

"Cyric will never reign over this realm again, but a new god must take his place," Gwydion shouted. "That's the way of things, and nothing we can do will change it. Still, that doesn't mean we can't make our voices heard." He pointed at Bone Castle, deserted now and crumbling swiftly to rubble without a god to maintain it. "The lord who rebuilds those walls will do so only with our permission. And we won't give that until we have a few promises."

"No more torture!" someone shouted.

"Fair trials!"

"Justice!"

The crowd took up the last as a chant. After a moment, the denizens added their inhuman voices to the clangor. The chant swelled, echoing over the Realm of the Dead until even the Faithless trapped in the wall ceased their wailing and took up the call. Kelemvor found himself caught up in the moment, screaming along with the rest until his jaw ached.

Finally Kel raised the jagged halves of Godsbane over his head. "Justice will be yours! Each of you will be given a new trial, a chance to lift the doom proclaimed upon you." A riotous cheer shook the diamond wall. "Those who once served Cyric, we give you a choice: join us in building a just kingdom atop the ruins of his mad empire or flee the city. Your master may yet be hiding in some darkened corner of the planes. Whichever you choose, you'll not be harmed." Another cheer rose, this one thick with the growls and monstrous whoops of the denizens.

Kelemvor tossed the broken halves of Godsbane into the Slith. A magnificent plume of darkness erupted from each piece as it hit the fetid water, but the billowing shadows faded when the river swallowed up the blade. "My prison is gone. Together we can shatter the chains Cyric forged for you, the links of suffering and tyranny that make this place a realm of strife. Strike the first blow for freedom! Open the gates!"

A sudden flood of energy washed over Kelemvor. He trembled for an instant as the cool, thrumming pulse filled his being, stretched his mind to its limits, then pressed beyond.

The entire Realm of the Dead spread before his consciousness like a map upon a table. Each burning building, each shattered street, lay open to his gaze, cold details of a ravaged city. He sensed the fires and the destruction, tiny pinpricks of discomfort that nagged his thoughts. He felt the chill passing of the nightmares as

they returned to Dendar's cave, the corrupt scrabbling of
Kezef's paws as he climbed the Wall of the Faithless, seeking an escape from the city and from the gods that milled
at the gates. The smell of the swamp, the whiff of brimstone in the air, the horrible stench of fear that permeated
everything. . . .

This was the nectar of godhood, he realized numbly. At
least it was for the Lord of the Dead.

Eyes wide with wonder, Kel looked out at the sea of
upturned faces. He saw the hope there, the terrible longing for salvation. The unspoken prayers of each shade and
denizen filled his head, granting him the might of a million
dreams.

Lead us, they pleaded. *Give us justice!*

Jergal leaned close to Kelemvor once more and spoke
for him alone to hear. This time, though, the ice had
melted from the seneschal's voice, replaced by a cool deference. *Shall I see to it, milord?*

"See to what?"

Your command, Jergal replied evenly. *Do you wish me to
open the gates to the other gods?*

At a nod from Kelemvor, the unearthly seneschal vanished, only to reappear an instant later at the massive
gates to the City of Strife. Kel could sense Jergal's presence there, feel his feather-light touch upon the grisly
doors. The gates trembled slightly, the cowards' hearts
quaking at the awesome task they had performed; few
barriers could bar one god's passing, let alone a triumvi-
rate's. Their job was done now, though. At Jergal's silent
prompting, the gates swung wide.

Mystra streaked above the city, a huge blue-white
phoenix. Magical light rained down from her, driving the
darkness and despair from every corner of the ruined
realm. The wind from her passing snuffed out the fires
still burning in the city, and her shrill cry of joy made the

cruel things that preyed upon the damned cower in their burrows.

Torm and Oghma trailed in Mystra's wake, flares so bright that none could look upon them. Their passing left streaks of fire arched over the necropolis. Like banners proclaiming Cyric's defeat, the twin flames lingered over the Realm of the Dead as the three gods settled in Bone Castle's deserted bailey.

Kelemvor leaped from the wall and walked to Mystra's side. She looked much as he remembered her—slender and graceful, raven-black hair cascading down her shoulders, a slight smile upon her full lips. Only her eyes were different, blue-white and flickering with power from the weave of magic.

They stared at each other for a time, neither speaking. Kelemvor was the one who finally broke the silence. "Cyric's gone," he said. "I don't know where."

Mystra nodded. "And Mask?"

"As near as I can tell, he was disguised as Godsbane all along," Kel replied. "Ever since Cyric stole the sword from the halflings at Black Oaks. Anyway, Cyric shattered the blade. That freed me, but destroyed Mask. He melted away into darkness, crying out for forgiveness. He really seemed penitent."

"That's unlikely," Torm noted stiffly.

"Perhaps not," Mystra offered. "After all, Mask read the *Cyrinishad*. Who's to say the book doesn't contain the power to twist a god's mind, as well?"

In the silence that followed, Torm remembered his manners. "Forgive me, Lord Kelemvor," he murmured, bowing formally. "We have not yet been introduced."

"No need, Torm," Oghma said. "Kelemvor knows who—or, more precisely, *what* we are. He could sense it the moment we entered his realm."

"*His* realm?" The God of Duty gave Kelemvor a skeptical

look. "Only Ao can bestow godhood, and he—"

"He will ratify what the damned have already decided for themselves," the God of Knowledge interrupted. "If I can recognize the wisdom in their choice, I am certain Ao will, as well." He turned to the new Lord of the Dead. "Tell me, Kelemvor, what do you plan to do for a clergy?"

Kel shrugged. "Gather together people who want to see the underworld ruled by law, I suppose. That's all the denizens and the damned want." He frowned fiercely. "I really don't understand any of this. I never set out to be a god. All I wanted was justice. I didn't do anything to deserve a reward like this."

"Reward?" Oghma asked, the sound of tiny bells chiming amusement in his musical voice. "What makes you think being made Lord of the Dead is a reward? The last two deities to hold the post went mad."

Kelemvor glanced up at the grim tower that would become his home. "I liked this all better when I thought it was a reward," he murmured.

At the wounded look on Kel's face, Mystra laid a gentle hand on his shoulder. "The title will be what you make of it, but don't doubt your worthiness for a moment. Sometimes heroes must fight to prove their mettle, sometimes they need be patient enough and wise enough to stay their sword while others fight around them. You did both." She slid into his arms. "Besides, I have your reward, Kel. I've been keeping it safe for ten years now."

They kissed, and as their mortal-seeming facades embraced, their spirits curled together in a far more intimate union.

"Come, Binder," Torm said. "We have other duties to attend to." He stalked away from Kelemvor and Mystra, puzzlement clear on his handsome features.

The Patron of Bards spared the armored god a wry smile. "You should mark these lovers well, Your Holiness,"

Oghma said, "not flee them. They are the stuff of poetry, of song."

"There are songs about my knights, as well," Torm corrected. "Fine, heroic lays that steel a heart for battle."

"I've heard them," Oghma drawled. "Nothing but Zhentish limericks when compared to a sonnet meant to steal a heart for romance." He chuckled at his own cleverness. "Maybe that's what's been wrong with us all these eons, no sense of passion. You should instruct your faithful to belt out a paean to a loved one each morning—you know, a song to their horses or their swords. . . ."

Torm ignored the barb and made his way to Gwydion. The shade kneeled at the base of the diamond wall, Titanslayer held point-down before him in a show of humility.

"I have done my duty, Your Holiness," Gwydion said. "I raised my sword against his minions."

"Your deeds are known to me," the God of Duty replied. "Look upon my hands, Gwydion. Tell me what you see."

The shade lifted his eyes, saw the reddish light from the sky warp over Torm's gauntlets. Tiny runes covered the burnished metal, symbols and glyphs of a thousand forgotten languages. Yet as Gwydion stared, the letters burned themselves into his consciousness, shouted their meaning to him on the voices of angels.

"I—I can understand them all, Your Holiness," Gwydion whispered. Tears streamed down his face as he repeated the myriad words for duty and loyalty.

Torm raised the shade up from the dirt. "Come, Sir Gwydion, I'm certain Lord Kelemvor will free you from this place. You've proven yourself more than worthy of my kingdom."

"I will obediently follow your commands, Holiness," the knight said humbly. "But I would ask a boon of you."

"Go on," Torm said. "It is my duty to listen to the pleas of my faithful."

"I want to be mortal again," Gwydion said. "I ask only for the days and months I had left when my cowardice drew Cyric to me that afternoon in Thar. I wish to live that time, however long it may be, as an honorable man."

The shade's impassioned plea had drawn the attention of the other gods. "I will release any claims this kingdom has upon his soul," Kelemvor announced. "Gwydion dared stand against Cyric. Without him, the cur might have escaped into the city."

Oghma cleared his throat. "If you'll forgive my earlier impertinence, Your Holiness, might I suggest a quest that your knight could undertake?" He sidled close to the God of Duty. "One of my faithful has taken on the dangerous task of carrying the *Cyrinishad*. Perhaps you could charge brave Gwydion to watch over her."

Torm rubbed his cleft chin. "If Cyric still lives, he will most certainly seek the book. Who better to guard its keeper than a knight who has stood against the Prince of Lies before? Tell me, Binder, where is this guardian now?"

"I don't know," Oghma murmured. "I've given her a holy symbol that hides her from the gods and all magical scrying."

The God of Duty turned to Gwydion. "As usual, we are left to fulfill our sacred tasks chained by the foolishness of others. The Binder will give you a mental image of the woman and the book she carries. You'll have to do the rest on your own." He clapped the shade on the shoulder. "No other of my knights could be more worthy of this quest, Sir Gwydion. I know you will pursue it with honor and courage."

Gwydion gasped when Rinda appeared in his thoughts. Pale skin, dark curls, and intense, sea-green eyes—he'd seen this woman before somewhere. Or perhaps it was the determined cast to her features that marked them as kindred spirits. I'll find out which soon enough, he

372

realized joyfully.

A burst of silver radiance settled over Gwydion the Quick. After bowing to his god, he began his long run back to the mortal realms.

The sounds of a solemn procession had begun to drift over the diamond walls, curling over the noisome waters of the Slith. Jergal appeared at Kelemvor's side, almost as if he'd been carried to the keep by the mournful chanting.

The ghostly seneschal held a roll of blank parchment in his gloved hands. Even before Jergal spoke, Kelemvor knew that the time had come for him to take up his mantle as Judge of the Damned. Soldiers and sell-swords and sick old merchants—the False and the Faithless had arrived in the Realm of the Dead to hear their fates proclaimed.

As the first of the shades shuffled into the courtyard, Kelemvor turned his mind to the decaying heap of Bone Castle. With a thought, he recast the twisted tower as a beautiful spire of crystal, a palace more suited to a god who intended to hide nothing from his faithful.

From that day forward, Kelemvor's court shone from within those clear, sparkling walls, a beacon of law and compassion on the dark plains of Hades. And all those who looked upon the tower knew that justice had finally come to the Realm of the Dead.

EPILOGUE

In a hope-forsaken tunnel at the heart of Pandemonium, Cyric awoke. The lamentations of every mortal in Faerun, the sobs of the desperate and the keening of the broken-hearted, found their way to that lonely place sooner or later. And the cold winds that blew through the endless labyrinth warped those plaintive cries, transforming them into a weird symphony, rich with the chords of madness.

As he rose from the smooth-hewn floor, Cyric became aware of a shadow—*his* shadow—moving with him. Darker than the utter darkness surrounding it, the shape mimicked the fallen god's actions, but not his form. The Burning Men had left their mark upon Cyric, scarred him so deeply that no magics could mask the ragged brands on his hands and face. Yet the shadow suffered none of these imperfections, its outline smooth and perfect.

In the overgrown garden that was Cyric's mind, the shadow's voice murmured soothingly—at least, the soft words seemed to come from the dark form trailing him.

The jabbering of his faithful and the cold, sharp complaints of his myriad selves made it difficult for Cyric to tell for certain. And before he could consider the notion further, the thoughts racing through his mind drew him away to other, more vital matters.

There was a new kingdom to build. After all, Cyric was still a deity—God of Strife and Intrigue, Patron of Murder. As such, he deserved a palace of suitable size to accommodate his horde of worshipers, a mammoth treasure house to store the spoils of his victorious war against Mystra and the Circle of Greater Powers.

The Prince of Lies waved his tattered hand, and a fortress began to construct itself there in the howling darkness. Yet as the foundation settled into the tunnel and the first few night-black stones piled themselves one upon the other, the shape of the keep changed, altered to suit Cyric's ever-shifting desires. The castle became a single tower, high and twisting, then a pyramid, a final redout from which the God of Strife could plot his revenge upon the traitors who had usurped the Realm of the Dead.

The redout vanished, too, when the fawning voices in Cyric's head reminded him that Mystra had merely done his will in bringing the City of Strife to revolt. No longer would he be forced to waste time judging the damned, listening to their simpering excuses, meting out feeble punishments set down ages ago by gods with little imagination for cruelty. No, Cyric had forced them to take command of the loathsome place and set the title Lord of the Dead like an unbreakable stock on the shoulders of someone else. As always, the pantheon had been puppets, playing the parts Cyric created for them.

For an instant, the Prince of Lies heard the babel of voices in his head chime harmonious agreement. None of them could deny his absolute supremacy over all the gods in Faerun. The *Cyrinishad* proved the truth of that, and

Cyric himself had read the tome very carefully.

All across the mortal realms, a disembodied smile appeared in the most squalid alleys and haunted, shadow-draped woods. Broad and sharp, glinting like a straight razor in the moonlight, it hinted at the mad god's pleasure with a world well-suited to become his earthly kingdom. The true meaning of the apparitions eluded even the most gifted oracles. They wove dire but vague prophecies around the chilling visions, but, as was their wont, the men and women of Faerun heeded them little and went on with their chaotic, mundane lives.

In the hope-forsaken tunnel at the heart of Pandemonium, Cyric began to laugh. The world was doomed, but it kept running anyway.